THE FATHER'S TREE

CRYSTAL JENCKS, MD

This novel is fiction. Names, characters, places and incidents are the product of the author's imagination or are used fictitiously. Any resemblance to actual events, locales, or persons, living or dead, is coincidental. In case any message is received other than that intended, either by ill-worded prose or reader distraction at inopportune time, let it be clear. The author loves the Lord God with all her heart, mind and soul, and believes Him to be all good, all holy, all perfect, and ever worthy of praise. Please refer to the Holy Bible for any questions regarding correct theology. Above all, when answers are unclear, please simply remember to ask God.

THE HOLY BIBLE, NEW INTERNATIONAL VERSION®, NIV® Copyright © 1973, 1978, 1984, 2011 by Biblica, Inc.® Used by permission. All rights reserved worldwide.
Cover Illustration and Formatting by Damonza.com

ISBN 978-1-7360925-0-7
eBook ISBN 978-1-7360925-1-4
First Edition
Printed in the U.S.A.

For my love,

that you would know how intense, how big you are to me.

You are the wax on my skis,

the water station at mile ten,

the haunches on my horse when she's straining at the gallop.

Yours is the smile I so desperately need

when I'm worn and feeling defeated.

Without you, this never would have happened.

Thank you!

Here's to simpler times,
when one so crushed in spirit needed only to hope
in the promise that comes from embarking
upon an adventure most grand,
and to be further blessed with the good fortune
never to return.

PROLOGUE

Jubair

WHILE MOST OF Switzerland slept, Jubair Talmuk, now three months into his one-year term as president, approached the trembling gray wall of his flat. It was close to midnight. Not a breeze disturbed the streets below, but whatever caused the clamor taking over his home had more than interrupted his rest. He pressed his ear against the textured paint; the noise came from the other side for sure. And it was moving closer.

"Ugh, again?" Jubair growled, pushing his palms over his ears.

The pipes in his building were always acting up. To Jubair, a busted pipe was annoying at best; at worst, it ruined clothing, carpeting, and sometimes left holes in the walls. It was messy. And Jubair hated messes.

He'd been resting in his favorite chair—it crushed velvet and as purple as Geneva's evening sky—gazing out his giant picture window when the hiss had begun. Though soft and barely noticeable at first, within a few minutes it shrieked, demanding attention.

Malfunctioning pipes shouldn't be this loud, Jubair thought, scanning the room. The plaster shook now, as if the sound had taken form and intended to steamroll its way straight through. Jubair stepped back, ducking as the pictures above him dropped from their nails. He winced when they landed, dreading the cleanup for shattered glass. The frames bounced at his feet, rattling loudly but still intact.

Soon everything shook, and Jubair could no longer focus on the agitated wall. The whole place jerked side to side, like a television screen caught between two wavelengths. Years had passed since a sizeable earthquake had struck the town, but perhaps this was another one. He was about to lower himself to brace against the floor when the wall suddenly bulged toward him as if whatever was on the other side was trying to push through. It ballooned so dramatically Jubair was sure it would burst, showering chips of paint and plaster everywhere. He shuddered and inched back, eyes locked on the wall, ready to jump away any moment. With a pop, the entire thing recoiled, undisturbed and still intact, depositing the form of a shadowy beast in its place.

Jubair gaped, heart pounding in his chest. A dragon, black, scaly, and smoldering, stood in his living room.

Cowering, Jubair raised his hands defensively before his face and waited for the attack. When nothing happened, he narrowed his eyes and peeked through his trembling fingers. Smoke thickened the air between them. Above him, its head blocked the light from the ceiling fixture, obscuring the beast's features. Its serpentine body was long, its back end somehow disappearing into the wall. But through the haze, its eyes were unmistakably clear—they glowed red and fixed, hungry.

"Jubair."

Jubair rubbed his face, testing his senses. His hands slid, damp from sweat, down his cheeks.

"Jubair," it said again.

"Me?" he answered weakly.

He wanted to run, but his legs felt heavy as boulders paralyzed, and when he tried to step away, they hardly moved. He tripped, almost falling, and turned again to face the thing. Hoping this was all a dream, he stood taller. If it wasn't, running wasn't a good option anyway. Dropping his arms to his sides, he stared it down, hands still shaking, struggling to calm himself. *This isn't possible*, he thought, reasoning the bourbon must be getting to him. He simply needed to close his eyes, and when he'd reopen them—

"I'm real, Jubair."

Jubair flinched and sucked in a breath, filling his chest with feigned confidence. It was still there.

The monster watched him quietly, then shook its head, clearing the steam from around its mouth. "Oh, please," it said, "relax. I'm not going to hurt you. I'm here to help."

"Who... why... do you want to help me?" Jubair stammered.

"Because we both want the same thing—peace and quiet. Order. And I believe if we work together, we will get that."

"To–together?" Jubair regained himself enough to step sideways. Something inside him jumped; he had control of his feet again! Edging his hand behind himself, he traced his fingers over kitchen drawers, searching for the utensils. He needed a weapon—anything other than just his hand—in case the beast approached.

His fingers fumbled against the meat thermometer. *This should do*, he thought, and grasped it tightly, wondering if he could distract it—*him?*—long enough to run, or if he'd have to stab it in the end. Jubair's mind swirled, weak from the nightcap and hazy from the smoke. Neither plan made sense, but then, this thing, this... *dragon*... didn't make sense. None of it did.

Jubair rubbed the back of his neck and took a deep breath. He'd just... talk. That would make things plain eventually, or if not, he could figure out something else. Steadying his hand, he forced one of his room-paralyzing smiles.

"Together. So, sir... what do you want me to do for you?"

"Ah, no worry. I wouldn't expect *you* to do anything for *me*. My ways are… complicated. You need *my* help if you want in. And trust me, you do."

"In? On what?"

"I want you to unite the world. Get humanity together, finally, so they can stand. You all need to be stronger. Together with *me*, you can be."

Jubair gawked. The thing didn't only talk, but it reasoned too—like a person. It spoke just as naturally as he did. Dazed, Jubair furrowed his brow, focusing on its words.

"You need to listen! Your people, divided as they are now, are going to miss an opportunity."

Jubair sucked in another breath and pinched his fingers together behind his back, regaining himself. "What do you mean?" he replied slowly. "How can I do all that? What opportunity?"

"You'll need to persuade some people to work together. The leaders of France and Germany and Israel, of course, plus a few more. Most of the others are insignificant. Troublemakers, really. In turn, I will give you reign over the UN. With my help, you will finally end the turmoil you can't seem to calm using just that smile of yours."

Jubair hesitated. "Who *are* you?"

The beast's words were enticing. It spoke of things Jubair had longed for ever since his boyhood. An end to all the bickering. Order. Unity. To top it off, something about its voice reassured him. It was familiar, like a memory he'd kept in the depths of his mind, in the place that held things he was fond of, things that filled him with warmth and comfort.

Jubair decided this was a *he* after all, not an *it*. The voice resonated raspy, but also deep, like a man's. Even without the monster's frightening appearance, he held an authoritative tone, which somehow calmed Jubair—just slightly—and made him want to hear more.

"Consider me a friend. An ally," the dragon answered.

His father. The beast sounded just like his father.

"Your name?" Jubair asked.

"Aren't you full of questions? Quite forward for being the one cowering with a metal spindle behind his back."

The monster flashed a golden claw, shimmering from atop one of four feet that, until now, Jubair hadn't noticed. "Now this is a weapon," the dragon said, and he licked it, tongue and claw igniting when they touched, in a burst of amber light, too bright to look at. He laughed. "Not *that* thing."

Jubair shuddered and took a step back. He had forgotten about the thermometer. Glancing around the kitchen, he wondered if his legs would work enough for him to outrun the beast—whose body, unfortunately, blocked the path to the door. The only other way out was through a window, fifteen stories above the street.

Jubair squared, fixing his eyes on the dragon. "Yes, well... you know my name. Why can I not know yours? You did say you were my friend."

"Fair enough," the dragon replied, staring back. "My name is Helel ben Shahar."

"Helel ben Shahar." Jubair rolled the name around his mouth, committing it to memory.

"Jubair, I came to give you something. You'll be needing more than what you have."

"Do I get a choice in this?" *If I don't, will you kill me?* Jubair closed his mouth to prevent the words from slipping out.

"I wouldn't worry. You and I should get along quite well." Lowering his head to Jubair's, the dragon puffed a hot breath into his face. It smelled acrid and sweet all at once—like spoiled fruit. He lingered there a minute, eyelids blinking from the sides like a lizard. Then, he turned and moved around the sterile room, his claws tracing the lines of the floor. "I tell you what. I don't have time to play around. Neither do you, though you may not realize it. Why don't you think about what I'm saying? I can offer you power and peace, Jubair, but I can also offer safety. In these times, and with what you're up to, safety is something you should consider. Let me leave you with the gift either way."

He jerked his head back once more and stared Jubair down. Flaring his nostrils, he snorted, blasting out glowing sparks. Jubair grimaced instinctively, but he gasped and sucked the embers into his chest. They burned. His eyes flew open at the pain, and he fell forward, clutching at the black tiles beneath him. He heaved, trying to expel the fire that seemed to have ignited in him. But each breath spread the sting deeper, beyond his lungs, into his belly and the flesh on his back, down through his arms and legs, until every inch of him felt singed, and he curled up on the floor, writhing in pain.

The dragon nodded, satisfied. Turning, he left the same way he'd come, through the wall, without a scratch of evidence he'd been there other than the pictures lying on the floor and the meat thermometer in Jubair's hand.

Jubair lay there another minute, trying to decide if any of what had just happened had been real. His hands still shook. He squeezed them tight, trying unsuccessfully to steady them. Pushing himself upright on the black-marbled floor of his designer kitchen, Jubair propped his back against a kitchen cabinet, the cold stone beneath his legs reassuring him he was awake and safe.

Puke. That was all he wanted to do—wretch, hurl, spew everything sour from his throat, just to cleanse himself of whatever was taking over his body. Jubair was sick, yes, and exhausted, and his stomach was bloated—so, so bloated—like he'd overeaten and then eaten twice as much afterward. He'd been down for days, achy and wracked with cold chills, curled up in his fancy, five hundred-count linens with his felt-lined blanket wrapped around him, sipping steaming mugs of chamomile. Nothing had helped. Even water turned his stomach and tasted like mildew and rust.

The serpent had done this; it was as if he'd injected him with poison. Jubair rolled over and stared at the shiny wood fan whirring above him from the slatted ceiling, but it made his head spin, worsening his nausea. He squeezed his eyes shut.

Something had changed in him. He felt sick, yes, but also... restless. Energized. Eager. He wanted to start something that ended in violence. He wanted to charge at someone, anyone. But not just that. He needed to punch and kick, and kick some more and *run*—run fast and far. And while running, he'd pummel his way through anything or anyone in his path until all the energy pulsing through him ran out.

If he could only find a way to stand first.

Aching for a breath of fresh air, Jubair tried to sit again. But his head swirled as soon as he was upright, and he tipped backward. With a grunt, he scooted toward his pillow, propped himself as high as he dared, and shut his eyes.

Pinching his lids tight, he raised his forehead, trying in vain to separate himself from the nausea. After a few moments, he gave up, ready to lie there until death if need be.

The phone rang, just as he was drifting off.

"Argh!" *Why was the phone always ringing?* Jubair smashed the pillow over his ears to drown out its shrill nag, but it was too loud and apparently had no intention of stopping.

He shot up and hurled the pillow at the phone, missing it and knocking a nearby vase off its stand. The vase crashed, shattering across the floor. Jubair could almost hear every splinter take its course—one skidding, another bouncing, another stabbing between the oak planks.

Shocked, he sat, staring at what remained of the vase—chaos.

I

Jack

YEARS LATER AND a sea apart from where things first started, the walls of an underground bunker shook ominously. Jack Barron furrowed his brow at a computer screen, his jaw clenched in frustration. Concentrating was difficult these days, even though the tremors were now familiar, more a rumbling background for the worrisome BBC news updates the satellite radio spat out. But two months ago, they'd decided to continue their work. The satellites still worked, after all, and to sit around worrying was maddening. So, there they brewed, studying again how and why the ancient Ubar civilization had escaped being found for millennia, while the buildings above succumbed to the forces rocking their shelter.

"Captain Jack, would you like a smoke break?" Rashid interrupted.

Jack rolled his eyes at the nickname. "Seriously? Dude, you're going to get black lung." *Or die*, he thought.

"Come on, I need to take out the trash, and Boss wants us to harvest more toiletries."

"Now? Didn't you feel that last bomb? They could be crawling around up there."

"Do you really think they'd be patrolling the same area they're actively bombing?" Rashid answered, shifting weight. His thick Egyptian accent was now easy to Jack's ear. "Please, I need an excuse to get out there, even if just for a few minutes. I want to view the situation."

Jack minimized the screen, slid his chair back, and stood, feeling the stretch across the rear of his thighs. He'd been sitting too long anyway. *Enriching work environment,* the ad had said, *perfect location for independent study and cultural advancement.*

"All right, let's go." He sighed, glancing around the window-less pit they now called home. Jack's team—the ones left—had been holed up in it for the last three months. It was originally built decades before as a secret retreat for the university's famous founder, Ahmed Lutfi el-Sayed. No one even knew the place existed until two years before Jack's recruitment, though it was thought to have been used during World War I.

Rashid unbolted the heavy steel doors, inviting in a gust of dry heat from above as the two stepped out. To the left, a thick cloud of smoke expanded, creeping closer. Its source could have been anything—a sandstorm, fire, air bombs. To the right lay what remained of the University of Cairo. The library still stood, mag-ically intact, as did a few other buildings and half of Kakyoin's Water Tower. It had all been transformed from its prior glorious mix of industrial silver-gray and green to a new landscape of yellow-brown destruction, covered in dust and ash.

"Prof says they should have the perimeter moved out another mile by the end of the month," Jack whispered, scanning the area to the north, where the food court sat.

Rashid nodded solemnly, eyes intent on the latest smoke plume pushing its way around them, further enriching the air with carbon dioxide and ash. "Well, the explosions do seem farther out than last week," he mumbled, then sucked a breath in and squared off to Jack. "So, food court or The Cook?"

Jack laughed. The Cook Door restaurant was a longer walk,

but it also contained Rashid's favorite treat of late—milkshake powder, which, when mixed with water, was loads better than the canned peas and ketchup they'd be getting from the food court.

"You're so fat. Toiletries were the request, not junk food."

"Aww, come on. We're risking our lives out here," Rashid pleaded. "And what about you? You're speed-aging from all the stress. You practically look thirteen now! I'm just saying we need to make it worth our sacrifice."

"Dude, the only stress I have right now is you." Jack turned to punch Rashid in the shoulder. But Rashid's face had darkened at the word "sacrifice," and he now stared ahead, blank-faced. Jack nudged him gently. "Hey, you okay?"

Rashid shook his head and refocused. "There's more fresh air this way. The Cook it is."

The two crept forward, dodging the view of any drones by keeping to the shadows and piles of rubble.

The battle here had not been going on when Jack had taken this job. But two years before, a meteor shower hit Burma. NASA hadn't even seen it coming. It obliterated much of Asia and parts of Africa. Fiji was devastated, and the impact caused an earthquake, waking the supervolcano in southern Japan. Casualties were so high WHO stopped counting. The ash cloud rising from the eruption wreaked its havoc, destroying crops, blacking out the sun, and poisoning the rain in the surrounding two thousand miles. There were photos online of the bleak gray horizon. Noon looked like two in the morning, and even night appeared darker with no stars or functioning streetlights to brighten the sky. The refraction of light through the stratosphere, now rich with sulfur and who-knew-what other gases, made the moon look red. Alas, natural disasters only aided the cause of the corrupt, and while the world and her spirit were recuperating from it all, the wicked started in on her injured frame, and the war had begun.

The clanging of metal against stone jarred Jack out of his

thoughts, and he flinched. Rashid had tripped on a steel sign, bent and ragged. It read:

Welcome to the world's center
for the advancement in Political Science,
Anthropology, and Egyptology

"Rash, where did you learn to walk? You sound like a drunk cow."

Rashid wrinkled his forehead. "Drunk cow? And when was the last time you heard one of those? Is this another of your strange America sayings?"

"No, that one came from my abundant creative brilliance. Don't hate," Jack answered, grinning.

"Shh! I'm not hating, but you're louder than me. Do you want some fake ice cream or not? Because we won't get it—or the toilet paper—if we die first."

Just as Jack rolled his eyes, the sky flashed, illuminating the fog to a sickening yellow tan. The air cracked a few seconds later, delayed as if it were choreographed to hit the men as soon as they released their held breath. Hunching down, Jack shot a glance over his shoulder. A boulder tumbled in the distance, pluming dust from its impact. A building to their right fell, shaking the ground beneath them.

"Now, Rash, go!" Jack yelled and sprinted into the restaurant.

"I got the TP; you get the food," Rashid answered, making a beeline for the janitor's closet.

In fifteen seconds, the men had retrieved their treasures and left out the back door this time. They'd have to circle the university now, just in case whatever dropped the bomb had eyes on them. The deal was never let the drones see the bunker. No matter what.

The men ran through the alley, keeping as close to the struc-

4

ture's brick walls as possible, until they came to Ahmed Zewail, the street separating them from the part of campus they needed to get to.

"Go for the awning!" Jack hissed, though the awning had all but been destroyed. They smashed their backs against the building and scooted sideways under the shredded cloth.

Another boom filled their ears as Cook Door collapsed to their left. The streetlights shuddered, the two nearest the restaurant toppling back onto the building, tearing chunks of sidewalk up with them.

"What?" Rashid whispered. "Are you serious? That place had my jam!"

"Ha!" Jack blurted, then forced back his laugh. "It did? What kind of your jam did it have, exactly?"

"Had my jam, you know... *my jam*."

"*Was* your jam, Rash. That place was your jam." Jack answered. "And now it is jam-packed with its outsides." He searched the sky for the drone that had unleashed on them but couldn't see anything through the fog of falling dust.

"We need to wait," Rashid said, as if reading his mind. "They're still up there. If we go now, we're toasted."

"Yeah, you're probably right." Jack slid down to his heels and sighed, trying to calm his nerves.

They waited silently for a few minutes until the adrenaline was too much for Jack and his legs jiggled impatiently. He cocked his head towards Rashid, eager for distraction.

"So, uh... Have you heard any news about your family?"

"Not yet," Rashid said. "The part of town where we lived is now leveled. I'm holding off on hope until they let us leave this place." He paused and stared up at the sky. "I can't."

Rashid's wife and daughter were home when the first bomb had hit. He'd initially tried to leave the campus, but the artillery and destruction had been unpassable. Jack had found him in the main parking lot, his trembling hands scrounging through the debris, desperately searching for a way to get through to his family. Jack practically had to carry Rashid to the bunker, amidst exploding rock and screaming students. Since then, from what Jack could tell by overhearing Rashid's phone calls—which were rare as the phones only occasionally worked—his friends and family had no clue as to their whereabouts. It was as if they'd been erased.

The two men remained there an hour, watching the smoke plume they had spotted before. From here, it was obvious where it had originated—across the Nile, where the FREA rebels had been collecting—and executing—prisoners. The murky cloud silently swallowed the university, dropping a powdery mist around them.

"They're gone," Jack said, only in part referring to the drones. "And I'm officially too hot, Rash. Let's get back in."

"All right, Captain. Let's go find some dead guys."

Jack gave Rashid a sideways glance. Even though he knew he was referring to the gone civilizations they spent their days searching for, the ash, silently coating their sweaty necks likely contained more *dead guys* than they'd find in their entire careers.

11

THE DEVIL STOOD across from the Lord in their usual meeting place, in a plane out of man's reach, where only angels roamed. A giant metallic stone was wedged between them, the only ornament in the otherwise empty space.

The Lord said to the devil, "Where have you come from?"

The devil, who was also Satan, the great deceiver and serpent, answered the Lord. "From roaming the Earth, going back and forth on it."

Then the Lord said to him, "The time is coming. You need to start if you are going to try to win over my children."

The devil's eyes narrowed. He leaned forward and pressed his hands flat on the stone, which was much too cool for his liking.

"You speak as if I have a chance but write in their Bible that we shall fight, and I will be defeated and thrown into the abyss for a thousand years! You have even recorded that, in the final battle, I lose again and will then be thrown into a lake of burning sulfur!"

"I have spoken," answered the Lord. "You do as you must. The time is coming whatever you decide." The time He spoke of was the end of days for man and the beginning of the end of Satan's reign on Earth. He turned to leave.

The devil raised his voice, desperate because of the Lord's decree. "I was a magnificent angel. The most beautiful testament to your power and strength—your creation! Am I not your child as well? Is it not expected a child to be rebellious at times? But people—who repeatedly rebel against their human parents *and you*, just as I did—are granted resolve. You say you are just, but this is not the case."

The Lord stopped and faced the devil. He was right. People *were* held to different standards than angels. He changed the subject.

"Have you considered my servant Isaiah? There is no one on Earth like her; she is blameless and upright, a woman who fears God and shuns evil."

Satan recoiled, then slammed his hands on the now-gleaming stone.

"Oh, not this again!" His wings folded tight against his back. "She is one of your weakest children. Her, too, you have put a hedge around. She has rarely felt loss, and has been blessed her entire life. Even her hands you have blessed in healing, so most of whom she has treated have lived. Of *course,* a woman always answered and never tempted will seem strong and upright. But strike just one thing, and she will surely turn from you."

The Lord said to Satan, "Very well, you may have power over her blessings. See if you can tempt her. But do not lay a finger on her." He paused, then added, "As for the rest of my children, you are not to present yourself to them in any deceitful form for the rest of their time. You have done quite enough of that. You are a snake, a sly dragon who seeks to burn up and devour, and so shall you present yourself to them from here until the end, with nothing but your speech and powers to deceive them any longer."

With His words, the devil's body fixed permanently to the form which he would keep for eternity. Before that day, he could take on any likeness he chose to tempt or deceive others according to his desires.

Then Satan went out from the presence of the Lord.

III

Isaiah

ISAIAH LAY WIDE awake, staring blankly at her phone, which sat a foot away on the end table. Why had she bothered to drive home to sleep? She'd already worked until midnight, finishing charts, messages, and refill requests, but was on call for both general medicine and obstetrics, so likely there'd be some reason for her to go in early. In the less than four hours she'd been home, three times already they had called. Despite her exhaustion, she was having difficulty getting back to sleep. When her husband had been there, with his warm body and strong arms to cuddle into, she had always fallen asleep quickly, no matter how often the thing went off. Isaiah touched her lips, remembering his thick, heavy kisses.

As if greeting her good morning, the phone went off again, beeping and vibrating all around the table. She startled; even though it had been five years since residency, their calls still shook her—the alarm was like a warning that someone somewhere was about to die, and each second she snoozed could be hastening it.

Please don't be OB, please don't be OB, she thought, grabbing the little monster, willing it to stop. She clicked the buttons haphazardly until she hit the right one. A fluorescent green light rewarded her efforts, illuminating the hospital line that beckoned.

Of course. OB.

She had one last baby to deliver before she gave up OB—obstetrics—for good. But this last mommy was the definition of high maintenance. She kept showing up with new emergencies, each time knowing all the right words to incite concern in an overcautious physician. She'd even shown up in Isaiah's office with typed lists of symptoms, interestingly like those on the internet-based diagnosis tools open to the public, for all the scariest pregnancy complications.

Isaiah tapped the green Answer button on the phone. "Hi, this is Dr. Robinson."

"Hi, Dr. Robinson. This is Sherry in Labor and Delivery. Tiffany Blanc is here. She's thirty-two weeks and three, G1P0. This is her third visit this month. She says the baby hasn't been moving, and her water broke."

Baby not moving. Come now.

"Is she on the monitor?"

"Yes. So far, heart tones are reassuring. No contraction patterns. We have a dry pad under her. Says she changed it herself when she was alone in the room because it was getting wet. Vitals are good."

"I'll be in soon. She needs a BPP—please get it ordered." And with that, scrubs became the outfit of the day. Again.

Isaiah encouraged her tangled, not-quite-too-greasy hair into a wadded-up bun and slid the blue linens over her curved hips. Getting ready took less than thirty seconds now, which was monumentally faster than the twenty minutes it used to take in the mornings under similar circumstances. Now she only had to brush her teeth, grab a Coke to turn on a few extra brain cells, and go. Before, there were bodies to shake awake, Spiderman sock mates to find, lunches to pack, and breakfasts to hustle down mouths that barely had time to say, "Good morning, Mommy."

It turned out to be another false alarm in the end. Tiffany waited for her with two friends this time, giggling and grinning through Isaiah's wasted hustle. The pad, her vaginal canal, everything was dry, dry, dry—no leaking fluid from ruptured membranes. Negative ferning, nitrazine, and amniotic fluid protein swabs normal, the biophysical profile ultrasound was perfect—another morning given up for the young woman's enjoyment.

After leaving Labor and Delivery, Isaiah headed down the sterile blue-and-gray halls to make her rounds before clinic. The good thing about being here early was she had more time to be intentional about her work, and if she could help someone have a little longer or better run in life, then she was happy to spend the extra time. The hours she spent didn't all feel like work to Isaiah. And no place had she worked before were results as immediate as on the floors of the hospital.

She sat at the desk behind the counter in the ICU and pulled out three patient charts.

"You're here early."

The night nurse was Ginger this time. Isaiah loved Ginger—she was thorough and kind, and just *good* at what she did. Plus, being still fresh in the world of medicine, Isaiah appreciated a nurse who gave gentle nudges of advice when she got nervous and graceful protocol reminders when she didn't see things clearly herself. Ginger knew how to help—and guide if needed—without making Isaiah feel like an incompetent idiot. She was the kind of nurse that could bring you to the point of finding that missing piece for a failing patients' recovery.

"Hey, yeah, on call." Isaiah shrugged. How did she always look so bright-eyed and pretty? Even after a night shift, her makeup was perfect—down to her neatly lined pink lips—and her blonde hair styled as if she'd just stepped out of a salon.

"Coffee?" Her southern accent smiled the offer at Isaiah.

"That. Would be… amazing," Isaiah answered, grinning broadly. She focused on the first chart and set her mind on the world of biochemistry and anatomy.

The first patient was a ninety-three-year-old man who presented to the ER septic and hallucinating about his wife, who'd been gone for twenty years. He had aspiration pneumonia on top of emphysema, and just for a little extra challenge, a new desire to die. His kids, of course, wanted no such thing, so the first task was to get him out of his delirium, to have a real conversation with everyone involved—including Dad—in his normal, lucid state.

Ginger set a Styrofoam cup next to Isaiah and sat on the counter next to her, eying the chart.

"He had a good night. I got to remove the O2 for a few hours after his neb, and his sats stayed up. He did try to hit me, but I sweet-talked him down."

Isaiah laughed. "Hit you or hit *on* you?" This man was the same one who had smacked her own butt once during an office visit. He was sick and on dialysis, so she hadn't fired him. Instead, she'd turned around and corrected him harshly, but now all the ladies taking care of him had to be aware.

Ginger grinned. "Does it matter? My persuasions got him to calm down, and look—no restraints!"

No restraints. That meant one less call in the middle of the night and one less trip in. Ginger was amazing.

"You rock," Isaiah said, sipping her coffee—the bone-thinning, stomach-wrenching, beautiful, eye-opening nectar that it was. After thumbing through the labs and telemetry readings from the preceding twenty-four hours, she folded up the chart and headed into her patient's room. As she entered, the blood pressure cuff hissed quietly, announcing another round of vitals data would soon be displayed on the monitor.

"Mr. Smith?"

"No one's home," the man grunted.

"Hmm, well, maybe I can talk to you instead?" Isaiah clasped the old man's hand between hers and studied his glazed-over eyes, which were purposely pointed away. "How was your night, sir?"

"Fine," he snorted. "When do I get out of here?"

Isaiah smiled, his first sign of hope. "You think you can get out of this bed today? We need you to walk and keep your oxygen up. Ginger can help if you think you can." He'd still need the oxygen to do it, but they'd get him out of bed and moving as early as possible. It was good for the lungs and sped recovery. Plus, patients felt better when they had a goal to aim for when they were this sick.

"Ugh… I guess." He finally glanced up and squeezed her hand. "Has my family been by to see me?"

"Every day."

"Well, damn. I guess the secret is out then. No hiding our love now."

She shook her head, smiling. "Nope, *you* are officially the talk of the town." Yes, old Mr. Smith was back to his old self.

After Isaiah left the ICU, she rounded on six of her partners' patients—her duty for being on call. She smiled as she closed the last chart, with its stable labs and even blood pressures over the preceding forty-eight hours. Clinic wouldn't start for another hour.

On the other side of the hospital campus, Isaiah unlocked the door to her dark, still-sleeping clinic and treaded to her office. Four people smiled brightly from a photo on the corner of her desk. Their skin glowed, golden from a week in the sun, and they stood leaning into each other around a sign that read *Cozumel*.

Isaiah winced. Not nine months ago, she was Mrs. Mommy, MD, the spread-thin hero of her surroundings. But now she was just Dr. Robinson, beloved physician in Small Town, Indiana. Not to say she wasn't grateful for what she still had—every minute of work kept her from imploding. But she ached for her family, for the warmth of her children's sticky smooth fingers, her husband's hot breath on her neck, her three-year-old's thick, dark eyelashes, tickling her own as they kissed goodnight.

Blinking, she took a breath, chased her family out of her mind—a strong step for her—and focused on the computer. CNN's cover story flashed before her. Another earthquake had hit Japan. Thousands more dead. She sighed and leaned back in her chair.

So many disasters had occurred lately, both natural and man-made, and they just kept coming. An update flashed about last month's tsunami. It, along with the earthquake, were aftershocks from the meteor strike—still, weeks later. They buried one hundred fifty thousand people last week, and there were more to come. The report said *thousands* or more dead and unaccounted for. All those numbers—in the end not even labeled as men, women, or children—just washed away. She thought of the people caught up in the tsunami's waves, ragdolls in the force of nature. It horrified her to imagine the children, their bodies slamming into cars or buildings underwater, screaming as frigid currents filled their delicate lungs, reaching for someone to save them.

Isaiah closed the screen and stared blankly at the wall, allowing her fatigue to consume her. She was tired, so tired. Lately, when the exhaustion came, if she wasn't busy, she just let it enter—let it fill her and chase out any hope that things would get better. The sorrow would drift in and lift her, helpless as debris, tossing her around and rushing her toward the seafloor.

Why, Lord? she thought. *Why let them all die?* Tears welled behind her eyes. She ruminated again on her own family, this time unable to shake the thought. She hadn't been there to save them, either.

Isaiah dropped her head into her arms on the designer wooden desk. Mass graves. Death. Sorrow. Monday.

IV

"INTERNET IS UP!" Rashid called from his corner of the bunker.

"Yes!" Jack said, spinning in his chair to face the desktop monitor. He opened his email first thing, hoping to skim his inbox before they lost it again. He longed to hear from someone, anyone, from home. The war had hit the US, too, but, for the most part, other than the constant vigils and the red, white, and blues now waving ruthlessly from every building, life there went on as usual. He scrolled down until he found a message entitled, *Help!* from an unfamiliar email address, EHarper@hotmail.com.

Jack Barron:

My name is Dr. Elise Harper. I'm a medical missionary with Salvage Health Inc. and a fellow scientist. I was given your name as a talented archaeologist and was told you are exceptionally good at interpreting satellite photography.

I need your help. I would like to speak with you directly. Is there a secure phone number I can try to reach you? Or could you call me when your phone lines are operational? I need help with an extremely important project, and am willing to compensate you by sharing profits if you find what I am searching for. You can reach me at the contact info listed below. Please respond to this message either way to let me know if you have received it.

Most Sincerely,

Your sister in Christ

Elise Harper, MD

964 36 377 7121

Jack furrowed his brow. *Sharing profits?* Well, that was open-ended. What could she want from him? The letter rang of wasted time and an unexposed scheme. But it never hurt to get a second opinion.

"Hey, Bossman, will you look at something?" Jack called, chewing on his lip.

"Ah, Elise finally wrote you, did she?"

Jack startled. His Archaeologic Dating Techniques professor already stood peering over his shoulders. The old man was full of surprises; he seemed to enjoy shocking his students. But Jack knew better than to underestimate him. Not many seventy-some-things with a cane could drag two stumbling, full-grown men by their shirt backs—through active artillery—to safety.

"Dr. Farenheim. You know about this, sir? What does she want?"

"Her parents are friends of mine. She's a bit... inimitable. She has this fanatical plan to find a cure for cancer and all things bad in the world. She thinks she's discovered directions to a Fountain of Youth, of sorts. In the Bible."

"Fountain of Youth, sir?"

"Correct. You're a Christian if I'm not mistaken?"

"Yes, sir." Jack sat up a little straighter. "But really?"

The professor smiled. "I thought her idea more fitting for another zealot of Jesus than myself. Given our current... predica-ment. If you wanted to undertake some extracurricular study with university equipment, I would okay it." His eyes twinkled. "I'll approve any paperwork coming across my desk."

"But, I don't understand."

"Well, actually, I don't either. But whatever she has in that brain of hers has kept her happy through all this. Hope is powerful, son." He patted Jack's shoulder. "This would be good for your mind and maybe for your colleague's too. Clear the fog, as they say." He dipped his head toward Rashid, who sat staring at his palms on the other side of the room, then turned and walked away.

"Thanks, Professor," Jack said to his retreating back. He fingered the wheel on his mouse.

Jack had never been a man of many talents. In fact, he considered himself generally boring, with not much defining him besides his love for all things old or extinct. He didn't speak another language or play any instruments, and he couldn't play any sport well enough to join even the Sunday-night leagues. He didn't even like bowling... and didn't everyone bowl?

But *this* was what he did. So far, this was what he was good at too. At barely twenty-six years old, he'd already made himself known to the archaeology world. He had publications pointing out—politely—how ancient sites could have been found much faster by using information gathered from space photographs, ancient writings, and a little word of mouth. The submerged Egyptian trade city, Heracleion, for example, was found in 2000. Its discovery took years of geophysical survey—ground-based, sweaty effort—along with sophisticated and expensive excavating. Using his system that he touted in his most recent article, it could have been easily located within a few weeks.

Up until now, though, his work concerned already known sites. This might be an opportunity to find something new. With everything going on, he had to believe a purpose to his work existed out here. Somehow, the war, in all its horror and turmoil, solidified this in his mind. Perhaps this was it—the thing he was meant to do.

18

Jack scooted his chair closer to the screen, squared his shoulders, and dialed the number at the bottom of the email. It rang once.

"Hello? This is Elise Harper."

"Yes, my name is Jack Barron. I received an email from you today. Looks like you sent it some time ago, but our internet has been down."

"Mr. Barron, yes! I have a proposal for you. I hear you're something of an expert in your field—and you're a fellow Christian."

"I am a Christian, but I'm still learning on the rest of it."

"Oh good, you're humble too." Her voice came out rushed. "Well, let me get to it. I'm putting together a team for a research expedition to find a very special place. Unfortunately, we don't yet know where we should target our search. I believe you may be able to locate it for me."

"The Fountain of Youth, ma'am?"

She laughed. "I see Brad let you in on my obsession. It isn't a fountain, though. Well, there *could* be a fountain, I don't know. But anyway, yes. Something like that."

Leaning back in his chair, Jack raised his eyebrows at the professor, who now watched musing from across the room. "So, what do you need me to find exactly?"

"I hoped you could help pinpoint the location of the River of Life. On your computer. Your satellite... deal."

"River of Life?" Jack hesitated. "I'm sorry, I don't follow."

Elise continued. "Okay, I've been in prayer, and I have heard from God. The thing that will heal us—all of us—is located where River of Life started. I can give you some general information— what I already know about its location—and I figured you could use your brain and experience to find it. You'll give me some coordinates, and my team will trace it back to its source. Or where its source would have been. Originally."

"Originally." *She'd heard from God?*

"Yes, like…" Elise's excitement was audible over the line. "Like when the earth first formed."

Jack rubbed his forehead in frustration. He had no idea what she was talking about.

"I'm sorry, I…" His voice trailed off. "We're in a war zone. I'm just trying not to get killed right now. At some point, the rebels might hit our hardware out there. Then I wouldn't even have what you need me to have for… whatever you need me to find. This is just… I don't think I'm your guy."

"I'm so sorry. But isn't this a better thing to think about than all that?" Elise answered. "Something good? Fun, even?"

Jack considered her words. He wasn't quite sure what the River of Life was, but rivers he could find—even old ones. And it would be fun. "I'm sorry, can you just explain this to me one more time?"

"Listen, I know this sounds crazy. All I need you to do is find the river's original route in the general location I send you and trace it back to its source. I can give you what I know, and if you could locate something fitting the description, I'd—we'd be—that would be just what we need."

"And would I be able to come along when you set out as well? In the field, I mean, later."

Elise paused on the other end. "Well, yes. Yes, of course! We would be honored for you to come. It won't be a big expedition—this trip will be just to *find* it and collect a few specimens if we can. But certainly, you can come. We'll wait until it's safe for you to leave. I believe your circumstances should be changing soon—I *know* they will be, actually. If you're coming, then certainly, they will be, of course. Oh good, thank you!"

Elise's response confused Jack. How could his commitment to come in any way affect the circumstances of the war? But he was hardly a man to pass up an adventure.

"Well, this will be interesting. Send me the details, and I'll see what I can see."

"Wonderful, thanks again. I look forward to hearing back."

The call ended with Jack's mind reeling. This was either going to be the treasure hunt of the century or a dead-end, hike-to-nowhere camping trip. He decided he didn't care; he'd go either way. His mind could use some resetting.

V

ISAIAH'S INBOX PEERED back at her as she sat at the computer to get some charting done before her shower. Four spam messages showed up for every single important email in her inbox, even in the hospital's Outlook account. How was that even possible? She skimmed the subject lines and origination addresses until she found one worthy of her time. Elise! Elise had written!

Hi Isaiah:

I'm writing from Kurdistan, Iraq. I just finished a two-month gig with Salvage Health. Wow, what a work God is doing here, even in this crushed society! I may or may not be PPD positive after this one, but what an amazing time!

God revealed a great plan to me, and He wants you to be a part of it too. Has He put it on your heart yet? We are needed for His service in the East.

It's a new day, Isaiah. When can I call you? I was thinking about 10 p.m. your time, 5 a.m. my time? You pick when works, and I'll call.

This is the day!

Elise

Isaiah's heart trembled as she read the words. A whisper of

air trickled down her arms and across her back, raising goose bumps in its path and filling her with restless energy. She wondered at the letter. Elise had always been eccentric. The two had met in medical school on an island in the South Caribbean, and Isaiah had been drawn to Elise's vibrancy, even from the start. She was enthusiastic at the very least and lived with unashamed confidence stemming from her desire to do everything from her love for God.

Isaiah sighed. For the love of God. How far had she come from that girl herself? She longed to live that way again. *Could I?* she thought. *Do you remember me, Lord? I miss you... I miss us. Do you still love me?*

God's answer filled her mind. *This is Me.*

She opened her eyes and gaped across the kitchen. There it was. She had her answer, simple as could be. She had done nothing but offer a three-sentence prayer, and yet, how long had it been since she'd heard Him, even sought Him? Work, family, cleaning house, organizing finances, work, apologizing for missed birthdays, exercising, work, work, work. Life was so full, even Sunday mornings had become just another time of catching up—apologetically for sure—but wasted, nonetheless. And now, here He was, loving her with purpose and a plan, and His lovely, pure, all-powerful voice.

This is Me.

She heard Him again, a gentle nudge back to the reality of Him.

She breathed deeply, staring at the email again. *This* was Him? Going to the East and doing what? Surely this was a call to share the gospel, which was definitely a passion of hers, but where? And for how long? The last time she left her patients for a month, three had died—two unnecessarily. It left her wary of leaving them again. After what had happened to her family, her patients were all she had left.

"Lord... what?" she whispered.

Lean not on your own understanding, Isaiah.

She held her breath, intent on the voice. Of course, His ways weren't always easy, nor did they always make sense at first glance. Was He trying to teach her to have faith? Or could this be a chance to reset her heart? Whatever this was, it was clear He wanted her in it.

In the past, He had done things like this to show that He was who He said He was. The memories of challenges He'd allowed her—which always had turned out for the good, she had to admit—were the memories she called on when things hurt, when she felt alone, or defeated, or ready for the slaughter. And now, for Him to love her so intimately that He would do this, create another chance for one of those memories—a time designed for and *by* Him, special for her... Well, she definitely could not miss out on whatever lay ahead. Smiling again, she embraced His words and the reminder of His love for her even when she wasn't looking.

Isaiah committed silently to go along with whatever her wild friend had in mind. She'd take this adventure and leave behind security because God had asked her to. She pulled up to the desk, straightened her spine, and leaned forward to write back.

Elise,

You are such an inspiration. I miss you! I'm on board. Let's talk Saturday morning your time, Friday night mine. I can't wait to hear about Iraq. Stay safe!

Isaiah

༺

Friday night at ten, she was still at the office, closing charts. Her eyes had been dried out for an hour now. They had always been her timer, telling her when to leave during these late-night work sessions. When the double vision started in or when she couldn't relieve persistent dry eye with repeated blinking, she'd shut down the Electronic Medical Record, no matter the number of open charts, unresolved patient messages, or results to review; she was done. Just as she checked the clock, her phone rang.

"Isaiah!" Elise's voice rang clear though half a world away. "How are you? It's great to hear from you!"

"I'm wonderful. Good, full of joy. I've never been more excited. God has been doing great work out here. I've seen *so many* miracles! He's showing up in the darkness, saving lives, and changing hearts. Isaiah, Salvage Health is *amazing*. They go where no one else does and help the poor and forgotten. I'm really blessed to be a part of it."

Isaiah smiled to herself. Elise was the same old genuinely dramatic friend she loved.

Elise went into detail about the compound she was staying in, the diseases she'd been slaying, and the midnight worship she'd been a part of. Tuberculosis had spread through the refugee camps, threatening thousands of lives, and she was there to fight it. Elise spoke quickly, her passion evident in every word.

Isaiah's heart sank. Elise's life overflowed with purpose and love—everything hers lacked. She listened quietly, chastising herself for her jealousy. *Thou shall not covet*, she recited mentally, stewing on the commandment she struggled with lately. This world was not for her, anyway—it was all for God and His glory. Her troubles would eventually end; this was just a season.

Seasons. She used to think this was just a pretty word Christians used to explain away random events. Now she knew it to be reassurance in the cycle of things—the start and end of the school year, the calendar flux through the holidays, everchanging waves of color and décor, spring changing into summer changing into fall changing into winter. Just like these inevitable shifts, the seasons of life were always in flux. A season was a place to rest with quiet anticipation for what would come next.

Isaiah's next season laid itself out through Elise's voice. It wasn't a mission trip after all. Elise wanted to go on a hunt for the Garden of Eden and harvest fruit from the Tree of Life. She wanted Isaiah to travel to the Middle East—now, at a time when the US Department of State had posted a travel warning not just to Israel, but also to the surrounding five countries. Her idea was for Isaiah to fly in all her fair-skinned, hair-flowing glory to a place where American Christians, even local Christians, were seen as opportunities for target practice. Nice.

Didn't I say, "Lean not on your own understanding?" She heard God's voice again. *I will give you the words you need. Have I ever failed you?*

He was difficult to argue with. So, despite her fear, she didn't.

Afterward, she pulled out of the manicured parking lot decorating the new hospital clinic. The sky was dark, starless. The streetlights shrank and disappeared behind her as her Subaru turned off the side road onto Highway 27, with its five empty, county-police-monitored lanes. Soon, she was the only light around.

Sleepy Town, USA, she thought with a sigh.

VI

"ALL RIGHT, WE have something here," Jack announced, switching the screen to infrared. A series of new lines, dark and winding, appeared on the monitor.

Rashid and Eva, the other graduate student staying with them, peered over his shoulder at the image. What seemed to be a river's remains dominated the screen, it weaving under one of central Georgia's mountain ranges. It was large and thick and had at least two discernable branches.

Jack grabbed a piece of paper and drew a map of his proposed River of Life and its branches. He needed to validate all four branching river systems to match the description Dr. Harper had given him, which came from the first book of the Holy Bible, Genesis.

> [10]A river watering the garden flowed from Eden; from
> there it was separated into four headwaters. [11]The
> name of the first is the Pishon; it winds through the
> entire land of Havilah, where there is gold. [12]The gold
> of that land is good; aromatic resin and onyx are also
> there. [13]The name of the second river is the Gihon; it
> winds through the entire land of Cush. [14]The name of
> the third river is the Tigris; it runs along the east side
> of Ashur. And the fourth river is the Euphrates.

"So the descriptions for the river say it has four headwaters." He said, tracing the branches on his drawing. "These?"

Rashid patted his back. "Captain Jack Barron, at it again, using nothing but stealth and stale coffee, has found the original river leading from the famed Garden of Eden! Stay tuned for his next satellite-imagery adventure."

Satellite photography had near saved Egyptology. In the 1960s, the only way to prove where rivers used to flow was through expensive fieldwork and land surveys. A few decades later, the infrared spectrum on satellite photography was found to be able to identify old, buried waterways—even those underwater themselves. That was because old riverbeds were rich in mineral deposits, which resulted in and were increased by plant life in an otherwise dry landscape. Biodegraded plant remains reflected light on the infrared spectrum; one only needed to apply infrared light to the satellite imagery, and miraculously, old river channels appeared where none existed. It was like seeing back in time. Since it had been utilized, money was spent more efficiently. Paying for people to stare at screens left more funding for the targeted, boots-on-the-ground archaeological digs of old.

"Yes, I see where it was." Rashid leaned farther forward, studying the screen. "But where's its source? This river supposedly originated somewhere underground, correct? Or at least in the Garden itself? So, there would need to be an underground tributary or at least have enough mountain springs to feed into it to make it that large."

"Yeah, there's that," Jack answered and shrugged. "I'll find it."

"Okay, call us when you do."

Jack clicked on a separate computer screen. He wondered vaguely if they'd actually found it. Speculation over the years as to the Garden's exact location ranged from somewhere in the Congo to multiple sites in northeast Africa and the Mediterranean, to the Mormon's site in Jackson County, Missouri. But

here in Georgia's mountain ranges and coniferous forests north of
Turkey, no one had suspected. Though here did make sense. The
Caucasus Mountains' thick, pine-laden forest seemed to pop out
of the surrounding desert, with its land rich and fertile. Millions
of acres sat, many yet to be explored by man, especially given
the turmoil in the surrounding countries.

He leaned back in his chair, calling over his shoulder. "Prof,
can I use GRACE?"

NASA's GRACE mission—Gravity Recovery and Climate
Experiment—had groundbreakingly introduced a highly exact
way to measure water beneath the Earth's surface. It worked
by measuring tiny variations in the Earth's gravity to evaluate
the underground water's mass. Since the original mission, private industry had launched satellites with similar technology,
mostly to help oil drillers find payloads. However, governments
occasionally used it to help drill wells meant to water cities and
farming endeavors. The University of Cairo had access for edu-
cational purposes. The River of Life would need underground
tributaries—a lot of them—and Jack hoped this would help him
find them.

"Sure. We don't need that computer right now for anything else."

Jack shrugged away the thought that they didn't need the
computers for *anything* right now. He pursed his lips and switched
on the screen.

In a few hours, he found what he couldn't believe. The River
Kura, in some places called the Mtkvari River, joined the Aragvi
River north of Tbilisi, near the town of Mtskheta. Using GRACE,
Jack could see the river started northwest of Gudauri, even farther
north from where one of its tributaries, the Tetri Aragvi, started.
Maybe a separate tributary started here.

He peered closer at the screen. It looked to have several
still-present underground sources, which sat east of South Ossetia, a province in Georgia. In the Caucasus, for sure.

"Unbelievable," he muttered, peering closer.

Another, more familiar underground water source lay beneath the Euphrates-Tigris basin. This one came and went over the decades. Jack magnified its location on the screen. There had been a time when scientists thought this region was drying up, and, with it, the hope for a lush, well-populated Middle East. However, time had proven them wrong as the region mysteriously filled again just a few years ago, and this could explain why. It could be receiving water from this underground system as well.

Jack read and reread the Bible verses Elise had sent him and redrew his map, pressing the paper repeatedly next to the images on the computer screens.

"Wait. Got it!" he exclaimed, then tore a piece of tape from the dispenser next to him. He stuck the new map to the side of the monitor and stepped back, arms crossed, studying the two images side by side.

The River of Life originally branched into four other rivers, the Pishon, Gihon, Euphrates, and Tigris. The Pishon could certainly branch off the Gihon south of what was now Yemen, as that area was known to have both onyx and gold mines. It could also be farther north, though. Another passage in Genesis located the land of Havilah across from Egypt, toward parts of Turkey, Syria, Iran, and Iraq, which together had once been known as the ancient land of Assyria. To the north sat Mount Sahand. Nearby flowed a small river, the Uizun, and it was said gold had been found there too.

If instead, the Gihon branched off the Pishon, it may have widened so dramatically over time that it now coursed to and through the Black Sea, through Istanbul, and into the Mediterranean.

The Euphrates and Tigris were simpler to find. In fact, the two famous Middle Eastern rivers were likely the very same ones he was searching for. They were thought to have been named this way because of myths and old lore—not specifically because they were the original rivers. But perhaps they were. And if so, they appeared to have survived the Great Flood and now joined farther downstream as the river Shatt Al-Arab, which flowed from there into the Persian Gulf.

Jack grinned; he had cracked the code. He had done what so many before him had not—found the origins to a several-thousand-year-old water system using satellite imagery.

"Rash, we did it!"

Rashid returned and watched as Jack flipped through the images.

"The Aragvi River. It joins the Kura," Jack stated, tracing the Kura River backward to where he thought the Aragvi started. "It got rerouted somewhere in time, but it seems like the Kura used to flow west, not east, to... look—the Mediterranean Sea. Thus feeding..." He pointed at a place in Turkey, to where the Kura River appeared to originate out of nowhere, then traced his proposed course, circling and tapping the screen at the point where Turkey and Syria met. "The Euphrates-Tigris River Basin."

Smirking, Rashid squeezed his shoulder. "Nice work, Captain."

"Who would have thought the basin originated north of Turkey? All this time, it was assumed it started in the mountains there, but see..." He pointed to the GRACE imagery. "There's an underground system. It flows from Georgia." He tapped the screen with his finger again. "So we follow *this* river and travel upstream until we reach the Garden. This is it!"

"Try not to break the expensive lab equipment with your woodpecker tapping on the screens, Captain," Rashid said, turning toward Jack. "Also, why do you keep saying *we*?"

"Come on, man. I know this sounds like a fantasy hunt, but I don't want to disappear with a bunch of strangers into dark forests and mountain ranges. What if they're crazy? I can't go alone."

Rashid pursed his lips and raised his eyebrows. "I believe the whole lot of you are crazy. Perhaps *I* would be afraid to go with *you*?" He grinned. "Or perhaps I could come along and after you are all eaten by wild sheepdogs, I can publish the paper demon-strating the river system find and be made famous."

"Yeah, see? There you go! We all come out ahead here. And if this lady is *not* crazy, and if *I* am not crazy, you get to see something no one has been able to see since the beginning of time. Either way, we get out of this place and get a little clean air."

Rashid's face melted. "Jack, you know I cannot go."

"Aww, come on. You need this as much as I do."

"Maybe later. First, I need to find my family."

That sealed it. Rashid would not leave without knowing whether his family had survived, and Jack would not leave with-out Rashid.

"So we wait. It isn't like this place hasn't been hidden a few thousand years already anyway."

Rashid nodded, unblinking.

"Let's go get some smog—I mean, air," Jack said. "My brain needs a break."

The two stood and headed out.

VII

IN A SECURITY booth on the other side of the world sat a guard with his feet propped on the desk, his tan button-down soaked in sweat and stuck to his armpits and back, waiting idly for something to do. At some point, he leaned forward, dropping his feet beneath him. The higher-ups had bought his crew cushioned pleather chairs, he supposed out of consideration, but on summer days like this, they just made things worse. He lifted his hat and wiped the dripping sweat from his forehead with his already-wet forearm.

"Ugh," he said as that only rearranged the moisture on his brow, then reached for a towel to blot his face. The clock read 2:52 p.m.—another five hours were left on his shift.

He radioed the office. "Asker, you there?"

"Copy, Cahil. What you got?"

"Nothing right now. When is that shipment going to arrive? I thought it was supposed to be before noon."

"It was," Asker replied. "I'm not sure what the holdup is. Let me check into it."

Cahil was glad to have met Asker. As the only two Turks working here, they had made fast friends. Most of the others were from Mleta, a small town near the preserve's border in the South Ossetia region of Georgia. Cahil had been on holiday there when he saw the flier listing the pay for the job. After shifts, he and Asker usually went to the main hall and sat with the others. There, they'd play cards until a fight broke out—or worse, everyone got bored—and they'd part ways, and Cahil would go back to his room to sleep six or eight hours before waking up to do it again. Weekends around the camp were interesting and full of parties, most without any occasion to mark. Georgians liked to eat and drink—always with the drink—and dance and sing, so there was never a shortage of entertainment if you liked that sort of thing.

Cahil swirled his flask. He had already filled it four times today but was still parched. He drank deeply, the not-so-cold water giving momentary relief to his thirsty tongue. As the last drops of his water dripped out, a dark green Toyota pulled in.

"Finally!" he said, standing to greet the day's first visitors. Outside the booth drifted a soft breeze. Several times, he had petitioned to sit out there but was always turned down. The booth, while offering protection from the sun, made the already humid air more stifling.

"Good afternoon, may I help you?" he asked.

"Delivery for the Retention Department. Packaged as directed. The escort that met us at the entrance is coming up behind us," answered the driver, who appeared to be in his early twenties. He motioned backward, to the cargo—a man with his hands bound behind his back and a black sack over his head. In the front passenger seat sat another man about the same age as the driver, wearing dark sunglasses and a tight face. He peered up from under the visor at the land before him. "What are you building out here?"

"A prison." Cahil had learned it didn't matter what he said to the delivery men as it always ended the same way anyway. So he had started just to tell the truth. For a while, he toyed with them and said things like "alien study facility," or "rocket launcher-developing company for the advancement of time travel," which was fun to say and usually rewarded him with some interesting responses. "Do you have any papers?"

"Huh, intense," the man answered, handing over a crisp manilla envelope and leaning back in his seat. "Where to from here?"

"A team will come up and take you back," Cahil answered. "Just a few minutes." He went back into the booth and picked up the radio. "Never mind, Asker, they're here. Send the drivers."

"Sending drivers. You got it, or do you need help?"

"Nah, the escort vehicle is pulling up now, and there's only two. We can take it from here," Cahil answered and clicked off the radio. He reached in the drawer and grabbed the plastic-coated metal cord he'd been issued at orientation. Tucking it in his pocket, he returned outside and motioned with a wave toward the sedan now stopping behind the Toyota.

"Okay, they're on their way. Have you been paid yet?" Cahil asked the driver.

"No, they said you would direct us to an expense processing department."

"Actually, we can take care of it here," Cahil answered. "Also, do you know your way back, or do you want escorted out too?"

"I'm afraid we'll need to be led out." The man was sweating now, as the steamy air pushed through his window. He looked around again, this time anxiously.

"Great," Cahil said, "you two can come into the booth to get paid while we wait for the others."

The men climbed out and followed Cahil inside. The escort driver, Levan, walked in behind them. Cahil raised his eyebrows at him. Levan was one of the easier men to work with, which made things fast. Though fast was necessarily good, as the only thing Cahil had to rush back to was an afternoon of being hot and bored.

Levan closed the door and stood, arms uncrossed behind the men, at the ready as usual. Eying him, Cahil pulled two red folders out from a drawer.

"Please review the forms and sign at the end if it all checks out."

He stepped back behind the shorter of the two and pulled a pair of black gloves and the cord out of his pocket as they opened the folders. To Cahil, the day was too hot to wear gloves, but rules

35

were rules, so he put them on anyway. He glanced over at his partner, who by now perched behind the driver, a cord wrapped in his hands as well, staring back, impatiently waiting for the go-ahead nod. Cahil gave it, sweaty fingers already sticking to the inside lining of the leather. He hated this part. He much preferred guns, but strangulation caused less bleeding, so was the director's preferred modus operandum.

The two men simultaneously shot their hands over the visitors' heads and hooked the cords around their necks, twisting the loose ends together like bread ties. Cahil's victim flung his head back, as per the usual, and jerked his elbows at him in defense. It only took a few jerks back and forth to knock his victim off his feet and out of orientation before the trachea snapped. Shortly afterward came the sudden heaviness, indicating death. If he could tighten the cord fast enough to squeeze the carotids, the process usually took less than a minute, as the loss of blood flow to the brain would make them pass out even before they suffocated. This one was soft and round in the middle, the typical eager-but-inexperienced recruit of a professional bounty hunter, and proved an easy kill.

"Done!" Levan dropped his man to the ground and undid his cord, then held his hands up like he'd just made the winning touchdown in an American football game. "Got the wipes?"

Cahil panted. "Yeah, man. Why do you have to make everything a competition? That's gross. These are people, you know." He dropped his driver on the ground and took a deep breath. "Check the top drawer."

Levan pulled out a couple of thick sanitizing wipes and cleaned his cord. "Whatever. You just keep to what you're good at, and I will too." Grinning, he tucked the bloody wipes into his victim's pant pocket.

A golf cart pulled up.

"All done?" Asker called out.

"Just about," Cahil answered. "Shipment's still in the car." Cahil handed his comrade a large black bag. The box he'd pulled it out of read, *BIODEGRADABLE,* in bright red lettering. *Go figure—they keep things eco-friendly while killing off the expendables*, he thought as he wrapped the now-limp man in a sack.

VIII

Jubair

Jubair Talmuk downed the last of his coffee, set down the empty mug, and squeezed the rim impatiently as he waited for the fat lady to stop talking. *How could anyone talk this much?* She was crying, too, a blubbering piece of blubber, going on about her husband and his recent indiscretions.

Jubair gazed at her, blank-faced, hoping she would get the message—but she didn't even hesitate. It was as if she just spewed... *whatever* she was going on about just for the sake of it, and it was so very tedious. He tapped the glass with his index finger, redirecting his energy from what it actually wanted to do, which was roll his eyes, push his hand against her mouth, and tell her to just, finally, shut up.

"Sir, I know he isn't one of your most elevated staff members, and maybe you don't know who he is for sure, but if you could—please—cut his hours back? He might be home more and realize what he's been missing out on, and then he might come around." Her makeup was sloppy now, black mascara smeared everywhere and her nose moist with mucous.

Jubair hated snot. It was a smorgasbord for infection, and it was so sticky.

She wiped her face with her wrist, smearing the slime under her nose and across her lips. It even dangled from her cheek—her fat, blubbering, sloppy cheek—waving with each contraction of her mouth.

"Really, ma'am, I must ask you to get ahold of yourself," Jubair said, rushing his words out when the lady finally paused for breath. "There's nothing I can do. He is obliged to work whatever hours he chooses. It's out of my control. He is passionate about bettering the world, you know. You should be proud of his devotion."

Her husband, Rick Vanderhaven, was a good worker and not afraid to bend the rules as was sometimes needed. Jubair wanted the man available and working for the cause as much as possible. One hardworking employee cost less than two average workers and meant fewer people to monitor.

Most of the wives of staff he had secured in this manner weren't quite as persistent, but of course, there would have to be some. This particular wife had scheduled an appointment with him and had proceeded to ask him, the *leader of the United Nations*, to ease up on her husband like she was his mommy, and the man couldn't speak for himself.

And Rick had been otherwise easy to secure. It was obvious to see why now, considering the woman standing before him. Jubair was doing this guy a favor by getting him out of this lady's house. All it had taken was a naïve twenty-something assistant who wore her skirts too short, batting her eyes at him when they worked late hours. After three months on the job, Rick was already messing around, enjoying the unspoken benefits that came with staying late and working behind the scenes for Jubair Talmuk's agenda.

The woman snorted, clearing whatever body fluid dripped down the back of her throat, and calmed down, pressing her lips together with new resolve.

"Okay, well... I see this is going nowhere. I guess I'll take my leave."

She turned around, pleasing Jubair enough he couldn't stop the corners of his mouth from raising, ever so slightly. As the woman left, she let his door drift behind her.

No respect to properly shut a door, he thought, his smile faltering as he rose to close it. Returning to his shiny maple desk, Jubair huffed as he sat down. He was almost re-settled when the phone rang.

"Hello?"

"Yes, sir, the Prime Minister of Britain is on the phone," his secretary said. "He wants to know if you are ready for the summit."

"Patch him through."

The receiver clicked, and Calan Tonto's English accent filled his ear.

"Jubair! How are you, my friend?"

Jubair sighed, smiling at something more positive to discuss. "Calan, hello. I'm well—just finishing up some HR business. How are you?"

"Bloody good! Getting prepared for the summit. Thought I'd ring you and check in on your proposal. Are you quite ready?"

"Of course. It can't come soon enough. The time to unite the world's politics is overdue. My hope is we'll get things started at the summit."

"Jubair, you're just what this world needs right now. I'm truly privileged to be a part of this."

"As am I, Prime Minister. Thank you for your support. We need each other for this to happen. Did you want to go over our agenda?"

The two men reviewed the upcoming summit's details and chatted a few more minutes before hanging up. Afterward, Jubair leaned back in his chair. He laced his fingers behind his neck and closed his eyes, sucking in a deep, satisfying breath. Things were going well. With all the turmoil spanning the last few decades, the world had become a messy place. His goal was to clean it up, and the summit was the next step to do that. He wanted to organize the UN into a stronger, more omnipotent group. This summit would help him start a unity movement, which ultimately would establish a new communication channel and diplomacy among nations to end the constant bickering and bloodshed—messes— that came from radicals trying to rule places not enough people paid attention to.

Secretly, he also hoped the summit would align him with countries with large population bases off the grid. Jubair had a smallish clandestine militia, left over from his time as Switzerland's president. He needed to secure more men. Many of the war- or natural-disaster-torn countries he helped rebuild could provide just that. Then, there were the refugee camps—just filled with displaced, hope-hungry people, ripe for his harvest. These would not be easily traceable, which, of course, was vital when one was building a secret force of any kind.

For the most part, Jubair kept things on the up and up. Being transparent helped him gain trust with other nations, and with trust came freedom backed by resources. He worked hard to maintain world leaders' confidence. Still, he also knew having a private stash of troops—to negotiate or eliminate as needed—maverick ambassadors, or countries for that matter, was also essential.

Later that evening, Jubair nearly collapsed through the door of his flat. It was after ten; he had spent the rest of the day writing petitions, attending meetings, and answering phone calls. He hadn't stopped for lunch or even to use the toilet. Relishing the silence of the night, he treaded to his bar and poured a nightcap, which he'd been craving since the crazy woman had left his office that morning. The amber liquid almost swirled over the edge, but he tilted the bottle back before it had a chance. He rubbed the silky countertop, relieved to have avoided the spill.

An hour and two double shots of bourbon later, the weight of the day melted Jubair into his chair, and soon he slept, head softly bobbing as if synchronized with the rise and fall of the streetlights below. He dreamed most days of late, and today was no exception. Tonight's was a familiar one—it started with him standing on a rocky cliff overlooking a mountain valley. Turning, he searched for the one he knew would be coming. As he pivoted, his view of the valley spun in the opposite direction. Jubair stopped, but the trees and rocks continued spinning—slowly at first, but gaining speed until the surrounding world raced in a colorful blur. His equilibrium twisted with it until he dropped his hands to his knees to keep from tipping sideways.

This time, his visitor came through the trees.

To his right, the leaves rustled. Then the dragon arrived, slithering through the shadows. His body was agile and hard; pure muscle rippled beneath the black scales. The beast stopped and raised his head—five, ten, fifteen feet in the air—towering over Jubair like a blade ready to plunge. Instead of teeth, he had a forked tongue, somehow beautiful, jewel-like, twitching in and out of his mouth. His bony front legs were ridiculously small compared to the rest of him, with awkwardly large, fist-sized joints, but the four-inch golden spikes adorning its toes commanded respect. Gems, shimmering blue, red, green, and purple, lay embedded along the ridge of his back, striking color against his shadow of a body. His back half was concealed by the forest surrounding them, but by now, Jubair knew what lay behind was no less intimidating—huge, powerful haunches and a golden-tipped whip for a tail. Here was a monster, when standing tall, that could be three times the height he now appeared.

"Jubair," the beast said, "are you okay? You look a little dizzy."

"Lucifer." Despite the lump in his chest, Jubair forced his greeting out as matter-of-factly as he could.

The serpent made a show of examining Jubair up and down. "Now, you know I prefer Helel," he said with a chuckle drawn out into a long hiss. "My, aren't you a sight. Still afraid of your old friend?"

Jubair shook his head, fighting the urge to step back. He forced his shoulders square and raised his chin, calming his trembling hands by pressing his fingers against his side.

"I see you are moving forward with your little project. But do you think you could focus on mine?" The monster's sarcasm was sharp.

"I—I thought I was?" Jubair answered, cringing.

"No, you are not to mount an army. It is *my* army Jubair. Leave its planning to me. Your job now is to clear the opposition. Well, and to romance the nations. I want the world fixated on you and your... good works."

Jubair stared at his feet. He felt exposed, like the day he'd been caught filling empty vaccine vials with saline in that tent in India. Even then, he hadn't been ashamed, but more irritated from getting caught. Back then, his easy smile and smooth talking had worked magic, and he hoped one day it also would with Helel.

"My work *is* good... sir." He never knew how to refer to him. Your honor? Your holiness? Your highness?

"Is it?" The dragon lowered his head and wrapped his body around the clearing where Jubair stood. "I suppose you might think so. Well, you can call it whatever you want, but remember, Jubair, your intentions need be only for *my* purposes. Man need only worry about his survival. They need not think about anything beyond each other on this world. If there is any greater thing they think of or want to be a part of, it must be me. There is no good, no God other than me."

"Yes, sir," Jubair answered. "Tell me what I should do."

"Oh, surely a man as intelligent as you knows the answer." Helel's voice was soft, almost sweet in its tone. "Just help them see themselves and each other. Finish the camp and remove the leaders who oppose you or who I indicate. From there, our work will succeed."

Jubair was glad for the promise of help; he hoped this meant Helel would keep him around. He breathed deep, strengthening his resolve.

"We are partners. I only want you to know what others would keep from you. Man can be colossally more than he knows, and you—you can show them what's possible."

The giant serpent withdrew into himself, shrinking to the size of a man. He was still foreboding, but more by his presence now than by his size. With a final glance, he turned from Jubair and left.

The dream ended, and Jubair awoke to his sterile apartment. Helel's appearance frightened him but not his message. Actually, Jubair liked what he heard and embraced it for the truth it brought—man *did* have such promise—but he didn't understand the dragon's recoil at his mention of doing good. Wasn't what they were doing just that? Helel wasn't one to argue with, but to Jubair, bringing peace to a world often torn by war seemed good. And wasn't preserving the cities—saving man's great works—good as well? Whatever Helel thought, Jubair's work was justified tonight, and that pleased him.

IX

THE MORNING OF the Summit, Jubair walked into a room brimming with energy.

"Secretary-General Talmuk, what an honor to have you here with us!" Jennifer Swartz, the organizer for the Conference of Nations, called to him. She was flustered, he could see. Though famous for being well-spoken and intelligent, he was also known for his good looks, with his six-foot, dark-complexioned frame and curly, manicured black hair. He had many female followers simply because of the dimples that appeared when he smiled, and he was always smiling.

"Ah, Miss Swartz, thank you. The honor is all mine." Jubair grinned, flashing his intense gray eyes her way. He reached out to wrap her hands in a warm shake. "I only hope our time together will be fruitful. Which leaders have made it today?"

"Not as many as we'd like, but more than last year. Here's the roster." She handed him a list of attendees, hesitating before letting go. "I believe they are mostly here for *you*, sir."

Jubair took the list and patted her hand. "Thank you. This day should be advantageous."

He scanned the countries. At least China and Russia were here, and Israel, of course. It was disappointing India hadn't made it, but it made sense Korea hadn't come as they were still recovering from a plague of mass bombings earlier in the year, initiated from within. Of course, most of Africa was too preoccupied to attend—Egypt with war and the rest with more war and poverty and disease they never seemed to break free of. Japan's Prime Minister had made it despite—or perhaps because of—the country being in shambles after the tsunami. The United Nations had all but crumbled away thanks to the destruction Mother Nature had dealt out these past several years.

Jubair settled in front of the massive conference room. The place bustled with greetings, handshakes, and deep belly laughs as men and women who hadn't seen each other in months or longer caught up. Whenever one of the attendants caught his eye or waved, Jubair would offer a half-grin or wave back, all the while musing what it would be like if they, "the best of these," were all who were left of humanity. Were they to be stuck together in some off-grid location, would they all prove to be as impressive, stripped of authority and resources? Who among the group would even survive if the luxuries of modern living were removed? He cleared his throat and tapped the microphone with his finger.

"My comrades, it is wonderful to have you all here. Shall we observe a moment of silence for individual prayer or meditation before we begin?" The room quieted at his words. He smiled broadly, letting his gaze settle on Germany, then the US, before lowering his brow, nearly closing his eyes except to watch his Rolex tick away the seconds. When it was over, he tapped his fingers on the table and lightly again on his microphone. Heads popped up, one at a time, focusing.

"Here we are together, strong and able, a group with the power to make something great out of our devastated world. May we find a way to help those who could not make it today. Death and destruction are harming our homes and threatening the peace we seek so fervently. Will you all join me to stand and challenge it? We need to reach out with whatever resources each of us has to spare and use those riches to lift up our brothers and sisters."

The room met him with a murmur of approval. He held his

head high, happy to have their audience, though he knew he deserved every bit of it. After all, it was he who had, at least temporarily, brought the Middle East out of what seemed like a century of war. Israel was still Israel, but Judaism and Islam were now at peace and had been ever since he'd begun his work in unification. He had convinced generations of enemies they were not enemies, but simply people living near each other who needed one another. Gaza was now a vacation spot. And though the war in Egypt continued, it was only a matter of time before he resolved that too. It was only over money and land, which were two desires much easier to placate than religious beliefs. Faith-based warriors had proven difficult for him to sway—particularly the Jews, Christians, and Muslims, as many of the other countries and religions were open to coexistence.

In the end, only six countries present had the resources available to fuel his revitalization plan. He petitioned the leaders for massive food drops, medicine and education funds, and, of course, for refugee resettlement. The leaders showed Jubair favor, and even those with limited resources offered funding or supplies or space if they had it available. If a few of the countries not present also pitched in, and if Korea could get on board, they'd have all they needed.

"Before we turn to Egypt, there is another issue up for discussion," Jubair announced at the close of the petition. "It is time to create a subcommittee, clearly." He swept his arm dramatically, motioning to all the empty seats around them. "Consider how few of us made it today. Too many leaders are home, managing their people. Too many cannot make it to every forum. I propose we streamline this organization—appoint a select group of representatives from each continent to sit in for the rest of us so when times are hard, as now, everyone's voice will be heard."

The Prime Minister of Japan shook his head, brow furrowed. "How would that be decided? How do we determine who is important enough to attend these meetings for all of those heads of state they would represent?"

"Oh, don't worry, Prime Minister. The meetings these representatives would be involved in would be few and only when—if—a majority of the rest of us cannot come. I propose we appoint one member per continent, except for those more-advanced continents with a superior Human Development Index—those should send two. After all, they are the ones who've been able to manage larger populations well, with longer life expectancy, better education, and of course, improved economics. Clearly, they should be given more input and have more weight upon decisions affecting us all. The more-advanced continents are likely better able to manage disasters well, as Asia has already demonstrated, given Japan still came today." Jubair locked eyes with the Prime Minister and nodded, then continued.

"Of course, there is the matter of Antarctica. Who should be the representative of a place with such a small and migrant population? Clearly Australia, with having such a presence there, owning several research stations and possessing the largest amount of land rights, would make sense. However, they would have two seats anyway, as they easily meet the other standards. It would not be right for one continent to have a greater presence than all else. Therefore, two for Australia shall be all I recommend if you agree. My suggestion, comrades, would be that North America, Europe, Asia, and Australia all claim two seats, and Africa and South America claim one each, for a total of ten leaders on this *Super Squad,* so to speak." Jubair paused again, letting his idea sink in.

"But, most importantly, each special delegate is mandated to *always* come. They must attend every forum, and if the majority of other nations does not arrive, even at General Assembly, of course, then the general leaders will be dismissed and will not attend as doing so would put an imbalance to decision making. However, in those situations, all ten *must attend*, or else the meeting will be canceled and rescheduled to when either a majority of the general or all the newly designated heads would be present."

Jubair raised a glass of water to his lips and sipped slowly, studying the room's response to his plan. Most everyone seemed to be taking it in without difficulty. Lowering the glass, he brushed his lips, and waited a little longer for effect. The next words he delivered slowly, with added emphasis. "So, you see, in this way, we will carry on. Even, as the great Martin Luther King Jr. once said, if we must crawl to do so."

X

Rashid

RASHID PEERED THROUGH a cracked windshield at the destruction that was now Cairo. He wiped his brow for what seemed like the tenth time and returned his sweaty hand to the wheel as he maneuvered around massive potholes and between piles of debris and cement chunks.

The battle in Egypt had lasted another seven months before ending in the spring, when Jubair Talmuk, the secretary-general of the United Nations, signed a peace treaty with Marcus Anan, the rebel force's leader. This was unheard of. Talmuk had recognized Anan's faction as a large entity, almost as if they were a country. He sat with their leader, discussed terms, and even paid out money to meet demands to end the battle. Finally, Talmuk had granted Anan a parcel of land in central Egypt to name and rule as he pleased—a new country surrounded by an old—and a place on the United Nations board. This gave Egypt a chance to strengthen her military and refortify while surrounding the new country, Anania. The treaty stated if Anan tried to overtake any other lands again, he would be immediately assassinated. Still, it also conceded that UN forces were not allowed to interfere with Anania's governance.

Anania became a dictatorship, with Marcus Anan as the leader, and the monies paid out had been spent to build an extravagant wall around the country, as well as a plantation for the new dictator. The new, twenty-five-square-mile country sat a kilometer away from the Nile's western border. It was large enough to develop communities, farm for oil, and build its economy but decidedly too small for any hope of nuclear testing or development.

The authorities had deemed the University of Cairo secure almost immediately, but it took another few weeks before the safety advisories were lifted for the surrounding regions. Jack and Rashid had stayed in the bunker until they could wait no longer, and today was their day of exit.

"Look at this place," Jack said from his shotgun seat.

Rashid nodded solemnly and glanced over at him. Jack was clearly uneasy, sitting with his hands shoved between his knees, shoulders hunched as if doing so would protect him from stray bullets. He shifted his weight on the stained upholstery and pushed his feet forward, crinkling moldy fast-food wrappers lying between a few unfortunately empty beer cans.

They'd borrowed the jeep from the north university garage. Its air conditioning did not work, nor did the speedometer, nor the right brake light. Also, its passenger window had been blown out by one of the bombs. But it still drove and had good tires, as well as keys hidden under the floor mat, so it was the vehicle of choice that morning.

"It gets worse every time we leave," Rashid muttered.

"Are you sure you don't want to wait a little longer? They could be anywhere."

Rashid hit the brakes a little too hard and turned to face Jack. "I can do this alone if you like, Captain. But I'm going now, with or without you."

"No," Jack shoved his chin forward, as if doing so would start the wheels again. "Let's do it."

It took two hours to navigate the less than three miles to Rashid's Al Duqqi neighborhood in Greater Cairo, west of the university. The destruction was overwhelming, and the city no longer recognizable. Gravel, dirt, and rubble predominated the landscape instead of neat rows of office buildings and restaurants. Occasional corpses cropped up too—or rather, parts of corpses— all dusty gray or black from ash and decomposition. Rashid stared out the window, gripping the steering wheel tight enough to leave an imprint in the cracked vinyl.

"Here!" he said at last, leaning forward. "We're here. This is our neighborhood."

Only nothing was left of it. The jeep made it another twenty-five feet before the obliterated road became unpassable. Rashid jumped out and stepped in the direction of his home. A large crater now lived in the center of a pile of stony rubble, the bottom two feet of which were lower than the original pavement. Rashid stared in disbelief, his breath catching while time held still. They'd hit his neighborhood—not just his town or university, but his own neighborhood. How could this be?

His knees weakened as the thought of his wife shook through him. Moyra. He spun around, suddenly frantic, searching for what remained of his house. There must be something left, anything to indicate what had happened to her and their daughter.

Rashid lurched forward to search through the rubble. His first step met the uneven ground awkwardly and he stumbled, and as he tried to catch himself with the next step, his foot slipped on the loose gravel and he fell forward. How would he find his home in all this debris? His head buzzed as if the bomb had just gone off, as if it had blasted around them and left him deaf to everything but the sound of the nerves in his ears dying. He pushed himself up and tried to balance himself, but fell again, this time landing on his face, tearing the skin from his forehead, though he didn't feel it. Somewhere in the background, he could hear Jack ask something. *Was he okay? What should he do?* Rashid ignored him; he didn't have enough in him to do anything but push forward. He searched the crevices, a stiff zombie with no life in him.

"Moyra..." he whimpered, his voice weak. His lips, his body were numb, no flowing blood to warm his limbs.

In the place where his home had once stood, green shards of siding jutted from the ruins—the emerald Moyra had chosen when they'd decided to paint it the week they'd moved in. *It reminds me of the first necklace you gave me,* she had said. He could still see her sweet smile, staring at the paper color swatch at the do-it-yourself store.

Rashid crawled forward, fumbling through piles of the shattered remains of his home. His hands shook as adrenaline fueled him on. Somewhere along the way, his heart had become loud, pounding against his chest. He willed it quiet, to better hear any sound from someone trapped below, but it wouldn't comply. The high-pitched ringing returned, quickly accompanying, and then replacing, the thumping.

Someone must be here! he thought, shaking his head to better concentrate, his fingers immediately raw from clawing through unforgiving cement and rebar.

Part of him hoped he would find no one, as that meant they'd escaped, though to where he had no idea. This end of town was nearly barren. Much of Greater Cairo, other than those captured, had evacuated; only those who'd been in hiding or survivors from the battle were left. People who had returned to the city camped in northwestern Egypt, clinging to family and neighbors, and no one he'd been in contact with had heard from Moyra or Nubia.

A familiar blue linen peeked out from under what appeared to be part of the basement wall—a six-inch-thick cement slab easily eight feet long. He grasped the cloth and pulled. It tore easily beneath his strength. The blue fabric—the sky blue of her Disney princess pajamas, the ones that had made her eyes dance when she'd opened them on her birthday because they were her favorite color—changed hue as it approached and disappeared under the slab. It turned a sickly brown, and deepened to black, crusted over with dried blood.

The ringing in his ears flooded his mind as he realized his daughter was here. It washed over his whole body, stealing any leftover strength from his limbs. He collapsed onto his side, the rough cement sanding off more skin from his forehead. His head swirled. The world was a merry-go-round out of control, and he was its lone passenger, clinging to the edge with nothing but his weight pressed against the ground to keep him aboard. Any moment he would fly off and sail into an eternal abyss or else slam into some lethal jagged wall—one last instance of pain to end his dismal path. Either way, his search was hopeless; he wasn't strong enough to move the rubble, and it had been blasted too long ago to hope for their survival. His family was gone.

"Rash, what is it?" Jack squatted beside him.

Too weak to answer, Rashid moaned and shook the fabric feebly in response.

Jack gathered him silently in his arms and squeezed tight. A chill overtook Rashid, while warm blood seeped from his forehead. A thin but deep line of tears trailed from his eyes, which stung and seemed full of grit. The salty liquid crept to his cheek, then raced down as gravity took hold, and joined the thick, cranberry blood from his temple—two streams merging to form a stronger river, one of life and death. The mixture flowed along the rest of his face and onto their shirts.

"Oh, Rash. I'm so sorry."

They sat that way for an hour, then two, until the sun tucked itself in for the night. Not until the sky turned dark gray, its purple hue muted from the lingering smog, did Rashid stir. He shifted his body off Jack's and onto the stone ground, embracing the rubble, fingers still laced around what was left of his family. Then he curled up on the unforgiving land and slept.

XI

A YEAR AFTER her phone call, Isaiah hunched over an open suit-case, finishing up her packing. Skimming the list Elise had sent her once more, she double checked her suitcases. Likely some—or even much—of this would be missing when she finally arrived, thanks to thieving customs agents in small airports without tight regulation in the "do not take things just because you want them" department. So she'd doubled up on and separated the hard-to-replace stuff.

She let a smile stretch over her face. Since the bombing took her family, Isaiah had cried more than she ate and spent many nights wide awake on her bed, flat on her back, staring through the ceiling. Sometimes, when she was filled with anxiety or trem-bled from imagining the pain and horror her family must have felt in their last moments, she'd get up and take a shower. She'd sit there just as flattened as in her bed, cross-legged, eyes fixed obscurely at the drain—or on a good day, the soap tray—and she'd stay like that, letting the water soak her until it lost its warmth. It'd trace its way off her eyelashes or nose, then down her spine and between her breasts, and disappear into the darkness behind the drain. Eventually, she'd turn it off, though often soap or shampoo had not touched her, and lie right there in the tub, curled up, with steam as her quilt, until she fell asleep, or not.

This morning, however, she stood in the shower, used shampoo and conditioner, and even ran a razor up her legs. Today, she started her new season.

To prepare the house for its sale, she had put most of her keepsakes in a storage unit. Only a few pieces of furniture remained for staging purposes, and a thin row of work clothes hung in the master closet. She'd given her notice to the hospital six months before. Whatever came after the expedition would not involve her home, this city, or maybe even medicine. The house would sell, she'd go on this trip, and that was it. Nothing else mattered as long as it was something new.

After the car was loaded, she walked through the 2,800 square-foot, hundred-year-old farmhouse, pausing in each room to embrace her ghosts—all the memories of her family—one last time. In her long, open living room, she felt her husband's heavy arms wrapped around her while they watched the fire together on frigid winter nights, hours after the chaos of the day had been kissed asleep. She saw their two sandy-haired sons doing handstands against the dark brown couch and heard their hysterical giggles as they crumpled against the leather together. In the kitchen, she envisioned the boys decorating Christmas cookies, sprinkles, and colored frosting smeared across the giant wooden counter, the floor, their proud noses. The scenes filled the house, the yard, the pastures, the rope swing in the barn loft. Never had she been so happy or so sad in any home she'd ever lived in.

Isaiah paused one last time, glancing around the garage, then slid into the front seat and drove away.

Travel to Iraq had been much safer since the UN had managed to facilitate a peace treaty among the countries and major religious leaders in the Middle East. No warfare, no murder, no revolt, had been the conditions. In exchange, the Jews had received allowances to have their temple rebuilt in Jerusalem alongside another mosque designed by the Muslim people. Of course, many other benefits existed for all people groups involved—not publicized—but this was the major outcome reported in the papers. Each group was allowed twenty thousand square feet on the same plot of land, and though the two buildings would share a courtyard, each was allowed to conduct independent religious services inside their respective buildings. Other than agreeing to be peaceful, the catch was that land in the holy buildings was to be considered international land—like an embassy for their faith on Jerusalem soil. It would be a refuge for their people even in future times.

Isaiah's plane arrived at Erbil International Airport without event. After deboarding, she stepped out of line and headed to another one at customs. She held her breath as they rummaged through her baggage.

"What is this?" The man narrowed his eyes at Isaiah, holding up a box of Tylenol.

"Tylenol," Isaiah answered, worried. "For headaches."

He peered at it closer, glanced behind him, then seemed to lose interest and dropped it back in the bag. He thumbed around the bags of saline tucked between her pants and the boxes full of glass antibiotic vials wedged behind her shampoo.

Isaiah shifted weight and rubbed her fingers nervously. Technically, these items could be confiscated and taxed, or worse, she could be in trouble with the law for bringing them.

"You're done, miss." The man zipped the case shut and eyed the next in line.

Isaiah let out a breath she hadn't realized she was holding. God had covered his eyes to the other supplies. *Thank you, Lord,* she thought, brisking away.

A white sedan waited in the passenger pick-up area outside the airport. A wiry woman covered in long blue fabric bounced out of the vehicle and waved at Isaiah. Like Isaiah, Elise stood just above five feet tall, but her tan skin hid any wrinkles, and she could easily have passed for a teenager. The silky black hair that normally danced down her back was wrapped now in a dark hijab headdress. Her giant black eyes were unmistakable, though, and they shone with recognition at her.

"Isaiah, you're here!" Elise beamed.

"Elise, hi!" Isaiah rushed forward and held her at arm's length for a moment before hugging her tightly. "I am completely excited. I can't wait to get out there!"

Elise grinned back. "Definitely. But we need to get you covered before we go anywhere." She pulled a charcoal cloth from her bag and handed it to Isaiah. "This will only be while we're here. No need to get imprisoned before we even get started."

Isaiah wrapped the law-mandated covering around her head. Her current hairdo was rather like a scramble of brown straw, so it actually improved things in her eyes.

"So what's the plan?" Isaiah asked.

"For now, we're going to get you settled in. Then this afternoon I figured I'd take you to see the hospital, and we can drop off any goodies you brought. We're having dinner with some of the other workers. They want to bless our trip. Tomorrow, we leave for Georgia."

They climbed into the back of the car. A tan-skinned man in a Red Sox cap turned around and grinned, showing off two deep dimples and a golden front tooth.

"Hey, Mustafa. This is the friend I told you about."

He craned his neck and nodded at Isaiah. "Welcome! It's nice to finally meet the woman behind all the stories." He winked at Elise, who rolled her eyes.

"Oh, stop!" Elise answered, turning back to Isaiah. "Don't mind him. We try not to let him out too often, but we needed an escort, and he was off shift, so here he is."

Isaiah laughed, immediately at ease. "Okay, but the real question is—did you tell him the *good* stories? Because if you did, I'm impressed he was brave enough to be the escort in the first place."

"Oh, really?" He raised his eyebrows in the rearview while swerving out of the lane to avoid a pile of cement.

Isaiah grabbed the door handle as her body swerved into Elise's. She shot a glance at Elise, not a little startled, and then out the window. The cars and trucks sped around them with no apparent lanes or sense of order other than that which came in a herd of cattle being rounded up.

"Ha! First time driving in Iraq, I see?" Mustafa laughed and swerved again, while hitting the accelerator. "Don't worry, ma'am. I haven't been in an accident since… since when was it, Elise? When was the whole chicken-in-the-road thing, again?"

Elise chuckled. "I don't think this is a good time to tell her your story, Mustafa." She turned toward Isaiah, who gave a half-smile, trying her best not to appear scared though her hand still squeezed the door. "It's fine, Isaiah. He can drive. There just aren't very many observed driving law-uh—" She caught her words as the car hit a speedbump, and something beneath them clanged loudly when they hit the ground again.

"Sorry!" Mustafa bit his lip and smiled bashfully. "Hope that wasn't important."

Elise laughed again, her eyes dancing. "Hope not!"

"So, uh, other than us, who will be coming along on this adventure?" Isaiah asked, her voice throaty.

"Oh! Yes." Elise chirped, clearly excited. "It's a small group. Besides us, there is the archaeologist from Egypt, Jack Barron. He's a Christian too. He'll help identify the site. And we have two local guides we'll pick up in Tbilisi."

"I can't tell you how much I've been looking forward to this, Elise," Isaiah confessed, relaxing again as the road widened and the ride smoothed out. "I know this will be fruitful. I can feel it."

Elise beamed. "I'm glad you're on board. We're going to change the world, Isaiah."

XII

THE HOSPITAL SAT in the heart of a tuberculosis camp, which appeared to be more like a prison compound enclosed in a giant chain-link fence. Elise showed off the hospital floors and explained the positive strides it had made over time. The patients still had to provide their own clothes and bedding, but they now received food while admitted. This was mostly to cut down on visitation and thus the spread of disease. Other third-world hospitals were usually swarmed with families carrying in crock pots and plates of rice and stewed meat for their sick loved ones. The number of exposed persons and therefore vectors for disease in those situations was astounding. The Iraqi government took years to agree to the hospital's plea to increase funding to feed the patients, but, eventually, it did—once the tuberculosis spread included a few officials' family members.

While they floated through Elise's home grounds, Isaiah barely heard her friend talk as she envisioned her hospital back home, with its fancy, art-covered halls and chandeliered entryways. The differences were astounding. Here, the bathrooms didn't have soap or even toilet paper. She had to force herself from staring at the thin wrists and rotten-toothed smiles of the twenty-somethings surrounding her. The sick wards were crammed with people; beds lined up in rows without walls or even curtains to separate most of them. Poverty was everywhere.

"Dr. Harper, are you here to help?" A man approached them, his frosted black dreadlocks pulled into a ponytail hanging halfway down his back.

"Sammy!" Elise blushed as her face broadened into a grin.

Isaiah nudged her gently, eyes sparkling at her red cheeks. Elise had a crush.

"No, I'm officially on sabbatical. This is the friend I told you about—Isaiah. She flew in from Indiana to join the expedition. We went to medical school together."

Isaiah reached forward and received his hand in a warm shake. "Hi, nice to meet you," she said.

"You too. So, are you as adventurous as our shining star Elise, here?" he asked. "Please try to make this unpleasant for her— I'm afraid she may like living out in the wild so much she never returns."

Elise punched his arm softly and shook her head. "Nah, I couldn't leave you *forever*. Someone needs to make sure you remember to calculate creatinine clearance on those little old ladies before dosing their antibiotics."

Isaiah heaved the giant duffel bag of medical supplies she'd smuggled through the airlines. "You wouldn't believe the way the customs man looked at me when he found the Tylenol. He didn't care a whip about the important stuff—didn't flinch at the syringes or needles—but those Tylenol packets almost got me arrested."

Sammy laughed, reaching for the bag. "We appreciate your help. Supplies quickly run short here. Every one of those Paracetamol tablets will go to good use, I promise you."

Isaiah warmed at the thought that something so small to her would make such a large impact. "You're welcome. I'm glad to help."

The three proceeded through the hall to the narrow medical storage room and spent the next twenty minutes unloading and organizing supplies onto tall metal shelves. Isaiah marveled at the expiration dates on the glove boxes—three years prior. Only some of the medications had familiar names. All were in limited supply. The physicians here had to be creative.

The supply room in her own hospital was easily ten times this size, maybe more. There, whole droves of equipment wasted away, expiring and disposed of long before they were even opened. She thought of her patients—many in their seventies and eighties, some even past one hundred—asking her about how to keep going with their lives of abundance. They came into her office with walkers and wheelchairs—several senile—with fingernails painted pristinely, hair regularly curled, wondering about the latest hearing aid. Here, much younger patients, many without close-toed shoes to cover their deformed, calloused, and dirty feet, struggled to survive. The idea of a cheeseburger and fries was foreign to these people—stringy chicken a luxury. Their houses didn't have four full walls, much less decorative scented wax burners. Life here, practice here, was harder but also fuller. Isaiah understood Elise's desire to work here. She understood... and wanted it for herself.

"Are you ready to check out the town?" Elise tucked Isaiah's hijab closer to her face. "We have *got* to tour the market."

"Let's do it."

Later that night, Isaiah hurried to keep up with Elise as they rounded a cement fence beside her quarters. Rows of motel-like rooms surrounded a sandy courtyard dotted with brush. In the center sat a small, open-air pavilion elevated on a wooden platform. A few picnic tables were scattered on the platform and a bench covered in massive blue pillows lined its edge. Sammy sat waiting for them, guitar in one hand, a white ceramic mug in the other.

"Good evening, ladies, my sisters." Sammy grinned, his teeth and eyes a bright contrast to his mahogany skin. "Come join us. Jenwa has made her specialty—pizza, Iraqi style!"

A tall, narrow-hipped woman with olive skin and long fingers was passing out dinner, but at his words, she turned.

"Hi! Grab a plate." Her thick pink lips broadened into a wide smile as she approached. She placed the tray down and hugged Elise. "I'm going to miss you." She held her at her arm's length, eyes sparkling. "We all are."

Turning to Isaiah, she pushed her hand out. "Hi, I'm Jenwa. You must be Isaiah?"

Isaiah nodded and shook her hand. "I am. It's nice to meet you. Thank you for having me."

"Of course." Jenwa smiled and returned to her tray. "We can't let two ladies of God leave on a mission like *this* without a blessing. I hope you're hungry—mostly because I maybe cooked too much." She motioned toward the dishes. "Grab a plate and dig in!"

Iraqi pizza ended up being like American pizza, except on pita and had sliced lamb instead of pepperoni. The type of cheese she used was difficult to ascertain, even for Jenwa, who had cooked it. "Market cheese," she joked when asked. The sauce came from tomatoes she found in the market as well. Isaiah was initially hesitant to eat because of the trip she'd taken to the fly-infested, bloody market. However, when she saw everyone shoving piece after piece into their mouths, she took a bite, and was immediately glad she did. The combination of spices was savory and rich—unlike anything she had tasted before, and soon her belly was overfull.

The group finished eating and relaxed back onto the benches for prayer, Sammy strumming his guitar to help them focus. As they quieted, the notes surrounded them, and Isaiah sighed deeply, soaking in the melody as it filled the air.

Soon their voices joined in harmony with the guitar. The words in the worship songs resonated through Isaiah. They found and defined the emptiness, the deep yearning within her heart that she had yet to identify words for on her own. The music defined it, then filled the emptiness the loss of her family had left—with comfort and purpose. Isaiah loved group prayer because God always showed up. He came most often as a whisper of the Holy Spirit. He was the warmth in her heart, the tingle across her arms as the hair follicles rose, the voice of intention when He shared His plans with her. In prayer, He reassured her; He lifted and strengthened her.

While they worshiped, a peace came to her as well—and with it, a message.

You are not alone. I see you.

God's words permeated Isaiah. She smiled; He was El Roi, the God who sees. Sometimes He felt unreachable, distant, even unreal. But in prayer, He revealed all that as false by the warmth that was His voice.

I see you, too, Lord, and it is my great pleasure to have you as an audience tonight, Isaiah prayed quietly.

They worshipped for two hours that night. At some point, Isaiah imagined a scene from the Bible, when the apostles gathered after Jesus's death and the Holy Spirit came to rest on them for the first time. There had been a wild rush of wind, and flames settled above the heads of everyone present. She closed her eyes and dwelled in the place she was tonight—a place mimicking that ancient event, with the desert gusts brushing over their bowed heads. The group's song brightened their spirits like the tongues of fire resting on those apostles that famed night and even seemed to illuminate the darkening sky. Their voices rang with abandonment. They didn't just sound this way; they felt this way. *She* felt this way. She was on fire, excited to jump into the service of this unreachable God who called her His friend and daughter in His holy book, His Bible. By the end of the evening, she was ready for whatever lay before them.

Afterward, the group hugged and parted toward their rooms.

"I'll see you at seven, 'kay friend?" Elise motioned toward the picnic tables on the wooden deck. "We have breakfast here usually around then, and, afterward, we'll head back to the airport."

"Great. I'm already packed, so it'll be easy."

"Make sure you get a shower. We've only got cold water, and bugs, but we likely won't get many real shower experiences in the next few weeks."

"Sounds luxurious," Isaiah teased. "Will do."

When Isaiah lay down, the bed swallowed her. She dropped into the mattress's soft fullness, happy to let the day and all that filled her thoughts fall with her—her mind sinking perhaps even faster than her body, which had more friction with its cumbersome mass. She released herself as she relaxed into it, a little more every second, until she realized she shouldn't be sinking anymore, that the mattress was only so thick, and likely wasn't thick at all. Why was she still descending into it? She flinched, trying to brace herself for the fall she knew didn't exist but imagined anyway. Except there was nothing to brace against, and she was still sinking. Her stomach and *soul* were being sucked lower than the rest of her.

The scene before her changed, from gray bedding to a brightly lit grocery store. She recognized the meticulously organized food lining the fat-tiled rows immediately—they belonged to the south-town Walmart in Fort Wayne, Indiana, the same store her family had been shopping in the day of their death. The scene was familiar; this dream had played itself for her time and time again since the bombing. She flew, zooming along the ceiling, scanning the world beneath her, anxious for the one part of the dream she cherished— the sight of her husband and boys picking through the aisles.

Her body stalled, either because she had arrived or because the force behind the ride was making an already-programmed stop. Before her were the sandy mops of her boys, drawing semicircles from above as they swung arcs around the front and back of the cart they clung to, and the gelled spikes of her husband's dark head, lifting a bag from the shelf. She craned her neck and willed herself lower, hoping to get eye-level with them and hear the children's giggles and Joseph's voice, which she imagined would be warning the boys to be careful on the shopping cart.

Usually any effort to intervene in the dream was a waste, and she had to watch from above, but today was different. Her body pushed forward, surging to the floor.

"Joseph!" she called.

Her husband glanced up and smiled, shock on his face. "Hi, Isaiah. I thought you were at work."

"I was," she stuttered, surprised at her hesitation, "but I wanted to see you guys, so I came."

"Well, good!" he answered. "Maybe you can calm these two down." His eyes darkened as he focused flatly on the children. "They won't cooperate, and we both know what is coming."

Isaiah reached for the cart, dragging it toward her, hoping to get them from the store before the explosion. "I will, I'm sorry. Come on, let's go."

Joseph grabbed the cart from the other side. "Isaiah, you know we can't come with you. We can't leave until the ride is over. You *know* that."

Isaiah was suddenly desperate, pulling back. "No, Joseph, we need to leave. Boys, let's go." She reached for her youngest, but her hand streamed through his arm as if he were a mirage. She tried again in vain, then grasped at her other son, who smiled up at her, his dimples completely oblivious to her frantic pleas. "Now—we have to go *now*! You guys need to follow me. I can't carry you."

Joseph frowned, his biceps straining as he clutched the cart. "Isaiah, talk to the man in charge. You can get this changed. We have to stay."

"No, I mean, I don't want to leave. I won't be back in time. I want to stay with you."

"Isaiah, go! You have to stop this! We'll wait here."

Isaiah searched his eyes, then turned to go and find the man in charge. Who would that be? It didn't matter. Once she put her mind to something, she always got it done. That was who she was. She worked hard, she got it done. She'd do this too.

Then she was flying through the store aisles, searching for the man, the guy, the person to whom she needed to speak to get them out.

She saw him in the produce section, only three lanes over. And he wasn't a man at all, but a dragon—a big black dragon with giant, sparkling wings and a gaping jaw, with red slivers for eyes and a pit for a heart. He stood next to a curly-haired woman who had dropped an apple from its display. The woman glanced around— apparently, she couldn't see him—and stepped away, intending to leave the fruit on the floor for someone else to pick up. The man, the dragon, the one in charge, swallowed her whole. She never flinched. She was there and then gone, his jaws suddenly giant with the bulk of her. He swallowed and turned toward another shopper, who was sampling a grape without paying.

Isaiah landed beside them and screamed at the dragon and the man who didn't understand the fate he was inviting with his taste. But they didn't hear, and then that man was gone too, devoured in one bite by the beast who was in charge.

The walls around them suddenly shook, and the floor buckled beneath the display of watermelons, spilling them everywhere. The fruit burst open, their blood-red juices and green rinds filling her view as the dragon launched himself into the air, headed toward her family. Isaiah spun, determined to chase him, but suddenly could not move her legs. They had become steel beams, inert against her commands. She strained until the linoleum beneath her dropped, freeing her legs from their heaviness, but then the floor fell away with each step. Pumping her arms, she raced for the right to stay above ground, before the breaking world swallowed her with the plunging tile.

As Isaiah turned the corner of the freezer section, the floor was suddenly solid again, and she sprinted, her feet swallowing the space between her and the dragon, who now hovered above her family. She hollered for them to run and for the beast to leave or to just *listen* to her because she could explain everything and help it with whatever it needed. But her voice was drowned out by the sound of the ceiling collapsing.

At the end of the aisle, she slid to a stop a second before running into the metal shelving.

"Stop!" she yelled at her husband, at the dragon, at the whole blasted store. Her family turned to her, obviously confused at why she should be so frantic.

The dragon also did, with just as plain an expression. *Didn't you know this was coming? Isn't this normal and usual, and right?* he seemed to ask with his beady eyes.

The monster opened its jaws and paused, suspended over Isaiah's family. It raised its eyes to her again as if to say, *Will you be joining us?* then swirled its tail, which was adorned at the end with a golden spike, around its head. A black mist followed the movement, filling the places it spun and streaming outward, seeping through the air around them first and then toward and past Isaiah. Soon the entire grocery was dark, save the area between its head and her family, which seemed spared almost like a bubbled barrier had stopped it from invading their space.

"Isaiah, come on! We're leaving," her husband said, his voice desperate. "You didn't do it. It's okay. We'll be safe here... together. Let's go, babe." He reached toward her, his eyes pleading.

"Joseph, look above you! Come out of there!" she called back, now surrounded in darkness.

"I can't see you, Isaiah. Where are you?"

Isaiah screamed again and darted forward, intending to hurl herself at the cart. She might not be able to touch her family, but they were all attached in some way to the cart, and she could move that. Once she was close enough to reach it, she leaped, arms stretched out to knock it out of the way.

The moment she was in the air, the world stopped.

The dragon perched, mouth wide, death dangling above her family. Her husband stood paralyzed, still confused, and her kids leaned back from the sides of the shopping cart, arms reaching for her and mouths frozen in wide grins. Isaiah hovered in the air like Superwoman, unable to move anything but her head. The only thing still in motion was the smoke circling her family. Wisps traced the area previously spared and then infiltrated, darkening it with the rest of the room.

A light appeared from above, glowing so brightly Isaiah squinted at its intensity. She searched the area in front of her, hoping it would illuminate the scene again, but it didn't. The light only existed in the place it was—a glowing orb with an agenda having nothing to do with the world around it. It drifted toward Isaiah. Hoping for one last glance of her babies' fingers, she ignored it and strained to see her family before they disappeared into the blackness. Then they were gone, and only she and the light remained.

"No!" Her voice rang clear this time, forcing her agony into the world. "Noooo!"

The light was on top of her. It was there and sucking, pulling her from her hips up toward its center. Folding in half, she was helpless against its gravity. Her shoulders dropped, heavy with the weakness of despair. The next instant, she was surrounded by the sphere. Eyes squeezed tight, she grounded herself in the sensation of it, then blinked, straining the muscles around her orbits to widen her lids. She opened them and found herself lying flat on her belly staring into the darkness of her room, arms tangled in the sheet she had loosened in the dream's struggle.

"What was that, Lord?" she wondered out loud. He didn't answer.

XIII

AFTER A HURRIED breakfast of hot sweet tea and sand-laden rolls coated with peanut butter, they headed to the airport with Sammy as their escort.

Elise grabbed Isaiah's hand. "Hey, friend, what's going on in that head of yours?"

"She's probably still working out those pizzas," Sammy cut in, grinning. "Don't worry. They will make it out the other end at some point."

"Ugh, seriously?" Elise rolled her eyes back at him.

Isaiah watched, glad for her. Elise had given her life selflessly to the service of others and, because of this, had put the simple, common pleasures of marriage and motherhood aside. She silently prayed for Elise's heart to experience love like she had and added for her never to lose it.

"I had a bad dream. It seems to be stuck with me."

"Oh, that stinks," Elise answered.

"What was it about?" Sammy asked.

"Sammy, don't make her relive it."

"What? Dreams are cool. Plus, maybe it will give us a picture into her soul." He wiggled his fingers in the air at Elise's face.

"It's okay." Isaiah shrugged. "I almost wonder if it was from God. It felt so real."

"Really? No way. That's awesome!" Elise answered. "Okay, I *do* want to hear it."

Isaiah described the dream to them. "It was intense," she finished. "So what say you guys? I've heard dreams are answers to questions we have but haven't figured the words to yet. What do you think?"

In the mirror, Sammy's lips pursed. "Well, in my expert opinion, some dreams arise from toxins accidentally consumed from spoiled lamb bought at dirty street-side shops."

Isaiah snickered at his expression. "Ugh, don't remind me. The pizza was good, though. I bet you guys all have stomachs of steel, eating this food."

Elise laughed. "My first month here, I lost five pounds—all dehydration from diarrhea."

"Yuck!" Sammy said, face crunched, flaring his nostrils wide. "I didn't think girls pooped."

Elise laughed again. "Well, Doctor, yes they do. And guess what? They fart, too." She grinned. "Well, most girls. I myself do not fart. I'm far too much a lady."

"I see," Sammy replied. "Okay then, *Doctor*, I certainly can't argue with that logic." He sobered, turning back to Isaiah. "Anyway, I don't know, but I prefer to believe dreams are less us working out answers and more us simply working out questions weighing on our minds."

Working out the questions, Isaiah thought. Which meant what, exactly? She'd let her family down—nothing needed to be deciphered there—and she had no interest in trying to convince herself otherwise. If they'd gone through the pain of a death as horrid as they had, she should go through the guilt of not being with them at the time. If the dragon and light were symbols, was she secretly afraid her family wasn't in heaven? And if that were the case and she was trying for them anyway, did she favor them above heaven?

Isaiah's heart dropped. God knew all. He could see all, deci-

71

pher all. If she were placing her love for them above a future with Him, what would that mean about how she felt about Him? Isaiah shuddered, remembering the familiar verse that had haunted her since she'd delivered her first son. *He that loveth his father or mother more than me is not worthy of me: and he that loveth his son or daughter more than me is not worthy of me.*

She hoped she was ready for this. She thought of the previous night of worship with believers she'd just met but now belonged to in spirit. The fire and peace she had experienced specifically for this trip had been almost palpable. Wasn't that real?

The car pulled to the curb. Sammy climbed out and unloaded the suitcases, every bit of his arms clutching them.

"We can carry those, Sammy," Elise laughed.

"Oh, no, you two just take care of yourselves and get what rest you can. I want you to come back to me." He paused, biting his lip. "To the team, I mean."

Isaiah noticed his dark cheeks redden as he hobbled away toward the airport. She lifted her eyebrows at Elise, teasing her.

"He's awesome," Isaiah said. "I do believe he may like you."

Elise grinned knowingly. "Oh, you do? Well, let's hope it stays that way while we're gone." She shared a glance with Isaiah, and the two rushed after him, arms locked in excitement like teenagers in a high school hall.

After a few hours, the plane landed at Tbilisi International Airport, in the capital city of Tbilisi, Georgia. The plan was to secure the last details of the trip with the guides, meet with the rest of the team a few days later, and leave. Their bags were heavy with supplies, so they were eager to find a room to dump them in. This airport was a bit larger than the one in Iraq, and much freer. They let their hair loose as soon as they left the plane.

"Ah, now *that* is better." Elise threaded her fingers through her hair, shaking it loose around her shoulders.

Isaiah wrapped hers in its usual bun. "Amen," she replied. "Iraq was scorching. I have no idea how the ladies can walk around in all those layers—especially without air-conditioning. I guess you'd get used to it, but seriously!"

They loaded up at the baggage claim and stopped at the airport gift shop for Isaiah. She had been collecting postcards and magnets for decades. One the shape of Georgia caught her eye, with a glossy picture on it of a mountain covered in pine trees. Her husband had always wanted a magnet when they went somewhere new, and she'd continued collecting them after he was gone. Their refrigerator had been adorned with colors and shapes of all kinds.

Two hours later, souvenirs had been purchased, the city had been navigated, and Isaiah and Elise had unloaded in their hotel room. They sipped tea at the hotel café, engulfed in catch-up chatter. Having a friendship so intense that even being separated by oceans and time did not diminish its spark was magical. The two spoke about Elise's travels and patients; her interesting, rewarding, and crushing cases. They discussed healing miracles that had happened after prayer and the laying on of hands and deaths that occurred after the same. Eventually, the conversation turned to Isaiah's family and the bomb that had taken them, and those that had destroyed other parts of the US. No group had yet to claim the attacks. The bombings had occurred nationwide, all slightly different but each one tragic. Kamikaze vans had been driven into thick pedestrian traffic, and suitcase and paper-bag bombs had been left at grocery stores, ball games, and movie theatres. The few perpetrators collected in the aftermath were never in one piece or able to be identified. It was as if whoever was behind the assaults had no goal but to incite fear.

Elise locked her dark eyes on Isaiah's. "How have you been? *Really* been, I mean?"

Isaiah gazed past Elise's shoulder, staring at nothing. "Not good," she said quietly. Her breath jagged, she pressed her tongue against the top of her palate, willing herself not to cry. "It hurts less, I suppose, but I can't imagine ever getting past it. I just don't understand how anyone can have so much hate." She slumped, confessing what she'd been brooding over for months. "I can't seem to reattach my heart to God, either. I know He loves me. I just... I know this sounds cliché, but I don't understand how He could let this happen. He is supposed to be *good*, and I am supposed to be *His*. He was supposed to protect my family. Was it wrong to be selfish for my family? Maybe He was teaching me not to love anything above Him, not to be selfish. I always prayed for Him to bless and protect them, and it was almost like He purposefully did the opposite. I know all things work for the good of those who love Him, and something about all this will be good in the end, but... but why them? Maybe His plan did need someone to die like that... but, again, why them? It's like He saw them as only numbers—pieces in some puzzle but not as people. Or souls."

There, it was out. She was embarrassed to reveal her lack of faith and anger at God to Elise, who always seemed so sure of His grace and goodness. But Isaiah wasn't sure anymore, and maybe Elise knew something she didn't. To Isaiah, her family had been sweet fruit. After the gift of salvation, they were her favorite blessing in life; maybe she did love them more than she should have.

Elise slid her chair next to Isaiah and squeezed her in a hug. "I'm so sorry, Isaiah. I wish this had never happened."

Tears flooded Isaiah's eye, and she let go, crying into Elise's chest until her shoulders shook. "I've been trying to get past this, but... *ugh!*"

Elise stroked her hair. "I don't know why it happened, but I don't think it was a punishment. And we can't even say God did it. It might have just been this broken world. I don't know. I *do* know your babies are safe now, for eternity." She paused, squeezing her hand tightly. "And Isaiah? I know He misses you.

He told me you are the one He wanted me to take with on this thing. *He* chose you, not me."

Isaiah sniffed loudly and calmed at her friend's words. A warmth washed over her, and a voice came with it. The voice was as audible as Elise's, though she hadn't said anything further. *I love you.*

XIV

THE NEXT MORNING, Isaiah peered out the passenger window of their rental car as Elise navigated traffic. "So, what are we looking for here?"

"It's supposed to be a shop with a blue canopy over the door and window. *Turkish Brothers' Tours*," Elise answered. "There," she spat, swerving into a parking space, bouncing the front wheel off the curb.

Isaiah grabbed the door handle, shooting a wide-eyed glance at her friend. "I see you picked up some driving skills yourself in Iraq?"

Elise laughed. "Perhaps. But I found it, see?" She pointed at the faded blue canvas dressing up a cinder-block building. "Are you ready to meet the men we're going to follow into the depths of the Georgian wild?"

A mischievous smile stretched across Isaiah's face. "Let's do it," she answered. "I hope they don't think we're nuts. Or should I say, I hope they don't figure it out until it's too late to turn back? Do they know why we're out here?"

"Not quite. I told them we want to buy their services for the next few weeks, and I gave them a rough idea of the region, but I just said we're on an expedition. They didn't ask anymore, so I didn't offer."

"Well, all-righty then."

Elise led the way inside. The girls glanced around the room, seeking signs of life. The freshly waxed linoleum floor seemed out of place against the dingy, cream-colored walls. Buzzing fluorescent lights filled the space with a sickening glow from above. A waist-high gate separated the front of the store from the back, but otherwise, the room was mostly bare. In front was a black desk with four chairs scattered around it, and beyond the gate lay two blue woven rugs, worn thin in the center, tassels barely attached on the ends. The walls were adorned with framed scenes of rocky cliffs, waterfalls, and mile-high pine trees. Near the desk hung a picture of a lone gray wolf, standing square. The animal was lean and matted, head lowered with lips curled in a snarl, its teeth peeking through.

Elise stepped closer to the picture. "It is like he's staring right at us," she said, touching the wild dog's face.

"He looks hungry," Isaiah answered. "I wouldn't want to be the one taking the picture."

"Well, it was a little unnerving."

A voice cut through the room from behind them. Both Isaiah and Elise turned to find a trim man with broad shoulders and defined features walking up to them, hands clasped in front of his abdomen.

"I did scare her off, but she was pretty persistent."

"Oh, hello. Are you Mr. Takir?" Elise stuck her hand out.

The man did not reach in return. Instead, he waved his hands from his wrists, keeping his forearms pressed against his torso. "Yes, I am Adira Takir. Are you Dr. Harper?"

"Oh, yes. Oh, so sorry. I see." She dropped her hand awkwardly. "Yes," she repeated, "I am Elise Harper. This is Dr. Isaiah Robinson. We're the ones you will be guiding for our expedition. We will have another joining us as well. Hopefully tomorrow."

Isaiah grinned. "Hi. Wow, that picture is amazing. Did you take all of these?"

"I did."

"Very cool. They're beautiful. I can't wait to see these places for myself."

"Yes, well, good. I am not sure this one you would have wanted to be there for, though. This wolf was very hungry. Anyway, my brother is in the back. He will be joining us later, I hope. Shall we go over the details of our tour?"

Adira walked behind the desk and sat, eyebrows raised at them expectantly, then reached into a drawer and presented a crisp plastic folder. He slid it across the desk, spread open to reveal a topography map. "This voyage, you want to follow the river up to its source, is this correct?"

"Yes, that's right. How long should it take?"

"Well, we estimate about a week. But as you two are women, we should likely have to double that, and we will also have to leave the riverside a few times as some regions are too treacherous for female hikers."

Isaiah snorted a laugh, immediately realizing she was the only noise in the room other than the hum above their heads. "Oh, sorry," she said, looking up. "We just are probably not as delicate as you may imagine."

Adira sighed, face otherwise unmoving, and blinked in her direction. "Dr. Robinson, you are to be under my protection for this tour. Meaning, you should probably take my advice as to the best dynamics and route. I have been through this area hundreds of times, and I know what we are up against. You"—he nodded deliberately toward the map—"do not."

Elise grinned, nudging Isaiah's foot with her toe, eyes dancing.

"Yes. Okay." Isaiah cleared her throat and shoved her chin sheepishly toward the plans. "So, two weeks in, a day or maybe a few days at the site, and then another two weeks back? Or can we float the river back and get home sooner?"

"Yes, this river is generally safe to float. However, I am assuming you do not have a boat at the top of it."

"Well, I brought a few inflatables. I know they're heavy, but if they save time returning..." She hesitated, suddenly unsure of herself. "Anyway, I thought it would be fun."

Adira tipped his head. "Well, it is possible. However, we should make sure they don't push us past our weight limit, which means no liquids."

"Mr. Takir," Elise cut in, "have you been that far upstream before? I mean, to the river's source?"

"No, I have not. There has been no need. It originates in the mountains. Its source is several slow-moving tributaries, and beyond those are more mountains and trees. This area you are wanting to go to is unexplored as far as I know. I am quite interested in what we find."

Elise smiled at Isaiah. "Us too," she said.

They signed papers and discussed logistics for another hour. As she stood to leave, Elise caught Adira's eyes. "I know there are cultural differences between us," she said, "but it is never our intent to be disrespectful to you or your culture. Please let us know if anything we do or say is confusing or offensive. We don't want you to feel uncomfortable. This will be a long trip, and I would like us to be a team here."

"I understand, Doctor. My brother and I will be fine. We are professionals. We live in Georgia, and certainly there are many cultural differences we are already accustomed to here. We will take care of your team and get you back safely as long as everyone works with us."

A second man, just as short as Adira, sauntered in from the back, wearing bright white tennis shoes glowing beneath his dark, skintight jeans, tears strewn erratically along the leg.

"Hey, ladies." He smiled wildly, revealing a row of crooked teeth. "I'm Mahir. I hope you weren't planning on leaving without meeting the brains behind our operation?"

Adira shifted weight. "Hi, Mahir. We already discussed the

details. We are hoping to leave Saturday morning. You made sure we have no tours booked for the rest of the month, right?"

"Oh yeah. Got it sir, yes sir!" He clipped his heels together loudly and saluted his brother.

Adira pulled open a desk drawer, removed a small bottle, and popped two pills, chasing them with a swig of dark tea. "Good. These are Doctors Harper and Robinson."

"Lady doctors? Isn't that something? What's this world coming to? You women are going to take over, I tell you."

"Yes, well, perhaps," Elise said. She and Isaiah exchanged glances.

"Are your husbands coming?" Mahir asked.

"We don't have husbands. Well, I don't. Isaiah lost hers to the war."

"Killed in battle?"

"Killed while shopping at Walmart," Isaiah interrupted, hands suddenly shaking.

"Hmm. well, kind of the same thing, isn't it?" Mahir answered. He lifted his ballcap and clenched it between his teeth, revealing long hair. He laced his fingers through the hole in the back of the cap, gathered his hair, and pulled all of it through into a low ponytail. Readjusting his hat, he tipped it forward dramatically. Peering down his nose at them with chin lifted, he smirked.

Isaiah stood up, boiling. "We'll see you soon, then," she said and spun around to leave.

They drove back to the hotel in silence. They both knew these were not the ideal hands to be putting their lives into for the next several weeks. Unfortunately, no other options existed. Elise had scoured the tour agencies and adventure companies for months. These guys were the best, and they'd traveled farthest into the terrain.

"We could consider another group," Isaiah said after a long silence.

"Ugh, I had no idea this was how it would be, but Isaiah, we need them. This is too important. Just stay away from the crazy one, follow the lead of the other, and we should be fine."

"Seriously, Elise, I don't know which one you're referring to when you say, 'crazy one.'"

Elise rolled her eyes. "You act like you've never stepped foot out of Mayberry."

"I've never been *to* Mayberry."

Elise grinned and swatted her shoulder. "We'll be fine. Let's work on cultural stuff tonight. I'll tell you what I've learned."

Elise and Isaiah returned to the room and showered, then spent the rest of the night discussing what to expect over the next few weeks.

"Don't spend too much time looking in their eyes. Well, Adira's eyes. I don't get the sense the younger one is very devout," Elise said. "Don't touch him unless you have to, and I mean *absolutely* have to. We'll be stopping five times a day to let them pray. I thought perhaps we could pray at the same time, but together. The archaeologist, Jack, is a Christian too. Hopefully, the three of us can stand together as salt and light."

Elise referred to one of Isaiah's favorite Bible verses, one from the book of Matthew that urged believers to stand out and help nonbelievers see God for who He is. *You are the salt of the Earth. But if the salt loses its saltiness, how can it be made salty again? It is no longer good for anything except to be thrown out and trampled underfoot. You are the light of the world. A town built on a hill cannot be hidden. Neither do people light a lamp and put it under a bowl. Instead they put it on its stand, and it gives light to everyone in the house.*

Isaiah answered, "Well, I *hope* we can be like light. Now salt, I know we can do that... poured right into a cut on their backs."

XV

AUSTRIAN AIRLINES FLIGHT 327 from Cairo to Tbilisi landed without event, right on time. Stepping onto the tarmac, Jack filled his lungs dramatically, then puffed the air out extra slow.

"Do you smell that, Rash? Fresh air. No ash, no gunpowder, no burning buildings. Just O2, nitrogen, and carbon dioxide. Nice."

"Yeah, I guess." Rashid gave him a half-grin.

The two made their way through airport security, grabbed their gear from the baggage claim, and headed out to catch a taxi. They were to meet "the doctors" the next morning for breakfast.

"Here!" Jack flagged a taxi with his palm out. When the driver rolled the window down, Jack leaned forward to negotiate price. The deal came to sixty lari, the equivalent of about twenty-five US dollars. Jack fumbled, trying to pull out the cab's pay from the few thousand lari wadded up in his pocket without showing it all, then climbed in.

The hotel room was fairly modern, with gray-tiled floors, orange porcelain lights, and a textured sink made of dark laminated wood. They plopped their bags against the wall, and Rashid clicked the remote, turning on BBC Television. The face of the former Swiss president, Jubair Talmuk, flashed on the screen as they announced more of his lifesaving, war-ending feats in the background.

The reporter adjusted his tie. *"The world is rejoicing in this man, who could not have come at a more-needed hour. The hope arising from Switzerland is powerful and contagious. With the new policies announced after the Conference of Nations this week, it seems hope will be continuing as well. World leaders have announced measures to end child trafficking, which still plagues many second- and third-world countries. They also announced plans to strengthen the United Nations, and many are hopeful Secretary-General Talmuk will continue indefinitely as head of its 'round table,' so to speak."*

"What do you think about this new secretary-general?" Jack asked, rummaging through the desk drawers, looking for a visitor's guide.

"Well, he got the war to stop. That is what's important to me. I do believe someone should assassinate Anania's new king, but, for now, I am simply happy to get out of Egypt."

"The guy, he… he is pretty amazing," Jack said. "Something about him, though—it doesn't add up."

"What do you mean?" Rashid answered. "He does nothing except for the benefit of others. He managed to stop the war that killed my family. I find that to be of good value."

"His eyes just seem empty," Jack answered.

"Eyes seem empty? Come on, Captain. He's from Iraq. He has dark eyes. Doesn't mean they're empty." Rashid tossed his shoes to the side of the television stand. "Now me, on the other hand, I would say my eyes have been emptied. As has my brain, and body. I need sleep. What do you say to a long nap, and then we can go explore the town?" He wrinkled his nose and threw Jack's bag at his chest. "Maybe first you take a shower, *then* a nap. You stink!"

"Genius doesn't need to shower. I'm just emitting my essence on the lesser-brained people around me. You ought to be saying thank you."

"Ugh, well thank you. Your essence has helped me to pass out even faster," he answered, then crashed face-first into the pillows.

Jack stood in the shower for a long time, letting the water hit him until his back went numb from its percussion. He thought about Rashid's words. The secretary-general did seem to be making a giant impact for the good. But he couldn't shake off the uneasy feeling. A few years back, he'd had the same feeling while gawking at a saltwater tank at the Shedd Aquarium in downtown Chicago. The sharks swam through the water with graceful confidence, but they were so robotic—more like darts propelled by some hidden intention than beautiful sea creatures. They seemed remote-controlled, their black eyes ornamental pits that white-washed any idea of connection or emotional presence. Jubair Talmuk had eyes like that—shark eyes.

✍

The next morning, Jack and Rashid walked to a local breakfast spot that was to be the team rendezvous point. A giant sign, reading, *Honey Bees,* was staked to the diner's brown, shingled roof. The windows were plastered with spray-painted pictures of pancakes, omelets, and ice cream floats. They walked in and glanced around the room.

"Do you think it would be weird if I ordered a cheeseburger?" Rashid asked, scanning the room. "It is the only thing that sounds good right now."

"Maybe, but who cares?" Jack answered. "Oh, by the way, I didn't tell them you were coming."

"What?" Rashid's eyes widened. "And when were you planning on telling them? Now? When this weird man comes to breakfast and orders a cheeseburger?" He dropped his shoulders. "No way I can order that now."

"Nah, it'll be fine," Jack answered. "It's both of us, or I'm not going. They'll have to agree."

"I'm not sure anyone is going to vie for your assistance in those shorts, my man. You look like you forgot your suspenders at home. Perhaps I should call you Steven Urkel rather than Captain." Rashid grinned and shook his head, glancing at Jack's beige canvas shorts, which landed two inches too high above his knees.

"Please," Jack answered, flicking up the collar of his plaid shirt. "These are my chick magnets."

Rashid rolled his eyes and squeezed the straps of his backpack. "*Chicks?* The only female those will attract will be either in her eighties or perhaps visually impaired."

Jack laughed and pointed at the far wall. "There. You think... is that them?"

Two American-appearing women sat across a large wooden table from two dark-complexioned men. The shorter man had neatly oiled curly hair and broad shoulders. His lips were tight, and he kept both hands on the table as if he were commanding it to be still. The other had a baseball cap on sideways and sat sprawled out, one arm draped over the seat beside him, the other holding a milkshake.

"Not sure. Let's go ask."

They walked up, and Jack locked eyes with one of the women. "Hi, I'm kind of hoping you're Doctor Harper?"

She smiled broadly. "I am. Are you Mr. Barron?"

"I am." They shook hands, and he turned toward Rashid. "This is my comrade in arms, Rashid Al Hassad. You've never met a better translator."

"Oh. Hello." Elise's face flattened slightly. "Do you live here?"

"No, I actually, uh... Hi, nice to meet you." Rashid shook her hand. "The bombings in Egypt destroyed my home, so now I am a resident of fate. Jack and I work together, and he invited me along."

"Oh, wow. How horrible. I'm so sorry." Elise answered, her eyes fixed on his wedding ring. "Okay then, I suppose we can swing that. Do you know what the plan is? Are you on board?"

She turned to Adira before Rashid could answer. "One extra—we can swing that, don't you think?"

Adira shrugged. "More people, more time. It is your choice." His eyes rested on hers firmly as he added, "More pay, of course."

Rashid interrupted. "I know what you are looking for, and I am ready. I am also quick. Actually, you may need me to keep this man on target," he nudged Jack with his elbow. "He may get slowed down by his poor choices in extremely awkward clothing."

The other woman giggled a little too loudly. Eyes widening, she shot a hand up to cover her mouth, then reached for her orange juice, locking her eyes on the glass.

Elise half smiled at her. "So sorry! This is Dr. Isaiah Robinson. We went to school together." She gestured toward the men across the table. "And these are our guides, Adira and Mahir Takir."

"Hey man," Mahir said, nodding toward Rashid. "Welcome aboard."

Jack pulled up a chair and sat down too quickly, knocking over the water at his place. "Oh, sorry!" He laid down a napkin, which soaked through in an instant, doing little to eliminate the spreading pool of ice and water.

"Okay, no coffee for you, apparently," Mahir said, standing as he shook the water off his lap. "Waitress!"

A not-quite-five-foot-tall, curvy woman with a swinging brown ponytail and fake eyelashes rushed over with a thick rag and mopped it up. Mahir reached over, pretending to pick up ice cubes, and brushed her petite hand with his. She glanced up, blushing.

Mahir smiled back. His voice dropped an octave deeper. "Thank you."

Adira rolled his eyes, turning toward the group. "Let's get this laid out."

XVI

Lazarus

IN THE HOLLOW quietness of the cottage, Lazarus sat, watching the leaves flutter through the closed windows—the only evidence of the wind outside. A storm was brewing, and he loved storms. They were yet another reason he was glad they had decided to move here. Israel had a nice temperature for sure, but the weather tended to follow the same pattern—hot, dry, warm and dry, cool at night, and dry. After decades of living through days that melted together this way, he realized they needed the weather cycle to keep things interesting. Years were hard to keep track of to begin with, and weather patterns helped prevent a person from going mad from the monotony of it all. Plus, storms displayed the magnitude of nature's power. They reminded him of how small he was and how big the world's ruling forces were.

He stood up to get some fresh air before the activity of the evening. The others would be back soon. Their return would chase away his peace and flood their tiny wooden cottage with the scent of mud and sweat. He had a surprise for them today—a pedestal. They already had more furniture than they would ever need, but he was an expert carpenter by now, and he loved to watch a chunk of wood transform into something beautiful. Anyway, they had been working on this project of theirs with fervor, so he kept carving away.

The door swung open and Salome toppled in after it. She came in sideways, arms full of tree limbs they had collected that afternoon. The wind pushed the door all the way open and greeted Lazarus by blowing his brown-black strands across his face. John followed her in, a soft, waxy leather bag slung over his right shoulder and a homemade spear in his left hand.

"We have mulberries!" he announced proudly. "Here, observe, and be glad." He grinned and dropped the sack onto the table, its contents spilling out immediately.

"John!" Salome scolded, maneuvering to shut the door quickly despite her armload of wood as the wind rearranged the whole room. Once closed, she made her way across the cabin and dropped the sticks in the corner pile where they kept kindling.

Lazarus shook his head and smiled, grabbing the bag from the table. "I see, boy. Now tell me how, after all these years, you still manage to spill something at least once a week?" Peering inside, he said, "These look good. Where'd you two find them?"

"*I* found them," John answered, "and I'm not telling where. It's a secret. I don't want Salome going out and eating them all, and then we don't have any left to make jelly."

Salome had her hand deep in the sack now. She rolled her eyes as she popped a handful of mulberries into her mouth. "Like Father wouldn't just show me if I asked Him."

Lazarus stepped around the two kids. "I finished a pedestal today," he announced. "We can extend the path another few feet."

"Where is it?" Salome asked, fruit suddenly forgotten. She smiled in excitement; Lazarus never let her see the pieces until it was done, and this one had taken several months to carve out. She would be expecting extravagance.

"Out back. Let John help you if you plan on putting it in the lineup."

Salome darted out the door before he had finished his sentence. She was for sure strong enough to lift it, but now she would need to carry it almost two miles to get it to its spot. Because Lazarus had made so many pedestals and there was nowhere left around the homestead to put them, the kids had decided to arrange them in a long line through the woods to mark a trail. *The Way to Wander*, Salome had named it. It started at the edge of their clearing and plunged straight into the woods. They had chosen the mountains' general direction to have less likelihood of anyone stumbling upon them and, therefore, their home. Wherever it would finally lead, they had yet to discover. Thus far, over a thousand carved columns were installed on either side of a dirt path the kids weeded out and tilled as they added each new marker.

A pang of nervousness shot through Lazarus as the two left. He knew by now they'd be fine; no permanent harm had ever befallen them. But he still worried about their safety when they were out exploring. He thought back to the times they had been injured—once John had nearly severed his right arm clear off. Lazarus had tied his arm back in place with a rope he'd made from braided bark and nursed him back for weeks. He remembered how shocked he'd been that John remained intact after all of it; he had thought for sure that would be the end of him. However, here John was, two arms complete, with strong hands skilled at pulling braids and sneaking frogs under Salome's pillow at night.

Lazarus scooped up the leather sack holding the berries now lying forgotten on the smooth counter. He put one in his mouth and pressed it against his palate with his tongue, savoring the sugary-sour juice spraying the insides of his cheeks and feeling seeds find the crevices between his teeth. He closed his eyes and tipped his face to the ceiling. *Thank you, Father, for this bittersweet life.*

XVII

Adira

"ARE WE READY?" Adira announced more than asked as Jack and Rashid stuffed water bottles in their backpacks. The others stood alongside a black Range Rover, its rusted fenders a stark contrast to its four thick, all-terrain tires. "Make sure your packs are light. Bring only what I wrote on your list and no more. You will be surprised at how heavy a few extra ounces can become three days into this."

"Are you saying I should not bring my magazines?" Mahir asked, one eyebrow lifted in pretend sincerity. He held a withered, partially torn issue of *Penthouse* in his hands. "How about just one? They keep me entertained when my energy drops," he added with a smile.

"Mahir," Adira sighed, "you bring what you need, but I seriously doubt anyone here will want to touch your... entertainment when they get heavy, and we are not leaving garbage in the forest."

Elise glanced at Adira and raised her eyebrows. "You said this would be professional. What is this?"

"He's innocent," Adira replied. "He just likes attention."

"Innocent or not, he needs to rein it in. We aren't going to trust him if this is how he's going to be."

Adira stiffened. "Doctor, you can trust my brother with your life. He may be... eccentric, but he knows the forest, and he will not cross any important lines."

Elise bit her lips together, hard, and shook her head. She slung her pack on, its giant mass towering over her tiny shoulders, then answered, "Fine. Let's do this."

Adira watched as she strode to the back of the vehicle to help load the rest of the gear, then followed to do a final supplies check. They had dried food, water filters, bug repellant, thin plastic tents, and so much more. Isaiah had convinced him to bring the rafts once he'd seen what she had brought. They were actually nicer than he had thought they'd be—only thirty ounces in weight, and once inflated could carry 350 pounds easily. Hopefully, they'd provide a fast—and easy—return.

A few hours later, they bounced along, shoulders rubbing as Adira guided the SUV carefully up the ragged dirt road. The one-lane path was barely wide enough to call a road. Evergreens towered above them, darkening the view though it was not yet midday. Occasionally when they passed a meadow, the vehicle would fill with light, then the land would roll away and the flower-speckled green would melt into brown nettles and gray trunks again.

Elise was the only one who didn't lose energy on the drive, drilling Adira with questions about the landscape and animals as they traveled. "So I've read a lot, but how much of it is true? Are we going to see bears?" She perched forward from the middle row, arms resting on the back of his seat and Mahir's.

Adira shook his head. "Maybe. Actually, with us following the river, we are likely to see a few. Let's hope they are not interested in us."

They hit a rut in the ground, launching the Range Rover a few inches in the air. The team bounced out of their seats and slammed back as they plunged forward.

"Yeehaw," Mahir exclaimed. "Good driving, big brother! I knew you learned a thing or two from me last trip."

"Never again will I let you drive out this way, Mahir." Adira's eyes sparkled as he grabbed his brother's cap off his head, then popped it back against his face.

"Nah, I'm an excellent driver." Mahir spun around to address the rest of the group. "Last trip I scored our dinner on the drive out—possum. Yum!" He sat back, amused.

"Yum," Rashid answered, facing his window. "Let's try to avoid death for now though, okay man?"

"Yes, let's do that." Adira said, then lifted his eyes to the rearview mirror. He wasn't sure this group could make the entire trip. The women seemed tough enough, at least in spirit, but Jack was all brains, and the other guy, Rashid, worried him. Something far-away dominated his countenance, and the fact he was here on a whim made him a liability. Adira was also uneasy about the whole point of the trip. The leader, Elise, hadn't shared why four strangers were hiking into unknown lands together. But his job was simply to get them to their destination and back, safe and alive. He had cleared the calendar for five weeks, hoping to return in under three. But hikers could be irrational, and sometimes they took on minds of their own. Occasionally, clients even tried to go their own way, alone. He worried this group might end up that way. As long as he was paid, he didn't care if they were mad, but he sure as hell wouldn't be answering to any high and mighty American relatives if these crazies didn't come back from their little adventure.

The team bounced quietly for another hour before the road became unpassable, blending from dirt and gravel into dirt and gravel and foliage. Adira pulled the Rover fifty meters into the brush and parked beneath the speckled, brown-and-white branches of twin birch trees.

"Well, we are here." He turned to the passengers. "Everyone ready?"

"Absolutely," Elise said, beaming. She peered up at the birch and whispered, "Beautiful."

Mahir glanced at her, amused. "So, uh, you like trees, do you?" he drawled. "They don't get many of those out in America?"

"I haven't been in America for a few years, but I'd say... yes, Mahir. Trees have captured my attention of late."

The group climbed out and prepared to hike away from civilization. Boots were laced, bug spray applied, and backs were loaded with packs, tents, and canisters. Adira and Mahir covered the vehicle with branches, then joined the others to check gear.

Soon, the six beasts of burden disappeared under the green canopy, along a path that came and went but usually existed as just a trace of trampled dirt or broken twigs. They hiked with energy, full of jovial voices and get-to-know-you conversation.

The men learned about the origin of Elise and Isaiah's friendship. They both had attended Domoin University, a Caribbean medical school, and met at the student-based church. They had formed a fast and deep friendship and bonded during late-night prayer sessions every Thursday on the island's black-sand shores. They lived there for almost a year and a half before traveling back to America for their clinical rotations, living as roommates until graduation parted their ways.

The conversation eventually turned to Jack and Rashid. Jack spoke first of their studies together in the university and then of how they had spent the last year and change of their lives. But after Rashid revealed his tragic situation, the hum of conversation fizzled out.

Adira listened in silence. He used to engage more with the clients on these tours, but he cared less about connecting with them as the years passed. Anyway, he never shared his story—it didn't lend itself to going over well. *Yes, well, I spent two and a half decades pillaging villages and killing innocent people for a cause I didn't believe in under a leader I never met. Perhaps you have heard of my work?*

He was not ashamed of his time in the brigade, but he would erase it if he could. He had met many men who'd served as he did—initially just to prevent the death of a loved one—but after a time, they continued because it was the only life they knew. There was a sort of community in it all. He had embraced victory and mourned the death of friends alongside those he'd served with. Those he killed became faceless eventually—they had to, or he could never have continued in the work. He could have escaped a few times after his initial subjugation, but the loss of his family had pulverized his spirit, and he never found the strength to try again.

Adira had finally left the regiment honorably—if one could call it such—when he was aged and injured out of usefulness. Initially, he'd returned to his old village, which by then was deserted. He'd stayed anyway, in the same home in which he'd been born, alone, for another seven months. Eventually, the silence and heat were too much to bear, and he left, searching for a new home in a less war-torn locale. That was how he made it to Georgia. His brother he'd found in a bar one night, without even looking. In one of his weakest moments, Adira had been there drinking to forget, while Mahir was there drinking to remember. They had hugged fiercely and laughed and talked for hours while the roughneck men of the town bellowed drunken "It's finally the weekend" melodies in the background. Somewhere in their reunion, they decided to join forces and start the guide company. In less than a year, his new routine was to spend his days by his brother's side, soaked in DEET and solace, entertaining rich tourists. The Georgian countryside was radically different from the desert Adira had served in for so long, and it kept his mind on the *now,* which was monumentally more pleasant than the *then.*

After some time, Jack broke the silence. "What about this

Jubair Talmuk guy? I hear he wants to authorize the UN to regulate other countries' policies. Do y'all think that'll happen?"

"Oh, who knows. He is certainly impressive, though," Isaiah answered. "Seems like he has good intentions."

"I disagree," Adira responded. "This man, he gave a terrorist his own country—*paid* him to shut down. The better thing to do would have been to imprison or even assassinate him."

Mahir glanced at him and raised an eyebrow. Guilt rose in Adira's chest—his link with Anan could qualify him for the same proposed fate. After all, the man had been his foreman for the best of his former career.

"I agree with Adira," Elise said. "Since when do we give terrorists what they want? Doesn't that just teach them to continue to terrorize? And won't it encourage others to do the same?"

Rashid furrowed his brow at her. "Remember, this war was going on for decades—like, over fifty years. This group essentially just kept growing and killing, growing and killing, and now they are confined to a small area encircled by Egyptian forces." His voice rose as he spoke. "The whole world is watching them. They don't have enough room to move or hide. The problem with groups like these, the guerrilla warfare groups, is they're hard to track... to *pin down*. I think Secretary Talmuk pulled an ingenious stunt here. He took their power completely away and made them think they won. No way the FREA or the SRA or any other group is starting from there now."

"Here," Adira said, interrupting the discussion. "We can stop here."

They had been hiking for nearly three hours and had long since left the forest. The trail blurred into sandy colored grasses and gray-brown shrubs that filled an otherwise barren foothill before them. The sound of water came from the distance, off to the north.

"I could go another hour or two. Are you sure?" Isaiah asked.

Adira sighed. "My hope is you will feel that way most of the first few days." He dropped his sack on the ground beside his feet, signaling the end of the discussion.

"Right. Okay," Isaiah relented. She slung the thirty-pound pack off her back and squatted to sit against it. She pulled out her canister of water, polishing it off. "So where do we get water for the rest of the trip? Should we be to the river soon, you think?"

Adira tilted his head back and studied the sky, then gazed in both directions across. "Usually from here it is about another hour, maybe less depending on the terrain. It is just under four kilometers, but there are several hills."

"Hmm," Isaiah answered, shaking the last few drops of water onto her tongue. Rashid stepped up next to her and opened a granola bar.

"Mind if I sit here?" he asked.

"Please, go for it," she answered, scooting over.

The group's energy was still high, just as Adira had hoped. He sighed again, searching the meadow for wildlife, still considering Isaiah's challenge. If it weren't for people, he would enjoy every day of work. Sometimes he thought he'd let them make these choices, just to prove to them how much they needed him. Something about rich vacationers paying all this money to walk in the trees made his throat curl. It might be because he grew up in such a poor town or lived with so little during his time in the regime. Maybe it was all of it. Whatever the reason, he was used to pushing aside his repugnance and listening quietly to their politeness-inspired comments about how lovely his accent was or how impressed they were at his "cute little country." He gave them half-hearted smiles, even when their words came extra slow or a little too loud, as if he were dumb or deaf or both.

The group ate energy bars and gorged on water for another fifteen minutes. Elise sat with Adira and questioned him about the wildlife. He was surprised to find her energy improved his mood.

"What will the mountains be like?" she asked.

"That part is fairly steep but safe in the summer. Once the

snow comes, I usually don't take tours that way." He liked to visit those wintery paths himself, though, to soak in the way the trees were wrapped in snow and icicles, every branch coated in thick white frosting. With the sun reflecting off the snow, the air would get so warm you could take your jacket off. The sky was often deceivingly bright, summer blue with little to no clouds, and the ones that did float by were the fluffy cotton ones. To look upon those days, you would believe it was the middle of June.

"Well, let's hope we have no snow then," Elise said, winking. "So," she continued, changing the subject, "tell me you aren't the least bit interested in why we're doing this? I mean, a group of otherwise strangers asks you to take them deep into the uninhabited wilderness, and you don't even wonder why?"

"Madam, I only worry about getting us all there and back in a safe and timely manner. After that, I worry only about getting paid." Adira was tempted to wink back, but instead, he nodded and turned to his brother, who'd been sipping on his "special canister," which Adira knew contained Mahir's favorite liquor, chacha.

"Hey, brother. Can you save some for when we get there?" He rose and took the canister away from him. "Do you think it may be a little early to start clouding your mind and weakening your stride?"

"Why do you call me out, *brother*? Chill, Adira. I'm just trying to help ease the tension of having so many westerners around. Anyway, shouldn't we share with them proper Georgian culture?"

"Fine, well, leave some. Please." His expression checked Mahir, who twisted the cap back on. "I am going to pray. Are you coming?"

"Yeah, yeah, I'm coming." The two stood and detached their mats from their backpacks, then wandered off.

XVIII

LAZARUS SCOOPED STEW into bowls. Salome had cooked, and her soups were always the best, likely because she used salt, even though it was a luxury, as getting it meant a long trip to town.

"I am *so* hungry!" John grabbed a hunk of warm bread from the counter and sat at the table in the room's center.

The others joined him and ate, savoring the steaming mix of herbs simmered with fresh potatoes, onions, and carrots. Lazarus watched the two children, trying to decide how to share his news with them. He had known something was coming for a while now, but they needed to be prepared as well.

God had a way of preparing him for assignments gradually. He often primed Lazarus by refreshing in him whatever skill was needed most for the job. The skills were life lessons about love, or patience, or generosity—things that still sometimes came hard for Lazarus, even though he had been alive so long. It was odd, how hard it could be. Because he was eons older than his fellow humans, he saw them as children. And because they had such limited time to get things right, it was easier to have compassion for them. However, their selfishness and violence, and their often-superficial tendencies, made his jaw clench in frustration. At times, he'd forget his compassion and even want for their punishment. When this happened, God had a way of correcting him—sometimes gently, with a whispered reminder in his heart, and sometimes harshly, even causing him physical pain to distract him.

Lazarus cleared his throat. "Father revealed something to me today," he announced, waiting for the children to look up. "We are going to have a visitor."

John stopped chewing. "What? Yes!" He recoiled and gave a sheepish grin. "Not that you two aren't good company, but... fresh faces and voices! I have been wondering what's been going on in the world lately. When will we meet them?"

"I don't know, but I believe it will be soon. This one is special. He is on a mission from Father, and we need to keep him safe and help him finish if we can."

"Keep him safe? From what, like, the wolves? From getting lost? Is the war starting again?" Salome asked.

"Do you think he'll have a gun?" John was leaning forward now. He had seen guns many times, even had one for a while, but Lazarus had thrown it out long ago. They had no need for it out here, and it had made Salome nervous.

"I again don't know. I'm sorry." Lazarus shrugged and turned to Salome. "I am pretty sure the war never stopped, though, *Flore*." He called her Flore because she was always picking flowers to decorate her hair and the cottage. To Lazarus, she, too, was a flower, delicate and innocent as the clusters of purple gentiana growing on the mountainside. God had given her as a gift to him and John—to make their world softer, he knew, and sweeter. He viewed her as his daughter, even though she was only slightly younger than him by now. She had died at only twelve years old, so she was still mostly a child in every way. She still played with butterflies and cried when they had to kill anything—usually a predator trying to harm them, as they no longer hunted or ate meat. Sure, she had become more temperate and wiser over the years, but, in form and essence, she had neither grown nor aged. "As for guns, he might, but I don't think so. I think he will be weak and need us very much."

"I can clean the guest room," Salome offered. "Should I leave a doll for him? Maybe he will be lonely and want one to make him feel better?"

"Salome," John laughed, "grown men do not want dolls." He shook his head, eyes fixed on Lazarus for validation.

Lazarus smiled. "I have to agree with John on this one, Flore, but it is nice of you to think about it."

Salome shrugged and took a bite, suddenly embarrassed. "Some men might want dolls. I made one for Lazarus, and he liked it."

"I do love that doll, and I *am* a grown man." He laughed, lifting both hands in defeat. "You got us."

"So do we get to tell him," John asked, "or keep it secret again?"

"This one we get to tell. He isn't a brother though. Father has a message for him. For it to be received, he needs to be prepared. Therefore," Lazarus concluded, "we tell."

"That doesn't always work out so well," John said. "Remember the man who thought we were crazy? God had a message for him, too, but he missed the whole thing. And that other guy— Salome's mom's friend. He found out all on his own, and see where he ended up."

At his words, Salome dropped her shoulders and sank heavily into her chair. Lazarus rubbed her back. "Flore, why do you still get sad over this? Your mom was only trying to protect you."

"Really! And it was for-e-ver ago. You don't get over things well, Salome." John sighed. "But I guess you've heard that before too."

"It's just... he died because of me. He didn't even get another chance to meet Father, and now he never will."

Lazarus tapped her nose with his finger and slid the jelly they had made earlier in her direction. "Eat, Flore. Life is sweeter than you know."

Their secret, their outrageously precious mystery, was that they were immortal. They were, as far as Lazarus could tell, the only ones on Earth still alive despite having died. And he had searched. Two thousand years was plenty of time to look, and he had never found another. They might have been out there, of course. They could be in seclusion as well. The fact none of them aged made them rather conspicuous in relation to the rest of the world, so they remained in hiding. He and these two children, they just kept on living. And living. And living. They would breathe, eat, and sleep, or not, and just keep going. In the beginning, when they hadn't realized their new lot, they all lived in their original communities. However, once a few locals learned something was different about them, the three were forced to keep away from the public eye, and since getting together, they chose not to make outside friends.

Which wasn't to say they each didn't have their run-ins with being discovered. Mary, Salome's mother, had even killed two people to hide the secret. A woman from their local synagogue had taken notice of Salome, as she and her daughter played and walked to the local well together. When Salome didn't age, but her daughter did, the woman got suspicious and started spreading rumors. A few people had believed her and came around to peek at the mysterious girl.

One man told Mary that Salome should be studied, and her gift made public. "She is a special treasure," he said. "She should bear many children whose lifespans would be long and special as well." He had offered to be her husband—all fifty-seven years of him—or else connect her with another suitable man.

Mary had become afraid for her daughter's future and decided to kill the woman who'd started the rumors, as well as the man who'd approached her. She had snuck into each of their tents one night and stabbed them both, wrapped up the woman, and dragged her to the home of the man. She staged the room as if the two had been sleeping together, placing their two naked bodies in bed next to each other. Then, Mary had cleaned and hidden the knife in the sands of the desert and burned her clothes and

101

the smock she had used to move the body. Their corpses were found the next day, and that had basically been the end of it. No one suspected Mary, and though there had been a great deal of shame for both families of the deceased, Salome was unharmed, at least in body.

From that day on, Salome was never allowed to play with neighbor kids again, except a few times a year, and always a new group of children, with the rule she was not to share her name or residence with anyone.

At some point, long after each had lived through the deaths of their families, the three had found each other—slowly and one at a time. They moved in together and lived their secret life ever since. During the Crusades, they made the voyage away from their Mediterranean homes into the wilderness of Georgia, which at the time was still called Gruzia. Times were scary back then despite having Father for comfort and protection. Salome seemed to tremble incessantly, which worsened with loud noises and strangers approaching or even passing by their door, and John was constantly talking about joining the rebellion, so Lazarus made the decision for them all to leave civilization completely, and here they were.

The group simmered in their excitement while finishing their stew, discussing how to prepare for the mystery man. Eventually, the fire was replaced by embers and the cold of the room took the rest of the heat, signaling time to get ready for sleep, which despite their regenerating abilities, the group still embraced every night. The kids hugged Lazarus and went to their rooms.

Lazarus set to the task of cleaning the kitchen, eyes easily accustomed to the dark. He was sweeping berries out from under the counter when he heard God speak.

He'll be here soon, Lazarus. Take care of my sheep.

Lazarus nodded. "Yes, Lord," he said, "we can't wait. Bring him anytime."

XIX

Elise

THE CRISP AIR and fresh scenes invigorated Elise as the group continued that afternoon. The soggy ground held tracks of all kinds, which proved to be great entertainment as the day carried on. They found deer prints, lots of deer prints, and bird eggs. Later, when they were again in the forest, amidst the pine needles were even bear droppings—a giant brown-black splattered pie, speckled with red and brown berries. For several hours, they pressed on, chatting easily along the way—especially Isaiah and Rashid, who surprisingly had a lot in common—until the light lowered in the west, bathing the landscape with its dusky orange glow. By the time they stopped for the night, the sun was surrounded by sunken clouds, its edges blurred and hidden.

They found a flat area to pitch tents along the rush of the river, protected from its mist by giant sycamore trees. The group sat circled around the campfire and ate their dinner of cheese and beef jerky until the sky was black and the stars shimmered off the undulating face of the river. Spirits were high, and it seemed everyone was refreshed from the exercise and fresh air. Even

Adira's smile came easily and lingered through breaks in the conversation.

Elise wondered if Adira would stick around when the trail got sticky, which would likely be at the end. The cherubim would need to be dealt with too. Unless, perhaps God made their entrance easy, and the legendary defenders of the Garden wouldn't be there after all. If they were, Elise was at risk of losing her guides once they reached their destination. She planned to separate from the brothers once the group got close, leaving Adira and Mahir to camp alone for a bit, and then rejoin them later. Of course, the option of them coming along sounded more reassuring and certainly safer, but for that, she'd need them to know and be on board with her plans. Either way, Adira did seem well suited for the role he now played, and she trusted God, whatever was in store.

Elise locked eyes with him and cleared her throat.

"This is probably a good time," she said, sitting a little taller. "I wanted to explain to you two what we are doing out here because we need a plan once we get closer."

"All right," Adira answered. He folded his hands across his knees and raised his eyebrows at her. "What is it you want to say?"

"We are searching for the Garden of Eden," Elise said slowly.

"The what?" Mahir asked.

"The Garden of Eden. You know, from the Book of Genesis," she answered.

"Oh wow, we're going to be out here forever." Mahir shook his head and tossed a rock at the fire. "You guys are cracked. You know we charge by the day, not by the mile, right?"

Adira stared at Elise, brow furrowed. Huffing, he pressed his hands firmly against his eyes, then wiped his face, pulling the skin taut. His voice came out slow, strained. "I don't think we have enough supplies for what you are proposing."

Jack looked up. "By *supplies*, do you mean booze? Because that's not really essential."

Mahir's face reddened. "No," he replied. "Our *other* supplies will last a month at most, planning for mishaps and surprises like getting lost or injured tourists. They are not meant for wandering around aimlessly hunting for magic gardens."

Adira glanced from Mahir back to Elise. "What my brother is saying is you have our services out here for up to two weeks before we need to head back, as supplies can run low and health and safety become concerns."

"But... do you know the legend?" Elise persisted. "Do you know what we plan on meeting once we get there? Will you stay with us the entire trip?"

Adira closed his eyes in a three-seconds-too-long blink. "Hmm, yes. I believe there is to be a large river, a giant tree, and paradise within its borders."

"Yes, but perhaps we'll also find a few angels guarding it... wielding fiery swords," Elise said.

Silence followed her comment, everyone's eyes landing on her and Adira—except Mahir, who was drinking again from the celebration bottle. He closed the canteen and leaned over his knees.

"Then what? You want us to fight magical angels so you can pick flowers?" he asked. "Or do you want to fight them, and we'll wait for you?"

"I'm hoping we won't need to fight," Elise answered somberly, then glanced away. "We may need to sneak in, though. Of course, you would do what you felt best. I just—we just need you to get us close and home again." Her gaze returned to Adira. "Please?"

Adira reclined on his elbow, letting the pause in conversation lengthen while he studied the fire, twirling a leaf. Sighing, he glanced back up at Elise and cocked his head. "Two weeks. We guide in, and we guide out. We don't recommend or do anything that puts our clients or us in danger."

His words satisfied her. "All right, I'll take it."

"What made y'all decide to do this?" Mahir asked. "Are you Christian scientists? Jewish? Catholics?"

"We're Christians," Elise answered.

"I'm none of the above, though," interrupted Rashid, wiping water off the edges of his mouth. "I don't believe in religion."

Isaiah turned to face Rashid. "You don't believe in religion or in God?"

"Religion. I'm still out meeting the jury on the whole God thing."

Mahir snorted. "See, Adira? I'm not the only one. And this man is hunting for a Biblical fantasy! Dude, why are you out here? Tell me not for the free refreshments, because I am definitely not sharing now."

"I believe we may find something." Rashid shrugged. "The account of the Garden is not only in Christianity, or even just the Bible for that matter. It's in several other cultures, ones separated by generations and oceans. Stories can't be across so many people groups without there being some basic truth behind them. Even if the garden is not there today, I'm searching for its bones. I'm here for discovery."

"A true archaeologist," Isaiah said.

"The refreshments aren't bad, though, Mahir." Jack grinned and raised his flask, which was topped with a Redi-straw, filtering the river water. "A toast to the pursuit of the mysterious, the hidden, the possibly not even there!"

"Here, here!" Rashid said, raising his too. "As the great Captain Jack once said, we just like playing in the mud!" He swallowed hard. "Anyway, this idea of God... well, I don't know. We're extraordinarily complex beings. The concept of evolution seems a little far-fetched to me. Obviously, life appearing as a result of a giant explosion, then evolving from primordial soup is as much a leap of faith as the existence of a creative being. But believing in that being still leaves the question of where it came from. And we're back to the same original square.

"But the Big Bang theory goes against the first law of thermo-dynamics—that energy, and therefore mass—cannot be created or destroyed. I'm a scientist. I like my assumptions to follow truths we already know. So I guess I'm saying the existence of God seems as likely—or unlikely—as the other ideas out there. Anyway, I'm still trying to figure it out."

He kicked at a rock. "It *does* seem to me though, if God is real, he basically created us as pets and then just left us here. Poor pet ownership. And if not pets, then we were, what—designed for his entertainment? So, for fun, he's watching us enslave and"—his voice broke—"*kill* each other? I'm not interested in worshipping that kind of God."

Isaiah nodded at Rashid, her shoulders slumped. "There is a lot of pain in the world." Her voice had gone weak. "I can see how it would be easy to feel as you do."

Elise shot a glance from Isaiah to Rashid. "We're created for fellowship with Him, not as pets. And God didn't create sin—man did. God came to save us from the pain of the world. Satan was the one who came to kill and steal and destroy, not Him."

Mahir stood and brushed the seat of his pants. "Hey man, God or no God, people die. They go when they're ready to go, not when you're ready to let them." Pulling his cap from his head, he rubbed his hair, suddenly somber. "Sorry about your family. Believe it or not, I know how you feel." With that, he took another swig from his canister and turned away. "Now, I'm out. I've got a hot date with a foam mat. See you in the morning."

"Yes, I am ready for bed as well." Adira sighed and nodded toward Elise. "Get your rest. And remember—no embers still burning when you give up on the fire. Put it out with river water if you need to."

Elise watched them walk away. They were wary of her and the others, but she had a goal, and she always reached her goals. On top of that, this one was consecrated. And why would it not be? God had chosen her to be a healer, and this tree was the ultimate healing tree. He wanted her to do this. He had revealed it to her one night in prayer. Though she didn't understand why now, of all times, He would allow re-entrance into the sacred garden, she was thrilled to be the one He allowed to go.

Elise matched gazes with Isaiah before turning toward Rashid and Jack. "You guys want to close up shop now too?"

"I'll stay up for a while yet," Rashid answered. "Thanks."

"Me too," Jack added.

"Not me," Isaiah answered, shrugging. "I'm beat."

As they rose to disappear into their tents, Elise watched Jack bump Rashid with his knee, and overheard him whisper, "You okay?"

"I'll make it," Rashid answered, staring at the blazing campfire. "I'm glad I came."

"Good, me too."

XX

ADIRA LAY AWAKE hours after the others had drenched the fire and gone to sleep. The crickets were too loud, or perhaps his mind was—or maybe it was both. Either way, the conversation earlier had gotten to him. Specifically, Rashid's story and the way his voice caught while sharing it. It reminded Adira of a time decades before—the last day he had seen his parents. When he closed his eyes, Adira was thirteen all over, and he could hear the woman again, choking on her tears just as Rashid had choked on his words. He could see her too, her and her baby, and Tatter with his dirty mismatched rags and stolen shoes, pointing his rifle at them. That moment, with her crumpled over her knees, all the strength she had routed to her arms, trying to keep her newborn lifted above her head, was the moment everything had changed.

"Hold her, or you'll both die!" Tatter had commanded, laughing.

The desert wind had blown the woman's tunic against her arms. The light flannel brushing against her made her falter and seemed to turn her task more impossible. When the baby began crying, the woman's tears fell faster, and that's when the praying started. Her jagged, desperate breaths filled Adira's ears while he watched, because the soldiers had made him. Her arms shook as she whispered fiercely, calling for strength from Allah, all the while cupping her baby's squirming bottom. The only comfort she could offer her child was her extended finger, tracing the length of the little one's arms to hold her tiny hand.

But eventually, the woman had failed.

"My sweet. My smiling bundle of velvet and drool," she whimpered. "I love you." Then she collapsed, and the baby rolled down her arms into her breast. The woman had wrapped her within her torso, hair spilling out from under her headdress to cover them both in an ineffective shield of love.

"Ineffective," Adira muttered, wide-eyed again, staring at the peak of his tent. That was what he had called it in the end. Later that night of long ago, he had lain wrapped around Mahir on a cot in their cement prison, and the word had popped into his thoughts as he remembered her. It was fitting; she had obviously adored her baby, and yet, after everything—after all her powerful love and care and passion—their lives had evaporated in an instant.

He wondered why he didn't brew on shooting his parents. Of everything that happened that day, it should have struck him the hardest. But it hardly crossed his mind. If he tried hard to remember, he could still hear the crack of the bullets, could still see his mom. But although he knew her eyes must have been pleading, drowned in tears, he couldn't see her that way. She had whispered to him in her last breath—something about how she and his father already forgave him. She had said their love was undying, and to *do* it, because knowing he and Mahir would live brought her joy. He knew she said those things—but when he tried to picture her, all he could see was her smile. Her mouth full of big, happy teeth, and eyes squinting practically shut because whenever she smiled, she did it with her everything. Eventually, he decided it was really the best thing—his beautiful mother should stay that way, so he stopped focusing on his parents and their last night. But the other woman—she, he remembered down to that trembling, resolute finger.

Afterward, the men had loaded them all in the back of a jeep, which he now realized was probably leftover from the Americans a few decades before, or maybe the French. The drivers were from Uganda, soldiers who had originated in the style of the famed Joseph Kony. They had made their way to Turkey and prayed on small, isolated villages like his, Kathre, which was separated from communication networks and defense resources. He and the others had been taken to be slaves—child-soldier slaves, meant to do the bidding of whoever told the men in the front what to do. He had watched his friends, most of them male, tremble in the jeep bed's corners, even the strongest pruned in fear.

But then there was Manal, his saucy best friend. She was the girl who outran all the boys in the yard and was constantly being corrected by her mother for fighting or speaking out of turn. But she wasn't the same Manal. She stood naked except for her hijab, which hung limply wrapped around her shivering body instead of on her head, where it belonged. Dried tears painted her face, but the deep red against her olive thighs was still wet—the blood evidence of what had been her fate prior to the decision to let her live. Adira had tried to meet her gaze, but her eyes were glazed over. He thought she might fall over any second. Seeing her broken that way had turned his surrender into rage, and even as the jeep bounced along to their prison camp in the middle of the desert nowhere, his fists tightened.

Adira's mother had always told him to watch after his brother, to keep him safe because he wasn't as strong, or as smart, or as much of anything compared to him. That day, he stepped into his mother's words for all of them. Or rather, he had tried. He had tried, when he shot both of his parents, to save Mahir the pain of pulling the trigger. He tried again when he stood up in the back of the jeep and addressed them all—and convinced them he would keep them safe and together. He had told them, nervous but determined, they would *all* make it. They could, if they only stuck together.

To encourage them, he had invented their secret symbol—the symbol of Kathre—to share with each other in the days to come.

"This. They'll never see it. This is what we'll do." He curled his lips in and bit down on them. "When you see another one of us do this, remember we *will* escape."

Around the jeep, scattered faces mimicked him until everyone was doing it—everyone but his Manal. Adira stumbled to her side and touched her shoulder, making her shudder, her eyes suddenly wide, as if he were a monster there to take what remained of her soul.

"Manal." He had spoken softly, worried she might hurl herself right out the back of the vehicle. "Manal, it's me, Adira. The men aren't here. Please, look at me."

Her eyes flickered, then twitched in his direction, focusing on Adira. He bit his lips together.

"Manal, see this? When you see me do this, it's me reminding you that we're getting out. Together." Again, he did it, gripping both of her shoulders. "Can you show me? Can you do this? Manal... this means whatever they do to you *will* have an end."

Glancing at his lips, she had breathed a deep, ragged breath and copied him. As her teeth bit down, she melted into him, tears spilling out over her cheeks. She grabbed Adira's shoulders in turn, as if to suck strength from the action, then nodded. Adira had smiled weakly back; she was still in there.

The group shared their symbol often while at the prison camp. Every time Adira saw it, he had remembered where they came from and whose side they were on. And he remembered his promises.

Eventually, he tried again when he formed the escape plan. And later still when he did it—he got them out. Had it not been for the soldiers, he would have been able to go too.

The way the gas pedal had felt beneath his foot that day had never left him—it wasn't exhilarating like when his father had let him drive the old Volkswagen, but terrifying. Once the others were secure in the back, he had slammed the pedal with all his strength. The jeep lurched forward, even before Manal's belt was fastened in the passenger seat beside him. But then the soldiers appeared, jumping in front of them and aiming their rifles directly at the cab.

"Bend down!" Adira shouted at Manal, ripping the wheel to the right.

The men shot at them, shattering the windshield, but Adira kept trying. He turned the wheel back, aiming for the biggest one. The man leaped away.

"Manal!" Adira had yelled, "Grab the wheel!"

She obeyed, robotically, and he slid against the door, preparing. He remembered the disorienting heat from Manal's body pressed against him. It intoxicated him, so much so that he had kissed her goodbye. Or maybe he had just wanted to and, in the end, only imagined it. But he thought he did, right before he grabbed the door handle, opened its latch, and clutched tightly as it flew open. His body swung out, glued to the handle until it made its full arc outward, and he let go. The soldier staggered backward, but Adira slammed into him, and they fell. The jeep left, Mahir staring from the back with the rest of them, his face stamped in horror over the tailgate.

Adira rolled over. Yes, he did try, and Allah had been merciful in the end, granting him life again, with his brother by his side. And he had kept his promise to their beautiful, sweet mother.

XXI

JUBAIR TALMUK GREW up the only son of a working woman in the heart of Sankt Gallen, Switzerland, though he hadn't been born there. His childhood was spent in his home country, Iraq. His mother, Talani Talmuk, became a widow when he was seven years old, when his father was killed as a jihad warrior in the state of martyrdom. Though considered a blessing from the great Allah, his death crushed Jubair's mother, who had genuinely loved him. She went from being an energetic woman of Islam and all things a good Muslim wife should be, to a darkened spirit who could never again look in the eyes of anyone she passed, not even Jubair. His good-night kisses and hair rustles, warm embraces on the couch in the evening, and sweet surprises from the market all vanished with the abrupt change his father's death brought. At some point, her love for Allah evaporated as well. All the prayer mats in their home were rolled up and shoved in the back of a closet.

The two moved in with his Italian-born grandmother and aunt, shortly after the news had arrived at their front door. His grandmother was kind enough, and she absorbed Jubair while his mother absorbed her new work as a seamstress for a local shop. She managed to keep Jubair from battle training for a few years before the local school noticed his absence. By then, it no longer mattered, as the fighting had quieted enough for the family to escape into nearby Turkey as refugees. Eight months and close to one million annihilated lives later, the war officially ended.

The years advanced for Jubair like the rush of high tide from the great Atlantic. Switzerland eventually accepted his family as official immigrants, and they never left. In the summer of his twenty-fourth birthday, he graduated from the Universität Bern with a political science degree. From there, he joined UNICEF and worked to bring vaccines to third-world nations. He often referred to his time with them in political speeches.

"First-world problems are a mark of inequality and should refocus us on eliminating third-world problems. And since when should there be places in the world? Especially based on the economy. Why should the world be in a race?" he had said once. "If this is a race, it is an unfair one because those in the last place do not even know they are competing." He clung to the fame that came from feeding hope to the masses and, at some point, decided to make this his platform when he ran for President of the Swiss Confederation, which, of course, he won.

Eventually, he rose even further in the political world and held the position of secretary-general of the United Nations. He finally felt he'd "arrived," and things could not have been more exciting. He was building a world of unity and peace. A *clean*, single-minded world, as had been his dream since he was eight years old, crouched in his jida's closet, hiding from the men who wanted to take him away to join the fighting. His intentions were being realized—slowly, yes, but surely.

Jubair sat on his velvet chair, gazing out the window. The busy street below was filled with crowds of people who had places to be and others to love. He surely had plenty of places to be, but he envied the people as love he did not have. He did try to keep in touch with his mother through phone calls and a flight back home every year or two, but her mind was near gone, and he tired of constantly reminding her who he was and that his father was not coming back. He had dated a few times in college but wasn't into the whole physical-intimacy thing—too many body fluids and awkward smells—so he had stopped after only a few encounters. He had some acquaintances, sure, but in his line of work, relationships needed to be calculated. He embraced those who could further his agenda and didn't waste time on those who couldn't, unless not doing so could damage it.

He thought of Helel. Perhaps *he* was a friend. He certainly knew Jubair better than any other. And they did spend quite a bit of time together. They argued and teased each other like friends did and even shared a common dream. But love? From what Jubair had observed, love seemed something entirely different, more hard-won and committed. Even though he needed Helel, and, in fact, looked forward to their visits despite the uncertainty they brought, he realized Helel maybe didn't need him at all. He had the feeling he could achieve the same results, enjoy the same banter, with anyone else.

No, he was alone. But he figured it must be that way if he wanted to change the world for the good. Because if he did love anyone, if he had a family or people he needed to attend to other than himself, he'd never have gotten this far into his plans. He'd probably have been too distracted, too stunted in his available time, and the world would have kept spinning and fighting and destroying itself, one day at a time. So alone for him was good. He was good.

He picked up his cell and dialed a number, focused again on another task from his to-do list.

"Hello?" The accent on the other side was distinctly African, his voice rising and falling melodically with each word.

"Yes, Jaakko, this is Jubair Talmuk. I'm calling to check in on our project."

"Yessir, hi! I have some new information. A group of locals have been scouting near our camp. It is outside the national park and normally quite desolate, so I am not sure what their interest is. They may be a small problem."

Jubair sighed, irritated. "I'm interested in the materials and timeline only. When can we expect an operational facility?"

"Yes, sir. Sorry, sir," Jaakko answered. "The first few buildings and prison are already functioning. We have only to finish the bunker. Should be done within the year. We can expect complete operational status by then. Much of the compound is inhabited and useable, though, and your guests are very well secured."

"Thank you. *That* is more what I want to hear. I hope to come for a tour in the next few months. Keep the good work going. We need things completed soon. I'll leave it to you to keep stray... *problems* addressed. It is a shame the area is so treacherous, so many lives have been lost over the years."

For a moment, Jaakko held quiet on the other side of the line. "Yes, sir, I agree," he said and hung up.

Jubair flipped to BBC World News, mildly irritated at the conversation. Perhaps things weren't as promising as he hoped. Jaakko would handle it, though, he told himself. They had placed the prison as far off-grid as he could manage, in an area rarely visited even by locals. The next best place was the Arctic, which had already been done. This he needed to keep secret, at least until the time was right. Helel had told him he would reveal when the UN was complete with only those who would be loyal to the plan, and so far, the word had not come.

Helel had also said he was displeased Jubair was building an army there, too, as he had wanted it only to be a prison. But Jubair knew better. If there was no force behind his ideas, no power behind his words, the respect would not be reciprocated, no matter his track record for diplomacy. Besides, the dragon hadn't done much about it other than voicing his opinion, and should the beast ever become a safety hazard, having a little gunpower behind him could do nothing but help.

He focused on the screen and a story about riots breaking out in the streets of Israel. The two-timing Arabs were going to back out on the treaty, he could see it already. Not that the Jews were any better. They, with their pious, "We are chosen, you are dirt" mindset. No wonder they attracted the hatred of their neighbors. Why would they not share? Land was land; this whole business with the temple and sharing the grounds had been so hard for him to negotiate because of their high and mighty attitudes. But he had managed it and drawn their treaty, and they built their temple, as he promised they could. Now, they had decided to pick a fight with their neighbors all over again. Why could they not let others do what others did and have their own space too?

Jubair turned off the television and dialed Calan Tonto. This needed to be dealt with, fast.

XXII

DESPITE THE IMPROVED light, trekking along the river proved surprisingly difficult given the number of moss-covered boulders. The thorns and shrubs were dense close to the forest's edge, so the group mostly stayed on the rocky path.

Rashid struggled the most with the rocks. He and Jack trailed a good twenty meters behind the others. Even though his endurance was lacking from all his time spent sitting behind a desk, he was in fair shape. His greatest difficulty was getting his tendons to comply with the uneven ground. He had twisted his right ankle twice already, and it ached whenever he put his foot down at the wrong angle. Stiffening his torso, he tried to hide his injury from the others.

"Hey, Rash. What do you think of our little adventure?" Jack asked, interrupting his concentration. "This beats LED screens and fluorescent lighting, am I right?"

"Aye, Captain. And your apparel is much less awkward when covered in sweat and accented with dirty knees." Rashid leaped from one boulder to the next. The one he landed on shifted, and he tipped sideways, nearly falling.

"You all right? Should I tell the authorities we need a break? Or can I carry some stuff from your pack for a while?"

"Nah, it's these rocks. I twisted my ankle back there. It isn't bad, just slowing me down a bit. I could still kick your ass in basketball if given the chance."

"Rash, everyone can beat me in basketball."

"I know. Tell me—why is that? You are ten feet tall and from Midwest America. Is it not, like, one of your core classes in school? English, math, science, basketball?" Rashid answered, laughing.

"You got us pegged," Jack said.

Rashid caught his breath, bracing for the next insult to his leg.

"That's it," Jack said. He trotted ahead. "Hey, Adira. I need a break, man. My feet are hurting bad. And maybe we could keep to the forest more? The land is flatter there." He huffed and grabbed his knees.

Adira raised his brow, then glanced back at Rashid. "All right, let's rest here," he announced, stopping the rest of the group. "Then we'll head into the forest for a while. The going is slower there, but Jack here is tired of rocks, it seems."

Rashid rested next to Mahir on the driest boulder he could find, overlooking the now-low river. Its edges were mostly mud, the nearby trees' bases still dark brown-black from when the flow had been higher. No foliage survived the ebb and flow of the flooding, so otherwise the bank was covered in only gravel and rocks.

"Pretty." Mahir said. He turned to Adira. "Hey, you don't want to get your camera out for this, do you? Isn't it lovely... the way the sun bounces off the... moist-ness?"

Adira rolled his eyes. "Thanks, I'll pass." He turned toward the others. "If you brought cameras, we'll have nice views soon."

"I think it's lovely already," Elise piped in. "Don't act like you weren't splashing through the puddles back there, Mahir."

"It *is* lovely." Adira nodded. "A river is still a river, especially when you grew up in the desert."

"It feels like an adventure to me." Elise smiled back at him.

"Like we're discovering hidden secrets, walking on the ground usually unknown to everyone but the fish."

Mahir snorted and shook his head. "Now it all makes sense."

"Hey, how far you think we've gone, Adira?" Rashid asked.

"We're probably averaging over twenty kilometers a day," Adira answered. "Not bad. Not good. We've had pretty easy going so far." He tipped his head at the mountains and rock cliffs before them. "*That* is going to take longer to get across."

Rashid considered the steep brown giants. "Where will we sleep then?" he asked.

"In tents," Mahir answered. "The trick is not rolling too much in your sleep. You wouldn't want to fall off any of those campsites."

When the team resumed hiking, it was slow going, just as Adira had warned.

Rashid gripped the nylon straps of his pack and eyed the peaks in the distance. He hoped he was in good-enough shape for this. It was supposed to be over sixty kilometers each way, and the mountains needed serious consideration. He had climbed before—several times—but always on day treks, and he usually hobbled for a few days afterward.

Georgia was a jewel, though, with breathtaking landscapes around every bend. Before Jack had brought up the trip, he had barely even thought of this country, and now here he was hiking its mountain ranges. He dropped his gaze to stare at his feet, swinging his shoulders from side to side with each step. Closing his eyes, he breathed deep, focusing on the steady rhythm of crunching feet on the forest floor. The day's exercise had already warmed him enough for sweat to saturate his hat and roll down his forehead. He smiled. For the first time in over a year, he felt loose, relaxed.

Rashid walked in front of Isaiah. She seemed as detached

as he felt. He had overheard the two women talking the night before, and learned she had also lost her family in the war. It was better knowing she was here; he wasn't the only wild card along for the ride.

"So, Indiana," Rashid said, striking up a conversation. "Where is that, exactly?"

"Oh," she said, puffing between words. "It's one of those states with a lot of farms and a few big cities. Fly-over country."

"And you are a doctor too? What kind?"

"Family practice. General medicine."

"Nice."

"Thanks," Isaiah replied. "You work with Jack, huh? I always wanted to be an archaeologist."

"I hear that a lot." Rashid smiled. "Would you believe I always wanted to be a doctor?"

Isaiah laughed. "Well, aren't we ironic?"

Jack stepped backward and bumped Rashid with his pack purposely, giving him a wink.

Rashid rolled his eyes. "Captain, are you wanting to make this trip twice? We are heading that way." He kicked Jack behind his thighs, sending him forward clumsily.

Isaiah laughed. "It's pretty impressive you guys found this. How'd you do it?"

"It was all Jack, although he won't admit it. He is the master of the satellites," Rashid heaved, lurching up a steep clump of dirt. "Aren't you, Captain? Tell us how you did it."

Jack smiled. "Well, anyone could have, really. The trick was the mountains. They weren't here back when the Garden was."

"Earthquakes?" Isaiah asked.

"In part, yes," Jack answered. "The Caucasus Mountains were originally formed when the Arabian Plate moved north. There used to be a sea in these parts, you know—the Tethys Sea. Anyway, that closed when the tectonic plates were doing their thing, and when that happened, the Arabian Plate crashed into the Iranian Plate. Another, the Eurasian Plate, was also sliding—twisting, really—and it hit the Iranian Plate. Then all the rock bulged up, folded on itself, and the Greater Caucasus formed. The whole thing also pushed up the volcanic activity in the south, in the Lesser Caucasus, which obviously complicated things a little—which meant more rapid change later. So I had to reverse all that in my mind before evaluating the satellite images. And, here we are."

"Huh. And here we are," Isaiah echoed. "Earthquakes... got it." She laughed nervously and raised her eyebrows at Elise, who shrugged back.

Rashid glanced up at her and winked. "He's a genius. Don't worry. If he is sure, I am sure."

Isaiah grinned back weakly.

"You know, Jack, I also did a little research before we left," Rashid continued.

"Of course you did. I'm not the only nerd in this group." Jack gave a mock bow to Rashid. "Pray tell me, what did you learn in your studies?"

"Well, we are actually walking up *the river*. The all-time mysterious river." He smiled. "Do you know where the Aragvi got its name?"

"Let me guess." Jack pretended to think, tapping his finger on his chin and pinching his lips. "It has to be something about Eden or Paradise or the Great Beginning or something to that degree, right?"

"Ha!" Rashid shook his head. "Good guess, though. No, Aragvi means 'river.' And as we are chasing the Aragvi River, we are therefore chasing the River River."

"Really? Nice."

"Yessir. On top of everything, you might have solved a debate in the geology community. You ought to write a paper."

"What debate?"

"They can't decide on the actual origins of the famous

River River. So, if you are right... Well, I want my name on the paper too."

"And ours!" Isaiah chimed in.

"Hey now," Mahir interrupted. "If we find anything at all, you can write a paper and title it 'Mahir Takir Proved Wrong. Once in a Lifetime Occurrence, Caught Live!'"

Adira broke through from the front of the line. "Hello back there—would you like the other history of this land?"

"Yes!" Jack sped up to the front of the line, nearer Adira. "I was hoping we'd hear some."

"We are near Gudari, which is commercialized, mostly for the skiing, but also, as you can see, for hiking. A lot of people like to parasail, too. That might have been a good idea for your purposes, actually." He nodded up to the mountains. "Gets a good view of everything from above. We do have a lot of protected reserves and parks. But where we are going, there is no reserve. There are a few roads scattered around—even a few villages—but a lot of this area is just wildlands staying wild. The government used to try to repair the roads, but eventually, they stopped throwing money at them, as the parks were meant to be natural, and most of the villages have been abandoned anyway."

"Why were they abandoned?" Jack asked.

"Because they've been damaged. The land is unstable. It's too steep, we get landslides, always have."

"Will we see any of them?"

"Not on this route, no. We'll follow one of the old roads at some point though. Mostly we'll be invading nature in all her splendor." A tree branch whipped back from Adira's hand to Mahir behind him, who wasn't paying attention, and struck him in the chest.

"What? I'm awake," he snapped, looking up quickly.

Adira chuckled. "My trusted partner here knows where a few special spots are—if we make good time, we'll stop for some sightseeing on the way back."

"Yeah," Mahir answered, "the waterfalls here are rad. There are even underground palaces in the caves. Maybe we can find one." He glanced over his shoulder at Jack. "As long as you promise to help protect the ladies from whatever's inside."

Jack gave a nervous grin. "What's in them?"

"Depends on the season. Usually nothing but water, bugs, and bats, maybe a few snakes. But in the spring and fall, the larger animals go in sometimes to nest. We found a wolf den in a cave a few years back. We lost a tourist, but you saw the lovely picture Adira got, so basically, it ended up a win-win."

Rashid watched as Elise, who had stepped up next to him, rolled her eyes, then quirked a brow at Adira to call out the lie. He shrugged, smiling, and shook his head.

"Mahir," Adira said. "Stop with the stories." Turning back, he added, "We aren't going to get eaten. Don't worry. My brother likes making people nervous. What he did not tell you is how stunning the caves are. Several have high ceilings and rivers running through them. They're well taken care of, so the stalagmites are pristine. The entire cave system hasn't even been completely explored yet, they're so extensive. It is unlike anything you have seen before."

Isaiah and Elise met eyes.

"Rivers, huh?" Elise's smile flooded her face. "What do you think, Jack? Should we check it out?"

"A-to-the-Men," he answered. "I'd like to examine one of the old villages too, if possible. How old are they?"

"Thousands of years. There isn't much to them anymore, though. The forest has grown over a lot of the earlier ones. The ones with paving are easier to check out, but my guess is those may be a little boring for you," Mahir answered. "I'm not sure we can fit it in though since we'll be wandering around looking for some long-lost garden."

"Hey, what was that?" Jack said, hesitating and turning to his left.

The group stopped and searched in the direction he pointed. A single tree, young and thin-trunked, swayed as if pushed aside. The cracking of a branch sounded in the distance behind it, but otherwise, the forest had gone silent.

"Why is the tree moving?" Rashid asked. He stepped back. "There's no wind."

"Probably a squirrel." Mahir shook his head. "City people." He bumped Adira with his shoulder. "Come on. We have places to be." They pressed forward, all except Rashid, who lingered, watching the trees.

Just before he had decided to move forward again, several bushes to their left rustled, then swayed abruptly, as if waving. The plants shifted forward, spreading apart as six men in black tactical gear rushed from behind them, holding rifles trained on the group. Rashid hid behind a tree, then watched as the others startled and bunched together, hands raised.

"What the—" Mahir spouted.

Adira stepped away from the others and cleared his throat. "What can we do for you, gentlemen?" he asked, scanning them up and down.

The men gave no answer. Instead, they advanced, surrounding them tighter, training rifles at their chests.

"You guys don't need all that firepower for us," Mahir said. "We're just hiking. Minding our own business."

"Get down!" the biggest one said in an American accent. His giant jaw tightened as he waved a handgun between them and the ground.

They complied, hands shaking—all except Rashid, who squatted, locked in place, watching. But the men never glanced his way. Instead, they secured the others' hands together with what looked like zip ties and directed them out, three of the soldiers leading and three behind, guns erect, with Isaiah and Jack near falling from trying to move fast enough.

Adira appeared calm through it all, carefully obeying but

watching the soldiers the whole time, not even pretending to look away. The big one jabbed him in the side with his gun and blurted out, "Eyes forward. Move it, wog!"

Adrenaline rushed through Rashid. They hadn't seen him! A thick cluster of brush sat to his right. It would cover him better if he could slink that way. He stretched his leg toward it, toe pointed as if afraid to touch the ground. When he shifted weight, so did his giant pack, throwing off his balance, almost making him fall over. He shoved his hands down and rebalanced, his fingertips pressed into the cool earth, their crunch against the pine needles seemingly gunshot loud. He snuck behind the bush and slid the pack over onto its side. Squatting next to it, he gingerly positioned the branches in front of his body. Rashid cursed his lungs as he watched the others—his breathing was so *loud*! He tried to steady it, slowing his exhale, but it only came out more jagged. Surely, they'd find him.

But they never did, and the men led the others away through the thick foliage, their heads bowed in defeat beneath the dimming sky. Long after they were out of sight, the sun's rays, brilliant pink and gold, burst their final defiance until the horizon consumed the last bit of light, and he was alone.

XXIII

RASHID CROUCHED, NEAR motionless, for what felt like hours. He didn't dare even shift weight for fear of being heard and captured. When the adrenaline wore off and his thighs finally weakened, he practically collapsed onto his back against the cool ground. Above, stars already filled the purple sky. He peered around, afraid but in part hoping to see someone else. He was alone.

Why am I still shaking? Rashid scooted against his pack. He'd have to camp there for the night as he obviously wouldn't be going anywhere right then. Surrounding him were trees, a soggy riverbed, a rocky shoreline, and more trees to camp under. The forest afforded more cover should there be any further uninvited guests. He pitched his tent low, between two giant bushes, and ate his dinner inside—dried meats and fruits and what was left of the water purified earlier that day. He laid out his sleeping bag and slid inside, resting his head on his only comfort—an inflatable pillow.

Two hours later, Rashid stared wide-eyed at the top of his tent, wondering at the difference a couple of local guides had made on his sleep. Every creak the forest made frightened him. What had resonated as melodic and beautifully wild earlier now sounded threatening, as if each noise could be the last he'd ever hear.

Rashid woke to an aching neck and the canvas of his tent

draped lazily across his face. He jerked sideways, afraid he'd been found and was being suffocated. He waved the tent away and kicked the sleeping bag off his legs all in one movement. Unfortunately, he also kicked the stake tethering the tent, and the whole thing collapsed.

"Aargh. Get. Off. Me!" Rashid flailed his arms and rolled sideways, tangling himself further. The strings holding it down wrapped one of his feet, and soon he was bound. "Seriously?" he grunted, then sighed deeply, refocusing himself before scrambling backward and shrugging off the tent.

He scanned the area. Day was coming—the sky already a faint purple, even at its peak—and the trees were visible now for a good hundred meters in every direction. He was still alone, though, and lost. How he would ever find his friends again?

He could try for the direction they had been taken, but their captors had guns, big ones, and he yielded a backpack stuffed with camping gear. The soft rush of the river was to the right; he decided instead to follow it back. They were only a few days out after all, and there was some chance of being discovered by other hikers.

After packing his gear, he stumbled to his feet and set out. Forcing himself not to look behind, he picked his way through the rocks to what was left of the river. He filled three canisters with water and iodine tablets, then screwed the lids on. The water ran steady, splashing white caps at its edges. *It'd be nice to have one of those rafts right now,* he thought before moving on, alongside it and down in the direction it flowed.

Rashid hiked nonstop all morning, traveling as fast as his ankle would allow. Near noon, when the heat set in and the sun blared from straight above him, he noticed a break in the trees across the river. A path stared back at him. Not like the one the team had followed—the dirt thin, barely noticeable through the foliage—no, this one was wide and well kept. The ground was flat, heavily trodden, and appeared to be lined with stones on either side. It plunged immediately into the forest opposite him. He gaped. How had they missed it yesterday? A path like this could mean people were nearby. Perhaps he could find help today, maybe even within the next few hours. Getting to it would mean he'd need to cross the river, and it could be a waste of time, but he couldn't believe this obviously manmade beacon could lead anywhere other than somewhere good.

Rashid waded cautiously into the water, which shocked him immediately with its icy chill, but he waded forward anyway, hesitating once it reached his chest. This was likely about to get very deep, very fast, and the weight of the water pushing down-stream felt much stronger when he was this deep. Cursing under his breath at the mass of his pack and the poor decision to keep his boots on, he figured it was too late for second thoughts. A step forward, and the ground dropped away. Instantly, the water enveloped him, and he sank, pulled under by his bag.

Fighting the current, he paddled madly, boots heavy and bulky in the tide. He brushed his hands across his chest, feeling for and unlatching the keep of his backpack. Rolling in the current to get free from its weight, Rashid squirmed out from under the pack and dropped it, immediately regretting the loss of all his comforts and tools but needing more the breath in his lungs. Once free, he pointed his chin upward and kicked, hard. When his face broke into fresh air, he gasped, filling his lungs before bobbing back under. Again he forced himself up, but then something solid and sharp stabbed him from behind, gouging deep into his right flank. Relentless, the river pushed him along, but the object stood grounded, tearing through his clothes and flesh, and folding him forward in pain. He screamed impotently into the water. As he did, the current spun him around and freed his torso, allowing a moment to steal another gulp of air and open his eyes. A splin-tered tree limb peeked ominously from below the waves behind him. Rashid spun around again, flailing his arms ahead, hoping they'd find first any further obstacles.

Less than fifty yards away, the river bent to the left. As if waving hello, soggy, foam-covered leaves flopped with the river's undulation, caught on a pile of broken tree limbs. Rashid winced, knowing if he got too close, his chance at another injury was high, but without stopping, he'd drown. He'd have to get to them. Trying desperately to paddle its way, he reached sideways, but the chill had saturated through his skin and numbed the muscles beneath, and now his arms were heavy from the cold. *Like logs,* he thought as he forced them up, lifting them one by one. He pushed his hands forward to grasp the wood, hoping to find it solid. It was. For a minute, he hung there, sucking air into his burning chest while his legs drifted behind him downstream, waving at the water as it flowed away. He grunted, determined, and pulled himself out toward dry ground, inch by inch, until he collapsed onto the pebbled shore.

Rashid lay flattened on his back, eyes closed, clawing the earth greedily, as if letting go would release him back into the angry river. He took a deep breath, realizing what people meant when they spoke of air being sweet. It was, and so was the land. Firm, reassuring, *strong* land that kept water where it belonged and let grass and trees grow and gave man reassurance at his place in the world. He sucked in the sweet air, and at once the pain in his side returned.

He groaned. A warmth spread from where he had been stabbed, waking up the surrounding numbed skin in its wake and spreading its hot, stinging punishment to the rest of him. Maybe this would be his end. His family was gone anyway—perhaps he'd soon join them and go wherever people who died went—if there even was a "where" beyond this life. If he did die out here, no one would mourn him. For all he knew, Jack was already dead, and as of now, Jack had been his only person left.

Rashid hated that he had convinced him to come on this trip. What good had it been? Not one of them would make it to Elise's fantasy garden, so it had all been for nothing. And

131

now the others were gone, and he, their only hope at rescue, laid feeble on the bank of some ruthless, piddly river, in the heart of this little-known nature reserve in an even lesser-known country. Staring at the meager path he had wanted so desperately to get to, he realized he was the same as the rest of it—little and unknown, and apparently fleeting.

XXIV

THE VAN BOUNCED through the forest, knocking Isaiah sideways and backward into the others as it crashed through the underbrush. She peered through the narrow window behind them to watch the path, but soon darkness concealed everything besides the occasional flash of moonlight off the scattered fluttering leaves. She had made out part of what the men said in the walkies, though most of it was in another language. "Cargo" the one who spoke English had repeated, one time while staring straight into her eyes.

Cargo. Isaiah wondered. *Lord, what is this? When did I transform from a daughter of the Most High into a package to be delivered?* She had heard of tourist kidnappings for ransom—money-making schemes. But Elise told her this was not an issue here, and Georgia was well-known as being generally safe. So what was this then? Perhaps it was a display of the battle unseen by people, the one raging continuously between good and evil—spiritual warfare. If that were the case, then God should be coming to their aid soon. Or perhaps not. Perhaps instead He would leave her and the others, direct His energy somewhere more important for the cause, and add them to his long count of lives lost, just more numbers blown through in battle.

From beside her, Elise whispered. "No weapon formed against me will stand; He holds the whole world in His hands." Isaiah leaned back, trying to embrace the Bible verse Elise quoted, one she herself had memorized in the past. It was meant to bring comfort, and rouse faith. But though Elise's zeal was plain, and Isaiah knew faith should be powerful, today the words just sounded like nonsense.

Squeezing her eyes shut, Isaiah tried to block out thoughts of what lay ahead. Death, maybe. Probably. She thought back to the first time she realized her own mortality, the year she had turned twenty, in Panama City Beach, Florida. Ironically, it happened shortly after her baptism, on the same night. For hours she and her friends had been body surfing—she exploring the ocean for the first time in her life. The water's power was intense, but she had felt invincible, soaking in her new freedom as a bonified Christian. The waves enveloped her, lifted her and rolled around her all at once; it felt like she was dancing or flying or both. The ocean was an endless salty playground, and she, a princess of its master.

But then came the wave that didn't respect her new place in its world. Instead of proceeding through the normal course of the others—rising, rolling, breaking, then sucking—it grabbed her and slammed her face first into the sand. Without allowing two seconds to recover, while she was still underwater, a new current came and swept her away. Her body twirled wildly out of control until she thought for sure she was going to drown. When it finally weakened and the tide resumed its former pattern, she fell out and struggled to her feet, only to find she had travelled an easy 200 meters down-shore from her friends.

So, being a daughter of God didn't always mean protection.

Suddenly tired, Isaiah closed her eyes and grabbed Elise's hand. Trying again to embrace its words, and calm at their meaning, she finished the rest of the verse Elise had started. "I'm holding onto your promises, you are faithful."

Elsie squeezed her hand, but Isaiah barely felt it for the turmoil in her thoughts. *This too will end. God did not send you on this mission for nothing. He is faithful.*

Then the van stopped, and a military man climbed into the back with them. Without a word, he wrapped blindfolds around each of their faces and left as quickly as he'd come. The vehicle lurched forward and drove another few minutes before stopping once more. Car doors squeaked open and slammed shut, and the murmur of men rose, until a loud creak announced the hatch opening again.

"Out!" a voice hollered, grabbing Isaiah by her shirt back and tapping her in the back of the knees with a baton. Despite the hustle, she stepped cautiously. The soldier led her away until the ground changed from soft and earthy to crunchy, obviously sandy or graveled. The air changed too—to the smell of damp soil and stone. As they continued, a dizzying electric hum filled her ears, indicating some type of human establishment. The soft scrape of an ill-fitting door against its frame came next, and the ground changed to flat and solid—cement.

In another moment, the floor dropped abruptly away. Isaiah nearly stumbled down before the soldier trailing her grabbed her shirt to steady her.

From behind, Adira yelled, "Stairs, be careful!" His voice echoed through what sounded like a narrow hall.

A few steps after reaching the bottom, the man unbound Isaiah's hands and shoved her forward. She fell this time, into the clammy lend of a clay floor. Behind, the others grunted, their voices surrounded by the muffled thumps of their bodies hitting the ground as well. The loud creak of old hinges came, and the crash of a heavy metal door, and the world went as silent as it was dark.

"Where are we?" Isaiah asked, climbing to her feet and pulling the cloth from her face. But the surroundings were still as black as with the blindfold on. She rubbed her eyes to see if it would help her vision. It didn't. Inching sideways to investigate, her fingers found the cold, rough surface of damp cement. "Where are we! Who are you? What do you want?"

"We're underground," Adira answered. "This place is sturdy. We must be in a prison."

"Prison? What the hell?" Mahir retorted. "A pitch-black prison? For what? Hiking?"

"I don't understand. I thought Georgia was safe.".

"This is a rebel prison. I don't know what they want with us, though," Adira said. "If they only had meant to rob us, they would have done so and, at most, left us for dead."

"Now what do we do? What do you want?" Mahir shouted angrily. "We didn't *do* anything! And where the fuck do you expect us to piss?"

Adira interrupted him. "Brother. They aren't going to answer. For now, we are safe. Save your energy."

"Where's Rash?" Jack's voice interrupted. "What is he going to do out there all alone?"

"He's better off than we are right now," Mahir grumbled.

"Not by much. He's out in the middle of nowhere! And it'll be night soon. All he has is his pack."

"And his freedom. Calm down. He just needs to follow the river back and find the path from there. He's supposed to be smart, right? We're the ones in trouble right now. He's the lucky one,"

"Mahir is right, Jack," Adira said. "He'll be fine. As long as he doesn't come looking for us. Having him out there gives us a chance at being found, if he goes to the authorities. This is better."

At his words, the door creaked open. A crack of light appeared, followed by the blue rays of a high-wattage LED flashlight, blazing at their faces. The blinding light blocked view of what lay behind it, but also revealed a gift—a tray holding food and a pitcher of water. The man behind the flashlight hurled a large plastic bucket in as well, bouncing it off the back wall. As it rolled to a stop, the door slammed shut, blanketing them again in darkness.

"I guess we know where to piss," Jack said.

XXV

"You know how tiny we are? When you think about the universe. The smallness of our enormous galaxy in it, you realize our giant Earth is only a sneeze." Jubair furrowed his brow as he spoke, intent on the breathing dollar sign who sat before him. "Or more of a droplet in the spray of a sneeze."

He pressed his lips together and waited. Pope Elijah the First was tedious. He was open-minded, sure, which was easy to use, but he required these *oh-so-long* meetings to maintain their connection. If Jubair could have done without these, he would likely have been a happier man. But these days he needed his support.

"Interesting thought," Elijah mused. "Yes, though. You're right."

He took a sip from the golden chalice in his hands. Jubair recognized the cup as the one on display in St. Peter's Basilica the year before. Its ornate curves were bejeweled with dozens of diamonds. Jubair wondered how the meeting to procure it must have gone. Did the pope himself attend? How much persuading did it take to convince the head curator His Holiness needed the prized artifact for his own collection, to sip spirits from while in his pajamas? Jubair sighed, suddenly tired, and refocused. Elijah probably just nodded and mumbled the poor man into compliance.

"What I'm saying is *we* are small. The change I propose

seems huge, but in the grand scheme—in light of the universe, of eternity—it's really very small. Very manageable."

"Hmm." The pope nodded. So... slowly.

Was he pretending not to understand, just to drag things out? Jubair pressed his fingers together, trying to distract his irritation from coming out in his words. He had been at it for nearly three hours with this man, and his patience was drained. He would have to leave soon, or he may not be able to maintain his composure.

"What about the Christian church?" Elijah finally asked.

"Which one?" Jubair snorted. "The religions of the world are so scattered these days. Only a few are still intact and thriving."

"You do have a point. Still, their numbers are worth considering. It's a shame they cannot come together for this."

"The Christians are rather plastic, don't you think? Their faith is artificial. They robotically go to the show every other Sunday morning, then return home and live as if they'd never seen the program. There is truly little heart there. And the ones who *do* have heart, well, they're just the flower children of the twenty-first century, walking around high on music, chanting about their drug of choice, Jesus. They're not actually *doing* anything. We need a people who will *act*, Your Holiness. We need the Catholic Church." He paused, holding his gaze. "We need you."

Jubair watched as the pope considered his words. The man was soaking it up. This afternoon may not have been such a waste after all.

The dragon stood on the shore of the sea. And I saw a beast coming out of the sea. It had ten horns and seven heads, with ten crowns on its horns, and on each head a blasphemous name. ²The beast I saw resembled a leopard, but had feet like those of a bear and a mouth like that of a lion. The dragon gave the beast his power and his throne and great authority. ³One of the heads of the beast seemed to have had a fatal wound, but the fatal wound had been healed. The whole world was filled with wonder and followed the beast. ⁴People worshiped the dragon because he had given authority to the beast, and they also worshiped the beast and asked, "Who is like the beast? Who can wage war against it?"

Revelations 13:1-4

XXVI

RASHID LAY FACE up, dying on the bank of the River Aragvi. The sky had already changed from bright and sunny to star-filled, then stayed that way as he drifted along the edge of consciousness. At some point, when he was more aware than before, the glow of early morning seemed to localize somewhere behind him. But it kept dim much longer than it should have, teasing him with a never-progressing promise of noon.

That would be pretty, he thought, *an eternal sunrise.* But the air was hazy and too thick, different than the usual crisp clearness of sunrise. Then something cracked, and a familiar popping came from behind him. Fire. He tried to sit up and look, but his side immediately punished him for it. He fell back; everything throbbed. His side, his head, even his fingers, which, for some reason, were now swollen to twice their normal size.

"You're safe." A man's voice came from behind him, near where the fire should have been. "Lie down," he added.

Rashid swiveled his head, arching his neck backward. "My friends, they took them," he said. "My pack. I... I almost drowned."

"You're safe." The voice was kind, deep, and a little tired. "I found you yesterday when I came down to check the nets."

"Can you help me? My friends. My side. We need help."

"I will help in whatever way I can," the man said. "We're a little separated from the rest of civilization here, though. I don't know where your friends are or where they went. Who took them? What happened to you?"

Rashid managed to prop himself up on his good side and scooted his legs around to see the man's face. Every flexion hurt, and it seemed the muscles in his side were connected somehow to the rest of him, because the pain shot everywhere when he moved.

"We were hiking, and some men came. They had guns. They didn't see me, so I escaped." Rashid took an aching breath. "I saw the path across the river, and I tried to cross to get to it, but the water... it won."

"I know. The river appears a lot calmer than she really is," the man said. "Did you say guns?"

"Yes, several—men, I mean. And guns. Several of both."

"Huh. There haven't been many with guns this way for years. Hunters come through sometimes, but not usually."

"People hunters?" Rashid asked.

The man shook his head thoughtfully as he handed him a metal cup. "You think you can keep some water down?"

Rashid took it gratefully and drank deep, his tongue brushing against the sweet, textured metal. He lowered the mug to examine it. It was made of copper, but its original color had oxidized and was now dull, gray-brown and green, with obvious hammer marks from when it had been shaped.

"Wow. This is impressive. It must be four thousand years old." Rashid traced its lip with his swollen fingers. It looked to have belonged to the Bronze Age.

"Well, give or take a few dozen decades, but yes. It's held up rather nicely, I'd say." The man raised an eyebrow and peered at Rashid from under his lowered head. "Course, that was long before me."

Rashid took another sip. "Nice."

"So, what's your name?"

"Me? Rashid. Sorry, how far are we from town?"

"Maybe a two-day hike if we move quickly. But I don't think

you will move quick." The man handed him a piece of flatbread. "Here, eat."

"Thanks," Rashid said, taking the bread. *If we move quickly.* How could he even walk? "Do you have a car? Are there any roads out here?"

"No car. The roads are mostly dirt and overgrown. We don't have anything fancy out this way. But perhaps we can carry you? Or maybe we can help you get stronger and take you back after? He reached his hand out. "I'm Lazarus, anyway."

"Nice to meet you," Rashid said, shaking hands. The move pierced him, and he cringed. Before he could steady himself, he vomited, spewing out the bread and water. "Ugh, sorry."

"It's fine. Just rest." Lazarus answered.

But vomiting had made Rashid shaky, and he was afraid if he laid down again, the pain would keep him there. "You said 'we.' How many are you?"

"Just a handful. We don't have much, but you're welcome to stay, if you need. To build up your strength."

"How did you... come out here?" he asked, hoping this Lazarus would do most of the talking.

"Well now, that *is* a story. Though, I don't believe, son, that you are ready to hear it yet."

Rashid turned toward the strange answer. Why did he call him *son*? Lazarus was obviously only in his late twenties, with smooth, even-toned skin and curly black hair pulled back at the base of his neck. He had a dark complexion, almost like Rashid's—which was ironic, as they were in a country laden with pale-skinned people. But he appeared harder than the other locals, with his calloused hands and nubbed, dirt-filled fingernails, and thick, muscular torso, without a trace of luxury anywhere to be seen.

"Try me," he said as he maneuvered back. He was exhausted, and all he cared to do at this point was rest in the warmth of the very lovely, very manmade fire.

"It may make you feel uneasy if I tell you. It seems any time

I share it, people leave and never come back. Let's save the story for another time."

Rashid cocked his head. "Should I be afraid here?" he asked.

"Oh no, not at all. I'm here to help you, Rashid. I'm sorry I was a little late getting here, but when you are as old as I am, time starts to lose its definition. You tend to be late quite often."

"How old are you?"

"I actually don't know, I stopped counting long ago. I can safely say I am much older than I appear, though, as are the others. I'm not quite sure why God chose us to age so very gracefully, but he did, and... well, here we are."

"You are so old you don't know how old you are?" *Is he for real?* Rashid thought, hoping the man wasn't crazy, not when he was this weak and hoping desperately to have been rescued. "Okay, how about *why* you came out here?"

"We came to be alone. Georgia was close enough to our homeland that we could travel without much money, and this area has everything we need to live off the land. Plus, you can't beat the views."

Lazarus stirred the fire with a stick, allowing a few more pops and crackles to fill the space between their words.

"I'll tell you. Part of the issue with sharing our story right now is I might not remember all the details. Like which things belong in what order."

Rashid's eyebrows crept up.

"Son, when you've been around this long, the difference between real life and dreams even gets hazy." He sighed. "What's for sure real is you and your family, and your maker. And that is sometimes all you can count on."

Lazarus went on to explain how he had happened upon Rashid's body the previous morning and had cleaned and dressed his wounds with leaves. He had been back and forth from his cottage a few times already. It turned out it wasn't sunrise after all but after sunset.

Afterward, the two men rested quietly by the fire, Lazarus encouraging Rashid to sip water, and Rashid working to keep it down. Long after the sun went to sleep and the air cooled to its evening chill, the forest began to stir.

Lazarus shook out a cloak and wrapped it around his square shoulders, then stared into the trees.

"In the morning, we'll head to the house if you are up to it," he said. "It is not good to stay out here exposed like we are. You should be strong enough by then if I help you."

"I'll be glad to move out again," Rashid answered, hoping he had the strength.

XXVII

I**T TURNED OUT** Lazarus was strong. After ten or more failed attempts at walking, Rashid gave up and let Lazarus carry him. He had wrapped his lean arms around Rashid's torso and knees, then draped him over his shoulders, making Rashid cry out in pain. But Lazarus held on anyway and headed back via the path carved through the for rest.

By the time they arrived at the cottage, Rashid was nearly asleep. He woke to two children, swarming them at the doorway.

"Hello," sang out one of them, a young girl with rosy cheeks and a giant smile. "Welcome, we're so glad you made it!"

At the sight of her, Rashid pushed up, straightening on Lazarus's shoulders. "Nubia?" he asked, reaching out.

Giving a quizzical glance to Lazarus, she stepped forward. "I'm Salome," she answered.

Rashid's fingers brushed the black hair framing her face, and he squinted, confused, studying her. Her hair was curly, not straight, and her cheeks filled her face when she smiled instead of sinking deep into dimples as his daughter's had. Rashid's face darkened, and he dropped his hand. "Hi. Thank you for taking me in."

"I'm John," the boy said, his head craned around Lazarus. "Do you have any bags?"

"No. I'm afraid the river stole it from me," Rashid answered.

Lazarus slid Rashid onto their couch and sucked in a wanted breath. "Can we get you something? A blanket? Water? Food?"

"A blanket, thank you."

"Don't be shy now, put your feet up." Lazarus pulled a tightly knitted blanket from a cupboard and handed it to Rashid, then turned to the others. "Flore, go get the soap and a tub o' hot water, but not too hot. John, a new set of clothes. We need to get this man cleaned up and fed for the night. Rashid, you rest. We'll take it from here."

In an instant, the little house bustled with activity, all focused on Rashid. His shirt proved difficult for them to remove as it stuck to the edges of his injury despite Lazarus having cleaned him twice already while at the river. After his bath, he sat quietly while Salome and Lazarus cleaned and dressed his wound again. The surrounding skin was swollen, red and purple and hot to the touch. A foul green discharge oozed from beneath ruddy tissue edges. Salome shrank back when she saw it, but after a glance from Lazarus, stood taller and steadied her hand while she washed. Afterward, Lazarus coated the sore with leaves, which instantly soothed Rashid's stinging skin.

"Wow, that feels great," Rashid said, smiling.

"Change those every few hours," Lazarus directed the kids, "unless I get to it first."

And they did—all night and for the next three days. Each time the leaves were removed, pus was drawn out with them. At some point, Rashid asked Lazarus what kind of plant the leaves came from, but he just shrugged and answered, "Eh, it's green."

❧

By the end of the fifth day, Rashid perched on the edge of the bed as Salome again finished up his wound care.

"Oh, so much better!" he said, reaching his arms out and rotating his torso back and forth. The tension in his muscles released satisfyingly with the stretch. "You've really helped, Salome." His side no longer seeped, though some new black tissue had formed in its center, and the edges were still yellow and rolled. The swelling in his legs had decreased, and he could now drink a whole cup of water without vomiting it up afterward.

"You're welcome." She beamed. "I'll be back. Maybe later today, you can come out and see the rest of the place."

"I'd like that."

As soon as the front door closed behind her, it opened again and John breezed through, carrying a handful of tools. He glanced at Rashid and grinned. "You up? Any plans today?"

"Heal, I imagine. Work on beefing up my pipes."

John's forehead wrinkled. Shrugging, he said, "We don't eat meat anymore."

Rashid smiled. "No, that means to make my muscles bigger. These..." He held up his arms and flexed for the boy. "Meet my pipes."

"So you have metal in your arms?" John pitched forward, intent on Rashid's biceps, and reached to touch them, hesitantly. "They make your muscles bigger? Can I see?"

Rashid laughed. "No, it's an expression. It means I'm going to work on getting stronger. There is no metal in my arms, John. The pipe is the muscle." He rolled his sleeves up as if to prove his point. "See? Normal, sexy, sculpted arms. No metal or cow involved. Just me." He rolled his biceps in and out and shook his head, chuckling.

"Oh." John's faced flushed. "I see. Well, I already have perfect arm muscles. So, yeah." He grinned and started toward the door. "I'm going to go now."

After he left, Rashid stood and stretched again, but, this time, it caused his side to spasm, folding him over in pain. He limped to the table in the center of the room and stopped to lean on it, out of breath. This was going to take longer than he thought.

A murmur interrupted him, coming from outside. John must

have found Lazarus. Or perhaps Salome. Their voices rose, too loud for casual conversation. *Were they fighting?* Rashid wondered, hobbling to the door. He cracked it, hinges creaking and the heavy wood scraping noisily against the floor as it opened. Wincing, he paused before peeking out, sure he'd been heard, but nothing happened and instead they grew even louder.

John and Lazarus stood at the far edge of the yard, a chunk of wood and the tools they'd been using on the ground between them. Lazarus was on his knees, eyes closed, and arms extended in the air, like he was expecting to catch something meant to fall into them. But above him was nothing except a tree, barely rustling in the nearly still air. John, positioned in front of him, sang brazenly, his eyes open. Rashid could not make out his words, but by the expression on his face, which glowed with a mix of excitement, joy, and pleading perhaps, they seemed important. Rashid turned his neck, forehead pressed hard against the door, trying to look around without opening it any farther. No one else was around.

He shut the door, alarmed at what he'd seen, and leaned against it from the inside, staring at the ceiling. This place was odd. These people were not right. Why was Lazarus on the ground? Why was John singing at him? Rashid stepped forward, filled with a resolve to get out before he wound up as their dinner. Or worse. The pain in his side grabbed him, though, sending him to his knees. He shuffled up and back over to the couch. For now, there was nothing he could do. He was stuck there.

XXVIII

At first, when the bearer of the light brought them food, no one in the cell ate anything for fear it was poisoned.

On the third day, after the tray was deposited, Elise picked it up, reciting solemnly as she did, "therefore, do not worry about your life, what you will eat or drink. Is life not more than food? Look at the birds of the air, they do not sow or reap or store away in barns, and yet your Heavenly Father feeds them. Are you not much more valuable than they?"

She started in on the food, taking only a few bites before pushing the tin tray to the others. They each ate, and though Mahir snorted at her, finished what was left.

Soon, time blended together without the sun's glow to differentiate day from night. There were noises, however, and these the group clung to for sanity. They decided it was day when they heard active sounds—rustlings and footsteps overhead and what sounded like a bathroom, too, with flushing water and a lingering drip that never seemed to stop. They stayed awake when the noises were active and slept when they quieted.

And every day came a visit from the great white light, bearing a new metal tray, a pitcher of water, and an empty bucket to replace the one full of excrement. Most days, they tried to speak—sometimes pleading, sometimes not—to whoever hid behind the light, but the men never responded.

Then, one day, when the door cracked, Mahir flung the bucket at the open space, coating whoever was there with urine-soaked feces. The door slammed shut and didn't open again for days, leaving them without food or water all that time, until their lips cracked and they had to lick the walls to get what moisture they could from what seeped through its pores.

When the bearer of the light finally returned, he brought friends. Three flashlights entered and surrounded Mahir, one immediately kicking his legs out. Then they pounded on him, each of their beams bouncing in the dark as they delivered their blows. Adira and Jack rushed them, but the men with the lights could see, and they could not. Composite rifle butts slammed into their faces, forcing them back. They beat Mahir until his grunts softened into passive puffs of air with each kick.

For what seemed like hours after, the others sat by his side, until Mahir's breathing had slowed and he stirred, groaning loudly.

"Brother? Can you speak?"

"I can. But my tongue is swollen. I think it tore," Mahir answered, his voice muffled.

"Why are you so hotheaded?"

"I don't see you trying to get us out of here," Mahir grumbled. "I assumed Adira the Great would step in and free us during my... distraction."

"Why? It's useless." Adira answered, his voice tired. "We are in a prison. You can't fight your way out of prison, Mahir. You just have to wait."

After that, no one engaged the light bearer again. Instead, they submitted to the imposed schedule, learning to appreciate the few seconds of illumination that came with the daily meal, which most often consisted of mush though sometimes included a few pieces of stringy or grizzled meat, cold of course, and bland. Sometimes it was moldy. Eventually, they learned to stomach the food and even eat with fervor. For weeks, when they spoke, it was only in cautious whispers. They spent most of the time in silence—even Mahir, who seemed to have run out of words.

XXIX

THE WEEK AFTER they brought Rashid in from the river, Lazarus stood, cleaning the dark wood of the kitchen counter, while Rashid rested by the fire.

"How are you feeling?" Lazarus asked over his shoulder.

"So much better," Rashid answered.

It was plain to see their nursing him had helped; his strength was returning and the pains wracking his limbs had almost disappeared. "Well, good. I think you'll be able to get outside to walk soon then."

"That would be nice."

Lazarus' gaze lifted to the aging tan-and-green curtains covering the window before him, then drifted past them until his eyes blurred, as he wondered what to say next.

He felt a nudge as a gentle command fill him. *It's time*, it whispered. *Tell him.* The voice was familiar—it belonged to the Father. Lazarus had long ago learned to follow His biddings. They always led to some good end, even though it sometimes took pain or time to get there. This one was not unexpected. The Father had prepped him for this man from the city for a year now, and since they had first met, he'd been anticipating sharing a message with him. But he'd resisted blurting it out, waiting instead for the Father's bidding. Now, finally, it was time.

"Do you know what a psalm is, Rashid?" Lazarus asked.

"Sure. It's a poem from the Ketuvim section of the Jewish holy book, the Tanakh, and the Christian Bible."

"You remind me of a psalm." Lazarus paused, letting his words sink in. "It says, 'I am a stranger on Earth.'"

Lazarus reached again for the curtain in front of him and traced its edges with his thumb and forefinger. Salome had made them from fabric she had found in his keepsake box, years ago. It had come from his mother's favorite tunic. The cloth was stiff and thin now, but he remembered well how it had felt originally, soft against his cheek, thick to absorb the tears he had released over the years. The tears had come after the deaths of his wife, friends, and, eventually, his mother, whom he found on the ground moments after her passing. He never got to watch the light leave her eyes that day, but, as he lay there, head on her chest, he had felt the warmth fade from her tunic for hours after she was gone.

"Do you ever feel that way? Like a stranger on Earth?"

Rashid furrowed his brow, then turned his face away as if he hadn't heard—or perhaps didn't want to have heard—what Lazarus said.

"It goes on, you know." Lazarus persisted, studying him. Bright light from the window edged through the space between the curtains now, widening as it entered the room.

Rashid sighed. "Does it?"

"It goes on to say, 'Do not hide your commands from me. My soul is consumed with longing for your laws at all times.'" Lazarus paused again, longer this time. "I suppose, as you said, we are a little like pets to God. Just a little. Pets do tend to long for their masters. So it is with us and our God."

Rashid stiffened. "How did you—"

Lazarus saw the fear in his eyes. "You did not see that path by accident, Rashid. Neither did those men not see you by accident. God made this appointment here, for us, and those were His steps to bring you here. I have something to tell you. From God."

"I don't believe in God." Rashid's voice cracked. He shifted weight and slid his feet down from the couch, glancing around the room.

"Sure you do—your heart witnesses of Him by its longing for Him even as you say those words. That's why you are like the psalmist. You feel alone, don't you, Rashid?"

Rashid looked up, clearly trying to still his now-trembling hands. "I'm not sure what you mean. I am here with you right now. Look, Lazarus..."

"You know, you don't need to be afraid. I've lived a long time, but I know the rest of you aren't so lucky—especially in these times, the way things are..." Lazarus's voice dropped. "Listen. I don't feel like wasting your time. If a man tells you he has a word from God for you, you listen. Few get it handed to them this clearly."

Eyes wide, Rashid nodded.

"The man who wrote Psalms had a longing for the Father, just like you. He misunderstood it as loneliness at first. At some point, he realized what he needed was God. Back then, everyone thought the way to God's heart was through following His law. It still is, you know, in a way. Jesus came as the fulfillment of the law—He never said it was abolished. God still loves His law; it's His way of showing us who He is, His nature. He loves that we can know Him for who He is. I guess in that way you can relate, huh? Wanting to be known?" Lazarus shook his head. "Forgive me. After so many years, I have a lot going on in this brain of mine. It's sometimes hard to stay on track."

"Huh," Rashid said quietly. "I guess I haven't thought much on the idea of God actually existing. I've thought about what belief in a god does to people, though. They get fanatical. Religion makes people kill. And die. Entire civilizations, they'll build and destroy 'em—all in the name of some unseen entity."

Lazarus watched Rashid's mind spin. "Yes, well, about your message. Actually... well, I guess I sort of already told you, didn't I?" He chuckled, tipping his head down, still shaking it, and added, "It's funny how He uses us even when we think we're making mistakes. He sure knows what's going on."

"Sorry? I don't understand."

"God knows you feel alone, like you don't belong here anymore. But you do—because He made this Earth and you are His child. Of course, a child belongs in his Father's house. But the emptiness you feel? The deep sorrow—the one you think is from loneliness or the loss of your family—it isn't that. It's your heart testifying it wants you to be united with your creator, who wants you to know Him too. And you can. Through His law, through His word. You need to *learn* Him to get that unrest rested."

Lazarus turned back to the window above the sink and pushed the curtains the rest of the way apart, wide. Sunlight blazed into the room.

༄

"Hmm." Rashid rolled over, closing his eyes at the brightness of the sun's beams. Lazarus had clearly fallen off his rocking chair. The things he said were crazy. And how had he known about the conservation he'd had with the others? Unless maybe he'd been following them during the hike. He must have. Could this man be a part of the group that had taken his friends?

But he and the others *did* seem to genuinely to care for him, all without pay. Their kindness comforted him, though on some level, also made him wary. Lots of people *seemed* kind, but from his experience, most wanted something in return. Except for his wife and daughter—who was essentially his wife in smaller form—people had disappointed him. Sure, he had known some nice ones, but it was easy to be nice when everyone was friendly to you, generous when you had more than you needed yourself. Once things got hard though, once being kind cost them something, people tended to change. But this man and his family hadn't changed. They'd just taken him in, in all his life-disrupting weakness and shaped their whole world around helping him.

Rashid shifted his gaze to the fireplace and the dancing blue and orange flickers. Fire was all-consuming; the wood attested to that. While everyone's attention was on the flames, the wood popped and splintered away into nonexistence. He realized he'd been feeling rather like the wood, shriveling away steadily into black coals, with only a smothered voice to glow his defiance. But now, with this group of people who all believed in a higher power, it almost seemed like he could do so too—and maybe be heard, and maybe not burn up after all. He understood their desire to believe—perhaps if some magical being was out there, and it heard him... perhaps all this could go away, and time could reverse, and Rashid could have been home that day. He could have taken his family away before the bombs did.

Lazarus was right. Rashid did feel alone, and empty. The things he'd said were more than words. They seemed to wake up something in his mind, an old truth he had somehow forgotten—something similar to but more real than déjà vu resonated through him. Goose bumps swept down his arms and across his back. Despite the chill, his chest seemed warm and full, and he felt somehow reassured that he was seen and not alone after all.

He lay down, ending the conversation. Before he drifted off to sleep, his last thoughts were of how odd it was that such simple words could be so powerful.

XXX

IN THE WEEKS that followed, Rashid warmed to the Lazarus and the children. They were odd, but never did try to hurt him, and eventually his small talk, at first wary exchanges of appreciation and acknowledgement, became more fervent conversation, like when he updated them on what was going on in the outside world. The three were unfamiliar with what computers could do now, and had never even used a cell phone, which astounded Rashid. He also shared with them details about the natural disasters wracking the world, and also the war, including the loss of his university and home, and why he had come their way to begin with.

"I'm an archaeologist. Egyptologist, actually, but who doesn't love a good treasure hunt?" Rashid had said with a sheepish shrug and smile. But his smile faded almost as fast as it had come. "I suppose the mountains have pirates too, though, don't they?"

"Do you remember much about those men? Did you catch an accent?" Lazarus asked.

"It was clearly not Georgian, if that's what you mean, or Arabic," Rashid answered.

"It shouldn't be. The war hasn't reached Georgia so far as we can tell—much less South Ossetia, which is the closest heavily inhabited place to here," Lazarus replied. "The Russians won the battle over that land over a decade ago. It should be fairly peaceful now."

Rashid nodded. Lazarus was right; the fight in the Middle East wasn't supposed to have reached this far. There had been war in neighboring Turkey, though, as well as in Syria, Iraq, Egypt, Southeast Russia, and most other parts of the world. The fight was recently between the civilized countries and FREA—Free Radicals Encouraging Armistice—which was an ironic spinoff of Joseph Kony's LRA—Lord's Resistance Army—and a fizzling ISIL—Islamic State of Iraq and Levant, as well as some other unknown entity. The irony was not just in its name but also that both groups originated from opposing religions.

Their union proved neither group was interested in their decreed religious purposes, but in land, power, and money. FREA had claimed its purpose was to reunite the world in peace and purity, but to do so required the subjugation of all lands to an ever-changing set of laws decided upon by their self-appointed leader, Marcus Anan. FREA had been the ones responsible for the University of Cairo bombing. They had spread terror attacks seemingly everywhere—from shoot-outs at ballgames in the US to suitcase bombs in the buses of Europe and Asia.

Rashid described the recent compromise made with Anan.

"So, you are saying the Secretary-general got everything to stop by simply giving the man his own land? How is that even a UN matter?" Lazarus sat, mouth partly hanging open, brow furrowed in confusion. "How could a man responsible for decades of terror be paid off so easily? What about all his military officials? What do they get?"

"Well," Rashid said, "it is said he traded their names and locations as part of the negotiation. They were all assassinated by the UN."

"*That* I can believe, if he genuinely wanted to stop the battle. But I don't believe the rest of it." Lazarus stood and helped Salome make dinner—roasted potatoes with bean-and-root salad—as they spoke. He scrubbed vegetables in the sink while she chopped herbs at the table.

"Well, I'm glad he did it," John cut in. "I was tired of all the news from town being about hate."

Salome stopped her chopping. "You know it's the way of the world, John. Always has been. Can you remember a time when it wasn't?" She frowned as she rolled a handful of green onion together to slice. "It will start again."

"Tragic words for such a young girl," Rashid said, glancing from Salome to Lazarus. "Unless she, too, is older than she appears?"

He wanted more information on his hosts. So far they had yet to speak about their origins. They were obviously a family, fashioned as a father and his two children but not related by blood.

"That she is," Lazarus answered, leaving his vegetables and returning to the old table. Across from Salome, Rashid and John were playing a game John had taught him, like checkers but with faster-moving pieces and far more rules. John looked up eagerly.

"So are you ready to hear our... peculiar story?" Lazarus asked.

Rashid considered his question. In his whole life, he had never met anyone like these three. They were wild and odd. He still wasn't sure if the older one had all his mind intact, but otherwise, the three possessed a rare innocence. And, because of them, Rashid's body had strengthened, enough that he had even started pitching in with the chores. He could now clean house, navigate the forest, and chop and carry wood.

What about them could he have possibly been afraid of? Now, he was fond of them—so much so, he would stay with them in their happy, hidden lives forever if they invited him to.

"I'm not afraid of you," Rashid said. "And anyway, if you folks wiggle out on me, now I can run."

Salome giggled. "And tell him about Father, Lazarus. He needs to know about Father too."

"Yeah, for all your talk about this Father fellow, I still have not met him. Is he away?"

Lazarus smiled at Rashid. "No, Father is never 'away.' He is our God—and yours, too. He's the one who told us about you. Last year."

Rashid leaned back again, confused. Out of respect, he decided to listen, the way he did when his demented uncle used to talk to him about the people in the room that only he could see.

"You know, Rashid," Lazarus said, "things are going on in the world that you have never seen or heard of. Some are difficult to believe. Doesn't mean they aren't happening."

Salome and John nodded.

"It's true," Salome said. "He's right. You can know about it all, though, if you choose to. But you do *have* to choose to."

"Well, I want to hear it," Rashid answered.

"Well, then. I suppose you've heard of the man Jesus Christ?" Lazarus got a far-away look in his eyes when he said the name, and paused for an instant—as if he were reliving some wonderful moment from his past. "Well, I knew him well. He saved three people in this world—after they died, I mean. He's surely rescued too many others to count. But as far as people who had *already* died, whom he brought back to life—there were three." A half-smile crept onto his lips.

Rashid cocked his head. "Three," he repeated, scanning the others.

"Yes, three." Lazarus's smile broke into a grin, and Salome giggled again.

"Jesus Christ, from over two thousand years ago? The one and only?"

"Yep," John said, leaning back in his chair and balancing on the two rear legs, stabilizing himself with the toe of his shoe. He nudged Salome's side, just barely, with his outstretched hand. The girl's giggles erupted into full-blown laughter, which made John snicker and almost fall out of the chair. "She's like a faucet—just bump the lever." He laughed.

Rashid stared at them. Lazarus had started in, too, chuckling unapologetically. The three rolled around as if they'd told some ridiculous joke... *Were* they joking?

Salome held her hands to her heart, tears shining out the corners of her eyes. "Isn't it the most fantastic, wonderful thing? And we found each other!"

Lazarus reached for Rashid's shoulder. "Rashid, son. This is our story. And the Father is responsible for it all."

He shared with Rashid about their "father," God, and described their secret of immortality. He told of the radical healing they'd experienced—both physical and emotional, through the years. He spoke gently when he introduced the pain they'd each gone through when losing their loved ones. In the end, the key to their healing, he said, was not their magical rejuvenating powers at all, but in how they considered the situation. When they remembered their late loves as sweet blessings they'd been given for a short time, instead of someone they'd lost, they healed. They had learned to embrace their "Father" as their ever-present security instead. Afterward, Lazarus shared what he said was the truth about heaven and hell, and what eternity meant for people.

"It's all there in the scripture," Lazarus said. "Though I don't suppose you've read much of that, have you?"

The truth was Rashid *had* read much of it. Of course he was interested, and he'd read the oldest, most intact collections of ancient writings available. But he'd read them out of curiosity—just like he did when examining the hieroglyphics on Egyptian tombs—as fascinating clues exposing a world long gone, not as something he himself should believe in.

"Let me get this straight. This God you are describing—He uses bribery, a chance at immortality, and the threat of an eternity of torture to make people love him?" Rashid snorted. "Sounds rather desperate. He must not be very likeable."

"Desperate. Hmm..." Lazarus appeared to contemplate the word. "Perhaps," he replied slowly. "I suppose a parent might be desperate for their children."

Rashid looked toward the wooden floor, smooth from Lazarus's fervent sanding. This point he understood. He, too, had been desperate for his child. Would he not threaten her with consequences to protect her from costly mistakes and reward her for doing well? The consequences their god was offering were much more dramatic than his toward his daughter, however. Kisses and extra dessert were nothing compared to an immortality full of joy and peace. But then, so was eternity more dramatic than poor manners.

"Rashid," Salome said, "this is real. *We* are real." She had given up her cutting and was standing next to him now. The young girl reached for his hand and clasped it between hers.

Her palms were velvety and smooth—like a baby's—though she used them to chop wood and climb trees and pick berries. How could it be she had not one callus? In many ways, the three of them were archaic—their clay dishes, their simple home, even their language—all of it old. And how on earth could any man have carved so many pedestals, even in ten lifetimes?

He felt it again—a chill, followed by warmth and a strange knowledge that their words were true. "You guys are giving me goose bumps," he said.

"It isn't us," John answered with a grin. "Cool, though, huh?"

Rashid gaped. Had they all lost their minds? Could he have stumbled upon a cult? But watching them, he could see these three believed every word they'd said. And it seemed to bring them peace, or something even bigger—happiness. Maybe there was something to this religion thing after all, if just for them.

"Let's say I believe you," Rashid said. "How did you all *meet* this God?"

"I've already told you, Rashid," Lazarus replied. "Don't you remember our talk? Faith comes from hearing the Word. The Word, Rashid, is *Him*. It's His law, His Bible, His voice in you now."

"That's right," Salome interrupted. "He does speak to us. You have to listen though. He yells sometimes but not usually. If you don't pay attention, you'll miss Him."

"So, like, what?" Rashid said. "He'll be a voice in my head?" The words came out extra slow, emphasizing his point. "You want me to try to listen to a voice in my head?"

"Yes," Salome answered, smiling. "Sometimes, that's Him. But rarely. Sometimes His voice is just something you *know*. An assurance you were never taught. Sometimes He speaks like a warmth over your arms when a thought pops in your head or when you hear someone else say something." She grinned at Lazarus and nudged her elbow in his direction. "Like him."

Rashid glanced at Lazarus. The man *knew* things, it was true. *He told me about you last year.* Lazarus's words resonated through Rashid. He'd said the words so confidently, not at all shy about how strange they sounded.

"To me," John interrupted, "Father feels like he is stirring up my bowel." His face was sincere, as if he were trying hard to relate.

"Your bowel? Like your guts? He stirs up your guts?" Rashid tried to contain his laughter, but it built up too quickly and, with a shake of his torso, burst out. "Sounds more like you may have a problem with gas!"

John grew red-faced and shook his head. "No way. My stomach is strong. I can eat anything."

Rashid wiped his eyes, still smiling at the boy. Something inside him crumbled—a wall? Before thinking, he asked the question bothering him most. "But why can't He just *be here* like the rest of us? Visually, physically, in voice... everything?"

Salome smiled. "A blind man cannot see," she replied, "so what good would it be for him if Father were always visible? A deaf man would never experience Him if He came only in sound, and even if he experienced hearing, he would not comprehend it without having been able to hear long enough to know how to

162

interpret language. Even our sense of smell fades over time. And God is not something to be consumed, so we do not taste Him."

"Yeah, I'm sure someone as powerful as God could make himself obvious to us if he wanted to—senses or not. He made Earth obvious to everyone. No one disputes we are on Earth or that we are here together, why not do the same with his presence?"

"Who knows," Lazarus said. "Did you always explain everything to your daughter, Rashid?"

"No, not always, but I did when I could. Sometimes, she wasn't ready to understand or was unwilling." Even as the words left his mouth, the truth of what Lazarus claimed struck him.

"Well, there you go." Lazarus spread out his hands. "Some things to us are a mystery because of who we are to God. And they'll stay that way for you until it's time or until you become something else to Him. Like this—just knowing when He's speaking to you. Until you seek Him, even this might stay a mystery."

Hours passed as the group shared with Rashid their lives. With every word, he became more sure they were telling the truth. His worry melted away and was replaced with an excitement for new things. For a moment, Rashid forgot he was mourning.

XXXI

To Lazarus and the family in the woods, the few weeks Rashid stayed with them were an instant. They lived happy, slow lives, absorbing him as one of their own, up to the day he was to leave.

That morning, Lazarus found Rashid packing his bag.

"What have you in there so far?" he interrupted, walking up from behind him.

"Oh, hi," Rashid said, turning. He lifted the backpack and scanned its contents. "I've got those clothes you gave me, salted rolls stuffed with cheese and several of the *most perfect* apples Salome could find." He hugged his pack at the words "most perfect" and grinned broadly.

Lazarus smiled back; though Rashid's leaving broke her heart, she had still found a way to make it beautiful for him. Losing his company would be hard on them all, but today needed to happen.

"How's your side?"

Rashid slid his hand under his shirt, revealing the raised pink scar on his flank, the only evidence of all he had been through. "Really great. I'm good as new, thanks to you all." He paused and met Lazarus's eyes. "Thank you. You saved my life. In more ways than one."

"Our pleasure."

Rashid glanced down at Lazarus's boots, raising his eyebrows. "Nice kickers," he said.

"Kickers? Hu." Lazarus considered the shoes. The leather was smooth and strong and had just started to form around his toes. They'd been sitting in his closet for ages, but today the hike would be long and rough, so he had worn them. He met Rashid's gaze again. "You don't need to worry, you know. The Father is guiding you. All you need to do is step out in faith, and He will make sure your feet land on the right path."

"Bold thing to say, coming from a man hiding in a forest all these years," Rashid answered. He bit his lip apologetically, as fast as he had said it.

Lazarus took a long, loud breath and nodded. "You are correct. I'm not as bold as I should be by now. But I *am* right." He tossed Rashid a sack of candied berries. "The wildflower wanted you to have these too," he said. "She made them for you."

Rashid grinned. "Thanks." He tucked the sack into the backpack's side pocket. "I need to find my friends. That's where I'm going."

"See? You're already getting it," Lazarus answered. "But before you do, I need to show you something."

When the two started out, the sun had just peeked over the horizon, revealing the day's first display of clouds. They walked along the path John and Salome had carved out with the pedestals.

"Did you really make all these?" Rashid asked, tracing the grooves running along the tops of the pillars as they walked past.

"I did. Though John helped with several."

"They're all beautiful. Masterpieces."

"Thank you," Lazarus answered quietly.

As they walked, Lazarus studied the trail, praying silently. *How long ago did Your design for this path begin? Did You share its purpose with the children when they started it?*

He had always thought of the carvings as a fun pastime, but last night he'd had a dream revealing the Father had had a plan for it all along. In the dream, he'd been shown this very path, the one the children had been forging for centuries, with no apparent direction in mind. The images were vivid but dizzying. At first, he floated rapidly through the pedestals. He saw his and Rashid's hiking boots, crunching dirt under their feet. At the path's end, there had been another trail, this one much narrower and without pillars, cutting through the forest. This they followed next, the scene rapidly changing but dotted by several landmarks—a broken tree here, a collection of white flowers there.

At some point, their two sets of feet had turned into four, then eight, then more than twenty. And they were no longer just boots. In fact, most were bare feet—some bloody, some calloused. There was the crunching of twigs underfoot, the pillars, the landmarks, and the dream ended with shouting and light and blood—so much blood—all flashing before him. He had caught glimpses of a few faces—mostly older men, though some young ones and a handful of women were mixed in too. A few were dressed in some sort of uniform. Throughout the dream, Lazarus heard Father's voice, whispering instructions. Today, he was to take Rashid to the trail's end and return home. But this path would be used again with Lazarus as its guide.

The two continued in silence, Lazarus brewing wordlessly on what wonders lay ahead.

XXXII

Rashid studied Lazarus as they walked. He looked disturbed, which was uncommon for him. Perhaps he was sad, as was Rashid, at his leaving. He wondered if anything he said could make it better but decided to let him work through it. The man was certainly strong enough to handle this. And anyway, if he did say something, Rashid might tear up himself. So instead, he closed his eyes and inhaled deeply, experiencing one last time the scent of the homestead—fresh dirt from the stirred-up ground beneath them, wet pine from the dew resting on the pillars and Lazarus's sweat, which was gross but still part of it all. He glanced up to soak in his final view of the column-lined path, and ran straight into Lazarus's back.

"Oh, sorry." He stepped away and regained himself.

Unaffected by their collision, Lazarus stood still as the pedestals, whispering something under his breath.

Rashid cocked his head. "What's that, old man?"

But Lazarus didn't respond. Instead, he plunged forward into the trees, his stride suddenly huge. Hesitating, Rashid glanced around for some clue as to what had spooked him. The forest was silent. Leaves fluttered in the soft breeze, bouncing sun rays between them. Nothing appeared off; the morning was perfectly beautiful. Rashid shrugged and jogged after him.

He caught up quickly, though Lazarus still charged through the foliage.

"Hey, what's going on?" Rashid asked. Lazarus didn't answer but instead pressed forward as if he couldn't hear him.

Without warning, he stopped and pivoted, examining a cluster of flowers. Mumbling something to himself, Lazarus scanned the area and took off again. Rashid chased him, trying hard not to be smacked by every branch that flew backward after the burly man plowed through. At some point, he realized they were following a path—a thin, winding game trail, which emerged, disappeared, and reemerged right where Lazarus led him. For over an hour, they moved this way, Lazarus often pausing to study a tree or mutter something, then taking off again.

"You've been holding out on me," Rashid puffed after what felt like another kilometer of trying to keep pace. "What other superpowers do you have? Man, I can't keep up!"

"Rashid." Lazarus stopped and turned around so quickly their faces almost rammed together. "Listen, I *need* you to keep up. Right now, we have a goal. You need to put your legs under submission. Have you not heard the words of the great teacher, Paul? 'But I keep under my body and bring it into subjection; lest that by any means, when I have preached to others, I myself should be a castaway.'"

Rashid leaned forward, hands on his knees. He tilted his head up, sucking air through his wide mouth. "Riddles, Lazarus. Don't speak to me in riddles. I can barely take a deep breath right now, much less decipher riddles!"

Lazarus laughed, his eyes sparkling, expectant.

"Breathe, son." Lazarus patted Rashid on the shoulder. "We're nearly there."

"Where?"

"You'll see." He waited another few seconds before continuing on, a little slower this time. "Now come on."

Rashid followed, trying his best to keep the man in his sight.

At some length, Lazarus's steps slowed, and he slouched forward. "We're here. Quiet now."

Rashid caught up and bent down behind a tree, heartbeat skipping with the feeling they were not supposed to be there. "What is it? Where are we?"

By then, Lazarus had also crouched, hiding from whatever they were there to see. "I'm not sure, but God revealed it to me last night. The path we have been building all along, I never knew where it was to lead, but now I know. It's for them."

They lay flat on the dirt, branches masking their faces. Below them lay a large compound, which seemed to exist *under* the forest, as if someone had uprooted all the vegetation in the area and simply planted it back on top of the buildings in front. The place must have been ten acres across, and it contained a series of cement buildings, gravel paths, and a barren courtyard in its center. The rooftops were painted shades of green and decorated with trees, while the irregular courtyard was painted blue gray. Around it stood scattered boulders and more trees. It looked like a large pond, and if Rashid had been any higher the whole area would pass for a patch of forest. Men stood about, wearing gray-and-tan uniforms, sunglasses, and large guns.

"I'm thinking that people aren't supposed to know about this place," Rashid whispered.

Lazarus propped himself up on his thick elbows, squinting at the area below. "What are you hiding down there?" he mused.

Rashid motioned toward the courtyard. "Look—something's happening." A long line of men filed in from the side and stood in rows in the center. Their movements were robotic as they hit their final positions. A man in a gray-and-red outfit circled them stiffly, gesturing his arms about as he walked. He snapped together, facing the formation. With another wave of his arms, the group turned as one to the left, then the right, then dropped down to their bellies to press out push-ups.

"It's military," Rashid whispered again.

"See there." Lazarus grabbed Rashid's chin and turned it toward the back of the complex where a narrow, windowless building stood. Next to it perched a wooden scaffold, and next to that was a large bin, lined like a giant garbage can.

"Is that a gallows?" Rashid peered closer, his heart dropping in his chest. "We shouldn't be here." He scooted back and searched for the quietest route away. "Let's leave, Lazarus."

Lazarus didn't move. "Wait," he said. "I want to learn the layout. We might need to remember it."

Rashid scooted forward again and followed Lazarus's lead. Only one narrow road led in and out, barely one lane wide. He spotted what appeared to be a guardhouse to the side of the road near the rectangular area. Behind that, a barbed-wire-topped fence lined the entire compound, forbidding entrance or exit by any other route. Altogether, there were eleven structures, varying in size and form. Two narrow buildings lined the courtyard's sides. A giant garage with doors big enough to let a tank in and out stood near a smaller building, which angled into the dirt, more like an entrance to something bigger underground. Two small cottages were right next to this structure, between which was a yard enclosed by tall brick walls, containing a patio decorated with gardens and a lap pool. The other buildings were plainer and strewn about around the rest of the area.

Rashid turned toward Lazarus. "How did you know this was here?"

Lazarus shrugged. "I didn't. Father showed me last night in a dream. He told me to bring you here."

Rashid shook his head. He still didn't fully understand the connection this man had with God, but here they were.

"Do you think my friends are down there?"

"Maybe."

Just then, voices and the sound of crunching leaves came from off to their right. Someone—or rather several someones—were approaching. Lazarus caught Rashid's eye. Holding his gaze, he jumped to his feet. "Do you trust me, Rashid? I need you to."

Rashid sat up, searching nervously through the brush for the sound's source. His throat swelled, making his voice crack. "What's going on, Lazarus?"

"There's more. Your journey is just at the start. I am taking you to your next step in the walk Father has for you. Have faith, son. Call on Him and trust Him. Trust me."

Rashid had always been reserved and polite; his mom had raised him to be that way. But now, taking in this half-crazed brown man, hair wild and eyes open so big the whites showed at every edge, Rashid suddenly wanted to run. An angry shout curled up in his chest. But he couldn't let it out, not with... *whatever* was going on down the hill so close. "I don't understand you," he whispered harshly instead. "Stop preaching to me about your imaginary friend! What are you saying?" Rashid climbed to his feet, holding his hands out in front of him.

Lazarus cocked his head to the side as if to consider Rashid's words, but then something rustled in the bushes behind them. He jerked his face over his shoulder. "Shh!"

Rashid followed his glance and scooted forward. The rustling drew closer; had he exposed them? The urge to run suddenly rose inside him.

"I'm leaving, Lazarus." He said, hesitating for just an instant before sprinting away, into the trees, before whatever made the noise showed itself.

"No, Rashid, not like this. Listen!" Lazarus called after him, but Rashid had no intention of seeing whatever was coming their way. He heard Lazarus grumbling from behind, and then footsteps as he started running too.

In another moment, Rashid felt a tug as something grabbed his bag from behind and swung him off his feet to the side, right into a tree. He hit the trunk with a thump and fell in a pile on the ground.

"Oomph!" The air had been knocked from his chest. Rashid grunted, trying to fill his lungs again, but before he could, Lazarus was on him.

"Forgive me, son. This is going to hurt." Lazarus pulled his fist back and, before Rashid could raise his arms to defend himself, punched him in his left cheek. Rashid's body bounced away from the steel knuckles. "Relax. Everything will be fine."

Standing, Lazarus yelled out in the direction of the voices. "Here, help!" He bent and tore Rashid's shirt, then took a branch from a nearby bush and whipped his chest twice, ripping the skin jagged. Crimson blood crept to the surface. "Do not fight them," Lazarus said quickly. "Trust me, Rashid. Trust Father!" He stood and spun around, bolting before the approaching soldiers burst through the nearby brush.

"Lazarus!" Rashid cried. "What are you doing?" But he was already gone, and now three other men were fast approaching. They were dressed in black like the ones who'd taken his friends all those weeks ago. One shouted out to him in a strange language.

"Hi," Rashid sputtered, still dazed. "I'm lost. Can you help?" He patted his chest and spread his hands out, trying his best to appear harmless and in need.

The men eyed him. Rashid knew he was a sight with his torn shirt and freshly injured chest, and hot blood oozing from the swollen cut under his eye. He had not shaved in weeks, and his hair was stringy from sweat.

"What you are doing here?" the closest one said, narrowing his gaze at him. He put his hand on a pistol holstered to his hip.

"Hey, hey, hey, watch it—I don't know. A man brought me here. He said he needed to show me something, and he hit me and ran off."

The soldier considered Rashid for a minute, then dropped his hand from the gun and glanced at the others, spitting orders at them in the other language and motioning toward Rashid. "Come," he finally said, his accent musical, like the Georgians he had met in Tbilisi, but also assault the air the way Russian words did. The men grabbed Rashid and pushed him roughly up the tree he was leaning against until his feet were under him again, scraping bark chips into his shirt and down his back.

"Thanks, guys, I got this," Rashid said, shaking them off.

They let go and stepped back. The shorter one extended his arm out as if welcoming him into the woods the way they had come. Rashid stumbled sideways, regaining his stance. He considered running but eyed the guns and instead stepped hesitantly in the direction the man indicated, then fell in line with them. Through the trees they headed, following a narrow weaving path, which led directly away from the compound.

As they trekked along silently, Rashid's mind raced. Why would Lazarus have attacked him? His words came back—*Do not fight them, trust me.* What had he known? Rashid wondered if he'd ever see the family from the woods again, and what his new companions would do with, or *to* him. He glanced around at their stone faces, slowing his steps, and with them the sluggish rhythm of crunching pine needles beneath his feet. He breathed deep, filling his chest with courage. He could do this.

"So, uh, sir?" He spoke up, addressing the one who seemed to be the leader. "Do *you* speak English then? Aw Rubama aerabi— *or perhaps Arabic?*" Can you tell me where we are?" The man stopped and looked right into Rashid's eyes, his own narrowed with determination. Reaching into his holster, he pulled out a black pistol, waved it at the compound to the north of where they stood, and then wagged it forward, toward where they headed. The angry, guttural sound of his language filled the air as he spoke again, this time much faster.

"I'm sorry. I don't understand you," Rashid answered, arms up, palms facing the man. "Please put the gun down. I'm no threat."

The man eyed Rashid again, head to toe, then pointed his chin away. Rashid thought he really should have studied the language before coming on this trip. He tugged at his shirt, trying to cover his bare skin.

"Hey guys. I'm sorry. I didn't mean to trespass. I'm just moving through." He stepped backward, arms held up in defense.

Shrugging, the man tucked his gun away and turned to leave.

Rashid relaxed, then asked, "What is this place?"

But they didn't answer. Instead, they stared forward, intent on wherever they were heading.

"Maybe, can you tell me which way to the nearest town? I can take it from there."

At his words, the man, who Rashid imagined to be the leader, stopped. His shoulders rose in a slow sigh. "No, you come," he said. "Come... us. We take you."

Rashid followed more willingly this time, as ease from the threat of getting shot being put away. The trail contracted as they hiked, until the surroundings became a redundant backdrop of gray bark cloaked with green fuzz. *What was the rule about moss?* he wondered. *It always grew on the north side of trees—or was it the west?* He huffed. It didn't matter; the moss seemed to grow any way it pleased around here. From tree to tree, it had no pattern.

When the compound was long behind them, their pace slowed. Perhaps the men weren't with the ones he and Lazarus had been watching after all. Could they have been spying on the secret barracks as well? If so, what were they doing in these parts?

One of the others grunted and glanced at Rashid long enough for him to glimpse his gray, pitted skin and mouthful of rotten teeth.

"Oh! Don't brush much, huh?" Rashid said, figuring the man couldn't understand him anyway. He pinched his lips together and nodded. "I get it. Who wants to waste time on hygiene when you could be doing much cooler stuff, like guarding mysterious buildings in the woods, right?"

A loud popping noise broke through the air. Bark splintered

off the trees around them, and fountains of dirt plumes sprayed from the ground. The men dropped, clearly alarmed. Something tugged at Rashid's leg, sending a sting that shot to his toes. He spun around, stunned, trying to figure out what was happening, but when he took a step, his leg collapsed. With a grunt, he fell, his face slamming against the dirt and dried leaves.

Soon Rashid's ears rang, deadening the chaotic noise from the background. Rashid groaned; it was happening again. Then the ringing took charge, dulling his senses until, in the next instant, the world spiraled around him. Though the ground was secure beneath him, he felt disoriented, like he was floating in midair. He turned his head to the right—a bad move as it made the spinning worse—and discovered a pair of wide, yellowing eyes staring back at him, surrounded by dingy gray skin. The man they belonged to lay staring at him, dead still except for an occasional blink.

A tree limb fell behind him, and as it hit down, someone howled in pain. He jerked his head over and cussed in a harsh whisper at whoever it was then turned again to lay immobile, facing Rashid.

The soldier's hat had fallen off in the commotion, releasing a bunch of thick, shiny hair across his head. Rashid thought it funny how, just then, with bullets flying above and foreign strangers with guns of their own crouching beside him, all he could think about was what nice hair it was. He closed his eyes and relaxed into the ground, blocking out everything else. This man who looked sickly or drug addicted or whatever had such a lovely, well-groomed mane, all hiding under his black cap. What a surprise that was.

Soon, the popping slowed, and the one in charge hollered something in his language again, and belly-crawled into the underbrush. The soldier next to Rashid scrambled after him, as did others. Rashid contemplated leaving them all but felt another tug, this time on his arm. As if a well had opened beneath it, a crimson stain appeared and spread almost immediately on his shirtsleeve

"Okay, so I guess I'll stick with you guys," he murmured, crawling after them. The dingy guy gaped at Rashid like he'd lost his mind, then, seeing the leader eying him, kept moving.

They squirmed back and forth through trees, staying as low to the ground as possible. The skin on Rashid's chest tore as he scooted along, dragging his torso over sharp branches littering the forest floor. He didn't feel their thorny stabs so much as friction tugging him back from safety, impelling him harder and faster after the men.

A few minutes later, the forest became dense again, and the soldiers slowed. They sat up and leaned against the bark of the thicker trees. The one with the gray skin sat up and stared at Rashid, mouth open, sucking in air. He pulled out his gun and aimed it directly at Rashid's bloody nose.

"Hey man, I'm not going to hurt you—*I'm just passing through*," Rashid half yelled, eyes wide. He lifted his hands in defense again. If only he could get them to understand; what was wrong with this guy? The other two spun around, and one made a hushing sound, his finger raised angrily to his lips.

The leader said something to the man pointing the gun, and he lowered it, keeping his eyes focused on Rashid. With his face twisted in anger, he spat a response over his shoulder. As he spoke, saliva shot out from a gap where a tooth was missing and landed on his gun barrel.

Rashid dropped his shoulders with an aggravated breath. "Look, I'm happy to leave. I just need to know how to get out of this place. City? Town? Normal people? Will. You. Show. Me. City?"

The leader grabbed Rashid's shirt near his wound, pulling it out to peek at the bullet hole, then tightened his mouth and shook his head. Huffing, he tossed the cloth away and pointed at the forest.

"You. Die. You come."

Rashid stared back, worried. The man was right; he probably couldn't get out even if he knew which way to go. But with them, he was at their mercy, and they all appeared rather suspiciously like the ones who'd stolen his friends the other day, minus a few rifles. "You can't help this," he said. "I need a hospital."

The man shrugged his shoulders and turned to go, waving his hand at Rashid as if he had given up on him.

"Wait!" Rashid called, desperate. He placed his hand on his chest, trying a different approach. "Rashid."

The man stopped and rolled back to look at him again. He jabbed his own chest and answered, "Vepkhia." He pointed at the others, one at a time. "Boris. Andro."

"Got it," Rashid smiled, nodding at each one as he spoke their names. "Vepkhia, Boris, and Andro is the hair model who hates me."

Vepkhia reached for his arm and helped Rashid back to his feet. The three men turned once Rashid was up, and walked into the woods again, this time slower. Rashid shrugged and followed along, a bloody dirtball now, half-blind from Lazarus's love tap. His legs still worked, though the one with the gunshot wound was much weaker and insulted him whenever he put weight on it. He sighed. At least no one was shooting at him anymore.

The group hiked along silently, Rashid struggling to stay within eyeshot. He was exhausted but the pain in his leg kept him awake. After a while, though, the leg numbed and became heavy, his feet sloppy. Occasionally, the world-spinning would begin again, and he'd have to stop and grab his knees, eyes squeezed tight, counting the seconds before his presumed collapse. Somehow, he never fell—though at one point he did tip over and butt his face into a nearby tree. Even then, the others kept moving ahead, seemingly oblivious to his struggle. He had pushed himself off the tree and pressed on, phasing in and out of alertness until they finally stopped. When they did, he found himself leaning on a cement utility building surrounded by a dirt lane, which led in the opposite direction they had come. Rashid piqued at the road.

"Home," he whispered, his good arm propped on the building.

He looked at the men who had accompanied him. Vepkhia nodded—a glimmer of encouragement—until Andro's yellow grin filled his vision again and a thud echoed through Rashid's head as a fist slammed into his face.

XXXIII

"YOU STILL DON'T have them all?" Jubair was having difficulty listening to Jaakko drone on with his excuses. He needed a current assessment and the next step in his plan. Nothing else. Why did this fool insist on pointing out all his own shortcomings? Was he wanting to be disposed of?

"Twelve, yes. We have twelve, sir. Your honor. Sir." Jaakko's face was solid, emotionless.

Four men in camouflage trousers, olive T-shirts, and baseball caps lined the wall behind Jubair. They stood at ease, with their hands behind their backs, feet eighteen inches apart, eyes forward. Jubair would have preferred to travel without so many escorts, but Calan was on his back recently about security. Jubair had relented, though he made Britain foot the bill. Well, actually, he hadn't *made* the man do anything. He'd simply *allowed* his friend to protect him in whatever way *he* felt comfortable.

"Fine," he said. "Just one more. You still have two weeks. That is very manageable."

"We'll try, sir, but he's hidden. Our intel cannot find even his family. It's like… like he just vanished, sir."

Jubair tapped the thumb and forefinger on his right hand together, slowly behind his back, pressing them firmly enough to feel the muscles in his forearm contract each time. The man before him was a bumbling idiot. How difficult could it be to gather thirteen rogue rebel militia leaders when given the supplies this man had on top of a four-month timeframe? It wasn't difficult—not at all. Jaakko had no sense or apparent skill for his job. He needed firing, which Jubair planned to do as soon as he found a suitable replacement. But this job needed to be completed first. He'd already invested too much time and money to start from scratch again.

"Look, Jaakko, I don't care how you do it, just do it. And fast. And quiet. That's it."

Jubair turned to leave. One rebel leader was all that remained of the force he'd already proclaimed to have squashed by giving Anan his own territory. He needed the entire militia eliminated, or else he'd lose credibility.

"Oh, I almost forgot." He turned once more toward Jaakko. "How about the local insurgency? Have you found them yet? I don't want our treasures discovered."

"We have not. A few soldiers approached the compound recently. We shot them, sir. Multiple times. We're pretty sure we injured them, fatally."

"Pretty sure, as in they still got away?"

"Yes, sir."

"As in, maybe even took pictures before they got away?"

The man dropped his gaze. "Possibly, sir."

"And did you think to follow these soldiers? To find their camp?"

"We tried, sir. We've been combing the area. Nothing's out there."

Jubair fumed. The local resistance was proving to be more of a problem than he had anticipated. If they weren't stopped soon, word might leak out about the compound and its contents. For years, Jubair had been collecting people of importance and imprisoning them here. Wives and grandchildren, even beloved parents—only the beloved ones—of any world leader who resisted Jubair's decrees. Promise of their pain or death had done well in securing compliance. He hadn't done it to be cruel; he just needed the whole world to support his efforts. The entire existence of the new era he planned rested on world peace, world unity. Any outliers were ripples in the surface of his otherwise pristine masterpiece.

"I see." Jubair dropped his tone and stepped toward the desk. He lifted his hand and inspected it. Then, sucking air in through his nose with a loud, drawn out breath, laid his palm against the smooth wood, still following it with his gaze. "Nice. This is a nice desk."

"Yes, it is, sir." The man stiffened at his approach.

"I know this is hard"—*for an idiot*, Jubair finished in his mind— "but remember *why* we're out here. Why we're doing this. Unity. Order. The *end of war*, Jaakko. Can you imagine a world where your children can grow up without fear of senseless suitcase bombs? Where they can go to, say, a rugby match and sit in the bleachers, in peace, without having to plan an escape route in case terrorists attack that day?"

"Yes sir. It is a great goal, sir."

"But if we get found out, if this place is seen, that will all go away. We'd be back to all the horror. I need you to act as if your children's futures depend on your success." He raised an eyebrow at Jaakko, who now trembled. "Because we both know it does, don't we?"

"Yes sir!" Jaakko thundered, snapping to attention.

"Very good. I'll be expecting your phone call soon then," Jubair said and turned away.

Still seething, he stepped into the hall. He didn't like threatening people, especially his own staff, but sometimes it needed done. Brisking away, he decided to tour the grounds. He needed some reassurance after such a depressing meeting, and seeing the rest of the compound in smooth operation should help.

His mood lifted almost immediately when he entered the prison. It had been constructed first. By now, systems were well established and the building itself broken in. Everything there was polished and in proper order. He paused when he entered the cell room, which was also the main area. The room's center was dropped—its floor lay thirty feet beneath him—so despite having entered on the ground floor, Jubair now found himself walking among the rafters, traversing a long catwalk that wrapped around the entire room.

He smiled at the neatness and consideration of the area below. The prisoners weren't housed cruelly, not at all. They shared one large common area, and each had their own bed, all welded to the floor in the center of the room. They were supplied with two bolted-down card tables as well, where they could play board games, eat their meals, and keep company with each other. He had even approved a walled-off bathroom for bathing and toileting. The roof to the bathroom, like the rest of the cell, had to be open to the people above, of course, for proper surveillance, but at least it afforded some privacy between the prisoners.

Jubair squeezed the handrail before him, then patted it confidently. Things were indeed better than Jaakko had painted them. Each person below was a symbol of accomplishment. Each accounted for a world leader who agreed, despite their own selfish desires, to relent for the betterment of others. They were his trophies. He didn't intend to ever return them, of course. At some point, all the prisoners would have to be executed to keep his persuasion tactics private. Though when and how the executions would take place hadn't been figured, or even thought much about yet. Perhaps he'd wait until the new laws were signed, then kill the dissenting leaders along with the prisoners. That seemed a terrible waste, though. Maybe, he thought, it would be better to keep them instead, as encouragement in hard times.

XXXIV

ISAIAH SIGHED. "ALL I want is a shower." She leaned against the wall next to Elise. "A long, hot, soap-sudsy, drenching shower."

"I'm sorry, Isaiah," Elise answered.

"Why? You didn't lock us up in here."

"No, I know. But I wanted this to go differently."

Isaiah snorted, a loud burst in the otherwise sleeping room. "Me too."

"Here, here," cackled Mahir from across the cell. "You got an apology for me, too, princess?"

"Mahir," Jack broke in, "aren't you supposed to be our guide? Why should she apologize to you?"

"Look, Dr. Digs-in-the-Dirt, you should have been able to see this coming too. You're the one with the satellite imaging and all the secret intel about where random militia camps are. You should have known."

"Guys, stop," Elise said, raising her voice, though somehow without sounding angry. "This was out of everyone's control. We're just living our path right now; we need to accept it. Do the best we can with what we have."

Adira's voice cut through the dark. "Dr. Harper is correct. This will be over soon. They have to talk to us at some point."

Isaiah worried at Adira's words. "Talking" could mean anything. Perhaps leaving them alone would be a safer alternative. "You know how I *really* feel? Scared. Worse than scared."

"Oh great, a woman trying to figure out her feelings. This should be good."

"Mahir," Adira hissed.

"All right, whatever."

"Well, I am," Isaiah said. "It's like… when you're driving along, just driving, and red-and-blue lights start flashing behind you. And then you see the cop car in the rearview mirror." Isaiah paused. "The thing is, you're wondering, what did I do? You know you did *something*, and there's a punishment coming, but all the rest of it…"

"Well. I feel like… like when you actually *are* caught and then forced in an underground mud pit. Like by strangers with guns," Mahir said. "Oh, wait, yeah, we are."

Isaiah sighed again, closing her eyes.

Just then, the cell door opened, and the light shone in as usual. This time, however, came a heavy rustling until, with a thump, something fell into the center of the cell. No one stirred until the door closed again.

Isaiah crept forward. "It's warm. I think it's another person."

"Hello?" Jack's voice broke through the darkness. "Are you… okay?"

A weak moan rose from the pile.

"Rash?" Isaiah felt Jack rush over, edging between her and the body. "Rash, it's me. It's Jack."

"Captain," Rashid breathed.

"Yes, you're here! We thought we'd lost you! We thought you… Well, we hoped you escaped," Jack answered.

"Captain. I found you guys." Rash said weakly. "Where are we? It's so dark… am I blind?"

"No, we're in an underground prison. We've been here a while, not sure how long."

"A prison. Fitting," Rashid uttered.

Isaiah scooted to his other side, eager to hear what he had to say.

"Where have you been?" Jack asked.

"I, uh—" Rashid roused. He pushed forward, knocking into Isaiah's side, then wretched, vomiting in Jack's direction, over and over, until Isaiah could smell the sourness of bile and the thick metallic scent of something worse. Blood.

"He's throwing up! I think... docs, what's happening?" Jack said, his voice suddenly desperate. "Rash, are you okay?"

"Oh, man. Sorry. Ugh. Sorry. I... was shot. I don't feel right. Need to lay down. Mind if I... a nap?" Rashid dropped back, his torso limp against Isaiah. "So glad I found you all." He huffed, then quieted, his breath coming heavy and deep, as if he were already asleep, silent except for the sticky whistle of his exhalations.

Isaiah touched his forehead. "He's clammy. Rashid, can you stay with us?"

He stirred but didn't speak.

She shook his shoulder softly. *"Please,"* she whispered, the words trembling on their way out. "What hurts? How do you feel?"

"I feel..." he answered, his hot breath coming heavy and slow. "I feel... with these." He held up his hand, fingers shaking, and pressed them against hers. Even this seemed to exhaust him, though, and he dropped it as soon as they touched.

Isaiah closed her eyes at the contact. She couldn't see two feet in front of her nose anyway. "At least you're in good spirits."

Jack rolled Rashid the rest of the way onto Isaiah's lap. "Can you help him?" he asked.

"I'll try," she shook him awake again. "Rashid, I'm going to examine you. Where are you hurt?"

He moaned. "They shot me. My shoulder, my leg. Careful." He lifted her hand and placed it on his right arm to guide her. She examined him carefully, her fingers delicate, tracing his body. His shirt quickly changed from soft and flexible to thick and stiff, evidence of drying blood. She inched closer to where the fabric was torn, and probed the area beneath it, light enough just to note the texture change and feel him recoil in pain.

"Sorry. I think I found it." The cloth was wet at the tear. He was still bleeding. "I need to bandage it, will you let me?"

"Kay."

Rashid stiffened as she shifted him, pulling the hem of her shirt out from beneath him. She slid her shirt off, bit the seam of her sleeve and pulled until it gave and she could tear it away. Rashid's head, clammy and cool, eased against her bare belly. The temperatures of their two skins meshed, neutralizing the heat she knew she emitted. She felt him melt into her with his next breath, deep and relaxed until she tightened the cloth around his bicep, and he winced again.

"Sorry. One more. Which leg?"

"Here." Rashid directed her hand toward his thigh. "It seems they wanted me neutered."

She reached to find the tear in his pants, which was close to his groin. "I see. Well, let's be glad they missed, then."

This time when she touched him, he didn't recoil in pain, but instead flinched. The nerve that managed sensation where the bullet hit was the same nerve that controlled sensation for his entire groin. It could have sent an unexpected pulse to his other thigh. His muscles twitched, flexing his legs and belly forward and together.

"Wow, oh... sorry," he said softly.

Isaiah's cheeks warmed, embarrassed for him. "Don't be. It's perfectly natural. Kind of cool, really. You want me to do it again?"

"Sure. No! No... but am I fixable?"

Isaiah traced to the back of his leg, and found the exit wound, then ran the length of his leg to his feet. The bullet had missed his femoral artery, and the vessels, in general, weren't injured, at least to no measurable degree, as his pulses were fine and his feet were warm. This wound was barely bleeding.

"I'm not sure," she replied, "but for now, this is what we can do." She tied the other sleeve around his leg, then slid her shirt back on. "Okay, you can sleep. Just stay here, I'll watch over you."

Rashid rested his head back against Isaiah. She flattened her palm against his brow and left it there, heavy with the weight of worry. He was sick, and she could do nothing about it. Being a physician only came in handy when supplies and medications were available. In this case, with the only tangible tools being her body and the mud on the ground, her MD seemed rather worthless.

She realized the entire group could end up this way or worse. Were they to die? Was God even on their side right now? Maybe He didn't want them doing this after all. He had certainly not been shy in allowing her pain lately—testing, refining, whatever you wanted to call it—but had she lost favor with her Heavenly Father? Was this whole thing a big mistake? She had barely even prayed about this trip. She had just done what she always did— run toward what felt right. Though she had felt *so sure* of this from the start.

Isaiah stared into the dark, confused. She thought of Elise— surely, she had heard from Him too. *Hadn't she?*

Rashid slept for hours. When he finally stirred, Isaiah had almost drifted off with him, and had lain down, wrapping him in her arms so his wakening would alert her.

"Doctor."

She sat up.

Jack interjected, "Rash! Welcome back!" His voice was clearly worried. "Are you stronger now? Can you tell us where you were?"

"Out looking for bad guys," Rashid answered. "By the way, I did crush that. How about you?"

Jack choked back a laugh. "We've been planning this surprise party for you. You're late, you know."

"Such a good friend." Rashid pushed up in Isaiah's lap, then gasped and fell back. "What is this place?"

"A rebel prison," Adira said from across the room. "These men are soldiers, although I am not sure who they are with. They have no reason to want us, which makes me think they may not know what to do with us. We must have come close to their camp, and so they had to take us to avoid being found."

Mahir spoke up. "Yeah, we're stuck."

"Is that Mahir? Are you all here?"

"The one and only," Mahir replied, "though I'm feeling out of sorts without my liquor. The food is nasty, and the drink leaves a lot to be desired."

"I would be sure to write up a formal complaint on checkout." Rashid grunted as he shifted sideways. "Ouch!"

"What happened to you?" Isaiah asked.

"You mean other than being shot?" Rashid answered. "Before that, I was impaled by a giant tree while our cherished River River tried to drown me."

"Wow," Elise cut in. "Praise God you're alive!"

Rashid sighed. "Why is everyone so fixated on God these days? *I* made it. God had nothing to do with any of this."

"Well, whatever you want to call it, you should be dead," Isaiah answered.

"Nah, not Rashid." Jack's voice trembled. "He's like a cat. You can't kill him."

"Don't you mean cockroach?" Mahir interrupted. "Cats, you can kill. Cockroaches can survive anything."

"I don't understand how you didn't die after the tree issue," Isaiah persisted.

"I met this man in the woods. He and his kids live in some

cabin out there. They took me in and nursed me back to health," Rashid answered. "But I don't know why, because then he decided to try to knock the light out of my head and leave me out there."

Jack chuckled. "So are you saying you still have light in your head, my friend?"

"Much like the phenomenon of the rare woman crushing on you, most of your western sayings don't make sense. If they did, I'd be much more fluent in them," Rashid answered. "But basically, I survived... sort of."

"Maybe he's getting help?" Elise said, her voice hopeful.

"I'm afraid not. He even called to these guys—as if he intended for them to take me. There will be no one he goes to for rescue. He wanted me here." Rashid took a deep breath. "At least I'm with sane people now. That man was not normal. It's a wonder he did not try to kill me in my sleep."

"Wow, man. Intense," Jack answered. "Glad you're here, anyway. Hopefully, the good doctors can get you feelin' better."

"Yes," Adira said. "At some point we need to plan our escape, and everyone needs to be as strong as possible for that."

"Escape?" Mahir asked. "But you said we couldn't, how?"

"Through the door," Adira replied. "It's the only way out, and it opens predictably."

"But who knows how many are waiting on the other side? And they have guns." Isaiah felt her nerves bundle up in her chest, a thick pressure pounding where her heart was supposed to be.

"Rashid knows. He just came from there."

"Yes," Rashid said. "This place is huge. Only a few people were out there when I came, but the setup is big enough for many more. There is a road outside, though. If our timing is good, we can escape."

Rashid told them what he remembered of the building, though it wasn't much. He had blacked out when one of the guards punched him and was already inside when he awoke. He said the exterior of the building appeared to be a utility shack, but inside it seemed a lot bigger. A row of dirt bikes was parked along one wall. In the back corner, a few tables were lined up in an otherwise large, open area surrounded by corkboard decorated with maps and pictures. The guards had carried him to what first appeared to be a janitor closet, but when the door opened, it revealed stairs plunging into the dark earth. The cellblock.

"This sounds promising," Adira said quietly.

"He had me at dirt bikes," Mahir quipped.

୬

The prison guards changed the routine after they added Rashid to the cell. They brought more water, soap, and bandages, and a handful of pills, which the doctors hoped were antibiotics and fever reducers, every twelve hours. Meat came, too; just one piece, but daily.

The group accepted the trays gratefully, and Isaiah and Elise did what they could to heal Rashid, who had lost much more than blood from the bullets. He became septic, his body inflamed at the new assault, burning and chilling without any pattern. His limbs swelled, and he trembled violently at times, often right out of consciousness. He spent hours a day sleeping, sometimes fitfully, sometimes not, and when awake, he often still lay close to sleep.

As the days progressed, his responsiveness trickled back in, until one day he became strong enough that the fog cleared from his countenance in the way an early-morning mist evaporates from over a lake, burning away abruptly the moment the sun's rays change from bright to hot.

It happened while Isaiah was replacing his bandages.

"Am I going to be as strapping as I was before, you think?"

Happy to hear his voice again, she laughed. "I have no idea. I may be bandaging your skin wide open for all I know."

With a gentle tug, she tied the cloth snugly around his leg. The truth was he was healing well, but Isaiah wasn't one to bestow hope until she was sure. The bullet had obviously hit a tendon, but to what degree it was torn, she couldn't know without an MRI, which clearly wasn't available here. He already had more strength in his leg, but depending on the amount of tendon still attached, any running or jumping could cause it to snap and leave him without a functioning leg permanently.

"Well, Doctor, I am grateful you are here."

She smiled. "Thank you."

XXXV

ANOTHER DAY, SEVERAL angels presented themselves before the Lord. Satan hoped this was an opportunity to renew his standing on high and so he also came with them.

God listened to all their concerns and, to each, spoke His reply. One angel, who was ordained to be among those who would gather God's chosen from the ends of the Earth, was requesting instruction on how and when he was to carry this out when God glanced up and saw the devil standing behind him.

The Lord stopped His discourse and spoke to him. "Where have you come from?"

The devil answered the Lord, "From roaming the Earth, going back and forth on it."

Then the Lord said to him, "Who are you, who tempts my children and hides among my Holy Assembly? Do you not know even now your plans are failing, and mine are taking hold? What of value have you to say to me? Should you not be out crawling on your belly among the thorns, eating dust?"

The devil raised his voice. "I was *chief* of your Holy Assembly! Why are you surprised to see me sneaking up in this way, when you have made my path more difficult than any of your creation? And so, even now, your great daughter Isaiah is preparing to fail you just as I have before. Look and see."

The Lord did not falter, saying, "No, your heart has deceived you. Still, she maintains her integrity, though you incited me against her to ruin her without any reason." The Lord narrowed His eyes at the other angels, signaling them to move away as the devil had many more things to say that might tempt them. He continued, "Have you considered my servant, Adira? There is none on Earth like him. Even before he takes on My heart, he is already blameless and upright, a man who fears God and shuns evil."

"Oh, but he does not!" the devil replied. "A man will give all he has for his own life. Surely, if you stretch out your hand and strike his own flesh, he will curse you to your face."

The Lord said to him, "Very well, he is in your hands. But you must spare his life."

"And what of Isaiah?" the devil asked.

God eyed the crowd of angels growing behind him. "You may carry on as you wish," he replied, "though she, too, must maintain her life, whatever you do."

Then Satan went out from the presence of the Lord.

XXXV

FOR THE SIX cellmates, the rhythm of their lives became their strength. The prison's noises—the leaking and flushing above, the squeaking, heavy drag of the door—blurred from expected to anticipated, the same as the sun's rise and set would have if they could see them, welcoming the expectation of morning and chasing away the afternoon lull.

One night, sometime after dinner was eaten and conversation had reached its end, Elise sat staring into the blackness around her. Her face was damp with the freshness of dried tears after a good cry. She had been praying again, as she had done repeatedly every day they had been imprisoned.

Lord, what are we doing here? She wrapped her arms tight around her legs, pulling her knees up high, and dipped her forehead forward to rest on them. She sat still, listening, but God had been more mysterious in His communication lately. Normally her prayers were answered—one way or another—quickly, and often boldly, but since they had been locked in the pit, she hadn't heard a thing. She knew He was with her because she still felt His presence when she was worried, but otherwise, He had been utterly silent. Maybe this whole thing was some type of strengthening lesson for her faith. Perhaps He wanted her to rest in what she already knew and charge forward despite any further reassurance. She knew she could be rather like a toddler toward Him—constantly tugging at His leg, asking questions and pleading for His attention. This could be His way of helping her grow up.

After another moment, when she had decided to move on, sighing the way she did when she ended her prayers—because devotion time was sweet and she enjoyed every bit of it, even when she left with the same questions—she heard Him. His words came assuredly and were so clear He could have been sitting beside her.

Humble yourself. Pray.

His voice came as a surprise. It rushed at her, washing over her near-parched spirit. She smiled; He had answered! But what did He mean, pray? She *was* praying, all the time. Did He want her to lead the others to pray too? Isaiah would do it, and maybe Jack, but Adira and Mahir, not so much.

She had never been good at sharing her beliefs with others, or even talking to others about them. The truth was, she wanted to. She loved Jesus with all her being, but to tell someone they were wrong and she was right on any topic other than medicine, where she had authority simply because of her training, was difficult for her. *Serve your people, Lord?* Yes! *Love you, Lord?* Yes! *Go to the darkest, most impoverished parts of the world and live equally impoverished to help those who need it?* Yes, yes, yes! *Stand up to a man of another culture and tell him he'd been fooled by the Great Deceiver? That* was outside of her comfort zone.

Plus, there was Isaiah and Rashid's pain to consider. Elise would never understand how those two felt, nor would she ever want to. But the problem was, if people in pain didn't turn to God for comfort, they tended to slink into a dark existence. And going in after them was tricky; should you say the wrong thing, they might retreat deeper and build walls to keep you out, suppressing further hope of emergence. But Elise knew if they realized they were not alone, that they had the God of the universe, the King, the Creator, *the Great Comforter* with them, their pain would be so much more bearable. She wanted this for these two. *Lord, give me your words*, she prayed silently.

A warmth approached on Elise's left.

"I've been thinking," Isaiah said, scooting next to her.

Elise smiled. Isaiah always referred to her prayer time as *thinking*. "Me too," she replied.

"What if we did like Paul and Silas?" Isaiah's voice was just above a whisper.

Her words caught Elise off guard. Obviously, God *did* want them all to pray together. Where else would this be coming from? Paul and Silas were two followers of Jesus who'd also been imprisoned, but while there they had prayed for rescue. God heard them and sent angels down to free them.

"They got prison walls to fall down," Isaiah persisted. "Maybe we could too?"

"You know, for all my service in the name of God," Elise murmured, glancing toward Isaiah's voice, "my faith is still small."

"Mine too, Elise," Isaiah said with a sigh. She waited a long moment before speaking again. "We clearly had enough faith to go on this trip, so we do have something there. We just need *more*. We need… enough to shake a few prison walls. How much can that be?"

Elise nodded. "Wouldn't that be something? Shake the foundations down like the great Paul?" Paul and his friend Silas's feet were even locked in stocks, but when the earthquake came, knocking the walls down to free them and everyone else from their cells, these too were broken open. Elise wanted to have faith like them—to believe something so fully that God granted her request just because He said He would. But she hated to step out on a limb; she was always so uncertain as to whether it would support her weight, much less bear fruit.

"So, we need faith," Isaiah said, as if reading Elise's mind. "Faith comes from hearing the Word, right? Well, then, that's what we ask for. We need to hear from God."

Isaiah was right. They didn't need to call these men and their faith out. She simply needed to gather with her sister in God's name. They only needed to invite God into the cell. He would introduce Himself. "Let's do it," Elise said.

She closed her eyes and prayed silently, thanking God for the answer to her question and inviting Him in. *Fulfill your promise, Lord! Come into this place!* Then, she introduced a new sound into the air.

"Bless the Loooord, oh my so-ul," she sang out, "and aaall that is within me, ble-ess Hi-is hoooolee-ey name!"

Her voice rose, carrying her apprehension with it, until it reverberated off the walls of the chamber and returned to her, striking her skin as if it were physical—like the waves of the tune had taken form and bounced off her.

She kept singing, loud enough to drown out any rustling feet or dripping water from beyond. *"Bless the Loooord, O my so-ul, and aaall that is within me, bless Hi-is ho-olyyy name!"*

Isaiah joined in after the first verse—softly at first, but with clear, loud words by the end of the next. Before the third verse had finished, Elise felt a new body approach. A hand squeezed her shoulder as it settled next to her. Jack. He hummed along with them, unfamiliar with the song, though by the end he had picked it up and was singing, his deep voice echoing in her ears. When the song ended, the three sat quietly. It seemed for a moment they were done, but then Isaiah's voice burst into the darkness.

"Come Thou fount of ev'ry blessing

Tune my heart to sing Thy grace

Streams of mercy never ceasing

Call for songs of loudest praise

Teach me some melodious sonnet

Sung by flaming tongues above

197

Praise the mount, I'm fixed upon it
Mount of Thy redeeming love!"

The melody filled the space around them, the words spilling from Isaiah without hesitation. The three sang loud and long, worshipping their Lord with the abandonment that comes easily once you have officially laid yourself out in front of others

"Here I raise my Ebenezer
Hither by Thy help I've come
And I hope by Thy good pleasure
Safely to arrive at home
Jesus sought me when a stranger
Wandering from the fold of God
He, to rescue me from danger
Interposed His precious blood!"

Elise felt toward Isaiah and grabbed her hand, squeezing tight. Reaching back, she found Jack's hand as well, then pushed the two together, clasping them between her own. She moved behind Jack, searching. When she found the arm of the next person, whom she knew was Adira in part because he recoiled at her touch, she grabbed his hand, too, and joined it to Jack's. She connected everyone in this way, dragging a stiffened Mahir and encouraging Rashid, who's palms were weak and wet with a now-rare cold sweat, until they were all in a circle, holding each other's hands. Though there came groans and irritated sounding huffs from the guides, Elise persisted, ignoring the boundaries she had previously been so careful to avoid.

When everyone was placed, she pushed herself between Isaiah and Rashid and sat down, voice ringing without falter.

"O that day when freed from sinning

I shall see Thy lovely face

Clothed then in the blood-washed linen

How I'll sing Thy wondrous grace!

Come, my Lord, no longer tarry

Take my ransomed soul away

Send Thine angels now to carry

Me to realms of endless day!

"O to grace how great a debtor

Daily I'm constrained to be

Let that goodness like a fetter

Bind my wandering heart to Thee.

Prone to wander, Lord, I feel it

Prone to leave the God I love

Here's my heart, oh take and seal it

Seal it for Thy courts above!"

Elise led the three Christians in song after song until nearly an hour later. The circle stayed intact—the others surprisingly compliant, perhaps partially out of shock and partially from curiosity. When the singing finally ended, Elise raised her eyes, stared into the dark, and prayed, pouring her heart out as if she finally saw God right in front of her. She spoke to Him like a friend and a Father between recognizing Him as her Lord and master. Isaiah and Jack prayed, too, loudly, shouting praise and requests into the cell until no more could be said.

Then, they sang again.

XXXVII

THE UNITED NATIONS' secretary-general was nervous. He had been preparing for the press conference that was to be aired not only nationwide but to neighboring countries as well. The speech itself didn't bother him—he addressed his nation on a regular basis, which was one reason his popularity was so high; he *talked to* his people. No, he was uneasy about Helel's satisfaction with what he was to say. He'd worked on the address for hours and believed it was in line with what had been requested of him, but recently the dragon had been more agitated than usual, and things that had previously pleased him seemed to make his mood worse.

Ms. Swartz stepped into his line of sight, her golden hair almost as bright as her eyes. She shone up at him like she were a puppy and he her beloved master. "Your Excellency, sir. We're ready for you."

People often got this way around Jubair; his presence electrified them. He grabbed his jacket at the cuffs and shrugged, shaking his arms loose in the sleeves, trying to release some tension. If he could influence people who barely knew him this easily, he could please a moody animal. Heck, in his youth he had hunted and eaten sand vipers and desert black snakes for fun. What was one more serpent?

Jubair sauntered out into the bright lights and flashing cameras surrounding the speech platform. Reaching for the podium, he broadened his face into his trademark, charismatic grin. The crowd purred in response. Then he raised his hand in a gentle wave, leaving it up to calm their excitement.

"Good afternoon. What an honor to be here today to share with you all my hopes and plans for our tomorrow. What a great, great honor. Thank you!"

The press erupted in applause. A few whoops escaped the mouths of the more enthusiastic reporters. Jubair feigned a bashful chuckle, dropped his head, and glanced up again, his dimples somehow deeper, eyes sparkling. He had them. This was too easy.

"The war has reached too deep, gone too far. We need to unify our country. We need to unify the world. And come together as one people—no, one *family*." He closed his lips and eyes, dipping his nose further for effect, and arms spread wide, gripped the podium until his knuckles whitened. "We must... for the sake of our future."

More applause, more cheering, right on target as he nodded along.

"But we all know this, don't we?" He didn't wait for them to quiet down. "We do, we all know it. The question we must explore is *why* haven't we been able to in the past? What has been our repeated failure? How can we join hands in this kinship?" He scanned the crowd, face serious, chin now lifted high. "To have a truly open mind, one must cast aside all their past experiences and prejudices. And we all have prejudices, even if we don't want to admit them. Don't we?"

Jubair surveyed the crowd. Murmurs rose with most everyone clapping in agreement. This was working out well. "We need to transform our thinking into open-mindedness, accepting all races and cultures. Stop dividing ourselves, *allow* ourselves to be as one. But how can we unify when so many want to tear us apart? When so many won't change, but instead would judge—the racists, the prejudiced. What if we extracted these—from our midst? Remove the toxicity!"

A voice broke through the applause. Elenore Bongol, a journalist for the magazine *Christian Today*, well known for its doomsday warnings and ads requesting money for millions of charity organizations, waved her hand from the crowd.

"Mr. Secretary-General, sir! A question." Her petite frame was all but swallowed up between two other big-bellied reporters. "How do you suggest we go about this?" she asked. "And follow-up question—what do we do once these people have been extracted?"

Jubair was perturbed. He had not finished his preparatory speech. He wanted to reel the crowd in further before answering these inevitable questions. Of course, it had to be a religious fanatic to interrupt.

He furrowed his brow in feigned concentration. "I suppose since they want separation anyway, we could certainly give it to them."

"Meaning what, sir?"

"Meaning we remove them from our greater society. Give them a land all their own but properly governed, of course, so they don't try to wage war on the rest of the world... again." He allowed his voice to drift, and lifted his hand, frowning at it like it had slapped him when he wasn't looking. He wiped a pretend tear from his eye and turned to regard the pesky woman again. "It seems we have all lost someone to this war, haven't we? If some want to fight, let them fight amongst themselves, away from those of us who are more interested in peace, coexistence, technological advancement, and the arts and sciences. Let us instead turn our focus to our future and to the good that can be!"

The crowd shouted approval, thrilled by the hope of his new prospect. Elenore scribbled in her notebook, struggling to keep the pen in her hand as the men jostled her, their arms in the air, clapping and hooting in praise. She raised her hand again.

"Sir, where..."

But her voice was too small, drowned out by hungry cheers.

The praise went on for several minutes, reignited every time Jubair smiled or waved a response. He had done it. He had edged his plan into political acceptance, with apparent full support of the masses. Even the conservative correspondents seemed lovestruck.

Peace was something only dreamt about for decades now. His determination had not only raised him up from his losses, but would be the thing to remove the atmosphere of fear and anguish that had befallen humanity and replace it with harmony and progress.

Jubair smiled genuinely. Perhaps Helel's idea wasn't a bad one after all. Even as he'd announced it, he was shocked by how reasonable and just it sounded. After all, he intended no violence; its purpose was for the betterment of civilization. How was this in any way different than sending criminals to a prison? It wasn't. Except, instead of prison, they would enjoy their own type of freedom, in a society allowed to flourish so long as they did not bother the rest of the world. No, the idea wasn't bad, but *good*. Today, despite his parading and staged virtue, *he* was good. And that felt... acceptable.

From the outskirts of the assembly, an object streamed through the air. Too small to be spotted, too fast to be averted. The Glock that fired the 40-caliber hollow-point aimed at Jubair's chest let out its own clap, though not in celebration. It was no more noticed than the tiny journalist now leaving the gathering.

XXXVIII

ADIRA SAT ON his knees, listening to the others from his corner of peace and reason. They were praying again. He felt decades older than he was, mostly because he was so often surrounded by adults who acted like children, and today was no exception. He certainly didn't despise them, nor did he feel sorry for them. Their foolishness simply exhausted him. So many people were easily distracted by senseless things. Some could enjoy the pleasant distractions, though many more were plagued by more damaging ones. For his part, he had been privy to both and could spot those who only had only been exposed to the former. If religious, they were often zealots; if not, they were big spenders. But most were loud-mouthed and felt the need to improve or pity others, usually without fully examining their station. This group was clearly filled with this very type of people.

Adira focused on Allah. It should have been easier, existing with nothing to distract him besides a small group of simpleminded Americans, but he found it difficult to tune out their ramblings. He curled forward in the sajdah position, his forehead dropped face-first to the ground between his shoulders, arms relaxed at his side, knees, palms, and toes down and whispered, "*Subhana Rabbiyal A'la,*"—Glory to my Lord the Great—reciting his *Salaat al-Asr,* for he assumed it to be late afternoon and time for his third prayer of the day.

Rocking back onto his heels, Adira moved into the next phase of his prayer. "*Allahumma*"—he began, and went into the memorized verses asking for protection, mercy, guidance, and sustenance. He finished his prayers after repeating the motions several more times, then prayed for exaltation on Muhammad and his followers, as per usual.

Adira was ashamed of his *salaah*; he had done his ritual cleansing with dust, as there was no water to cleanse himself more properly beforehand, but he wasn't even sure if he was facing Makkah when he prayed. He'd been in this situation before though, and he was not one to grieve Allah. So despite his situation, he prayed.

When he finished, Adira was surprised to feel the warmth of another body close by.

"Hey, brother."

Mahir. Another adolescent. Adira shifted his weight and sat with his back against the wall. "Brother."

"Do you think He's listening?" Mahir asked.

Adira cocked his head, his exasperated expression invisible in the dark. "Yes, He is." Mahir was unbelievable. Did he not remember any of what they were taught growing up? Had his brother no respect, even here, in this place, with no one to call on but God?

"We are created to worship him," Adira added. "Why would he not hear us? Do you think being underground hides us from him?" *Of course, you do*, Adira thought. This was the man who had been drunk more days than not for all the years he'd known him since their reunification. Mahir would have been dead, save for *his* sacrifice and God's favor. This was exactly what Adira was weary of—this childish, self-centered existence people lived in, oblivious to everything going on around them. Oblivious to God. Oblivious to him.

The two sat silently for a few minutes until Mahir spoke again. "Interesting, being trapped here with this lot."

"It is," Adira answered softly.

"So what *was* that, the other day?" Mahir asked. "Did you… Did you *feel* anything?"

Adira sat quietly, pondering an answer. He, too, had wondered what to do with the strange episode the women had caused. It had been odd, but he had been polite about it. Of course, had they tried to connect his hand with one of the women, he would have let go. But he'd always wondered what the Christians did during prayer, so he'd remained. In the end, it was just as haphazard as everything else they did.

"Well, no," he answered. "I didn't feel anything, save for the awkwardness of being put in a situation I could not escape. I suppose they have us as their captive audience here, though, don't they?" he answered.

"Yeah, they do," Mahir said. "You know, I've never thanked you. For saving me. I know my life isn't much to brag about, but I'm glad you gave me a shot at it."

Adira blinked and turned to Mahir. "This was my duty. You are my younger brother."

"You didn't have to," Mahir persisted. "I felt bad. I felt like we abandoned you. I should have gone back for you."

"You would have been captured… or killed. I am glad you didn't."

"Still, I should've tried. I was just so shook up." Mahir's voice trembled.

Adira sighed. "No, you should not have. The life I led after we were separated should not be one two brothers share. Al-Hamdu lillāh I survived."

He thought of his brother and the sloppy mess he had become in his absence. He was, before and after, too weak for the life of a combatant. Most assuredly, his soul would have succumbed to the thrill of murder, and the result on Mahir would have been irreversibly destructive.

206

"I just want you to know—in case." Mahir's voice cracked. "Thank you."

❧

In the days following, when the noises were active, the Christians prayed, and Rashid and Mahir sat with them, meditating, filling the cell with their hope. They prayed to stay awake and for courage. They prayed for rescue and blessing. They prayed to maintain sanity. Adira prayed as well, five times every day in the corner, reciting his salaah, passionately at first, as a type of rebellion to the Christians. But his brother seemed to enjoy the time with them, and as Christian prayer was better than Mahir's previous choice in stress relievers, eventually Adira decided to encourage him. And so, he joined Mahir in the prayer group sometimes, quiet but present. Over time, Adira softened, and sometimes he even sang along. On the days they all sang together—Atheist, Christian, and Muslim—songs directed to God the Father, the Most High, the room filled with energy and the air became almost electric, the power of their voices was so strong.

Then one day the door opened, and the light lingered without depositing a tray. They waited, their apprehension palpable.

"Who do you work for?" a voice behind the light demanded.

Everyone was silent, as if shocked at the sudden acknowledgement. Adira felt Mahir jostle beside him, then nudge his flank. He sighed, clearing his throat.

"My brother and I work for ourselves. We run a tour business out of Tbilisi. We were guiding this group of foreigners through the area when you found us."

The door closed, leaving them stunned.

"Well," Jack declared, "I'd say that was a step in the right direction. Rashid, they seem to like you. You come, and now we get meat and clean water to clean our nastiness again, and then they speak to us. Where have you been all our lives?"

"Right here, my sergeant. Taking it as it comes."

"This is just the start," Adira interrupted. "Next come inter-rogations. Or they will dispose of us."

"Dispose of us?" Jack asked.

"Yeah. Doesn't sound good, bro," Mahir answered. "I think I prefer Option A."

"I agree," Adira answered. "We had better work out our escape plan. Before they choose Option B."

XXXIX

THE NEXT DAY, the door opened again. This time, three figures entered and grabbed Adira. They shoved a gag in his mouth and dragged him out by his arms, while blinding the others with flashlights in their eyes. As fast as it had been opened, the door banged shut.

"No!" Mahir called from the other side of the door. The thumping of fists pounding against the clay walls resonated into the hall. "Give me back my brother!"

Adira hesitated at the ruckus his brother made, imagining the desperation he must be feeling. But then he opened his eyes and the blazing light outside the cell refocused him. He slammed them shut again and squinted, peeking at a now-hazy world, waiting for his vision to readjust. The captors shoved him forward, down a blurry hall, and then upwards, over something rock-hard, but apparently jagged... *stairs?*

"Blaindi!" one of them shouted, tugging Adira's shoulders back before opening the door. The second one cussed under his breath, then wrapped a cloth around Adira's eyes, tying it tight against his skull. The familiar darkness soothed him as they bustled him forward again, through a creaky door that announced itself as they opened it. After more hurried steps, they slowed and pushed him backward onto a smooth, metal seat that rocked beneath him as he landed. A folding chair. The soldiers bound him tightly to it, crushing the stale fabric of his pants into his ankles. Finally, they removed his blindfold. He chuckled silently at their sloppiness; had he not needed first to get acclimated, he could have easily overtaken them.

Sucking in a deep breath, he strained against the tight ropes and evaluated his new surroundings. The air was thicker up here, fall was descending from summer's peak of humidity. It was fresh, too, cool and smelled of water mixed with metal or clay... were they still underground? The room he sat in was lined with either plaster or cement, he couldn't tell which. Rippled and gouged, the walls held no semblance of the makings of a sophisticated structure.

Three men accompanied him—the two feebles who'd secured him and another who watched, reclined behind a metal desk in the corner. This one's skin was rough and deeply tanned. All three wore black caps, but the man in the chair's was more weathered and pinched down low over his forehead. His expression was intense, deep lines jutted between grim eyes and around a pursed mouth. Adira tried to discern if the lines were temporary—from anger or impatience or both—or permanent residents of his face from years of squinting in the sun. He heard voices in the background and banging, even the crack of gunfire from somewhere beyond the dingy walls.

"Are you two done quite yet?" the man behind the desk said, his accent clearly American.

The others stopped and snapped to attention, facing him. "Yes, sir!" they bellowed, their accents definitely not American.

"Well, let's see." The grit-faced man stood, puffing air from his barrel chest. He swayed stiffly when he walked, side to side with each step, as if his hips ached, then stopped in front of Adira. Despite his gait, he was a solid man. He would not be easy to bring down should the need arise.

He bent forward and wrapped his beefy hands around the rope tying Adira to the chair. He jerked it up, whipping the chair and

210

Adira off the ground. Using only his wrists as a pendulum, he shook him. The rope slipped as Adira wagged back and forth, and he dropped decidedly a few inches as it gained slack. The man puffed again and cocked his head to the side to eye the soldiers. "This is shit," he said and tossed the chair aside. Adira slammed onto the cement floor, hip first. "I give you one job. There's *two* of you. Two of you together can't figure this out? Boy scouts could do better!"

They eyed each other, clearly embarrassed, then pitched forward, on point to try again when given permission.

"Boy scouts. You know? BOY... SCOUTS? Little children, camping and eating marshmallows in the woods. Weak. Little. Boys." He eyed them, somehow furrowing the creases in his face deeper. "Go on, then. Do it again," he said, sitting down with a huff as he leaned back in his chair. "Do it right!"

It took the men three more attempts before the rope held when tested. Every time, Adira was thrown to the ground, so by the end of their lesson in knots he'd gained a few of his own, scattered over his head and knees. When he was lifted for the fourth time, his head hung to his chest. This time when the brute wagged his wrist, the rope held and Adira relaxed, relieved. When the man dropped the chair on its legs, Adira flinched again, but also shot half a grin toward the two apparent recruits.

"Now git," the leader growled. "I'm going to do some interrogation, and you two are going to do some shoveling." He nodded toward the metal door.

When they left, the burly man cut the ropes with a giant switchblade hiding in his back pocket, making sure to hesitate before and after each slash, holding the knife an inch from Adira's cheek each time. When he was almost done, he dipped its tip forward, pressing it through Adira's flesh, puncturing his cheek slowly, then dragged it down just enough to produce a slow stream of blood. Adira caught his breath at the stabbing pain, careful not to move his face for fear of a deeper gash. After

211

a pause, the man grabbed Adira's arm and lifted him, swinging him off the seat and onto the floor once again.

"Tell me, what were you doing on our land?" he finally asked, towering over Adira as he crept onto his hands and knees.

More for effect than from pain, Adira flinched dramatically and looked up. "My brother and I are tour guides. We were leading a science expedition." He dropped his shoulders and craned his neck, peering up from beneath his brow, lip curled in defiance. "Is this not public land? We have as much right to pass through as you."

The big man waddled over, each step resonating against the tiny room's walls. He grabbed Adira by his shirt back and dragged him to the table, smashing his torso against its surface.

"I know you're not hurt. I can change that if you don't start talking," he said, his face wearing a question Adira wished he had the answer to. "Who are you with?"

"No one. Not anymore," Adira gasped. "I work for myself. I am a business owner. My brother and I try to live our days in peace."

"Fine then. Who *were* you with?" He grabbed Adira's sleeve with his free hand and slid it up, revealing a circular brand on the soft flesh under his forearm. "Or was this just a spring break stunt?"

Spring break? Adira ruminated. *These Americans and their wasted lives.* He thought of the obnoxious college-aged kids who spent a week or two in town every March, loud and high on themselves. Sometimes they made fun of him, mocking the *taqiyah* he wore atop his head when walking to prayer. They came in the winter, too, to ski the local mountains. Usually, they were busy getting drunk and calling out obscenities, trying to make a whore of any woman who would let them.

"I used to be a Free Radical soldier. But not now," Adira answered. "I have no issue with you or your men."

The man relaxed his grip and stepped away, allowing Adira the chance to fill his lungs.

"What shall I do to convince you?" Adira asked, genuinely gasping. "We just want to continue on our way. We do not wish to interrupt your work. Let us go, and you will never see us or evidence of our existence again." He stood tall, pushing his shoulders back and narrowing his eyes. "Please."

The giant took his hat off, revealing a middle-aged wisp of gray hair covering an otherwise balding head. He wiped his brow with the back of his rough hands. "Stay," the man said and left, locking the steel door with a loud clunk behind him.

He returned shortly with another soldier, a woman, who bore his same flat countenance but donned a black headdress and crisper uniform. Adira immediately recognized her. Her squinty eyes were unmistakable; he'd watched them for hours while playing *Bes Tas*—Five Stones—in their youth. He remembered them sparkling back then, full of joy and adventure. He also remembered them later, flooded with tears when the two were rounded up like cattle after their innocence had been murdered, and later still, closed gracefully in prayer when their captors were not looking. But mostly, he remembered them as they were the last time he had seen her: wide in determination and terror as she gripped a steering wheel, ready to drive their fellow villagers to safety.

Manal's eyes ignited, though only for a second, from behind her stony expression.

"This man bears the same brand as you. Do you recognize him?"

"Sir, no, sir!" she lied.

"He says he used to be a soldier. Do you think we can... repurpose him as one for us?"

Manal eyed Adira and curled her lips inward, biting down subtly. "Yes, sir! Better to kill him though, less trouble."

"Very well, thank you, soldier. You can return to your duties."

Her narrow eyes closed delicately as she nodded her response before leaving.

The man turned to Adira. "Well, you heard the woman. You are trouble, whatever you say. We're gonna have to dispose of you and your friends."

Adira filled his chest and squared his eyes at the man. "Inshallah, you will see you are wrong."

"Look, son, between you and me, I'm not one to kill civilians. But we both know there is more to you and your story than you are letting on." He shuffled to his desk, gripping the revolver anchored to his waist.

"Interesting weapon choice," Adira said, still thinking of Manal's lips.

The man lifted an eyebrow. "Do you like it? I find it more... amusing to have the challenge of only six shots when in combat."

"I am not fond of guns. I find they lead to death."

Adira had seen this man's kind years before in the recruits that had flocked from all corners of the world to join the jihad crusade. He was the type who left a safe, rich country like the United States just for the sport of murder. Adira had killed them, along with his Muslim brothers, when necessary. His fight had not been with Islam at the time, but executions were inevitable for a soldier. Kill or be killed was the rule. After escaping the regime, he mourned their souls, all but those of men like this, who needed to be exterminated.

"Yes, there is that." The man broke Adira's concentration. "Well, anyway, I've got things to do." He stepped to the door and beckoned to the two green soldiers. "Take him back. I have what I need."

Adira hit the cell floor with a grunt. Mahir shot to his side, grabbing Adira's shoulder, which made him flinch as his touch came just as the door slammed shut.

"What happened? Did you see a way out?"

Adira sat up. "I did." His grinned. "I'm not sure what exactly is going on in this place. It is some kind of secret military."

"There seem to be a few of those around here," Rashid said.

"What?"

"The men who shot me were from another militia. I completely forgot to tell you about the hidden compound. Or at least, that's what it looked like—the man from the cabin in the woods was showing me a camouflaged military base when I was shot."

"Dude, what?" Jack cut in. "When were you going to tell us? That's, like, a major twist on the whole 'lost in the woods' thing."

Rashid hesitated. "It hadn't even crossed my mind. These people out here are all crazy. I'm crazy for coming on this trip. What importance is it that some men are out playing G. I. Joseph in the forest?"

"Hold up," Mahir interrupted. "Knowing about a second militia hiding in the forest would have been good to know. Like for my brother, just now, during his interrogation!"

Rashid coughed nervously. "I… I'm sorry, really. I just forgot."

"Guys, I think Rashid has had a little to deal with lately. Can you cut him a break?" Isaiah chimed in. "Unless any of you know what it is like to lose your family and then almost your own life?"

"Well, yeah," Mahir snapped. "I'd say a few of us *do*. But those of us who do are trying to get out of here, while this jack has been sitting here for weeks with potentially helpful information!"

"Mahir," Adira spoke up. "It does not matter. I have a plan."

"Um, no. It does matter. You should have known that. We all should know. These guys are clearly in a turf war out here. They probably think we're with their enemy!"

"I know," Adira replied, "but the idiot who questioned me would not have believed anything I said even if I had known. Our way out will be escape. It's our only chance."

Jack interrupted. "Hey, Rash, it's okay. We know you have a lot going on. You obviously didn't do it on purpose."

"Whatever." Mahir's eye roll was evident in his words. "Death is life. Life is death. He needs to get over it."

"Listen," Adira whispered, his voice raspy. "Keep it down. I have good news."

Excitedly, he shared with them about his discovery, careful to keep his voice low.

"Who is it?" Mahir asked.

"Manal."

"What? *Manal?*" Mahir half gasped. "The chick you crushed on growing up? She's *here?*"

"She is," Adira answered.

"Wow. Interesting career choice." Mahir paused. "You'd think after…"

Adira cut him off. "Things happen to people sometimes. Not everything is a choice, brother."

"Can she help us?" Rashid asked.

Adira thought on Manal's lips, pressing together in the symbol of Kathre, in the same breath as recommending his execution. He was glad no one could see his face as he answered, because it would give away his uncertainty. "Without a doubt."

XL

Manal

MANAL'S HEART POUNDED. When she had seen Adira, she pictured him falling away again from a swung-wide truck door, decisively sacrificing himself for her and the others. She was a frightened little girl all over again, sitting in the driver's seat, wary of punching the gas and leaving her friend but petrified not to. It had been her responsibility to accept his gift for the passengers in the back. She had done it in the end, just as he'd wanted. Her tears had streamed for hours, fast and long, with the spinning of the tires across the Turkey desert beneath her.

And here he was again, now her captive! She needed to help him, but Bear was not likely to play along. The battle between them and the gov's was all that was on his mind these days, and his paranoia level was soaring. He wouldn't let Adira go—no way—no matter what she said.

"Lieutenant."

The beat, beat, beating in her chest paused. She turned to meet her visitor. The sergeant. "Sir."

Bear's eyes were narrowed. "Tell me what you know about our new prisoner."

She nodded, swallowing hard. "Well, sir, I do not know him specifically. It is the old unit I know enough about."

"Yes, I heard you were a member of FREA. What is their... retirement procedure?" Bear paused over the word retirement, as if the idea of it were a fairy tale.

"Sorry, sir, I was not involved with FREA. I was a captive of Islamic State and not around long enough to by privy to those details."

"Oh?" Bear raised an eyebrow. "How is it you came to leave, then?"

"Escape, sir. Few teenagers want to be a part of a murderous rampaging militia." She bit her lip as he blinked and sharpened his expression. She caught her breath, waiting for his rebuke. Why was she always blurting out her thoughts? In general, she was a reserved woman, but whenever an issue mattered to her deeply, her emotions always betrayed her.

"I see." Bear softened his gaze and looked away. "I need you to find out his story. If he's a spy, I'd like to use him. If not, I'm not sure we have much use for him and his friends."

"Friends, sir?"

"He's here with a group of five others. They were found on the edge of our grounds. He says they were on a hike. An expedition. But one of them was found close to the enemy's base."

Manal searched her thoughts. Could he still be working with FREA? She had believed him dead, so seeing him had given her hope again, but if this were true...

"Yes, sir, I will see what I can find out."

"Good. Report to me when you have some information. Tweedle-Dee and his twin will get you access to them." He huffed as he stood. "It wouldn't hurt if you taught those two idiots something while you were at it."

"Yes, sir, what would you like me to show them?"

"Anything, Lieutenant. Anything." He waddled away.

Manal found Boris and Andro at a table in the back of the

main hall, polishing the parts to their M16s. They weren't as dumb as Bear made them out to be, but they were edgy. Whenever the pressure was on, it was as if their training vanished and they were two raw shanks, approaching the orientation meeting years ago in General Elkara's home basement. Dozens of recruits were gleaned from that night, and since then, their forces were making a good impact on the Swiss base. When Manal had joined, her friends thought the whole thing was a cult in the making, based on paranoid conspiracy theory. But Manal knew better, even then. Switzerland had been planning something. She investigated and found the rumors discussed that night to be true. The supposedly peace-making country was building some type of military camp in Georgia, which was clearly not their land.

She remembered the stories of the battles between Russia and Georgia, when they were fighting over who was to govern South Ossetia and Abkhazia. She did not want history repeated. Manal had chosen to live here because Georgia was peaceful. The country was her shade in the desert, her planned refuge from the heat of the rest of the Middle East's fire. But if Switzerland was here, building a secret army and doing who-knew-what in giant buildings guarded by blokes with machine guns, her refuge was at stake. The way Manal saw it, the people of Georgia needed to take matters into their own hands now before the war came here too. If they could drive the camp's inhabitants away, they'd have a chance.

The problem was, some of the other soldiers seemed to be here for fun, the sergeant for one. Or at least he seemed to be. Manal suspected a tender heart under all the gruff and gunpowder, but so far, she'd only seen a few glimpses of it—so few, in fact, she had wondered if during those moments of tenderness, he was just tired.

"*Privet*," Manal said as she strode up to her comrades.

Andro whistled at her. "Not many women can wear a uniform like you, Manal."

He spoke to her in his Georgian tongue. By now she could decipher most words, though she could still barely speak it. Ignoring him, she said she needed to interview the prisoners. Andro nodded and slid the desk drawer open. Grabbing the keys, he stood and they escorted her away.

The door stuck a bit before creaking forward, heavy against Manal's palms. She peeked into the black room and beamed her flashlight on the prisoners, who looked like zombies from the movies she had seen in the city. Their clothes were dingy and tattered, and they cowered, arms raised, farther into the corner when the light hit them. Adira she found as one of two bodies huddled against the back wall. It was surely him; nothing could hide those broad shoulders. He sat next to another man with similar features but a leaner frame and hollowed cheeks. Mahir.

"You." She spoke sharply, staring straight at Adira.

Mahir flinched at her words, then half lunged her way like a dog that had been chained too long. But Adira squeezed his shoulder, and he relaxed back to the ground, drawing his face together in a threatening snarl pointed her way.

"Follow me." Manal turned stiffly, hands by her side, and whisked away.

❧

After they left, the door remained open, gently swaying, waving at the others teasingly. Rashid rose and inched forward to investigate, until Andro and Boris appeared, stepping from behind it and sending him reflexively back down. Andro met Rashid's eyes and gave a smirk, his fingers thrumming against his rifle which he held across his chest, while Boris entered and picked up the tin food tray and bucket that had been left behind from the last drop. Usually, this exchange was quick, completed before the sudden blindness from the light could wear off. But Boris took his time.

He stood tall, slowly eyeing the group while they watched silently in apprehension.

Rashid grinned sarcastically. "Goldilocks!" he called out. "So nice of you to visit. How *are* you doing? How's the family?"

The two men turned to each other and then back to the group, but said nothing. They stood there for several minutes, until Adira came clamoring down the hall, stumbling as if pushed. Andro pivoted sideways in the doorway, making room for him before returning to his prior stance. Adira fell on his knees next to Boris, and heaved, sucking in a breath with his eyes locked on the ground. Mahir rushed to his side, frantic.

"Adira!" He reached across his back protectively.

Laughing, the guards made their way through the doorway. In the last second before the light disappeared behind them, Adira glanced up and winked at Mahir.

The door locked, once again encasing them in darkness.

"What happened?" Elise asked. "Did they hurt you again?"

"No," Adira answered. His voice was clear, though it cracked just a bit as if he were trying to convince himself of his own words. "That was our friend. She will work out our escape." He shared the plan with them; they were to wait until Manal could take the vehicles out of commission, to give them a chance. Then, they'd run.

XLI

Mahir

LATER THAT NIGHT, Mahir slouched in the corner of the cell against the frigid cement. He found if he sat this way long enough, the wall would lose a bit of its chill and almost warm to body temperature. Should he move though, and shift his weight too much, then he'd meet a cold surface again and the process would need to be started all over. He could have slept warmly, huddled together with the others, as by now it was no longer awkward. But his brother stayed away from them at night, so, despite the cold, he chose to do the same.

The room was quiet except for the gentle sound of air being sucked in and out of his cellmates' mouths.

"Will you not sleep, brother?" Adira's words drifted lazily into Mahir's mind.

"Oh, hey. Yeah, I will eventually. It's hard without my nightcap."

"Still?" Adira said. "How unfortunate."

"Right? It sucks." Mahir turned toward his brother's scent. The whole place smelled like moldy dirt, but each of the team had their own distinct stench. The women smelled sweet and rich, like yeast and rusted iron. Jack reeked like a teen who hadn't discovered roll-on—all sweat and spoiled apples—and Rashid somehow smelled of olives. Adira's scent was bitter, too, but different from the others—harsher, like the grease from a gun. Mahir leaned closer to the wall, hoping the wet cement would purify the air from some of the stink.

"I'm not going back to drinking, you know. When we get out of here, I've got a plan."

"Do you? What plan is that?" Adira said, his voice skeptical.

"I'm going to invest in us," Mahir said. "I'm all in. Our business, our life. I'm going to make us a proper family, find a good girl to make babies with who will grow up and call you *Aam*."

"Sounds nice," Adira answered.

Mahir knew Adira had heard these words before, repeatedly even, over the years. At first, it seemed like he had believed him, hopeful for a better life for his brother. At some point, though, they had probably become just another spectacle, like the snide and self-centered outbursts that came with his drinking.

But this time was different. Mahir meant it this time. All the days he had spent meditating in the commotion of the Christians and their prayer had roused something desperate inside him. Before now, he had been empty. Ever since the day he'd left Adira on the dirt of the prison camp, he felt alone and worthless. Even when they reunited decades later, part of what he originally lost never returned, and he continued to live his hollow life. Existing simply because he existed, knowing at some point—just as simply—he would exist no more.

But the others, the born-again loons, had found peace by setting their minds on something good and high, out of reach even. He had decided he'd be born again too—into a new, passionate, *full* life. And today, sitting beside his brother, the one person who literally gave his life for him, he defined what that would mean. He had... hope.

"I want you to believe me, believe in me. You're all I got."

Mahir's voice was raw, desperate. "You're the most important person in my life."

"Well, brother, may it be easy for you. Either way, I am here."

"Thanks, bro. I know you are." Mahir leaned against the wall. "I hope I can be there for you, too, one day."

Adira's grin was almost audible. "My little brother is quite sentimental these days."

"I'm just saying," Mahir's voice leaped to a high-pitched tease, "I love you man!" He reached out, fingers wide, and pet his brothers face, then pushed him square in the chest and laughed.

"Aaand there he is," Adira answered.

XLII

THE NURSES WHISPERED outside the curtain about Jubair's approaching death. Too much blood loss, they said. Stroke took away his respiratory drive. Something about puss in his lungs from complications of the chest tube. Jubair listened to their secrets; he could do nothing else, anyway. The damned tube in his throat hurt—it felt like it was jabbing him at some unnatural angle, maybe trying to relocate things or tear his neck in half from the inside. If only they would adjust it or somehow get some water down there to relieve the dry burn overwhelming his entire body. But he couldn't tell them, he couldn't even indicate it to them because, for some reason, his eyes wouldn't open.

Jubair let his mind drift to distract himself from the pain. Unless these fools killed him with all their drugs and devices, he didn't believe he was going to die. He felt like he had drunk too much coffee and then been stuffed in a two-foot cube, crumpled up like a rubber-jointed contortionist from the circus. The last thing he remembered was the press conference. It seemed to have gone generally well, had it not been for the plucky, twit reporter asking questions she knew would get her in trouble.

He'd been shot, he knew, because he could still hear the loud crack from the gun's release. There had been satisfaction, annoyance, and then that noise. Then, he had woken here, in this bed, where his will had somehow been disconnected from his limbs, but pain and restlessness coursed through his everything.

The curtain slunk open, breaking his thoughts, and the slow thud of heavy footsteps approached. What sounded like rustling papers and the beep of a machine came from his right.

"He's been the same all week," a voice said. "I get a pupillary response and normal reflexes on neuro checks, but otherwise no cognitive change, even to aggressive sternal rub. It's like he doesn't feel anything." The airhead nurse, master of the torture chamber, was speaking again.

I'm fine, wake me up! Jubair thought. *She's full of nonsense!*

"Let's wean him off anesthesia and the vent support today, see what his lungs can do on their own," came the response.

Jubair felt the cube he was stuffed in grow another inch.

XLIII

A HEAVY CREAK woke Isaiah. It sounded like the door had opened, but the room maintained its black pitch. She lay still, eyes fixed on the emptiness above her. The blasted fear had returned, and for a moment she was numb. She tapped the sleeping body beside her.

"Pssst, wake up! Someone's here," she whispered harshly.

Elise stirred. "Hello?" she asked.

Jack groaned and stirred from beside them.

"Hey, heartthrob, you think you could manage to keep those biceps out of my face?" Rashid asked.

"Sorry, man," Jack answered in a groggy voice. "You know this isn't a gun-free zone, though, right?"

"Ugh, is that what you call those?" Rashid laughed.

"*Guys,*" Isaiah hissed. "*Shh!* The door opened."

Everyone fell silent. Except for the familiar dripping from above their heads, the air was still. Isaiah sat up, erect, unsure if they should get ready to run or cower.

"Up, now!" A woman's voice startled her.

The rays of a flashlight appeared, and cut through the cell, waving toward the open door. Their rescue had come.

"Let's go." the voice urged again.

Then they were all on their feet and following the beam out the door, through an unlit clammy corridor, and up a flight of stairs. The woman leading them shone the light on another door at its end, which was covered in chipped white paint with dirty brown and red smears at its center. Isaiah's stomach dropped as she realized what she was looking at. Some of the marks were linear, in the pattern of fingers. Someone had tried to claw their way out of here. She wondered how far they had gotten as their escort opened the door.

They surfaced one at a time, their hurried footsteps soft on the stone floor. It only took a few seconds for her eyes to adjust to the new surroundings. The place was not a storehouse after all, but a giant cave, with a ceiling too high to see and sharp stalactites dripping at its edges. Isaiah hung behind the others, trembling and afraid. She glanced around at the empty space. They had surfaced near a row of white doors lining a wall. A metal staircase ran up one side of the cave, leading to a wire platform in front of another row of doors, along the back and side walls. Where was the exit? She stood, waiting for guidance, praying whoever was behind the doors was asleep.

Isaiah watched as their rescuer darted across the open area fifty yards ahead. Adira trailed her, followed by Mahir and the others. Paralyzed by fear, she willed her now-heavy legs to follow and her breathing to quiet, but she was fixed in place, alone and far behind everyone else.

Something touched her shoulder. She jumped.

"It's me." Elise's hushed voice filled her ear. "It's okay."

Isaiah turned and seized her friend's forearm.

Elise laid a hand on top of hers. "We're going to get through this," she said calmly. "Come on, one step at a time."

Elise walked forward, pulling along a stiff, frightened Isaiah, still affixed to her arm. They moved with slow, heavy steps, Isaiah crouched forward into the darkness, flinching repeatedly, dodging imaginary bullets. The giant room shrank after they crossed it, then narrowed further until it became a rocky tunnel. By the time they made it out, Isaiah was covered in a cold sweat that rivalled Rashid's sickest moment.

They emerged into the dense forest, with nothing but trees and the black of night to greet them. Even the cave entrance seemed to have disappeared in the darkness.

Rashid scanned the area, confused.

"The road? The building? Where are they?" he whispered to Manal.

"About a kilometer and a half over there," she said, waving behind her. "We sometimes knock out our prisoners when we get that far and carry them in so they don't remember the path here. Security measures. You understand." She shrugged and tossed a backpack she'd been carrying to Adira. "Sorry, they'd already repurposed the rest of your bags. But I found your map, and I filled this one with a few more supplies. You have a blade, tons of matches, a handful of rags, iodine tabs, filtration water bottles, some food. A plastic sheet, one mat. Soap. Not much, but enough to get you through a few days, I think. We ready, then?"

Adira nodded, then motioned for the others to follow, just as Manal turned and disappeared into the dark. They picked their way through the brush, delicately at first, until they were far enough away that noise no longer mattered. Then they burst through the branches, carving out their escape in the wild moonlight. The cool breeze welcomed them, carrying the fresh scent of pine needles and the promise of coming snow. Ten minutes later, the forest broke open, revealing a one-lane dirt road, and they stopped, drunk from freedom and exercise-induced endorphins.

"Okay, what's our plan?" Elise asked, still holding Isaiah's hand. She sucked in air between her words. She turned anxiously to Adira.

"Well, it is up to you," he answered, huffing. "Are we returning home?" He caught Mahir's eye for a second before turning to Manal, who simply raised an eyebrow in turn. "We are officially back on the clock either way."

Elise scanned the group. Standing tall, she spoke matter-of-factly. "Well, I'd like to keep going. I understand if any of you want to turn back." Her glance sharpened, expectant, at Adira. "I'm assuming one of you will escort anyone who wants to leave?"

"I will," Mahir answered. He stepped forward, ignoring Adira's disapproving glance. "And," he added, "I'll get you back fast. I could really go for a shower."

Jack stared at Mahir for a moment, shrugged, and turned to Elise. "I'm game. Let's keep going."

Elise smiled at him and turned to Isaiah.

Isaiah grinned, trying to ignore the sensation of her still pounding heart. "You know I have nowhere else to be."

"Neither do I," said Rashid, stepping forward. As he did, he slipped his hand over Isaiah's free hand and squeezed, gently and just for an instant, then let go and patted her shoulder.

Mahir shook his head. "You've all lost your minds." He slumped, leaning hard against the trunk of a nearby tree, eyes closed. "Fine. I'll stick with you."

Adira sighed, exhausted. "Well, it appears we have a decision. And you"—he nodded at Elise— "are well into overtime pay." Turning to Manal, he asked, "Which way out of this mess? We need to get west. Our goal is to get to the river's mouth, and we would like to avoid any further combat zones."

"I can help get you back to the river, but then I need to get back," she answered, eying Mahir. "Follow me."

They headed back into the wood, leaving the road and all its promise behind. Isaiah watched it disappear over her shoulder, until the moonlight that had found its wet surface became just a flicker in the darkness. Turning forward again, she blinked the thought away.

XLIV

THE GROUP TRAVELED through the night, stopping for only a few minutes at a time to catch their breath and do a headcount. Despite the adrenaline pushing them onward, they were deconditioned at best. Everyone welcomed the breaks, even Adira, who had been distracted all night thinking on the dark beauty of Manal's eyes. She was the same as she had always been, though harder now in body and will. It suited her, though he wondered if she held to her Islamic roots. He doubted it. A woman who feared God was to be submissive and a good worker—which she clearly was—however, he could see that other than her headcover, she had abandoned proper adornment and modesty. He'd even caught a glimpse of her midriff at one point when they'd stopped for a drink. She, quite without reserve, lifted her shirt to wipe sweat from her brow. She was still his kindhearted, beautifully spirited friend, though. He planned to hike this way again someday, though next time by himself, to visit her. Perhaps he would wait and go in early spring, before the rush of tourists, or maybe before the winter ended yet this year. He could bring a peace offering to the sergeant, he thought. Fresh socks and wine could work. Or perhaps a fancy new revolver. He could do it. It would be worth the risk if it allowed him another chance to search for the bottom of those deep, dark eyes.

As he was thinking this, Manal suddenly stopped walking, then raised a hand and cocked her head, as if listening to the forest. To the right, he could make out what he assumed she was listening to—the soft rush of water crashing against and over resident rocks. They were back near the river's edge; it was time to leave her.

"Here, this is the end. You'll be safe from here." She spun around, so quick she almost collided into Adira's chest. He caught her arms to stop her from toppling forward. She hesitated and glanced up. Her face filled his vision, just two inches away. For an instant, they both froze, neither blinking nor breathing, fixed on each other. Then Manal gasped and stepped back.

"I'm sorry," Adira said. "I did not mean to be so close."

Her eyes met his before dropping to his mouth. "No, brother. I should be more careful." The darkness had waned enough he could make out her reddened cheeks as she forced her glance away. She raised her head, eyes drifting up again—slowly this time, as if to see if he was still watching her. He was.

"Do not be sorry. You have been our rescue."

"There was a day you were mine," she said, straightening. Biting her lips together in their symbol of Kathre, she hesitated, then reached forward and softly touched his cheek. "But, Inshallah, just one more look. I want to see you this way, when... My memories, they have been nightmares. I want dreams again."

Mahir strode up, face brightening. "Well, I see nothing has changed," he taunted, eying them both. "Can't say I didn't see *that* coming."

Adira winced and stepped back, suddenly rigid. "Yes, well... Manal, thank you for your assistance. Stay safe. Salaam alaikum."

Manal hovered a few more seconds before answering. "I should go, before they notice I'm gone. Don't come this way on your return. I'm not sure they'll be so lenient next time." She turned and picked her way through the brush quietly, without looking back. "Thank you. Alaikum salaam."

Adira watched her go. He cleared his throat after she was out of sight. Then he turned and hiked away as if nothing had happened.

XLV

MAHIR HAD BEEN silent most of the day, absorbed in the clear mind that came with sober hiking. He was invigorated despite the exercise, or maybe because of it. The mountains never smelled as fresh as they did today. Perhaps it was because of his new freedom—not just from prison but also from the influence of booze. His senses had been blunted for far too long.

He was reveling in his new ability to pick out the sounds of the birds amidst the wind whistling through the leaves when Rashid trotted up to him.

"So how did your brother know Manal?" Rashid asked.

"Oh, we grew up in the same village," he answered absently. "In Turkey—a town named Kathre. You heard of it? It's small, near the mountains."

"No, never," Rashid answered. "Sounds nice though. Safe, I bet. Out of the way of war."

Mahir snorted. "Nice, yes. But safe? Away from the war? I think not."

"Oh? I'm sorry. Has it affected you, too?"

"Well, that depends. Do you count ISIL coming up on us and slaughtering all the adults—or should I say, making *us,* their children, slaughter them—as affecting us? Cuz if you do, then yeah."

"Wow," Rashid said, clearly shocked. "I had no idea. So sorry."

Mahir shrugged. "People don't know. We were young."

"I'm glad you two got away. I heard they made combatants of their captives. Especially the children." Rashid paused thoughtfully, shifting his eyes away. "War can be hard on children. Perhaps harder on some than others."

Mahir huffed, irritated at Rashid's ignorance. "We didn't. Well, not from the jump. They kidnapped us and put us in a training camp. It was brutal. But most of us escaped before they made us... official." He thought it strange he was so open about this now after keeping the story in for years. Even when drunk, he hadn't told a soul. And now here he was, exposing to this dude from Egypt, whom he barely knew, the darkest secret of his life. Mahir continued, "I can't think what being in the army would've been like. They were monsters."

"Hopefully now things will be better."

"Yeah, I doubt it. Adira knows. He doesn't think it's over. Simmering maybe, but it'll start again if he says so."

"How does he know?"

"He couldn't get out with us. They made him a soldier... for, like, twenty-five years. He was there for the whole FREA transition and everything." Mahir wiped his brow; the talking was wearing him out. He glanced back at Rashid, who was suddenly still, staring blankly ahead. Mahir winced, cursing his big mouth. "Dude, he tried to get out," he explained. "He did. But when we escaped, he was caught. He *had* to work with them. The game is you cooperate, or you die. He just played the game—that's not who he is."

Rashid shook his head, then straightened, eyes set on Mahir.

"So you're saying your brother was a member of the parent group, the *founding group* of the ones who attacked... my home? That destroyed my world?"

"Well, yeah, but not on purpose," Mahir answered, worry mounting. "And he didn't atta—"

"And now we're following him through the middle of nowhere?"

Mahir watched as Rashid craned his neck, processing Adira's connection to the war. In a way, he was right; it was possible that had Adira not been there, both of their families may still have been alive. Glaring ahead, Rashid heaved a jagged, drawn-out breath and rolled his fingers into tight fists at his sides.

By then, the others had almost disappeared into the trees. Mahir called halfheartedly to them, though he wasn't sure if it was for help or as a warning. They stopped one at a time—like a slow-moving scene in a horror movie right before the worst of it hits—pivoting sluggishly toward the two of them, naïve and blank-faced.

"I'm serious, dude," Mahir said, shifting weight. "He's not like that. He had to."

Adira was the last to turn, grumbling in annoyance when he did. Rashid met his eyes and squinted, his body now trembling.

"Oh! Are *you* now irritated with *me*?" he growled. "You... animal!"

"Rash, what's wrong?" Jack asked. He followed his friend's gaze to Adira and back. "You need a rest?"

Then Rashid was in the air. Mahir jumped forward, trying to stop him, but Rashid tore right through him and plowed into Adira, knocking him off his feet into a wild rose bush three feet away. Adira was tangled in the branches, face up, when Rashid attacked again, this time with his feet. He kicked Adira's hips, rolling him face-first into the thorns, then lifted his knee and stomped, hard, on his back. Adira grunted as he crashed through the branches farther, deeper into the unforgiving thorns. Rashid's foot came down over and over, until Adira regained himself enough to grab it, two-handed, and shove Rashid back, twisting his ankle as he did.

"*Rash!*" Jack hollered from his side. "Get ahold of yourself!

What are you doing?" He reached for Rashid's shoulders in a futile attempt to stop him.

But Rashid seemed not to have heard him with his empty face and dark eyes fixed on Adira. He roared, desperate and loud as a jet engine, and kicked away Adira's hand, then blasted forward again.

"Help me!" Mahir yelled at Jack, trying to wedge himself between Rashid and a scrambling Adira. Somehow Rashid made it past him again, and then Mahir was on his back, impotent in the bushes too, watching even closer as Rashid unloaded on his brother.

"You!" Rashid bellowed, fists flying wildly. "You killed my family!"

❧

Adira realized at Rashid's words what had happened. He recoiled and leaned back, shielding his face with his forearms but leaving the rest of himself open to attack. Somewhere off to his side he heard Mahir, at it again, sloppily trying to save him. Adira managed his gaze sideways and stared at him, shaking his head—*no, I have this*—then groaned as another blow landed on his ribcage.

Adira had, years before, prayed for his own death. He knew he didn't deserve to live. The things he had done in the militia were unforgiveable, even though he had been forced into them. Sacrificing others for your own safety was a special form of selfishness, and he'd known as much, even as a boy. He tried to justify it to himself sometimes, reasoning he had saved so many from his town, and therefore hundreds or even thousands more as they therefore never became soldiers themselves. But always he had sorrow, always he knew his actions were unjustifiable. There on that forest floor, in that exhausted moment, as another man's grief materialized onto him, Adira decided to let justice finally take him. He grunted and moaned with each blow that made it through the other's attempts at restraining Rashid—*Mahir never listened*—but he lay still, purposely, flaccid against Rashid's anger.

"Stop!"

Tears flooded Rashid's eyes, but his fists still found Adira's bulk, easily and repeatedly.

Jack and Mahir finally got a hold of Rashid's arms and yanked him off Adira, then shoved him against a nearby tree. He strained against them, still thrashing; the last year's pain clearly blazing out against whatever flesh he could find.

"I am sorry," Adira breathed. "I am. So. Sorry." He locked eyes with Rashid and let his head sink back into the bush.

"For what? It wasn't you!" Mahir blurted out. "Y'all... you don't know anything about what it was like."

Rashid didn't answer. Rage and the promise of revenge shot from his sweltering eyes at Adira. His nostrils flared and his chest heaved, pulsing in rhythm with his breathing, the undulation of hate and breath. After a long moment, he relaxed against the lock the others held him with, exhaling as he did, and turned away.

Adira remained near frozen, watching.

"I think this is a fine place to camp for the night," Elise said finally, and plopped down, pulling Isaiah with her.

"Okay, yes. I agree," Isaiah replied, giving her friend a puzzled look. "We need to help Adira," she whispered harsh enough for everyone to hear.

Elise wrapped her hand around Isaiah's arm and shook her head. "Wait," she whispered back.

XLVI

ANOTHER HOUR PASSED before the tension left Rashid's muscles, and Isaiah felt Elise loosen her hold on her arm. She glanced at Elise, then stretched, scanning the group. Jack and Mahir had stayed by Rashid's side the whole time. Adira had already climbed out of the bush, slowly, his eyes downcast, and crept to a tree a few yards away. He now sat with his back against it and the others, facing the forest.

"Well," Mahir said, breaking the silence, "now that *that* is out of the way, I suppose we can get back to what we're doing." Keeping one eye on Rashid, Mahir reached into the backpack and pulled out a water-filtration canister, announcing he'd skim a drink from the river.

As soon as he left, Isaiah rose to assess Adira's injuries.

"No, don't," Elise said, grabbing her arm again. "We still need to be careful. I've seen the look on Rashid's face before."

"What?" Isaiah cocked her head toward Elise "When?"

"At our tent clinics. When the soldiers came in from the border towns for care, it's the same as how the refugees would look at them." Elise nodded at Rashid, as if it proved her point. "All their fear—and hate, really—was only held back by a thread. We had to have extra security on those days. Because sometimes they snapped." Elise released Isaiah's arm and inched away. "Go to Rashid," she whispered, "You're better at calming others than I am. I'll take care of Adira while you distract him."

"Hmmn." Isaiah pinched her lips together and leaned forward. Elise was right. She was good at helping people with aching hearts, mostly because she understood the pain so well. Her office had always been well stocked with Kleenex, and for good reason—patients frequently broke down during their appointments. Often, a person would be sitting in an exam room, discussing with her their tingling toes or burning stomach, and she'd recognize it—a catch in their voice, the quick dart of their eyes when mentioning a painful name or place or life event. She'd tease out their hidden burdens and help them identify issues that needed dealing with, knowing good physical health could only come when the mind and spirit were also strong.

She slid down the tree Rashid leaned against, close enough to intentionally bump shoulders with him on her way down. "That was intense," she said, staring into the forest. "Unexpected."

"Yeah, well, I guess this God of yours wants to keep throwing things at me." He sighed. "It seems everyone has some connection to this war."

"Seems so," she answered. After a long moment, she continued. "Rash, do you believe we're here for a reason? Like, there is a purpose to everything going on?"

Rashid's face was a stone, the wrinkles between his eyes and across his forehead fixed in place, as if this were his permanent expression. But Isaiah watched him twitch as her words hit him, their directness a blunt chisel. He turned to her. Seeing the pain in his eyes, she winced. Yes, she understood him. Isaiah possessed the same pain, in all the same places.

She thought of her family again, reimagining their last moments. Two years had passed, and her absence at their final hour still haunted her. Catching her breath, she stopped herself before she sank back into the familiar despair. Rashid had to be her focus now, not herself. Otherwise, she too would harden.

Then they might both freeze here in this way—two people, hearts full of granite, coursing its way through their bodies until it solidified them into permanent statues at the base of a tree in the middle of nowhere.

"What?" Rashid asked, breaking Isaiah's thoughts. "No... maybe. It feels almost like a game. Maybe the gods want to see how much pain they can put on one man before he cracks. But I can't take any more."

Isaiah fumbled her fingers on top of her knees; they shook already. Tears welled behind her eyes, and she shoved her tongue hard against the roof of her mouth to stop herself from breaking down. *Not now*, she thought frantically. *Why now? Lord, give me strength to help this man!* The heaviness had broken free from her heart and was spreading to every part of her. She didn't trust her tongue to work without her words being replaced by sobs, but Rashid needed comfort, so she attempted it anyway.

"Gods?" Her voice shook. Desperate for him not to see her brimming eyes and hot cheeks, she turned her head away and coughed. "How many gods are playing this game?"

"One that I've been told of," Rashid answered. He didn't seem to notice the weakness in her voice. "Apparently, he makes appointments for me and ensures I get to them—in whatever way is most painful."

"I hope He makes things better soon," Isaiah said.

She faced him and gave a half smile, watching Rashid's eyes glaze beneath his furrowed brow. Half expecting him to cringe, she slid her hand over his. When he didn't, she folded her fingers down and softly laced them into his, willing whatever comfort she could offer through a touch. He leaned her way and wrapped his fingers around hers in turn. Together, they sat, unmoving, until the sun dropped.

XLVII

EARLY THE NEXT morning, they left camp and climbed with the sun until midday, when its light hung above them, dangling like a ripe apple waiting to be plucked from its branch. Except for the heat, and the residual tension between Rashid and Adira, it had been easy going.

At noon, they took a break, and when they moved out again, the sky began to drizzle. The group, with their hot heads and sweaty backs welcomed the shower. From the back of the line, Rashid smiled as the rain gently soaked the top layer of his hair. Its gentleness distracted him from the awkward mood that covered them since the fight. He wasn't sorry for what he did, except maybe sorry he didn't hit Adira harder. But he was past it. He was past the pettiness of men who kill for their agenda, or fun, or whatever, and past the smallness of apologizing too. He was in a place that was real, and empty, and sad, and Adira was one of those that caused it.

He thought of his family—bouncing rays of sweetness and love, and of the beauty of Moyra's sparkling eyes when she smiled at him. He'd never seen eyes so deep, so dark and yet bright, anywhere else. When they had met and she smiled for the first time—now he could barely remember why, he was so taken at the sight of her—but when she had smiled it was like a magnet sucked every bit of his attention in her direction. He couldn't help but stare, awkwardly probably, but fully, into those beautiful shimmering gems. His daughter had eyes just as bright, though hers weren't as stunning, or delicate as Moyra's—hers had toned down with the addition of his genes. But they still shone and brightened up his worst days.

He lifted his gaze and stared at the back of Mahir, who sauntered through the forest like he owned it, and in front of him Adira, quiet, nimble, brisking forward without leaving trace he'd been there—did his feet even leave marks where he treaded? The man was barely there, barely here, barely anywhere. He could disappear and the forest would be the same as if he were still present. *He* was alone, spending his days hiking through the quiet, empty nowhere with no one but his drunken brother for company. Each day for him passed without having the eyes of a soulmate to get lost in, or the arms of a child to get tangled in. Did he even understand the pain he had caused so many? Mahir had said he'd shot their own parents. As a child. So even childhood he'd lost, with all its chance at happiness and carefree diversions. Adira would live a life of regret and pain and loneliness, without a trace of the pleasures Rashid had.

He could forgive Adira. And he could embrace the memory of his beauties the way Lazarus had said he and the children had embraced their losses through the years—as sweet blessings he got to enjoy for a short time. Losing his family couldn't take away the good he'd had with them—the sweetness of their lives—or the years of play and freedom he'd enjoyed as a youth. He was lucky.

The drizzle leaked over his nose now, dripping onto his upper lip and lining the edges of his mouth. It crept inside, wetting the tip of his tongue. It was pure, clean water, without a trace of the bitterness that the rain in Egypt held, with the smoke and fumes and whatever else they let off into the sky. Untainted. Innocent. He lost himself in its movement; it dripped in a slow but steady line down either side of his face, around his now-bearded jawline and then his neck, joining into one stream that fed down the front of his chest, drenching his shirt from the inside out.

Rashid's tears came then, but he was unsure if they even fell, as by that time, the sweet cleansing from the sky washed over his entire face.

ༀ

At the front of the line, Adira was also reliving his past. For him, the rain was heavy, a constant reminder of the weight of wrong choices he'd made in his youth. His exposure to Rashid had been painful but welcome, and he was glad for the weight of his secret to have been lifted. Closing his eyes, he breathed deeply. He had truly tired of hiding who he was from everyone. He wanted to believe he was not the same person, that he had left behind those actions for a cleaner life, more honorable and pure.

The truth, however, was his departure from the army was not voluntary, in fact it was cordial. Sure, he'd considered leaving many times while he was still young and in the early throes of combat—invading villages with gusto-laden bullets. But though in the end he hadn't, wasn't he a merciful soldier? Even while setting fire to homes and bombing the shops of countless Khabaz Ahmeds, had he not helped many people escape behind the blaze and smoke?

He thought of him, Khabaz Ahmed, the first man he had ever stabbed. All those years before, the morning after they'd arrived at the prison camp. The guards had brought in a truck full of corpses hardened by rigor mortis and lined the children up before them. The first body pulled from the pile had belonged to Ahmed. He had been the town baker and was famous for leaving out sweet breads for the littles after school. The soldiers at the camp had forced them to practice stabbing techniques on him, as well as the rest of the village's dead.

Adira remembered well the old baker's mass beneath his

knife. The first few attempts had been slow—not just because of death's stiffness, but also because it had felt to Adira like he himself was receiving the wound. Each stab he took at the old man's body sent sharp pains through his own arms and chest. After the first ten or twenty cuts, though, as the dead man's meat was softened by repeated assault, the blade entered easier. It had been the same with the army, too. Each passing day, every life he took became easier, more like a job and less like an act of cruelty, until, eventually, he had been nearly completely numbed. It eventually became strange to him that he continued to release prisoners and sneak children away during their decimating raids. This, too, he eventually did without emotion, which perhaps was the most disturbing of his memories—he had lost his sense of humanity. He wondered if he would ever fully recover it.

Adira did feel the tear he released. The fat droplet clung to the edge of his eye for a long moment, but eventually the impact from his hiking shook it loose. A stranger on his cheek, it was warmer and moved slower than the cool drips from above that seemed to miss his face for his sharp brow and new sideburns. It caught on the rise of his cheek, a swollen dollop of hope clinging to the skin above his wispy beard. He hadn't cried in years. Could this be a new mercy he was receiving? Could Allah be allowing him a chance at renewal, now, after so long? A smile stretched his cheeks and set the tear free.

XLVIII

IT WASN'T MUCH farther. Thanks to Manal, Jack had his maps again. His analysis had determined the river originated in the depths of the mountain range, and they had certainly neared the depths. Only a few ridges stood left to scale; they just needed to keep going.

Jack trailed second in line behind Adira, who was badly bruised but otherwise had escaped the beating with only scratches and a torn lip. When the team finally stopped to rest, the two huddled, planning their path per Jack's specs and Adira's knowledge of the general topography. He'd said he'd never been this far out, so everything from here was a gamble. After another few minutes, when the group's heavy breathing had quieted and they were again bloated with water, they moved on.

To cut the trek shorter, they'd decided to leave the river's side. This meant rougher terrain and no ready supply of water for a few kilometers. Other than the rhythmic puffing of breath, the group hiked silently, each person filtering what energy they possessed to their weak legs. Pine needles and twigs crunched underfoot. The lazy rustling of leaves overhead seemed to mellow time, dragging on them, slowing their charge.

During the tougher parts of the hike, Jack focused on the bird-song echoing in the background. Their chorus was light and airy, energizing. He listened as they cooed and were answered by others in the distance. How odd and sweet, he thought, that these creatures existed, somehow so connected despite their ability to soar miles apart, through the dimensions of the forest and the sky above. He copied their songs and called out to them, hoping to join their world, if only as an imposter.

"Hey guys," Jack stopped and turned to the group. "Listen—they'll answer me." Pursing his lips, he whistled sharply, the notes high and melodic, floating above their heads and into the trees. A reply came from the east. He chirped again, receiving another answer from the same direction.

Rashid shook his head. "Just when I thought you could not be any more of a dork."

Ignoring him, Jack did it again, hands on his hips, dropping the pitch lower and adding a warble. A new answer came from the south this time, followed by a black flutter of grouse wings.

Rashid laughed. "Jack, the Bird Whisperer. What other hidden talents do you have, my friend?"

"Such skill," Isaiah said, winking. "Perhaps if we ever see that wolf, you can speak to it?"

"Nah, I don't speak wolf. Much too simple a language to waste time on."

"Oh, I see," Isaiah answered, smirking at Rashid before turning to press forward. "Let's keep it complicated then, shall we?"

Before Rashid could follow, Jack grabbed his arm. "So, uh," he whispered, "I've got more." He hesitated, glancing ahead to make sure the group had moved far enough away not to see. "Check this out." He furrowed his brow and flexed his pecs. "What do you think?"

Rashid stared at him. "What am I supposed to be seeing here?"

Jack looked up, confused. "Watch my shirt, man. I think I can get it to ripple now." He tried again, this time straining so hard he pushed his tongue forward and bit it in concentration.

"Captain, you are literally just bumping your shoulders up and down," Rashid said, shaking his head in laughter. "Please—don't do it again."

"Come on, watch closer." Jack made one more effort. "This is tough stuff here."

"Seriously, there is no chest movement, at all, going on. We both know you and the pectoralis-es have no type of relationship. They do not hear or respect your requests. Leave the pectoralis-es alone."

Jack slumped and lifted his chin at his friend. "You. Are a hateful man. And for that, I will put these away."

"And cower in disgrace," Rashid added, cuffing the back of Jack's head. "Lead us onward, my disgraceful captain."

The scenery changed rapidly from green and wooded to near barren and rocky, brown and gray, and occasionally dotted with silvery brush and abrupt elevation changes. While the team was encouraged by the decreasing bug population, the increased grade and sun exposure exhausted them.

The evening took its time arriving, the work of the hike seeming to stall the sun in its course across the sky. The sun did finally go down, and the birdsong was replaced by that of crickets. They walked until Elise asked to stop, which ended up being eight times throughout the day. By the time she announced the final break, the team was overtired and hot.

"Let's camp here tonight, Jack," she said, leaning against a giant plane tree. "Can we? We're getting close, right?"

"We are," Jack answered.

"All right, everyone find a place to rest," Adira called. "Stay close! We're in bobcat territory now. Safety in numbers."

They divided up the remaining food, which consisted of beef jerky and a few MREs—Meals Ready to Eat. Other than that, they still had several packets of water-purifying iodine tablets left.

"From here we will need to forage for food. Tomorrow while walking, I need everyone to be on the lookout for some plants." From his pocket, Adira pulled a wad of withered greens and crumpled flowers. "These. Obviously, fruit—blackberries or mulberries—will work, pistachios, too, if anyone is lucky enough to locate them now." He scattered his finds along the ground for them to see. "These are all safe to eat. Dandelion, this type of clover, shepherd's purse, wild plantain, and this—" He pulled out an ivory stripe of young tree flesh. "This will be our main sustenance. You find it under the brown bark of the pine trees. Peel off the bark, then scrape this out." He popped it in his mouth and chewed. "The younger the tree, the easier it is to eat."

Elise tugged at her shirt and sat back on her heels, scanning the weary group, who were now all intent on Adira.

"Is everyone okay with continuing? Does anyone want to turn back?" she asked.

Adira shrugged. "We can head back, but as Mr. Barron states, we are getting close. I think none of us desire the pleasure of repeating this trip."

She smiled sheepishly. "I don't mind eating plants and drinking river water, but the rest of you don't?"

"I believe, Doctor," Rashid said toward the dirt, shoulders slumped, "we have all come too long to go back, as they say."

Jack laughed. "Too far, Rash."

"What?" His eyebrows bunched together "I was simply saying we don't want to give up now."

"Yo, dude. Are you, like, missing half your wit?" Mahir said, breath still heavy. "The phrase is 'Come too far,' not 'too long.'" He rolled his eyes. "Scientists."

Jack glanced at Mahir in disbelief, then turned back to Rashid, who stared off into space, apparently too tired to care about the insult. "That was unnecessary." He scowled at Mahir. The man had no boundaries, even sober.

"I am sorry for my brother," Adira interrupted, his voice calm but commanding. "He is clearly tired. We understand and agree with Mr. Al Hassad. We will continue on." He turned toward Elise, but for a moment darted his eyes to Rashid, who raised his brow in return.

Everyone arranged themselves under the plane tree, its trunk easily three feet across, while Jack draped the plastic sheet across the women's laps. Rashid fell asleep within minutes, wedged against the tree's rough bark, just inches from Isaiah on one side, and to the other, Adira.

XLIX

THE TEAM SLEPT fitfully. Though they stayed beneath the tree, nestled up against its bark and each other, the temperature plummeted in the darkest part of the night, and they were cold. The next morning, Isaiah woke in the break of dawn, to a stiff neck and the general feeling of agitation that comes in such circumstances. She stretched, feeling the release of tension across her back, and rolled over to scan the area.

Something was missing.

"Where's Adira?" She jumped to her feet. "Guys?"

The others stirred.

"Adira's gone. And the pack is missing." Isaiah announced, her worry mounting.

Jack stood and walked in the direction they had come from the day before.

"Adira?" He squinted east through the rising sun.

"I am here!" Adira shouted, climbing into view. His forearms bulged as he pulled himself over a boulder. He was even leaner than when they started, his veins now well-defined and muscle fibers practically traceable under his skin.

Isaiah caught herself before rushing at him.

"Water." He grinned and presented his pack. "I filled the bottles. We are going to need it today." He tossed the heavy pack to Jack, who lurched sideways, nearly falling over trying to catch it.

"We will not have another chance at water for a few hours. Drink now, and I will go fill them again before we leave."

They drank until every drop was gone. By the time Adira returned with the next fill, it was well into late morning. A muggy heat had diffused into the giant tree's shadow, warning them of the coming temperature.

They set out, hiking slowly, as the morning sun zapped their energy dry. By the time Adira announced their next respite, and the others ahead had stopped, Isaiah's tongue stuck to her teeth. Once more the forest surrounded them, and it sounded like they were near water again, too. She straightened her shirt, then flapped it, drying the sweat from her chest and relishing the coolness of the air against her hot skin.

"Drink," Adira said, stepping aside to reveal the river. It sparkled from below a canopy of green.

She glanced back. Again, Rashid paced last in line, his steps heavy. She bit her lip and locked eyes on him, silently praying for God to strengthen him. He stepped next to her and huffed, leaning against a tree.

"Mind if I camp here for a bit?" He stated more then asked, sliding down to rest.

"All you," she answered then went to fill a canister with water. After guzzling a full one herself, she filled another and brought it back to Rashid, who drank hungrily.

Raising his eyebrows, he nodded at Jack and Adira. "Our leaders plot the next leg of our adventure. Apparently, up ahead we have more hills, steep cliffs, and lots of stone."

"Sounds fun," Isaiah said, then leaned back beside him to listen in.

"Okay, so which way then?" Adira asked Jack.

Jack shrugged. "If we keep following the river, it should disappear into the mountain. There is a ravine going around it, but it also curves away. Even if we went that route, there would still be some climbing. It would add miles to our trip, and at this rate, likely two more days."

"Okay, so, straight ahead?"

"Well, no." Jack shifted weight nervously, scanning the horizon. "Sorry, but we need to hike that way." He pointed off to their right, where the trail was nearly vertical until it leveled out on top, easily a half-day's trek away. A clear divide remained between the two mountains on the opposite side of its backdrop. "Originally, the river should have come from over there."

"So the top looks to be easygoing, but getting up…" Adira's voice tapered off as he searched for a route. "I cannot be certain about what to expect. Those are untouched highlands. It may be difficult. Where is the next chance of water on those maps of yours?"

"There could be some along the way, spilling out in places from the side of the mountain. And after we clear the ridge, some streams, or even a pond is likely."

Isaiah watched for Adira's reaction. He nodded quietly and closed his lips, then scanned the group, his gaze falling on Elise. She rested a few yards away, her fingers tracing the water's surface. Her eyes were closed and she was humming softly, a hymn they had sung frequently during their time in prison. A faint grin spread across her face; she was praying again.

"Okay, we'll rest first, I want to reach the top by nightfall if we can" Adira answered, his eyes darting away as he walked off.

"'Kay. I'm going to go check on our rate-limiting step, then." Jack answered and ambled toward Rashid, who had already fallen asleep beside Isaiah.

"How's our man?" He smoothed out the rubble before he sat.

"Eh. Slow, tired. He needs good food and water. And a bed," Isaiah answered. "I think his heart is in the game though."

Jack nodded. "I was hoping the game would help his heart, actually."

"Yeah, I hear you."

Jack tilted his head her way. "You lost your family too, right?"

Isaiah closed her eyes in an exaggerated blink, her lashes a lock to hide the pain behind them. *Not again*, she thought. After a long moment, she looked up. "I did."

Jack frowned and pivoted awkwardly. "Oh, I'm sorry."

"It isn't easy to get over," she continued. "But distraction does help. At least it does for me."

Beside them, Rashid stirred. He pushed his legs forward and stretched, arching his back. "Are we there yet?" he asked. He straightened, glancing at Isaiah and then back to Jack. "Hello. Are you guys watching me? Is there a booger on my face or something?"

Jack smiled. "Isaiah here says you need rest. And food."

"Two things I suppose are in short supply today?" Rashid asked.

"That is an affirmative."

"I think rest is something we can manage," Adira interrupted, approaching again. His eyes were fixed on the ledge above. "I am going to hike ahead. I need to find a way up there that won't involve backtracking. You will stay here and take a break while I do. Mahir went to collect food."

"Well, I won't argue with you," Jack answered.

"Me neither," Rashid said. He stood, groaning softly before walking toward the river.

Isaiah watched him go. His strength surprised her. By now, she would have fallen out if in his shoes, but he kept pressing forward. She wondered if God was answering her prayer for him or if it was just the way he was made. After another moment, she rose to follow him.

"Where do you get your energy?" she asked, puffing as she stepped up.

He turned to her and smiled. "I don't know. But it keeps coming, so I'll take it."

"Well, I'm impressed," she replied, wiping sweat from her

brow. She pushed her hands through her hair, swirled it into a bun, and jabbed a peeled stick through to fasten it tight against her scalp. Giving Rashid a grin, she leaned against a lonely tree trunk by his side.

"Thanks." Rashid shrugged. "I'll take the break, though." He handed her a bottle he had filled with water. The river here was quiet, peaceful. "Want some?"

"Yes, please." She took it from him, her fingers brushing his accidentally. She was surprised to find the touch dizzying. The feel of another human after a day of hard work was strange to her. It seemed to spark a new, deeper kind of fatigue—one more even than her weary muscles were dealing with. A weakness that made her want to rest, *really* rest—the eyes-closed, head on his chest, feet on the coffee table with no concern for time—kind of rest. She offered a smile to Rashid and sipped from the canister before handing it back. "We're all nuts, aren't we?"

"Most assuredly," he answered, locking his gaze with hers.

Isaiah hesitated, holding his stare. His eyes were more intense than she had noticed before. They were intelligent—you could almost see the wheels spinning behind them—but also peaceful, and full, penetrating. Isaiah brushed her hands on her pants, though they weren't wet or dirty, then stepped toward a giant, smooth rock beside the river. She needed to sit.

"You coming back up?" Rashid asked, motioning toward the others.

"In a bit. Thanks."

After he left, Isaiah sucked in a deep breath through her nose. She held onto it for another moment before exhaling, letting her body recline against her elbows as she did. Mountain air really was sweet. A breeze cooled her face, drying the sweat lining her hairline. Her hands were sticky, her clothes thin and filthy, and her hair matted, but the elation from the hike had lifted her mood the way a good workout would. She felt surprisingly content, but also free and ready for adventure.

Before her, the water moved gently, shallow and interrupted by stones and the rise of land that in places almost appeared as if it would end the flow completely. Along these areas, the green of the forest boldly announced the soil's lushness beneath, soaking up whatever water was captured, distracted along the way, and blackening the soggy, root-laced ground. But at its center, the river streamed, determined and steady, intent on lower ground and the promise of future places.

She scooted up to take in the panoramic. Above hung an endlessly clear blue sky, filling the backdrop behind and around the brown and grey stone of the looming bluff ahead. And then rolled the silver water, lined with its brilliant green, black and then between it all red, the leaves above changing with Fall's impedance for growth. This place danced with color and texture and life. It was magnificent. She sighed, proud of her Father God, who had created this world in all its splendor—the most talented artist, who did things in real-time and 4-D, no less.

The pebbles glistened beneath her feet. She thought of them; if they had senses, they would be able to soak this in every second for eternity. She considered a verse from her Bible. *If I do not praise you, the rocks will cry out for you.* Sitting here, she could understand the phrase. Her eyes closed in prayer as she embraced its message. *Praise you, God, for this beautiful day in this beautiful country. Thank you for this adventure and the renewing of my spirit.* She lifted her eyes toward Rashid, who was now laughing and bumping shoulders with Jack. Her heart skipped. *Praise you for new friends.*

Adira's investigation led to a game trail that weaved up the mountainside gently, and even passed a stream along the way, fed from a weeping crack in the side of the rock, he said, deep enough to wash faces and fill bellies. The path meant some steep climbs, but generally left an open landscape with views a hundred yards to each side most of the way. By midday, the team had cleared the thick of the trees completely and the sun dangled above, trying to burn away any trace of humidity clinging above the foliage. Soon the clouds crept in around it and outlined its blaze, muting the rays and then moving down until they swallowed the treetops behind in a silvery mist. Then the drizzle returned.

The rain fell steadily, and though it initially had been a welcome reprieve to the hikers, it became more frigid as they climbed. Their clothes eventually were drenched, and the cold pelted through their now-useless second skins. Wind pushed the stinging rain against them at new angles and the raindrops became larger, more frequent. By the time they reached the climb's mid-point, the precipitation was mixed with fat, wet snowflakes and beads of hail. The wind had picked up as well, icing over the wet rocks until they became slick beneath their feet. The season had changed from summer to fall while they'd been imprisoned, but Adira had said he hoped they would still beat winter as the leaves had barely begun to change color in the forest. He had also said the mountains had a weather pattern all their own, independent of the valley and forest below, so this had always been possible despite the previous heat.

"So, Doctor," Rashid's voice gusted up from behind Isaiah. "Are you a missionary too?"

Isaiah's foot slipped on a loose stone covered in a fresh sheen of ice. She glanced back to find him much closer than she thought he had been, eyes filled with determination, rubbing his hands together.

"Not really, no. I mostly work in America. There is more cholesterol than cholera in my neck of the woods." She paused, flushed. "I have been on a few short-term trips though."

"Oh, yeah? Where?" he asked, grabbing a tree limb and holding her arm to help her scale another steep area.

"You know, the usual: Mexico, South America, Africa." She

half laughed, shaking her hands to help get the blood to her fingertips. "Warm places."

"Africa? Nice. Did you ever make it up near where we were, then? Egypt?"

"No, 'fraid not. Mostly I was in Mozambique, Tanzania, and South Africa. You know, in the bush. Where the people are like wild animals."

"Wild, huh?" Rashid shook his head. "You Americans."

Even as she said it, Isaiah knew her words sounded cold-hearted and racist. She didn't actually consider them as wild animals; she just thought of them as living in the most necessary way for their own survival, as wild animals did. And why wouldn't they? She would have, too, had she been in their position. The day she met the children in the bush—them clad in dirty, hole-riddled clothes without shoes, her in hundred-dollar hiking boots and bug repellant—they had struck her with the wild way they'd swarmed her for water, the pokes and prods at her torso. One had actually pinched her. She had been trying to distribute what water she had to their thirsty faces, but she'd had so little compared to their needs, and they all wanted all of it.

"Well, that came out wrong." She puffed. "I don't really think that. Sorry."

"Hey, it is fine. I understand. It's not easy to understand other cultures—much easier to judge their differences. I believe you are not the only one doing so these days." Rashid's words seemed to ignite in him a hidden energy reserve, and his thighs bulged, lengthening his stride and increasing the space between them. "Come on, Doctor, we're getting left behind."

"Oh, okay! Hey, I really didn't mean it," she whimpered after him, though only halfheartedly. Her lips were too numb, her body too tired to care about his feelings just then. All she wanted was a break in the hike, a warm bubble bath, and a piña colada, no matter how first-world spoiled brat it sounded.

"*Cold*," Mahir hollered from the front of the line. "It's sooo cold!"

Isaiah shook her hands again and sped up.

"Adira, my nose hairs have officially frozen, and these rocks are wearing even my buff self out. They're too slippery—it's like they're covered in half-frozen jizz." He pointed at a ledge fifty yards to the east, under which a shallow cave sat and a stream trickled. "I vote break time."

"Sounds good," Adira answered, and veered them toward it.

They crowded into the cave alongside the stream in the only space brightened by the few dim rays of sunlight that had escaped through the cloud cover. The stream would have been a godsend were it not taking up much-needed shelter room. Adira pulled out long strips of pine flesh and passed them around to hungry hands.

"This won't last long, enjoy it while you can," he said. The group huddled, eating and rubbing their hands together for warmth. They wrung out their tops and shook loose whatever water they could. A half hour later, weary and wet, they headed out once more, the hope of the sun's return igniting in them motivation to reach the top.

L

O N THE DAY that solidified the destiny of the world, the devil watched the Lord's angels move along the face of the heavens and Earth. The largest one came to him.

"Where have you been?" This was the archangel Michael, whom he had battled and been defeated by in the time before.

"I have been roaming the Earth, going back and forth on it," Satan answered. "And you? It appears you have been busy using the very wings you tore from my back." He frowned at the shimmering wings on the giant angel's flanks—four pairs instead of three. The larger flight pair, with golden-tipped scales, had once been his.

"Busy, yes," Michael said abruptly, arching his back in an exaggerated stretch. "But the time is nearing. Are you ready?"

"I will not be going down easily, Michael. I know God has plans to despise me further, but you and the others will see it does not have to be like this."

Michael raised his chin and observed the lands. The other angels hovered over their respective, predestined places, wispy-winged clouds where there was otherwise none to obstruct the intense blue of the waters and dark browns and greens of the Earth. "No, devil, you are mistaken. The Father was, is, and always will be. He can do all things, and no purpose of His can be thwarted. We have realized this, you have not."

"You could certainly have passed along if you truly believed that," Satan snarked.

"You are deceived by your pride still, after all these years."

"And what is so wrong with pride?" he replied. "Perhaps I can see something more because of it. Opportunity, Michael. A lion makes a better king than a lamb. I can see this. And you, I believe, are wise enough to do the same. Why do you desire to remain forever blinded by His light?"

"The light is a good place to be. Had only you realized as much before."

The devil glared at him, anger mounting. "I only tried to take my rightful place. And what would have been so wrong with that? At least I would have ruled fairly! Or don't you remember people have a chance at immortality and true understanding—at real power? They may yet listen and have sense enough to see the Father for who He really is."

Michael nodded. "I must go, brother. The harvest approaches. I can't say I won't miss our old times." He softened his heart, once more hoping for another end to their story. "If only things were different. Perhaps if you considered repentance? The Father may show you mercy."

Satan raised an eyebrow. "I am afraid such action is not likely." It was known to be true that angels, Michael included, did not have the power to know the devil's heart, and it felt to him to be torn, still possessing a pang of regret.

Showing Michael a vision of all the kingdoms of the world and their splendor, he said, "Perhaps instead you will turn with me and the others? With you by my side, our victory would be most certain, and all this I will give you. We could rule together!"

Then the Lord approached, and the devil removed the scene from Michael's sight.

"Servant," the Lord said to His angel, "why are you idle on this day? My children need you. Are you faltering at this most-desperate hour?"

"No, my Lord." Michael bowed low and opened two sets of wings to rise, the breeze they generated thick and warm. He saw Helel's eyes close as the draft hit his face, though his body otherwise stood rigid. "Till we meet again," he said. "May you remember that as relief when there is none to be found."

LI

ADIRA BREACHED THE cliff as the sun disappeared over its ledge. The approaching darkness signaled the time for Maghrib. He silently scorned himself; he had not knelt in prayer the entire day and needed to make them up, though first he had to ensure the others made it safely to the top. The clouds had finished dumping on them, but the wind whipped the remaining chill through his clothes. Judging by the burn in his thighs, the stragglers would be a good ten minutes behind.

Elise came next, stepping robotically, her eyes glazed over. Each of her hands rested weakly on a hip, as if this would somehow channel her energy to where it was most needed. Her last step up to flat ground appeared to be easier than she had calculated and sent her stumbling forward. She caught herself with a few running steps and Adira's shoulder.

"Oh, sorry." She stepped back.

Adira held his hand out to her. He turned to look across the plateau, as if his chin were an arm, waving to display their prize. "We made it."

Elise grinned between breaths and stood tall, taking in the respite. Then her face dropped, like she had suddenly remembered something terrible. "You don't suppose… it might be buried?"

"Hmm. I sure hope not, after all of this," Adira answered, disappointed in her frown. He had found he liked seeing her smile.

In fact, he imagined he'd be quite happy if he were the one to expose to Dr. Elise Harper's delight her improbable find in the wilderness. But she could be right. Jack had said the rivers all should have emerged by this point. From here on, the garden could be anywhere, even under their feet.

Where they stood, the area was surprisingly vast—several dozen acres at least. It could be larger depending on what the land chose to do to their left. The region to their right fell off abruptly to the steep walls they had just circumnavigated. For a good eight-hundred meters, the ledge was well defined, then made a sharp turn north and disappeared into the distance a kilometer or so later. The landscape before them was dotted with thin patches of snow, and yellowing brush, embellished with dying grass and scattered rock. Nothing broke the wind except their own bodies, so flat was the terrain. It certainly wasn't the beautiful oasis they deserved after such a difficult day, but it was dry—and for that, he was glad.

A raised area stood out a few hundred meters away, not quite near the ledge. Green shrubs wrapped around a giant, iced–over, rocky mound that shimmered in the reflection of the rising moon's glow, as if calling out to be noticed. It almost appeared to have been dropped in place from above.

There might be some cover there. If not, it would at least offer a protective barrier from the wind and serve as a lookout area for the night. He turned around just in time to see Jack and Mahir reach the ledge.

"Are the others close?" Jack asked over his shoulder.

"You would think so since we stopped, I don't know, fifty times to wait for them," Mahir snorted. "Jack, dude. They're grown, they'll get here."

Jack shrugged. "Well, it's getting dark. I want to make sure Rash didn't fall or something. Guy's always getting beat up," he said, clearly worried.

"Survival of the fittest, my man. Natural selection. Let nature take its course."

"Mahir." Adira's expression was half annoyed, half amused.

"What? It's science. Now I can't believe in science?"

Elise stepped up to Jack. "How far back do you figure they are?"

"Not sure. We spotted them a few times, most recently maybe thirty, forty minutes ago. When we turned by the giant tree."

"I am sure your friend is fine," Adira said. "He knew this was going to be a hike."

"Yeah," Jack answered apprehensively, then cleared his throat. "I do have some good news. This is the highest spot we need to go." He pulled out a soggy map, unfolded it carefully, and held it close to his face.

"Well, that looks like crap," Mahir said, walking over. "Why didn't you put it in the bag?"

Jack stood taller, fidgeting with the edges of the paper. "I was distracted," he answered. "I meant to put it away. I'll lay it flat later, it'll last."

"We made it!" A hoot rose as Rashid and Isaiah came into sight. They were surprisingly fresh compared to what everyone expected, bouncing over the remaining rocks like they were playing a game.

Adira sighed, relieved. Lost hikers didn't make for good reviews. He grinned and walked over, patting Rashid on the back and nodding in approval at Isaiah. "Thank you," he mouthed for only her to see. She smiled and nodded in turn.

A wind gust hit them, hard enough to make Isaiah step sideways.

"Whew, cold!" she said, bracing herself. "I suppose we're a little underdressed."

"I agree," Adira replied. "This should be the worst of it, however, assuming we don't get more precipitation while we're up here. Jack says this is as high as we go. Correct, Jack?"

"Right. I'd like to scope this place out though. This should be the final point up the main riverhead. We're far enough upstream to safely say the garden would either have been here or somewhere close." He waved northwest. "Maybe up there somewhere. No more than two or three kilometers. And from here, look..." He pointed. "It's hard to see, but there's the land in front of us, and then another valley. It's a slow grade down, but it's down for sure. And right now, down means warm." Jack smiled confidently at his good news.

"Oh, that sounds very, very good," Isaiah answered, arm propped on Elise's shoulders for support as she adjusted her shoes. Adira wondered if her feet were blistered, the way she hopped around. For sure, everyone would have to be soaked through to their socks by now. She stood again and searched the terrain before them, then turned to Adira. "I would love to take these things off soon. Anything in your magic pack that could get us a tent and fire to dry off by for the night?"

"Fire, yes, but it will be a short one. There is only so much wood up here. As for shelter, I would like to inspect the area over there." He pointed to the rock pile and dropped his bag to the ground, which hit with a thud thanks to the heavy wood and water he had collected along the way. Rolling his shoulders forward, he rubbed them, feeling three feet taller without the pack.

"It looks like something with sharp teeth lives there," Isaiah said, "and now it's dark, sooo..." Her voice trailed off.

Elise laid her hand reassuringly on Isaiah's shoulder. "We'll be fine. Let the men go check it out. Maybe we can collect some more wood and food before the light is gone." She turned back to the others. "If you found any chow along the way, give it to us. We'll get it cleaned and ready."

It turned out the rocks were uninhabited, at least for the time being. There were paw tracks, Adira told the others. Made by wolves, most likely. And mixed into the dirt were patches of another animal's fur, so old and brittle the color had mollified.

The cave was deep, and Adira and Mahir searched—and Jack, who came along either because he enjoyed leading or still didn't trust Mahir, Adira couldn't tell which—but after five minutes of walking downhill, as it generally graded that way, turning surprise corners, and dodging low ceilings, they still hadn't found its end.

The group settled a good thirty feet into the cave, listening to the wind swirl around them, broken by the Allah-blessed shelter, while the girls divvied up the food. Amidst their lot, they had collected plenty of greens and hazelnuts. Elise had even found berries somewhere along the way, carrying them in her hood for safe keeping.

The food sparked a new energy in everyone. Full-bellied and shivering now in anticipation instead of cold, they circled the fire Adira had made, which burned much hotter and longer than he had anticipated.

"Anyone else feel like we're at summer camp?" Jack asked, brushing his shirt front. "We should be singing songs or telling ghost stories."

"Umm, summer camp? Are summers cold in America?" Mahir asked, a puzzled look on his face. "Now I want to go there even less."

"I do, Jack," Elise said, her eyes flashing. "I, for one, am grateful for this place. And all of you. I could never had gotten this far without your help." She looked at Adira, then Mahir. "And you. Thank you both. I want to bless you for what you have done for us, for me. Would you mind if we prayed for you?"

Adira glanced at his brother. He had come to respect Elise. She had endurance and a kind spirit as well. He'd noticed her watching the others and could now recognize the change in her eyes each time she saw someone had a need—of rest, water, or even a hand to help crawl over a boulder. She'd spent much of the hike kicking aside rocks and enduring repeated cuts and pokes when pinching back thorny branches, to protect the others from their assault. Surely, allowing her to pray over them would be harmless. Anyway, a blessing from a good-hearted person was still a blessing. What could it hurt?

Adira nodded at Elise, silently commanding Mahir to comply.

"As you wish," he said quietly.

Mahir shrugged. "Knock yourselves out."

Elise grinned and lifted her hands, palms pointed at the two of them as if an invisible force were going to fly out and zap them. She closed her eyes and tucked her chin to her chest, furrowing her brow in concentration.

"Father, our God, our Beloved. We praise You for today. We praise You for our friends, for the time and experience they have given us, and for the protection they have provided when others tried to keep us from Your mission. We praise You for Your wisdom and grace, and for the blessing of being able to even be on this trip. We praise You in advance for the great privilege of being the first people since Adam and Eve to enter Your garden. Thank you! Thank you, Father! Thank you, Abba, Daddy, Allah, Jehovah, Jeeezuuus." Elise drew out his name as if she savored its sound, then dropped silent long enough to make Adira wonder if the prayer was finished.

Then, Isaiah sang.

"Praise God from whom all blessings flow,

Praise Him all creatures, here below;

Praise Him above; ye heavenly Host;

Praise Father, Son, and Holy Ghost."

Jack and Elise joined in while Adira sat, observing. They sang the verse over and over, each time louder and with more passion, until the words filled his mind as if he, too, had known them all along.

267

LII

RASHID CLOSED HIS eyes. *And now this*, he thought, though less in irritation and more comforted by the familiar chanting. He contemplated the Christians and their faith in this invisible God. They seemed so sure of His presence, just like the family at the cabin. Lazarus, with the things he and the children had said and done, had seemed supernatural. Perhaps God did exist, but who he was and what Rashid should do about it still confused him. Maybe he shouldn't do anything? Why did acknowledging him even matter? Perhaps he should be angry at this God if he'd had the ability to protect his family all along but refused to. Or perhaps, this God was just as impotent as everyone else, and only an observer of the Earth's activities and maybe not at fault at all; but if so, he'd be no more important to Rashid's current existence than any other invisible entity.

Show yourself if you are there! Rashid thought brashly.

He leaned back, scoffing at himself for entertaining such a naïve idea, then sighed and turned to lie down, planning to doze off to the others' song. As he reclined, a gust of air blew against his back from the cave's entrance. He sat up in reflex to the icy jolt, in time to see it blow their weak fire sideways. The fire dimmed under its weight and was almost smothered, when another airstream came in, this one reigniting it, stretching the flames longer with its icy fingers.

Rashid flinched back at the blaze. The fire stood nearly five feet tall for an instant, waving boldly, bright and hot, with the wind, which seemed to whip about the cave, scouring its walls for a way out. Soon the inferno danced and spun in a torna-do-like swirl above the pit, growing taller with each rotation. Rashid stared at it, wide-eyed as it bent toward him, its blazing yellow-and-orange arms whipping at his face. He gaped at the others. Mahir's eyes were huge, too, paralyzed by the sight, while Adira quietly repositioned himself, barely disturbed. The others remained unmoving with their eyes closed tight. The women's hair whipped across their faces and around their heads, and Rashid watched as the corners of Isaiah's mouth lifted in a gentle smile at the hot wind, like she was remembering a cherished secret.

"God, we pray a blessing over Adira and Mahir," Elise yelled above the roar filling the room. "Give them grace on their paths. Give Mahir purpose and meaning. No, God—share with him the purpose and meaning You already have for him! Send him love, and power, and a clear word from You! Show him, God! Embrace him in a way he knows can only be from You. Give him strength to lean on You for healing and nothing else!"

Rashid watched in relief as the fire bent away from him. It pointed instead at Mahir, who turned for an instant to Elise as she called his name. Mahir's gaze shot to the fire then lifted, tracing the walls of the room. Their eyes met. Was he afraid? It seemed this was the first time they had looked at each other this whole trip. Next to him, Adira opened his eyes and watched the fire, too, though he did not seem alarmed. He scooted back again, just slightly as if to avoid the heat, and glanced at his brother, apparently puzzled by his new expression. Rashid wondered at Adira. Could he not see what they saw? Could he be missing this?

"And Father, bless Adira! Make his days long, and full, and satisfying. Fill his heart with Your love and peace, in the sweet name of Your great sacrifice, Your son Jesus. Peace God, please! Peace—your peace—and none else! Give him forgiveness from the memories that haunt him! Bless his hands so whatever they set out to do, they bring forth only joy and healing from this day on. May he find You in a way he never imagined. May he hear from You too! Reveal to him Your word and truth. Make it hit him hard, make it obvious. In Your name, in Jesus's name, in the name of the Holy Spirit, who we know is here with us right now. Thank you, Father!"

The flame danced from Mahir to Adira during Elise's prayer. Adira sat stoic, unaffected by it all. Perhaps Rashid was making a bigger deal of the flames than necessary. Then the fire returned to the center of the room, spitting upward once again instead of around as the wind stilled, giving up its search for an exit.

Isaiah lifted her chin and sang again, this time a hymn that seemed to be their theme song. Rashid had heard it so often he had it memorized. For the first time, he joined in at its start, mostly from awe at what had just happened. He watched as Mahir wiped the corner of his eye and joined in as well.

"Come, Thou Fount of every blessing

Tune my heart to sing Thy grace

Streams of mercy, never ceasing

Call for songs of loudest praise

Teach me some melodious sonnet

Sung by flaming tongues above..."

They sang so loud the cavern walls echoed their voices. The song was robust, as fervent as the fire had been moments before, and seemed to warm the space the flames had previously filled. They sang the whole thing several times, until the fire weakened into glowing coals. Rashid mouthed the words, embracing their meaning. He needed to hold onto something, and this God—who made women with broken hearts smile and war-hardened men crazy for a life of peace—he *must* be there. He needed to be, and with him needed to be the chance to see his wife and daughter again. Because if not, what else was he to hope for?

"... Bind my wandering heart to Thee
Prone to wander, Lord, I feel it
Prone to leave the God I love
Here's my heart, oh, take and seal it
Seal it for Thy courts above."

By the time the fire died, Rashid's clothes had dried and his feet were warm. Cozy and contented, he was the first asleep. Surprisingly, he'd slept easily ever since the day the river had almost killed him. He preferred sleep lately too; not just because his body craved rest or because it helped time pass without having to deal with his sorrow but also because his family often visited him in his dreams. He could see them, hear them, even somehow *feel* them again.

He felt Nubia's wiry body wrapped around his torso and leg with one of her clingy four-limbed hugs, soft and warm as she always was. And Moyra's kisses were somehow still delicate but full, her lips velvety as fresh-plucked rose petals. The two felt so real in his dreams. They—and he too—were alive again.

That night Rashid dreamt, but not of his family. In his dream, he stood in Tutankhamun's burial chamber during the young king's funeral ceremonies. He watched as men adjusted his sarcophagus. To the side, workers painted the walls and arranged boat ores and a large golden shrine. No one could see Rashid, or if they did, they ignored his presence. He turned to wander through the ancient tomb's halls, studying the ornate fixtures, jewelry, oils, even food placed in jars all around. The colors were still vivid, the years and decay not yet taken toll.

He returned to the burial chamber and stepped close to a dark man with a long black braid and a tan tunic, who chiseled figures into the stone wall. Rashid examined the carvings, testing his knowledge of hieroglyphics. They spoke of Isis, the mistress of the sky, and of how she'd be breathing life into the king's nostrils in times to come.

The man doing the chiseling stopped, hammer mid-strike, and turned toward Rashid. Wondering if he could feel his presence, Rashid tried to catch his eye, but the man looked past him, as if something was coming from behind. Rashid turned around, but no one was there. The hall he'd just walked through had darkened and now shrunk away. He glanced back at the man, whose body now also withdrew. Rashid realized he was the one leaving, drifting up and away. He could soon see the entire tomb, with busy people in every room. Then the whole thing retracted, until eventually, he floated above it and all the land surrounding, filled with people mourning or working on some task to prepare the king for his time in the afterlife.

He lifted his gaze to the surrounding city and its buildings, fresh and undisturbed by centuries of weather. It was beautiful. He smiled, seeing the very thing he had studied for years to know.

A voice exploded into his thoughts.

"Rashid. This is all in vain," it said. The voice was big, a booming bass vibrating through his body. "All of it. Thousands of lives spent to honor a man who will never even see me. All this I can create or destroy with a thought."

The scene before him suddenly vanished, blanched white, and Rashid hovered in a giant vacant eternity, nothing present but his body and the voice.

"And without me…"

The scene went dark. A rushing sound mounted beneath him, and the ground appeared under his feet. It moved though, jostled like a sea disrupted by aberrant weather. Rashid's body lurched downward, making him flinch at the plunge. Instantly, he was submerged in water, warm as a standing pool in the hottest part of summer. He held his breath, afraid of drowning, but soon his chest burned, and his eyes bulged with the need to breathe.

Rashid gasped, sucking giant gulps of water into his chest. The fluid entered his lungs, but surprisingly came with the gratification of a deep breath. Puzzled, he took a few more cautious breaths. His lungs filled and emptied easily, as if he'd breathed this way every day since he was born. Blindly, he reached forward. The liquid was dense, thicker than water, but not by much, and his eyes stung from whatever was in it. Though he thought about closing them, the sting was more irritating than painful, and besides, he wanted to see what lay ahead. His body moved fast, coursing through the fluid feet first, straight down, then forward and down again into the blackness of the mysterious ocean.

Several minutes passed, and he was still moving, still unable to see. A few times he flinched, expecting something to come at him from the front or perhaps to hit some solid ground beneath him too hard. Eventually the liquid eased his anxiety, the gentle pressure and warmth of it calming his muscles and, with them, his mind. It made a soft whooshing sound as he whirled downward, its mass massaging his body and outstretched hands, wrapping itself discreetly around each finger and away as he sank. Soon his eyes became heavy and his head dropped back. A deep fatigue overwhelmed him, pressing on him from all sides, until he was only vaguely aware of his movement through the ever-so-soft, luxurious liquid. He nodded, almost asleep within his dream.

All at once, he burst out of the water. Now it was above, below, and around him all, but he was dry, surrounded by a bubble of air.

"This, Rashid—" The voice had come back. "This is what *was*. Do you not know none could have made the universe from this but me?" The scene around him vanished with a loud clap, and was replaced by blackness. Before him, the Earth appeared, a giant blue and green and white marble, swirling vibrantly.

He looked around, searching for the voice's source but found no one. "Hello? Who are you?"

"I am the before, now, and after. I am here and everywhere. Rashid, how long will you deny your Father?"

Helplessly, Rashid raced toward Earth. Fear mounted within him, but before it could take over, he awoke, recoiling as he opened his eyes. Trembling and drenched in sweat, he tried to sit up. His head spun, so once more he lay down and instantly fell back asleep.

LIII

AFTER A WEEK in the ICU and another in the general ward, Jubair had returned to work, trying yet again to mollify conflict. He had decided to make a bold statement on his first day back. Standing in the Jews' fancy new temple, perched near the curtain separating the Holy Place from the Most Holy Place—positioned behind the giant altar they were using to burn their sacrifices—he waited for the event to start. The crowd gathered before the podium, dressed in their spotless and gold-laden "holy garments."

Jubair fumed. The temple was meant as a peace offering, a way to unite a region in turmoil. They should have appreciated his sacrifice and taken the gesture quietly. Instead, these obstinate, simpleminded people chose to slaughter animals and burn both food and money—resources desperately needed by much of the world—on that alter in an inconsiderate display of their riches. They were angering the masses, which would not work.

"Welcome, everyone!" Miss Swartz beamed from the center of the temple court. "I am pleased to announce the leader of our United Nations himself, Secretary-General Jubair Talmuk will be joining us today. How fitting for him to be here, addressing the nations in this, a place dedicated to power from on high, after his miraculous healing!"

Jubair ambled out from behind the towering purple curtain and winced, reaching for the microphone. He was still in rehab, and though his pain was improving, the bullet had ripped through two ribs and the surrounding muscle. Bracing himself, he hooked his right hand behind his back, pinching his fingers together to distract himself from the pain.

"I'm back," he began, then stopped and lowered the microphone, waiting for the statement to be absorbed.

The crowd was silent.

"I am a little slower," he continued, "but with the impact of what happened, I'm also a little wiser. I thank God for my tribulation, as it gave me a chance to reflect on... well, on what really matters."

The courtyard exploded in cheers. He was the reason they and the Palestinians could finally exist peacefully in one place. Jubair smiled.

"Have you ever thought maybe we don't have all the answers?" he asked. "That there might be multiple pieces to this puzzle we call God? And maybe we all need each other to figure Him out?" He paused again. "Not that He is one we could ever fully understand, but perhaps our best hope of doing so is together?"

The crowd's murmuring rose in agreement. Jubair spotted Pope Elijah walking in. *Perfect timing*, he thought, and continued.

"God is close to, if not completely, unknowable. He is everywhere and nowhere to be seen at the same time, correct?"

Elijah moved to his side, nodding in agreement, his hands clasped together peacefully in front of his waist. Jubair shot a glance at the camera crew in the back, assuring himself they were recording. "Yes," he answered for the people. "Yes."

"Then why should we desecrate consecrated land? This divides us, stops us from being with each other. We need to honor one another in our actions and be considerate to those around us—not just to show love, but also so we can keep communication lines open, so we can tackle this mystery... together."

Jubair locked eyes with all the higher-ranking attendees, holding each gaze for a few seconds as he spoke—just long enough to let them know he saw each, individually. He held the regard of the most-decorated patrons a few extra seconds.

"Let's do this together, shall we?"

"Here, here!" Elijah raised his arms high and clapped, his hands pointing toward Jubair. "Yes!"

"I come to the next step in our unity. There will be no more wasteful sacrifice. No more burning of slaughtered animals. Let us, instead, share our sacrifices as offerings. To each other." Jubair spread his arms out wide, as if presenting the court to itself on an invisible silver platter. "I would be proud of that charity. God would be proud! And isn't God everywhere? Isn't he in each of us? Isn't he here, now, even in me?" Jubair stood tall, and gripped Elijah's shoulder. He glanced at the pope, whose face was set in agreement, and turned back to the crowd.

"Does he not approve of me? Of course, he does. He brought me miraculously back to life. Has he not chosen me? Perhaps he sent me here today to tell you this—to help unite this world, which keeps trying to tear itself apart. Perhaps—no assuredly, friends, *assuredly* he has sent me!

"I am here to help. Can't you see? Listen. Be mindful of these words. Clearly, if you believe in God, you can believe in this message I bring, which must be from your God, who dwells even in me! Now, in me! If you want to obey God and follow the message you proclaim, then let us use the sacrifices for the good of the people. Save this temple for your prayer and gatherings and as a beautiful monument to your faith—in God, yes, but also in humanity, which you believe God made, yes? Save this temple space. Transform it from a place of bloodshed to a place of honor for those who are here in the flesh, working to preserve humanity through peace."

Elijah beamed from Jubair's side, patting his shoulder enthusiastically. A lonely clap rose from the back of the courtyard, released from one of the cameramen. In another moment someone else joined in, and then more, until the awkwardness of it had faded and the sound rose in soft but steady encouragement.

"Oh, good—*good*. I'm so glad we are together in this. Now, I would like to offer a gift to the Jewish people. May I do that? May we?"

More clapping ensued, though many stood with their arms crossed. Jubair frowned at them and lifted his eyes to the eager ones who understood his message, whose applause echoed off the walls. *The future of the world.* He smiled. *Their voice is here!*

Jubair glanced at the pope and nodded. Elijah produced two buckets from behind him and extended them to Jubair, who took them, bowing graciously. He pivoted in place and carried them, one at a time, to the altar, which still smoldered from the most recent ceremony. Jubair reverently poured the first bucket, which contained cold water, onto the coals and waited patiently for the sizzling to stop. When the smoke cleared, he lifted a dripping rag of warm water from the second bucket and wrung it out, knelt, and proceeded to clean the blood from the floor. He rose and cleaned the altar grates.

When he finished, Jubair walked toward Elijah, who now stood next to a cameraman behind the altar. Calan Tonto had appeared from the crowd by then, and joined them and three other men dressed in military uniforms, as they squatted to lift a white marble slab, laced with gray and brown, and polished into the flattened symbol of the new United Nations. They laid it on the altar.

Then, stepping behind the stand, they lifted a sculpture, a gold-plated globe, procured from a local French artist, and placed it in the center of the tile.

"Yes." Jubair smiled, his heart full. "Now this altar is adorned with the hope of our age—a symbol of peace and unity. Is this not beautiful?"

Amidst the applause, a lone voice arose from where the silent, arm-crossed listeners stood.

"No, you desecrate our temple! You have no right! You are not even worthy to stand at the altar, and yet you put out our fire and defame it with your agenda?" The people around the voice shouted in agreement, until eventually the temple court rang with anger.

"This is a public building," Jubair yelled, suddenly irritated, "built by your United Nations. It will not be used to distribute hate. Guards!" Jubair waved at one of the uniformed soldiers. "Escort this man and these people out of here. Disturbance of the peace!"

It had been going so well. Why did someone always interrupt?

The pope took the microphone from Jubair. He coughed quietly into it and stood, until the people being escorted out had gone.

"Make note," he finally said, "any further desecration of this temple—in fact, any further hateful declarations anywhere—will not be tolerated. I am tired of the Church, of all churches, announcing their superiority in the name of God. Jubair is here in the name of God! We are the most powerful force on this Earth. Us—Earth's people. The leaders, your elected leaders and your fellow man, are the ones we should boast about. Any further blood sacrifices, any further acts of exclusion or judgmental proclamations—by any church—and you will be treated as an enemy of the people. You will be imprisoned or otherwise punished as necessary, according to the level of dissension expressed."

With that, Elijah signaled the camera crew to stop taping, put his arm around Jubair's shoulders, and turned to guide him away.

The crowd jostled. As if electrified by some invisible force, a stream of movement pulsed through it, originating from the side where the protestor had been taken. He was back, coursing through the crowd like a madman. The people separated, making room for him, as he charged toward the altar.

"Security!" Jubair hollered, but the guards now lay in a pile at the court's edge, writhing on the ground like snakes disturbed by an intruder. They clutched their sides, obviously in pain from whatever he'd done. *Another crazy one*, Jubair thought, eying the dark curls tight against the intruder's cheeks. A knife, tipped with crimson, peeked from under his black sleeve. Jubair was stunned. How had he made it through security with a knife?

Before he had a chance to refocus, the man was on the stage.

From beside him, Elijah gasped and tightened his grip against Jubair's torso. Jubair searched the temple for what support staff was left, half pleading for help, half wondering who had shirked their responsibility, or worse, aided in this. His other soldiers were nowhere to be found. To his side, Elijah dropped away as the intruder's fist crashed into his chest. As he fell, the pope tripped over the heavy cloth of his garment, tugging Jubair's arm down with him.

Jubair shook Elijah off and turned back, in time to find the man glaring at him, knife raised above his head. In an instant, he plunged it down, slicing through Jubair's shirt and the skin above his collar bone, into the soft base of his neck. Jubair's eyes widened at the pain. He collapsed with his left lung, as it suddenly decompressed, he desperately gasping for air.

From the side, Jubair made out the rustling feet of security as they finally appeared. They aimed their guns at the assailant, who was now on his knees between a rising Elijah and Jubair. At their arrival, the man dove under the alter and pulled a sword from its keep. Jubair eyed the shimmering sacrificial blade while he clutched his neck, trying in vain to ebb the flow of the warm blood drenching his fingers. He managed an angry glance at Elijah. It had been his job to have the stage prepared; how had he forgotten to remove a sword?

Elijah lunged at the assailant but was knocked away again. Soon, all Jubair could see was the blurred image of the crazy man, standing above him clenching the sword. His shoulders rotated wildly as he swung, and Jubair felt the tug of skin at the blade's contact, then the sudden blunt crush of his trachea as it razed his neck.

༄

Back on his knees, Elijah grabbed Jubair's hand and pulled what was left of him onto his lap.

Shots rang out, peppering the assailant's body. He fell onto Elijah, who crumpled in protection forward over Jubair's torso. Elijah wailed and tossed the assailant from his back with a shudder. Then, he spun around and grabbed the intruder's collar. As his chest filled with a raging breath, he faced the crowd and dragged the bullet-ridden body off the ground.

"This?" Elijah's strength surged with adrenaline as he yelled. He heaved the man at the top of the alter, knocking the idol over. "You all want *this*?"

Spinning around, he picked up the sword lying near Jubair's dead body. He raised it above his head dramatically and turned again to the audience.

"You want to make a sacrifice to your God? You want to spill blood in honor of him? Is that what your God is about? Spilling blood? Well, let's do it, then!"

His arms sliced through the air as he brought the sword down on his offering. The blade gauged first the abdomen, slashing through the man's holy clothes and deep into his belly. Intestines spilled upward through the wound, their yellow-pink flesh contrasting oddly against the perfect black and white of his outfit.

"Now leave, all of you. Leave or I will give you your war!"

With that, Elijah dropped the sword and stepped backward, falling again to mourn his friend, waving his hand behind him as if to shoo the entire courtyard away.

LIV

JACK ROSE BEFORE the others and wedged himself out from between Rashid and Mahir, moving slowly so as not to wake them. Through the night, they'd slept like the pack of wolves that had previously claimed the cave, bodies smashed against and piled on top of each other for warmth. He found Rashid's shoulder and shook it, hoping to have a buddy for his morning expedition.

"Rash, get up. Come check this place out with me," he whispered.

Rashid groaned, rolling over. "Ugh. Captain. Sleep." He buried his face in his arm, shaking off Jack's hand. Mahir scooted closer to Rashid, filling the void where Jack had been and pushing his hips forward, almost knocking him over. Holding the dark stone wall for support, he stood slowly, feeling somewhat disappointed. Rashid probably did need whatever rest he could get anyway.

With what little sunshine had crept into the cave, Jack had assumed it to be early morning. But it was obviously much later, he realized, squinting in reflex as he stepped outside. The sun had stopped rising and already hung high above his head. The air was warm too—almost hot. He needed to be quick if he was going to be back in time for the others to make it off the ledge today.

His long stride ate up the ground, taking him to the clearing's edge in what felt like just under a mile. A thick tree line sat less than four hundred meters below, a mangled roof of fall colors—greens, reds, and yellows obstructing whatever lay beneath. Jack gazed out at the land before him. Here he stood, on the other side of the world, lost in Georgia's mountain ranges, running toward eternal life—or perhaps now away from death. He supposed it was both. Either way, he was definitely not in Wisconsin anymore. The landscape was quite the contrast to the manicured lawns and neatly winding sidewalks through the suburbs near downtown Madison. No sprinkler systems or mowed lawns here. Decorative flowers, stone, and mulch were silly thoughts for this landscape. He inhaled, filling his chest with thin, cool air and the excitement of the day ahead, and turned around.

When Jack returned, Adira was outside, checking his bag.

"You look fresh," Adira said. "I take it you are ready to lead us today?"

"With you. From here, we are traveling blind. The other side of this is thick forest. Thick." He shrugged. "It's like the Bolivian rainforest over there."

Adira stared at him, blank-faced, until Jack shifted his gaze away. "You'll do fine, young man." He turned and swung the backpack over his broad shoulders, jumping to move it into place. "We've all just eaten. Are you hungry? Or are we ready to go?"

"I guess we'll go. I can eat on the way." Jack hurried into the cave to greet the others, the responsibility of leading them all driving him forward. Inside, a new energy filled the air. Conversation was easy between the ladies and Mahir. Even Rashid, who was stretching in the corner, seemed to have more strength.

"I saw the other side," Jack announced.

"Great!" Elise said, her smile growing impossibly broad.

"Yes, and it looks warmer!" He rubbed his hands together.

"It's dense though, we have likely undisturbed terrain ahead of us. The good news is we shouldn't get much snow."

"Shouldn't," Adira interrupted, "but we may, even with a valley to keep the worst away. Fall has arrived, and the weather in the mountains does not tend to play along in the fall. We should be prepared either way."

"We're close, I know it." Elise interrupted. "We will be there soon, snow or rain, it doesn't matter. The Garden is called paradise for a reason. It's worth the weather."

Mahir rolled his eyes. "Got it, princess. Let's get there, then. See this magic place." He stood and brushed loose gravel from the seat of his worn pants. "Ugh, and maybe let's stop somewhere to wash along the way. Manal did say there's soap in that bag, right, brother?"

"There is, but why don't we wait until we get somewhere warmer—with more access to a fire?" Adira replied.

"Fire, soap, mmm." Elise grinned again. "This day is sounding better every minute!"

"Well, let's get started." Jack headed out of the cave, the others at his heals.

They followed the sun northwest and passed over the ridge and down the steep embankment into the forest below. The undergrowth wasn't near as thick as the trees' canopy, so the going was quick most of the day. The air was warmer too, though the wind still occasionally blew bitterly in their faces. It was filled with the confusion of autumn scents, sometimes smelling of frost, sometimes of torn grass and peeling bark. Always, though, it smelled of damp leaves molding beneath their own weight as they gave up their vibrance for the nourishment of the very trees they had fallen from.

Jack sniffed loudly, the noise ending in an unplanned snort. The scenery was pretty, but he clearly had lost his tolerance to his allergens during his stay in Cairo.

"Captain... you, uh..." Rashid panted, lurching down another rocky grade. "Are you hungry, my elder chap?" He caught another breath. "It sounds like you are consuming body fluids to maintain your energy now." He offered a half smile, clearly fatigued.

Jack lifted the corner of his mouth in a weak chuckle and bumped shoulders with Rashid, looking downward. "Why, you want some?"

"Ugh, no," Rashid answered, "but I'll take aish baladi if you have any?"

"Fresh out." Jack's lanky legs pulsed forward, his mouth watering at the thought of the warm pita they had eaten so frequently during their late-night study sessions. "Perhaps we'll have apples later though!"

The land gently rose and fell, and everyone's energy lasted long into the afternoon. The crisp air and slow, downhill roll of the terrain had sent them coursing ahead more than once, their legs moving like steamrollers as the path opened its mouth between bushes and tree trunks.

They surprised upon a small lake just as the sun had nearly descended. To the east perched an amber wall of rock at least twenty feet tall, slick with water trickling from invisible cracks. One fissure, several feet wide, had opened from the pressure behind it and spilled steadily into the lake, whose water was clear enough to see straight to the pebbled bottom. The south bank was steep, the base of another mountain thick with vegetation, but the shore nearest the group was more welcoming and edged with sand.

"So, we obviously camp here, yes?" Elise asked, beaming.

Adira smiled. "This will work."

"What a beautiful day." She grabbed a dead log and dragged it to the edge of the clearing, as if to get camp set up before he could change his mind.

"Isn't it?" Isaiah added as she walked into sight. Her mouth dropped in an open grin as soon as she saw the waterfall. She and Rashid had pulled up the rear again. "Wow!"

Adira nodded thoughtfully. "The Georgian mountains are a too-well-kept secret, I'm afraid." He smiled as he stood, hands on his hips, inspecting the area. The bank was dotted with perfectly smooth boulders, gray, brown, and silver, glimmering like jewels with the last-offered sheen from the setting sun. It was a scene from a calendar. "What do you think, brother?" Adira said. "Could we sell a hike here?"

Mahir shrugged. "Eh, didn't we already?"

Jack peeled off his socks and stepped into the water. "Now *this* is a campsite!" he announced, wading through the traces of summer's heat still lingering near the water's edge

Grinning, Rashid plunged in after him. "Aaah!" he shouted, the splash catching everyone off guard. He reached the waterfall's base and held his hand beneath the streaming water. "Yikes, cold!"

"Rashid! Get in—you need a shower!" Isaiah laughed and waved him forward.

Rashid ducked his head under the tumbling water and shook it, drenching his shirt. It streamed over his face, falling heavily on his shoulders as he stepped in farther, disappearing beneath the gushing falls.

"Woo-hoo!" he yelled from under the downpour.

Jack trudged awkwardly through the water toward him, lifting his knees high in a slow but animated run. He grabbed Rashid by the chest and fell backward, then twisted his body to hurl him underwater.

"Look, two giant fish that forgot how to swim!" Mahir hollered at them.

The group played by and in the water for the rest of the day and stayed up late into the night, feasting on figs and fire-roasted fish, seasoned with the sage and wild onions they'd found growing in abundance around them. It was magical. After all they'd been through, all they'd done, this place seemed an impossible treat. That night, everyone slept deep and sound, with not a dream between them to disturb their peace.

LV

SATAN LAY CURLED in heap on the muddy floor of the Brazilian rainforest, squawking macaws and chirping oversized beetles his soundtrack. He'd dimmed his gemstones and camouflaged himself, so his skin was now a mixture of deep greens and browns, like the thick ferns and dripping tree trunks surrounding him.

He was brewing on the conversation he'd had earlier with Michael. He had lost track of exactly how long it had been since their original fight. Not that he kept count of years or dates anyway. That was something God did, and Satan—no Helel, for he despised the name Satan—planned on keeping his ways opposite the Father's, despite Michael's opinion. Their talk had been frank, reminding him of the closeness they'd once shared.

Their relationship had changed over the millennia but had always been based on candid honesty. He wasn't truthful with everyone, but with Michael, Helel found he needed to be. He didn't agree with Michael's position, but he did understand it; after all, they had served together as two of the original archangels. There was a time when Helel had been the closest to God in intellect and beauty. He had been complete—as close to perfection as an angel could be. He had allowed Michael to help him in governing the other seraphim, which was a great honor. The seraphim, who spent their days hovering above God's throne, worshipping Him, were the nearest to Him of all angels. Helel had been quite important, but so had Michael been to him. When the time came and Helel had reached enlightenment, realizing angels could be as great as the Father, he had asked Michael to revolt with him. But he'd turned his back on Helel, even fought him. And now, when Helel was willing to forgive and try once more as comrades before the final battle and all that was to transpire, his kindness was again refused.

Helel winced, thinking of Michael's words. *Are you ready?* He hoped he was. Should this world end, should he lose the Earth in this upcoming battle, where would he—a serpent cursed to spend the days on his belly—go? God's word spoke of a fiery pit, which was quite possible as the Earth was said to be replaced. His thoughts turned to God himself: the Father, the Eternal, the self-centered hoax he was. *Can't even make your creation everlasting*, he thought, knowing God could hear him.

"I could," Helel shouted into the silence. "I *would!* Lest such beauty be wasted, the innocent along with it!"

Me among them, he thought and dropped his head heavily onto the dirt. He folded his remaining two pairs of wings, which had been originally designed to protect him from the Most High's splendor when hovering above His throne. One pair had previously been used to cover his face, the other his feet. The appendages had shriveled since that ill-fated day when he first lowered them—purposefully—in the presence of God the Father, challenging Him for the throne. He did not understand why God insisted he keep the dreaded things. Without the flight pair, stolen by Michael, he was no longer able to fly, and these others seemed as useless as they were ugly. He had repeatedly tried and failed to amputate them, and each attempt was rewarded with their regrowth in their original splendor. He still had the power to shake mountains, lead legions of angels, turn black holes inside out; but this, he could not do. Over time, he'd learned he could at least shrink them. So, he did.

The leaves rustled overhead, releasing fat water droplets onto his face. He cursed silently, watching one of his angels approach from above. He liked resting in peace, and though eagerness could be useful, it was more often exhausting.

"Your Honor, Helel." An angel the color of ash approached. Samael. He would have been commanding in his presence if Helel cared for that sort of thing, because of his extensive muscles and steeply angled jaw, frightening even as he bowed low. Helel hoped this would be a short interruption. "Your servant has been attacked."

Annoyed, Helel turned his head away and closed his eyes. He deliberately left them shut as he considered this. *So, my friend's warning was sincere*, he thought. The near fatal wound of his chosen warrior was a supposed phase in the Father's announced plan, a sign the battle was soon coming. Helel had readied countless human warriors in the past to prepare for this "final war" the Father so often threatened. Some had been better than others; among the most memorable were several kings—his favorites being Alexander from Greece and the great Khan from Mongolia. For a time, he thought Napoleon may be his man, though he'd needed constant guidance because his will was far greater than his size. More recently was his most-prized one—the German—whose mind was so stirred up it had been easy to bend to Helel's pleasure. No, Jubair was certainly not the most impressive warrior, but he would do. For a game to begin, the players needed to meet at the gameboard, and as he finally had chosen a man who matched the so-called "rules" in the Bible, Helel figured they were officially sitting across the board from each other.

The game was about to begin.

"Sir?" Samael was still bowing, though he had allowed his eyes to creep up to Helel's face.

"Yes, I understand. You may rise. It seems the time may be nearer than we assumed, Samael. I need you to collect your army. We need to thin God's herds, strengthen our numbers. See to it no one interrupts Talmuk's healing."

"Healing, sir? He's dead."

"Dead?" Helel narrowed his eyes at Samael. His muscles tensed and the stones on his back erupted in color, suddenly brilliant against his dark flanks. What could this mean? Hadn't God said the injury to his player would not be fatal? He grimaced. "How—oh, forget it. This must still be the time. Do as I say. If Talmuk is already gone, then you have more angels available to carry out the rest."

"Yes sir. I will update you presently." The angel dipped lower, his forehead absurdly close to his feet, and stepped back before turning to leave. He bounded away, first along the giant fronds on the ground and then among the thick of the trees, soaring between dense vines and heavy branches high above the forest floor. With each ascent he changed color, paling until he bore no pigment at all. Swinging into flight like a stone from a sling shot, the angel's giant, invisible torso broke through the tree-cover and disappeared.

Helel watched him leave. What would become of his angels, Samael and the rest, should he not win? They were supposed to be thrown into the fiery lake with him. What would so many angels put into a flame bring? Would they turn against him for eternity for failing them? Did they realize the risk they'd taken when they turned away from God? Helel truly did plan to liberate every order of angel and man. He marveled at what the days would be like if everyone's potential were realized instead of smothered and constantly filtered toward magnifying the Father. Man was made in the image of God—Helel reasoned that meant they, too, could have the same power if allowed.

Helel puffed his chest, filling himself with resolve the way men did before charging into their own crusades. He had only one chance left, and he planned to use it well.

LVI

BREAKFAST THE NEXT morning had been more fish, roasted to a flakey, melt-in-your-mouth sweetness with crushed blackberries on a stone in the middle of their makeshift firepit. They even had mint tea, which had been heaven as far as Isaiah was concerned, sugar or no sugar. Full-bellied and grateful, she sat on the pebbled shore alone, watching the mist dance over the lake.

The waterfall had stilled while they slept, and though the rock it had careened down still shone, nothing was left to interrupt the pool except the breeze. The lake shimmered, as if a thousand tiny mirrors were connected and pivoted on their hinges when the wind brushed over it—though the air was so still, without the change to the water's surface, she wouldn't believe there was any wind at all. Somewhere halfway across the lake, the surface flattened out to one giant mirror, reflecting the tree-covered mountainside on its far end. The rocky bluffs rose and fell like a melody on a perfect summer day—when all the chores were done and nothing was planned or needed by anyone—the kind of day that filled her heart with ambition for dreams she had yet to imagine.

But it wasn't only the shine of the lake or the dark green of the pines that grabbed her. The entire east side was lined with groves of reeds, tall enough a grown man could get lost in them, bright green and lined up like rows of corn. A brown mallard sliced through the water then, on a silent stroll across its private refuge. Crickets and grasshoppers and the occasional rattle of a snake called in the distance.

A dragonfly arrived as the sun peeked "Hello" to the early morning, before approaching its throne. The insect was blue, at least four inches long, with a wingspan just as wide. It hovered before Isaiah, wings whipping through the air so fast they didn't seem to move at all.

"Welcome to my home," it seemed to say, hanging there in front of her as if sizing her up, trying to decide if she belonged there or deserved to even visit. It left in stages, bouncing between the reeds and fronds and dinosaur grass at her feet, then back to face her again. It disappeared as suddenly as it had come—quietly, and with no evidence it had been there save for Isaiah's thoughts, which were again lost in the slow change of the water from early-morning navy-and-gray to a perfect reflection of the pale blue and white sky.

I could stay here, thought Isaiah, *give life another go. Blend in with the world, with no one to hurt or disappoint. Or lose.* Except Rashid, maybe, because Isaiah understood he could be part of it—he needed peace as much as she did. They could stay as friends, or perhaps lovers one day. She knew she was starting to care for him. He might want this, and maybe her, too, and they'd build a cabin close to the lake's edge, small enough not to be noticed unless you knew where to look.

"Beautiful, isn't it?" Elise walked up, hands tucked in her pockets. "Like a postcard."

That's it. A postcard, Isaiah thought. "Wish you were here," it would read, and she'd address it to her husband. Isaiah closed her eyes, chasing the thought away.

"It is."

Isaiah glanced at Elise, then back to the lake, which was now completely smooth. A giant polished pane of glass. She dropped her eyes and marveled at the bedded ground through the clear water. The plants' fronds waved at her softly while the fish ambled around without a care.

"Well, I'm going to stretch my legs. Be right back," she announced, standing, then squeezed Elise's shoulder as she left. She needed to reset her busy mind with the smells and sounds of creation. Anyway, this was just the right type of morning to sing out praise for her blessings, and today that would be better done in solace.

Isaiah wandered from camp far enough to no longer hear the low rumble of conversation. A tanager—or was it a martin?—fluttered through the trees to her right. Adira had said thousands of varieties flew through here every year. His love for Georgia was obvious; one would have thought he'd been born here. How had he come to embrace this place so deeply when his native country was so close by? Could she do the same?

She thought of her own home, the one she had sold off and abandoned with such finality. That town had filled decades of her life—growing up, going to school, and eventually caring for the people that had raised her. And yet she had left it, left them, without a glance over her shoulder. Since leaving, she hadn't spoken to anyone from home. In fact, she hadn't spoken to anyone from her husband's family since the funeral, even though his mom and sister were always calling. They had even shown up on the doorstep a few times, though she had pretended not to be home, silently watching from the upstairs windows until their car exited the long gravel drive. It didn't matter—they had no responsibility toward her in the end—and it wasn't like she was keeping anyone from a child or anything. She just severed the relationships, thinking she was closing that chapter of pain for all of them. It had maybe even been a kindness.

Isaiah's eyes swelled at the memory of her former life. Being a mother had meant even more to her than being a doctor. In the end, though, she hadn't been a good one, so maybe it was best God left her alone, without innocents to rely so naively on her.

It wasn't her fault; no one could have foreseen the attack. Even if she had been there, she couldn't have saved them. Most likely, she'd have died with them. Instead of grieving their loss and blaming her absence, she should be rejoicing in the time God gave her with them and in His grace, protecting her from the same fate. But rejoicing felt wrong, and no matter what had happened that day, whether she could've saved them or instead just held them tight in their last moments, her job as a mother would have been better served. But instead, while they were being blasted by fire and shards of metal, she was busy laughing and eating cake at a lunch-hour going-away party for someone whom she barely knew.

Overcome by grief, Isaiah stopped and grabbed a nearby tree trunk. Her legs were suddenly weak, and her chest swelled, aching for her family. Tears streamed from her eyes, blinding her. Too heavy to stand up any longer, she surrendered to her sorrow, and slid down the tree until she became a crumpled moaning mess on the ground. Then the anger returned.

"Why, God? *Why?*" she yelled, face lifted as if He hovered there with her.

Would He even bother? Scorning herself, she dropped her head to the dirt. She was alone, and God was never tangible, anyway. What hope of comfort could she expect from an invisible friend? Groaning until her chest wrenched, she wept again, curled on her knees, soaking her face and hands in the dirt.

And who do you think I am? A voice came suddenly.

She recognized it as that of her Father, God. She had almost forgotten it existed; it had been so long since she'd heard it.

Must the head of a country be held responsible for every act of its people? Must he answer to every citizen for the turn of the weather? This world is fallen. You live in it. I am not here to fix the fallen world, but to save you for what comes after.

Isaiah held her breath. The words were blunt but true, and any message from God was a gift. Stiffening, she forbade another tear to fall. "Yes, Lord," she whispered, "and that you have done."

She wiped off the dirt and leaves stuck to her forehead then stood. Waiting for her feet to regain circulation, she scanned the area around her. The camp was supposed to be behind her, but unfortunately the area behind looked quite a lot like the area in front—and to the right and left, for that matter. Half-heartedly, she turned to walk in the direction she thought she had come from, this time registering every fallen tree and cluster of roots to not get any further lost. After a few minutes, she pushed through a patch of thorny bushes and found herself at the end of the forest.

The ground here seemed to drop off abruptly, with nothing past the rim of dirt before her but the clear, blue, Georgian sky. Despite her fear that the ground ahead was unstable, she was struck with the thought that this was the brink of the world, so she dropped to her knees and crept forward. She wanted to peer over the ledge, even if it meant crumbling down with it. *Wouldn't it be fitting*, she thought, her head spinning as fear took hold again. *A step into the quiet; an air-filled end to a now air-filled life.*

A valley lay below. Far, far below.

And what a valley it was—quite possibly the most beautiful place she had ever seen. Sunlight flooded the scene. It stood green, so very green, but also brilliantly colored—as if a rainbow had been melted and poured over emeralds. Golden stones scattered around turquois ponds dotting the giant basin, which seemed to stretch for miles. At the far end, a waterfall fed a narrow, cobalt river that rushed through the valley's center, toward her, and disappeared into the base of the wall she was perched on. Straddling the river stood two trees, easily twenty-five feet in diameter, bigger than the great baobab trees of Africa. Hundreds of smaller trees filled the valley, some lush with branches stretched high, others drooped like great weeping willows, many heavy with flowers or fruit.

Also, on either side of the river, the Tree of Life, with its twelve kinds of fruit, yielding fruit each month, the leaves of the tree for the healing of the nations. Isaiah mouthed the verse that Elise had attached to an email somewhere along the way in their planning. It had come from the Bible, in the Book of Revelation. The words had inspired her back then, indicating a once-and-for-all answer to disease. She stood frozen, gaping at the valley below. Could this be it? Could those be *the* Trees?

The bushes to Isaiah's left rustled. The sound was subtle, but it broke the moment. Before she could turn to look, there came a heavy thump, and her face cracked as if a baseball bat had smashed into her nose at the peak of its swing. She fell backward onto broken twigs and soggy grass and, dazed, searched for whatever had hit her. But her eyes wouldn't focus. Everything blurred, as if she were searching through moving water at a submerged world.

Something thick and black near her feet shifted, and within seconds it towered over her, covering her in shadow. She threw her arms in front of her face and rolled into the brush beside her, then scrambled to her knees. A loud rushing noise filled her head, and something knocked her legs away. Falling sideways, her mind screamed at time to slow down, frantic to understand what was going on. The black thing—was it a tree trunk?—shoved under her again, flipping her wildly into the air and slamming her face-first into the soaked ground. Then it was beneath her and on top of her all at once, encasing her body in its iron strength, squeezing tight with a vicelike grip.

Isaiah gave a futile squirm. She tried to scream but couldn't fill her lungs. The scene before her narrowed as her vision weakened. Then darkness edged out everything but the black tree, which now seemed to have fiery eyes and golden fangs. The world disappeared just as she was trying to decide if this was real or a hallucination.

LVII

AS ISAIAH'S BODY fell limp, the devil laughed and flung her over the ledge.

From below, four wings, heavy-laden with ivory feathers, spread wide and shot into the air beneath her. The beast they belonged to raised its arms, and a current of air appeared, catching Isaiah, slowing her fall. She landed in his shining, outstretched arms, which glinted, brilliant and opalescent in the sunlight. Then he raised his eyes, radiant beneath his wild golden mane, which had fallen forward in his rush, until they met Helel's. His wings didn't beat once, but remained open, thirty feet of rippling power, as he glided up the airstream he had charged to the top of the cliff.

"Enough!" the cherub's voice boomed as Helel landed. "What are you trying to do here? You have been banned from this place. The Father commanded you not to kill this one, and yet here you try. Now leave, and do not touch her again."

Helel laughed. "And what will you do if I stay? Brother, if you knew what she and her friends had planned, you would be saying something quite different."

The giant beast half sighed. "Leave us to our obligations, and we will leave you to be crushed beneath man's feet."

"Is this what you think? That I will be crushed? Were you not watching?" Helel fumed. "Humankind will be crushed, not me. Or at least, those who choose to align with the Father's foolishness will. The others will rule in power with me, eyes finally open to that which you work so hard to hide from them."

The beast laid Isaiah on the ground at his feet and pulled out his flaming sword, pointing its tip at Helel's face. "Goodbye, Devil."

Helel, still reeling, melted to the size of a garden snake. He turned to slither away, whipping the golden tip of his tail at Isaiah's head as he did so, slicing open her scalp.

"Oops. Forgive me, holy one," he chuckled, and disappeared into the brush.

⌘

When Isaiah woke, the world was dark. A lonely strip of light illuminated the ground, shining from behind her where the moon hung, full and bright. She pivoted, trying to get her bearings. When she turned her neck, a sting shot from the back of her head, punishing her and filling her ears with a loud buzz. The world was spinning again, and this time it made her nauseated. She pitched forward, leaning on her hands, sprawled flat on the ground to steady herself. Isaiah retched fiercely, which produced nothing as her stomach was empty, and was rewarded with a more intense throb in her skull. She reached up; her scalp was torn, wet. She brought her fingers back to inspect them, though she already recognized the sticky friction of drying blood. *What had happened?*

Isaiah faintly recalled feeling excited, though about what she couldn't remember. There was something else too—some recognition of God. She had encountered Him maybe, or something from Him. Scanning the area, Isaiah spotted the edge of the forest, with its drop-off under the moon, which now seemed to light the way into the empty sky as if it were an ordained path to her destination.

The valley! She remembered then—she had seen the Garden! She rushed forward on her hands and knees, afraid to stand for fear of toppling over. She peered over the ledge at the valley, gripping the grass for balance and feigned security. It was there! Even in the dark it was magnificent. The golden rimmed ponds and cascades of colors shone magically under the silver-blue glow of the moon.

Isaiah sat, fixated on the scene below, investigating every corner of her discovery. She was alone, save for the crickets singing boldly in the surrounding darkness. No one had seen this place in millennia, and now here she was!

She pushed back as a snowflake drifted onto her nose. More fell softly around her, dusting the leaves and pine needles, many disappearing when they landed on the soggy ground. Isaiah lifted her palm to catch the fat flakes, though they melted instantly once touched. She closed her eyes and stuck out her tongue, lifting her face toward the night, at peace in a moment she knew was designed just for her. A cool wind rustled the tree branches, still yet to fully shed autumn's leaves. She sighed again, a smile creeping through her lips; she was blessed. *Thank you, Father, for showing me this!* Isaiah prayed silently, her chest bursting with excitement. She couldn't wait to tell the others.

She scooted back and crawled up a tree to her feet. Her head throbbed, and something warm was trickling down the back of her neck. She bit her lip; it was dry. Her whole mouth was dry, as were her eyes for that matter—signs of dehydration. Had she fainted? Heights had always been a problem for her, perhaps that, coupled with the excitement and dehydration, had simply made her pass out and strike a rock in her fall. She traced her fingers up to the gash in her scalp. It didn't feel good. Tearing a strip from the bottom of what was left of her shirt, she tied it around her head, tight against the open cut to stop the bleeding. The pressure seemed to steady her, and she started back.

LVIII

Elijah

POPE ELIJAH SPOTTED Calan Tonto, sitting on the edge of a velvet couch in the family room at Celebrate Life Funeral Hall, forehead heavy in his thick hands. His black slacks were pulled up, exposing the socks he'd mismatched that morning. Both were nylon, one black and the other dark brown around the ankle. This one paled as it traveled up his leg to expose the face of the Star Wars character, Chewbacca, grinning naively out at the room. Beside Calan, two stone-faced officers in black blocked the doorway, standing as still as the Queen's guards in England. Pope Elijah edged through them, making his way to the pile of a man in Calan's body.

Calan straightened slightly at the pope's arrival, cocking his head sideways to acknowledge him. "So, where's God today?" he asked dryly.

Elijah stopped and bowed crisply. His red-and-violet hued vestment draped heavily on his narrow shoulders. Normally the pope would wear just violet to a funeral, but Elijah was making a statement. He had asked his seamstress to make a special vestment for him to wear today, one incorporating red, the color worn at the funerals of martyred popes. Jubair was not a pope, but as far as Elijah was concerned, he equaled—if not surpassed—one by his life's work.

"Celebrating the coming home of one of His great children, I suppose," Elijah replied.

"Yeah, I suppose." Calan breathed deeply.

"Well, he will be missed." Elijah groaned as he sat. His limbs felt stiff and heavy, like they had been replaced with logs. He wanted to lie down, as he'd been awake now for almost three days straight. He couldn't sleep, though not for lack of exhaustion. Phone calls and hundreds of arrangements needed to be made, and he had a speech to prepare. Above all this, an anxious fog seemed to have permeated the atmosphere, keeping him and half the world awake. "And you, Prime Minister? Where do you suppose God is today?"

"Father, you don't want me to answer that." He grimaced, and looked up, first to the pope's eyes and then down to his hands.

Elijah followed his gaze to the rings adorning six of his fingers. Calan likely thought he looked silly, and perhaps even wasteful, dripping with gold the way he did. But today he didn't care. He liked the jewelry. Each ring held meaning, and helped to hide his age, and add to the majesty of his position, which would amplify the people's respect for God. And wasn't that the point?

"Sure, I do," Elijah answered quietly. He shrugged, giving a half grin to the prime minister as he fingered the large gold cross hanging from his neck. "Every sheep is important to our Father."

Calan cleared his throat. "Yes, well, this is botched, this whole thing. So I imagine God, if he is there—or she, maybe… Well, if God is watching, likely there'd be some regret at not protecting such a great man. Probably Jubair was the one God would… should not have let die."

"God knows what He's doing, Prime Minister. Don't worry. In all things, He works for the good."

"You think so? Well, I don't mean this as a par, but Father, I can't see how this could ever be for the good." Calan sighed. "I'm sorry, I know you're trying to make me feel better. I'm afraid I'm not great company right now. I just wish this hadn't happened. Who will lead us now?"

"Oh, there will be another. You'll see." Despite his words, Elijah worried about the future of the United Nations. Jubair had been the heart of everything. With him gone, the alliance would surely be in shambles. Now, all the good he'd begun, all their giant strides toward peace might crumble. He wondered if now there might be a place for him, perhaps he could step in and encourage, lift the other leaders up while they healed and regrouped. After all, he had avenged Jubair, mightily, with strength and valor at that. Some might look at what he had done in the temple as hateful, a sin even, but he knew it to be righteous and an act of God. Anyone capable of enacting God's will on demand the way he did, surely would be valuable.

Sitting taller, he squeezed his knees, watching the rings pop up above his knuckles as he did. "Perhaps I can help?"

Calan squinted back at him. "Help? How? Do you know someone?"

"Well, son. I *am* someone, who knows *the One*. That might work for your purposes, don't you agree?"

Calan rubbed his forehead firmly. "Oh, wow. Father. We can't have another religious war on our hands. That's what Jubair worked so hard to change. It's why he died."

"I don't think you need to worry about that. God's message is one of harmony and acceptance. Peace, Calan. What that cult did was not peaceful. It was disruptive and arrogant, not to mention barbaric. They were trying to divide the world. I would never support such hateful behavior." Elijah shook his head. "My God is just, yes. But loving. I will spread a message of love and respect."

Calan cocked his head again. "The zealots, they need to be dealt with."

"And I know their language."

"But we can't have the masses expected to follow the teachings of one church."

"Free will, Prime Minister. There is no forcing the gospel on anyone, that is one thing I've learned in all my years. Each man has his own journey with God to complete. My job is and always has been as a guide, a helper, not a vehement fanatic. I've always believed in being tempered. Let me be a voice to help the world through this. Religious freedom is at stake here, can't you see that? Do you know what would happen, how much war would break out, if we polarize religion? As an example, and a leader to major communities of religious-minded people, I can help ease the tension, remind them of the value in tolerance." Elijah locked eyes with Calan. "Before things get worse."

Calan considered his words. "Father, you may be just the right man."

And I beheld another beast coming up out of the earth; and he had two horns like a lamb, and he spake as a dragon. [12] *And he exerciseth all the power of the first beast before him, and causeth the earth and them which dwell therein to worship the first beast, whose deadly wound was healed.* [13] *And he doeth great wonders, so that he maketh fire come down from heaven on the earth in the sight of men,* [14] *And deceiveth them that dwell on the earth by the means of those miracles which he had power to do in the sight of the beast.*

-Revelations 13:11-14

LIX

"I FOUND YOU!" Isaiah announced, breaking through the trees that lined the camp.

Elise looked up. Her face was swollen; she had been crying. When their eyes met, she jumped up and rushed forward.

"Where have you been? We couldn't find you!" Elise grabbed Isaiah's shoulders and, before she could answer, hugged her tight.

Isaiah beamed. "I'm fine. I got lost. Then… then I don't know, I think I passed out." She motioned toward her head absentmindedly. "But Elise—I have news. Good, great news!"

Elise spun Isaiah around and touched the bandage, which by now was caked to her hair. She sniffed, choking on the returning tears. "What? Good news about getting hurt?"

"No, not about that." Isaiah laughed and wiped her eyes. "The Garden, Elise. I've found it!"

"Found the garden? Wait… *the* Garden?"

Isaiah grinned. "Yes."

"Nice of you to make it back," Mahir said, stretching in a yawn as he sauntered up. "What's wrong with your voice?"

"Oh," Isaiah recoiled, suddenly aware of the state she was in—shirt torn exposing her midriff, bloody cloth tied about her head. "Well, who knows? I got hurt. I must have done something. Did you hear though? I think I've found the Garden!"

Mahir yawned again. "Yeah, I heard. Congratulations."

"Mahir, the Garden of Eden! I saw it! The Garden of Eden!"
Isaiah couldn't stop grinning.

Jack stepped up. "Isaiah, where? What makes you so sure?"

"That way." She pointed in the direction she had come from.
"Straight at the moon is how we go." She glanced around at the
group. "Well? Are we going or what?"

Mahir narrowed his eyes at her. "Now? It's the middle of the
night." He turned to his brother, who shrugged back. "Wolves?
Hello? Weren't you the same chick who about shit herself when
we had to sleep in the only shelter around because there might
have been wolves in it?"

"And there weren't any, I remember. I'm not afraid. We'll
be fine." Her eyes danced at Elise, asking for the agreement she
already knew she had.

Rashid stood up and brushed the back of his pants. "I'm
gaming."

Mahir rolled his eyes and looked away. Jack stood matter-
of-factly, obviously smothering his own laugh while he stared
Mahir down before he could spit out an insult. He handed Rashid
a walking stick. "Me too."

"Game, yes. You will be. Hiking along a *game* trail waiting
to be aced by *game* eaters." Mahir held his hands up and stepped
backwards. "Y'all crazy. We've been at this for months, what's
a few more hours?"

"I believe you've hit upon their point, brother." Adira stood
and placed a hand on Mahir's shoulder, squeezing lightly as he
did. "Let's go. I'm intrigued. Aren't you?"

Mahir blinked, gaping in defeat at the ground, which was now
dusted with white powder.

"And in the snow. Nuts." He huffed, falling into line with the
others as they headed into the black brush.

Isaiah had marked the path with broken branches every five
feet, so they found the clearing easily. By the time they reached
it, the sun had joined the skyline.

"There," she announced, hands on her hips. This time she stood tall near the edge of the cliff, chest full.

"Whoa!" Jack grabbed a nearby tree branch and leaned forward, peering down. "That river, it's perfect! It feeds right into the wall. There must be an underground water system, just like I suspected."

"How do we get down there?" Isaiah turned to Adira, who inspected the terrain.

She followed his gaze to the valley below, which was still green, apparently untouched by the snow. Their destination sat in a giant basin, with every side but one bordered by steep rock walls. To their left was the only approachable entrance, from between two swells in the land, a flat path of sand and stone and scattered sagebrush. Giant boulders lay scattered between the garden and the stretch of land as if dropped from above to mark it.

"There." He nodded toward the clearing. "Otherwise we would need to repel, and I don't have equipment for that anymore. We'll have to return the way we came and hike another hour or two down."

"Let's go!" Elise said, pulling Adira's arm and making him smile as they walked away.

LX

Zecheriah

BEHIND THE EASTERN boulders crouched two beasts: Zecheriah, with the face of a giant bird, and Ansiel, who wore pale skin, a small nose, and soft lips like those of the humans above. They sat at the best vantage point in the garden. From here, as the sun rose and flooded light through the valley, they could see everything from the tops of the stone walls to the smallest rodent under the most tangled blackberry thicket.

Entrance to the garden was not allowed, this was a clear order from the Father. It had been thousands of years since they'd had to deal with anyone attempting it—because of the mountain range, yes, but also because of the turmoil God had allowed in the surrounding areas, keeping exploration down. But it had happened before, and it appeared the people above were going to try as well.

"Perhaps if you had not rescued the girl, there would be less to slaughter," Ansiel—whose name meant the constrainer—said gently.

"You are right. I did not understand, though. I just saw Helel, and… he is never up to any good." Zecheriah gazed down over his golden beak. He twirled the smooth, amber handle of his sword, which was compressed per his will to only a few yards in length. It could extend as long as one of his wings if needed. "And he is a deceiver. I figured he was lying again."

"I know. Let us hope we do not have to fight them. But you know the rule. If any of them see us, they all must perish. Our duty is to keep this place sacred. They do not deserve entrance yet. We need to keep it ready for the time after. We must protect the tree, for their sake."

Zecheriah sighed. For the past several thousand years, every second of his life was spent protecting the garden. They had ruled over it since the time of The Cleansing, when man was banished from living there and its borders were secured by the Father from all except those allowed access per the discretion of these two, the heralded guardian cherubim. For the benefit of the children, he and Ansiel could be invisible as they pleased. However, if they got too worked up, if their energy were diverted too strongly, they would be exposed. This was one of Zecheriah's weaknesses. He could get emotional rather easily. He turned away, frustrated. In doing so, his head transformed from that of an eagle to that of a lion.

Zecheriah locked his eyes onto his essence, his "whirling wheel," pulsating on the grass beside him. The jewel-like beryl ring glowed brightly. It was covered in eyes, as were his arms and legs. He and this ring—they were so alike, but also so separate. And yet he was completely under its control. His every move was directed by what power inhabited the wheel, but he still felt detached from the thing. If the ring truly contained his mind, and he was simply its appendage, then why did he feel individual? This body he lived in couldn't simply be a tool. A tool didn't have a will—it just was.

He, however, knew he had a will—mostly because he needed to re-center it so often when faced with the task of hurting another. He never used to think this way. As the essence, he lived out his thoughts through the body of his cherub. He was a remote control for the glorious being God created for His pleasure. But over time, he felt less alive in the wheel that was him and more a part of the angel he controlled. This existence he had accepted for the honor of saving paradise for the children, but it didn't make sense to hurt the ones he was saving it for. Especially today, when he saw God's Spirit in the eyes of the one his brother wanted him to kill. How could that be what he was supposed to do? He closed his eyes, all of them, to calm himself; he needed to regain control.

"I don't suppose we could spar. It would help."

"I am sorry, brother. We must remain at the ready. If they choose not to make their way down here—which I pray is the case—we need to avoid giving them more reason to consider it."

Zecheriah turned his face up toward the cliff where the people had been perched. The wind picked up, rustling his feathers, which also appeared to have eyes, like those of the beautiful bird Adam had called *tevahs*.

On the breeze floated a familiar voice, that of Holy Spirit: *You know my children are among this group. Do what you must to keep the sanctity of the Garden, but if it is possible, take care.*

Zecheriah's heart fell at the words. He had never been a particularly spectacular cherub—if he had, he may have been allowed to be one of those at the foot of God's throne—but he did love the children. Cherubim were supposed to be the guardians of God's domain, meant to keep His Glory protected, but Zecheriah preferred to think of himself as protecting the children from God's Glory. They were, after all, innocents. They didn't have the wisdom that came from being around for so long, and most had no idea what was going on in this realm. They were fixated on their own world, their next meal, on staying alive, or on loving one another. Not enough of them dwelled on the idea of the supernatural, of this realm, of God and Satan and all the forces that made and sustained the Universe. They needed help.

He had been created a cherub though, and his job included helping the children in no aspect other than his current charge.

He filled his chest resolutely and accepted Holy Spirit's words. In doing this, his face changed yet again, this time to that of an ox.

Ansiel watched on. "Three faces in all of five minutes. Are you struggling with our orders again?"

"I was, but not now. You heard the Spirit?"

"I did. Let us offer them warning." Ansiel gripped his forearm. "Zecheriah, calm yourself. We have important things to do."

"I know, brother. I will be ready." With those words, he rose, turned his back to Ansiel, and faced the north end of the canyon. He spread all four of his wings, reaching them behind, toward Ansiel.

From behind him, Zecheriah felt a breeze as Ansiel stretched, returning the gesture. Then came the shock of energy, which meant the tips of each of their upper wings had intertwined. The sound of rushing water and wind, like that of the Great Flood when the deep had opened up and met the storms of the sky, resonated at their touch. Their bodies darkened from their original shimmering white to black and orange, still glowing but now the color of smoldering coal, ready to ignite.

ﰉ

High above the valley, the hikers were blasted by the roar rising from the garden.

"What is that?" Mahir hollered, pressing his hands to his ears.

"I don't know," Adira shouted back. The ground shook as the sound waves bounced off the canyon walls below. He braced himself on a nearby tree and grimaced. "Earthquake?"

"Let's get out of here!" Jack answered, nervously. He pivoted back toward where they had come from, tugging Rashid's arm before breaking into a run. "Now!"

The others hesitated, eyeing each other. Then Adira turned to follow Jack, and they trailed, stumbling as they ran across the hill, away from the canyon and the deafening noise.

In a few seconds, the thunder ended. For a moment, the only sounds the forest made were the faint rush of the river below and the group's panting after they had slowed down. Soon, though, this was joined by the soft rustle of leaves as grasshoppers resumed their bouncing between them, and, eventually, the world rang again with singing crickets and chirping warblers.

"Was that a warning?" Jack announced more than asked as the others caught up. He paced, shaking his hands.

"Jack, calm done. It was an earthquake. We are fine, everything is fine," Adira said.

Jack's eyes were wild. "No, that was not right. That was, I don't know... not right. I'm not sure we should go down there."

Adira glanced at Elise, who stood silently, brow furrowed, obviously deep in thought.

Mahir stepped forward. "Nope. Bony knees is right. I'm out. Something is wrong down there, and I'm not interested in seeing a bigger quake up close."

Adira squared off with his brother and lowered his voice, hands steadying his shoulders. "No, we have to finish this. Everything is *fine*. Trust in Allah, brother."

Mahir sighed, dropping his shoulders and looking away. "Allah, God, Jesus, Buddha, the magical Yeti! Why do you people keep referencing some mystical being that clearly isn't here or helping us? Reality check, brother! We're out in the middle of nowhere, and no one knows we're here. These people..." He waved at the others. "They're all nobodies! I'm not going to die for them. We go down there, and it's the end. That valley is going to rock loose."

Adira turned away. "Very well. I suppose if you want to stay at the camp while we go down, that would be a solution. We will be back, but I'm not sure when." Adira turned, nodding to the others, and started east.

❧

Ansiel nudged Zecheriah, waking him. "They are approaching."

Zecheriah lifted his wing, which had fallen over his head as he dozed, and folded it back, setting his face to that of an Eagle again.

"Good," Ansiel said. "You are thinking." He lifted the corner of his mouth.

Zecheriah nodded. He was ever grateful for Ansiel. The two balanced each other out, which was good because left to his own decisions, the garden would not have flourished as it had.

"I know. I feel them," he answered, rising to his feet and extending his blade to its full length. The sword blazed like harnessed lightning. He turned to stand beside Ansiel, hoping he would not have to be the one to strike the blow.

LXI

"THIS WAY!" ADIRA barked. They neared the end of the steep decline leading down to the canyon. It had been fast going, and their destination was already in sight. The others were excited again, their energy clearly renewed from the exercise, and if truth be told, so was he. He had never considered the possibility of Paradise still existing on the Earth. It had always been known as a far-away treasure, a reward for the hereafter.

Elise's excitement in particular was nearly palpable. She practically swung from tree to tree as she descended the slope. At some point, she abandoned the trees and sprung forward joyfully, arms as wide as her smile, as if she believed she would leap right off the hill and fly. Adira watched as she released herself into the pull of gravity and ran, accelerating the last twenty or so meters, into an almost out of control plunge downhill, legs roiling, and at the last of it shining her big smile his way.

Her eyes caught Adira unaware. How could they always sparkle so bright? Mahir had been right when he'd called her princess; that's just how Adira imagined her. She was a little girl dressed in a frilly costume, inviting them all to a tea party in the magic garden. Even though they were too old for such fantasy, her spirit intoxicated him, and now he was more than happy to drink from the empty plastic cup with her.

At the base of the hill, they stopped to regroup.

"That was fun!" Elise announced, hands on her head as she swallowed gulps of air. She bumped Adira's shoulder with her elbow and paced in a circle, catching her breath. "Well, sir? Wasn't it?"

He offered her a half smile. "A little."

Next arrived Rashid and Isaiah, trailing behind yet again. Rashid's right foot gave out from beneath him, sliding on loose twigs and sending his bottom to the dirt.

Isaiah scooted forward and grabbed his elbow. "Are you all right? You feel okay?"

"I'll make it." He shook her off and stood taller. "I'm fine, really. Just a little excited."

She pursed her lips and stepped back, bumping into Mahir, who had appeared from nowhere.

"Oops, sorry!" She turned, her nose only inches away from Mahir's. "Oh, hi!" She grinned and stepped sideways. "You came!"

"I did." He nodded at Adira, otherwise ignoring her. "Brother."

"Brother." Adira smiled and nodded. "Alhamdulillah."

"Hamduli-leprechaun."

"Hey, guys," Jack interrupted. "I think we're here."

They gathered around Adira, facing the entrance to the valley. Elise's smile faded into a look of wonder as she gripped Isaiah's forearm, her eyes wide.

"Something's wrong. This is too easy." She stepped sideways and scanned the valley. "The angels. The guards."

"Aaand now we are talking about guardian angels." Mahir plunged forward, exasperated. "Let's do this and leave. I'm not trying to be buried alive if another earthquake hits."

They followed him forward, their steps cautious. Before them, the landscape transformed from towering pines and junipers to thick ferns and flowers, everywhere flowers. Thousands of boldly colored petals were on display, all intricately shaped—dew drops, hearts, even angled, jagged spears. The ground was surprisingly free of undergrowth, save for the lush grass and miniature violets standing a few inches at most. Trees hung heavy with fruit—apples, figs, and berries—all plump and flawless.

"Now *this* I can handle," Mahir announced and strode forward. "You doctors do whatever you need to get done. I'm going to eat!"

As he took his next step, the air filled with the same roaring sound as before. It flooded Adira's ears, reverberating off his skin. Then Mahir's foot fell off, as if severed by an invisible blade hanging in midair.

He screamed and fell forward, clutching his leg. His ankle was now a smoldering stump, the end of it cauterized.

"Mahir!" Adira sprinted toward him, his mouth wide. He was almost to him when Mahir's head, tipped down to examine his leg, rotated completely forward, detached. It hit the ground with a soft thud and rolled toward the garden. In that instant, the grass indented in front of it as a sound like a blade slicing through the air pierced Adira. Mahir's face bounced off of nothing, suddenly on fire, and rolled backwards.

Adira stopped at the sight of Mahir's severed head. The eyes were only half closed, but his mouth was wide open. Already flames melted the skin at his hairline, pulling his lips taught and curling them back in a charred mess, exposing his teeth. Fat sizzled between the pink flesh of his muscles. What was once the face of his brother was fast dissolving into a grotesque, blazing skull.

"Please, no!" Adira howled, dropping to his knees. "No!"

But it was real. This was really happening, and it was not something new. His mind flashed to another time, when he had caused this same thing, when he had lit and then watched fire consume the faces of hordes of souls who had chosen not to follow along with the militia's ideas. He saw again the burning image of the eyes of a woman from a Turkish mountain village, one not two hours from his own Kathre. Her story was typical, her horrific end his daily grind. She had promised to work for them and even give up her body if they would only let her children free. They hadn't, though—rules of the militia—and she was chained to a building they set fire to. As that one burned, her eyes had pled, and he had actually seen her tears boil—desperate for them to enslave her if this one wish were granted. When it was done, her skull was exposed in much the same way as his brother's was now, in a blazing empty stare.

"Adira! Get back," Elise yelled, stepping up beside him, her hands tugging at his shirt.

Adira leaned against her, unaware of anything but Elise and the buzz in his head and the throbbing in his chest. His heart raced, pulsing blood so fiercely he somehow suddenly felt it through to his arms and wrists, until his fingers throbbed with each beat. He tried to regain himself, to focus on their situation. What was happening? He had an urge to grab his brother, and a lump somewhere in the pit of his stomach cried to be set free, telling him to get up and *go*. But when he tried, he couldn't move. His strength had abandoned him. From behind came more, something else—words—someone was shouting.

Jack. Jack was shouting. "Let's go!"

Elise grabbed Adira's face. Her palms, sweaty and cold, centered him as she turned it toward her.

"Adira!" Her hands and voice trembled, through the thundering that filled the air. She put her nose two inches from his and gripped his jaw tightly, until his eyes drifted to meet hers. "Yes, look at me! We have got to go. *Now.*"

Standing, she clutched his shoulders and turned him away from Mahir, then scooped her arm beneath his and tried to lift him. He didn't move. Next came Jack, clapping him on his back and grabbing his other arm. Rashid stepped up too and wrapped his arms around Adira's waist from behind. Then they were up and half pulling, half carrying him away, while Isaiah walked backward, watching the area as they left.

∽

Behind, though the group could not see them, the guardian cherubim loomed, both brimming in their own turmoil.

"Now! This needs to end now. We must stop them." Ansiel's words blared at his partner.

Zecheriah nodded. He inched forward on his copper hooves, wings wide, shoulders open, both hands clasped near his head on the handle of his sword. His face pulsed, between the appearance of a lion, teeth bared, mane wild, and a man, downtrodden and sad.

Ansiel urged him on. "You are not alone. Be strong and courageous, keeper of the most holy Garden!"

Zecheriah bellowed in anguish and swung his blade, skimming Isaiah's chest. The flames tore through her shirt, scorching her skin.

"Yeeeaaoow!" she shrieked. "Run, now!" She spun around and fell on top of Adira, who by now was walking. He stumbled, caught unaware. The others grabbed him again and hauled him forward and away, heavy and limp, his feet dragging, his mind lost.

Zecheriah hesitated, watching them go, impressed by their fearlessness—all risking their lives for this man who clearly loved the one Ansiel had stopped.

"Zecheriah." Ansiel walked over to his friend. "Please. Do this."

Zecheriah dropped his gaze. "I'm sorry. I cannot."

Ansiel sighed, then brushed Zecheriah's shoulder with his wing, dragging it along his friend's scapula, and down the length of his wing, until their tips entwined. The two angels darkened, their skin glowing in the way lava brews beneath a smoldering volcano, waiting to erupt. The air once again filled with the howling wind they released. Then, Ansiel sprang up, Zecheriah falling to his knees to watch.

LXII

BY THE TIME the group reached the edge of the forest, Adira, though still sloppy and disoriented, had regained his legs and scaled the hillside with the others. For once Rashid led, bounding forward between trees and exposed roots.

Just as the noise seemed muffled, and the space between them and the invisible terror started to widen, Isaiah's foot plunged through the ground. She fell, waist-deep in the dirt, gripping at the failing land.

"Aaah! Help!" she yelled, voice frantic.

Rashid spun around and ran back, seizing her arms. He pulled, bracing his feet against a nearby scattering of twigs, hoping they'd offer some traction, but instead dug useless channels in the earth.

Behind them, the noise crashed forward through the forest. Rashid spun around, worried at the sound. The trees popped and cracked, splitting apart as the deafening roar approached. He shouted for help, trying desperately to keep Isaiah and himself from falling into the hole, but the others couldn't hear, and the ground kept giving way.

He looked again toward where they had come from. Whatever was chasing them had almost caught up. It shook the trees and severed branches, catching them on fire and dropping them to the ground in a blazing trail. If they didn't hide, fast, they would all die. He grabbed at Isaiah again as her weight dropped suddenly, pulling them farther forward. The hole. The caves. Wincing, hoping he was right, he let go as gently as he could and watched her drop away.

Then Rashid ran to Jack and Elise, who still straddled a struggling Adira up the hill. He grabbed Jack's arm and pointed at the ground where Isaiah had fallen.

"Jump in! A hole! Caves!"

Jack blinked as his words took hold and nodded fiercely. The two grabbed Adira, suddenly full of power. In seconds, they had him slammed forward and shoved down. Afterwards Jack went, and then Rashid grabbed Elise's arm, and nodded reassurance at her, then braced behind her back as she slipped down after the others. Glancing up one last time, Rashid flung himself down.

Above him, a black snake with bright red eyes whipped its tail at a branch in the tree where it perched, cutting it free. The branch fell, heavy with leaves, over their way out.

LXIII

Ansiel

ANSIEL CHARGED THE hill. His now eagle eyes searched fruitlessly through the forest for the people. They were gone. He had failed.

"You looking for your victims?" Helel asked from the trees. "I believe they went that away." He laughed, pointing his golden tipped tail in the air and spinning it around senselessly.

Ansiel glared back, then, deciding to ignore him, turned toward the garden, which he could not leave unattended for long. And right now, Zecheriah as guard was the same as it being unattended. He raised his hands, commanding the air to rise with them, and form a chilled stream. It pushed forward through the burning trees and shoved all oxygen away, suffocating the fire.

Ansiel followed the stream back to the garden, where he found Zecheriah sulking, his head shaped now like an ox's. On one side of him rested his flaming sword, and on the other side his essence pulsated, the center wheel rotating and jerking on its axis, like a joint badly in need of oiling.

"The Father will not approve of this." Ansiel trudged up, shoulders heavy. He sighed. "You know when you are weak, Zecheriah, in the end more will have to die. You aren't being merciful. You believe allowing them reprieve is kind, but it is not. This will be difficult to correct. Our kindness to man is best administered in keeping this place secret, whatever it takes."

Ansiel stretched, trying to ease his mind. Beside his body, the center wheel of his own essence hummed as it spun softly. His wings rose as he let the wind, no longer his captive, flow through them, fluttering the eyed feathers loosely.

"I am sorry, you are right."

The eyes on Ansiel's essence widened, sympathizing with Zecheriah, until after a moment, when they narrowed, and focused on a form descending from the land behind. As they contracted, so did the eyes on his angel body, whose head had converted back to its lion form.

"Helel."

The jeweled snake approached, laughing softly.

"You are not allowed to enter," Ansiel warned. He glided forward to just inches from Satan's taunting gaze.

"Oh, believe me, I'm not interested." Helel jabbed out his forked tongue until it was millimeters from Ansiel's sword, then shook it in warning. He dragged it back into his mouth slowly, grinning, and sat on his haunches. "As far as I'm concerned there are much more valuable treasures out here. What have you got in there to tempt me? Fruit? Plants? An eternity of green, green, green? What a bore. Out here are the people. *They* are the real treasure, much more entertaining."

"They are precious," Ansiel answered flatly. "What do you want?"

"You should have let the woman fall, you know." Helel snickered again. "You"—he pointed at Zecheriah, now laughing so hard he lost his breath— "you thought you were doing her a favor, but then you tried to kill her anyway!" He closed his eyes, sides shaking hard as he snorted at his own joke.

"What. Do. You. Want?" Zecheriah said, now alert and perched next to Ansiel. The two stood side by side, towering over Satan, their upper wings extended out into a massive wall of muscle and power and flame.

"Oh, sure. As if the splendor God gave you two is not already filling this whole place! Drop your threats and glory, brothers—I am not interested in causing trouble. I only wish to ask a question. Or has the great Father disallowed that as well?"

Ansiel considered his words, then lowered his wings, hesitating after a few inches. "No, He did not."

"Thank you. I wonder if you would be interested in allowing the people through. For a price, of course. I know something that would be of extreme value to you both." Satan stretched his neck to his left and right before returning his gaze. "What I can share with you would allow you a new place in a world with no more secrets—no more injustice or domination of anyone over any other."

Ansiel's wheel darkened, transforming his face into an eagle's. He looked past Helel to the still forest beyond, and answered, "the Lord God has banished man from the Garden of Eden. Our duty is to guard from him entering. We cannot do what you ask. Nor would we desire what you offer."

Helel persisted. "Come now, you could be so much more than you are, both of you. Surely, watching over a meadow for eternity was not what you were hoping for when you awaited assignment in the time before?"

To their side, Zecheriah's essence pulsed. His outer wheel dropped forward as he kicked out with his copper hooves, knocking Satan in the chin. "Enough, be gone! Your answer is no."

Satan folded backward, losing his balance. He straightened, and flexed his jaw, chuckling softly again. "Fools and their losses! You will see. To deny such beautiful, innocent life a chance at paradise... it is not right. But I suppose justice and forgiveness are just words to you, not statutes you actually uphold."

"This life you speak of, is it yours or the people's? I have not known you ever to think of others," Ansiel said.

"Both. But why should it matter? Life is life. Why should one life be punished just for belonging to a race who was never perfect to begin with. We were, after all, created. Why should God create an imperfect being and then punish them for being that way? Why should I be held to a standard impossible for any of His creation?"

The edges of Ansiel's mouth dropped in pity for the serpent. He had reason to be bitter. Most of the Father's punishments were not permanent, but the rejection given to him had been.

"Helel, this conversation has met its end. Go now." With that, he and Zecheriah joined wings once more. This time, their union created an air current that emitted from their bodies in all directions, flooding the valley and pushing Satan with such force he slid away.

Helel grimaced, then curled his lips in a sneer. "I'll take my leave. But be clear, if necessary, I can and will crush you both." Then he turned, the cherubim's wind spinning him on his haunches, and slithered away.

LXIV

THEY HAD DROPPED into an underground lake.

Well, I'm back in the water, Rashid thought, swimming in the direction he imagined to be up for what felt like meters, until he broke the surface and gulped mouthfuls of dark air.

"Guys? You here?" He heard splashing to his left and turned to face it. "Jack?"

"No, it's Isaiah," came the reply. "Rashid?"

"Yes. Where's Jack?"

"I don't know. Anyone else there?" Isaiah called, her voice echoing off the walls. They were in a cave all right. "Where is the side of this place?" Rashid heard her swim, until her form appeared under the only light around, a beam shining down from where they had fallen. She grunted as she dropped beneath it, onto solid ground, heavy as a soaked towel. "Here, Rashid. The side is here."

"I'm coming!" He gasped and swam toward her voice, his shoes clumsy in the water. They caught on the mud beneath, soft but firm, and he scrambled forward, clawing with his hands until they heaved himself up and out of the pool. But instead of dirt, he landed on something warm and bulky, and clothed. A person. Rashid groaned, maneuvering around flaccid limbs. He rolled the body under the light, which was just to the side, until it illuminated the familiar pale flesh of his friend.

"Jack. Even in the dark you glow," he said, shaking him. There was no answer. "Jack?"

"Rashid?" Isaiah's muffled voice answered. "You okay?"

"I think so." He shoved Jack harder. "Jack!"

Beside him, Rashid felt Isaiah edge closer. He watched as her hand reached into the light and pulled Jack's T-shirt down over his exposed flesh. She scooted up and felt his neck, then leaned forward, placing her ear just above his face.

"He's breathing, pulse is good," she said, probing his limbs and torso. She pressed gently against his shoulders and finally behind his head, examining him. Her fingers came back covered in blood.

"Where did that come from?" Rashid asked anxiously.

"His shoulder. Head feels okay. I can't tell about his neck until he wakes. He might just be knocked out. Don't move him." She pivoted on her heels and pushed her hands to the floor, groping the dirt. "Elise? You there?"

Rashid stood with her, carefully, and squinted into the light. "How far did we fall?" Above, the ray was irregular and squirming on one side. Something was hanging near the hole they dropped through, which appeared at least five or six meters above. He grabbed Isaiah's shoulder. "Look. Up."

She obeyed, then flinched. "Elise, down here!"

Elise squirmed above them. It appeared that half of her rested on a ledge not far from the top, but her legs dangled feebly beneath her. Above, thin streams of light squeezed around the leaves and twigs attached to the large branch that lay across the hole they fell through, merging as they descended.

"Don't mind me," she huffed. "I'm just hanging out."

"Be careful!" Isaiah called.

"You guys think I can jump? Will you catch me?" Elise hollered from above. "Or should I stay, and you can come up too?" She panted, then swung her feet forward. They caught on the wall and bounced off. She tried again, softer this time, until she found it and braced against it, groaning loudly as she pulled herself up onto the ledge. "Hey, where's Adira?"

"I'm here." His voiced was weak but clear. "I'm fine. Stay there."

Rashid sat back down. He reached forward and rubbed Jack's body again. "Jack? Come on, Captain, wake up."

Jack moaned into the dirt. He pulled his arms closer to his chest and reached up to wipe his face. "Why is it so dark?" He pushed himself up. "Where are we?"

Rashid breathed a heavy sigh of relief and squeezed Jack's arm. "Hey, sit still. You were knocked unconscious. Let the good doctor check you out."

Jack leaned back down, bracing himself on his elbow and probed his head.

"My head feels fine. My shoulder hurts, but otherwise I think I'm all right."

"That's the adrenaline. You'll feel it in a bit." Isaiah scooted forward, and, sitting cross-legged beside him, reached up to his neck. "Tell me if any of this hurts." She strained as she examined him. "You should feel this if there's a problem. Usually."

"Nah, I'm whole, Isaiah. Really." He looked left and right and made a giant arc out of his head. "I can move it fine."

"It isn't just about being able to move it," she answered, gently cupping his chin with her hand. "Let me make sure. No headache? You feel nauseated? Ringing in your ears? You can see okay?"

"No. To all of it. Well—you, I can see. But other than this light, it's pitch-black down here."

She laughed. "Well, just sit still for now, I'm going to check you again in a bit. And tell me if you get any of those symptoms." She turned around. "Adira, you okay?"

"Not particularly, no." A light shot through the dark from where his voice originated. He had turned on one of the flashlights.

"What should we do?"

"Doctor, I do not know what you should do. I am not going back there." He whipped the light from her and ran it about their surroundings.

Rashid followed its beam. The cave was maybe twenty meters across at its widest point. Its sides were laced with tree roots and stones, but one was rocky. Many of the heaviest stones had tumbled down and formed a pile against one wall.

Adira stilled the light, lowering it lowered abruptly to the ground. "My brother. He's gone."

From Rashid's side Isaiah spoke, her voice soft. "I'm so sorry, Adira."

He didn't answer.

For a moment, no one spoke, and the cave seemed to go even darker as the reality of what had just happened sank in. Jack was the one to break the silence. "How did that happen? What *was* that?"

"The cherubim!" Elise cried from above.

"Elise, shh! They'll hear you," Isaiah whispered fiercely.

"Oh." She cringed away from the light. "Sorry!"

"Are the cherubim the guards you were talking about?" Rashid asked, eying the hole they fell through.

"They are," Jack answered. "Unbelievable." He shook his head. "You go your whole life saying you believe something, trying to be a certain way, hoping it's all true. Then it is, and it tries to kill you."

"Tell me about it," Isaiah answered.

"So, are you saying we have to go through them to get into the garden?" Rashid asked.

"We do."

"We'll never make it." He paused, swallowing hard. "We'll all die. Just as fast as Mahir."

"We might," she replied.

"Well, I don't think I want to go back, either," Jack said. "It doesn't seem like a fair fight."

"Hey, down there! What's the plan? I come down or you come up?" Elise quipped.

Rashid cringed, checking the hole again. This was not going to work. They were being too loud. And they needed a plan.

"You come down," Adira answered stiffly. "We rest in here for now. When it is safe, I'm leaving." He shined the flashlight to her left, on the wall of rock. "Go down this way, I'll guide you."

"'Kay." Elise leaned on her belly and reached her foot out to test the first rut, which was close. When it did not give way, she shifted her weight out, still holding the ledge, and squeezed her other foot over alongside it. She stood this way, looking frozen and confused, until Adira pointed out another hold for her feet. She snaked her foot out again and tested, then took hold of it too. Before letting go of the ledge, she peered down then grabbed a thick root from the dirt beneath it. Elise moved quickly from there, as if afraid in stalling something might give. Every shelf and root held, though, and soon with a thud, she dropped to the ground near the others. "Okay, well that's done. We are all officially trapped underground. Together."

"For the time being," Adira answered.

VXV

THE GROUP WAS more tired than they realized, and the grief from Mahir's fate, along with the gloom of the cave, subdued them until they were as drowsy as the evening. They nestled in the corner, hoping for security in a palpated wall, and cozied up to each other for sleep as was now their habit. They dozed all day, and even as night stretched her arm over them, her purple and black sleeves blanketing their bodies, they still slept in the embrace, breathing deep what little fresh air made it down into the pit.

Adira slept alone, or rather tried to, in the false assurance that the two meters separating him from the others provided solace. It felt like isolation either way. He was frustrated, sad, and angry at everyone, his brother included, at what had happened.

He'd actually believed Mahir's words in the cell that day when he promised to start over. Mahir had always had big dreams that never panned out, but this time Adira was sure it'd be different. It was supposed to finally happen; he was going to settle down, marry and grow their family. Make him an aam.

They had known an *aam*, or uncle once, as boys. He had always seemed so *big*, so full of life. He had been kind, often surprising their grandmother with flowers when she was sad, missing her husband, and was always trying to make the family laugh. Once he had filled empty Coke bottles with chilled beef broth and passed them out, claiming them a special treat he had found discounted at the local market. His mother had fallen for it, her eyes wide as roti after she took a drink. They had all laughed so hard that day, hard enough to make his sides hurt. But in the end, his uncle met the same end as Adira's parents. His enormous, silly, vibrant life had vanished with a shot to the head.

And then entered the militia.

Adira scowled. All he had done with the regime he did for Mahir. He had done it in the hope that he would know freedom, and of course one day have a chance to live deeds worthy of paradise. Now, because of these foolish tourists and their fanatical ideas, his brother was gone. Adira leaned back and turned his cheek against the cold wall. He breathed deep the scent of earth and water. This he loved and had wanted to share with Mahir too. The beauty and peace of Allah's created world was not just a reminder of Him, but a gift, and far better than the cloud of intoxication Mahir had lived in.

His brother had been a fool; he died a fool's death.

"It is Allah who has made for you the earth as a resting place, and the sky as a canopy, and has given you shape and made your shapes beautiful and has provided for you sustenance." Adira quoted softly one of his favorite passages from the Quran, then pressed his face against the wall harder, until his neck ached against the unforgiving earth. He wrenched his eyes shut, a prison for any tear that dare attempt escape.

It had all been real, though, hadn't it? What had happened to them, to him, was what he proclaimed by his faith after all. He believed in Eden, the *Jannat 'Adn*, as well—to him and his fellow Muslims it was their hope for paradise after death; the eternal reward for those who were worthy, and chosen, if Allah be willing.

Adira was suddenly tired. So tired he could imagine even falling asleep and never waking. He relaxed as he considered the irony of their situation; his brother lying at the foot of where Adira had worked his whole life to have the privilege to rest. He, in turn, might lie dead in this cave—which was a grave of sorts— and the place his brother would never have the privilege to rest.

LXVI

IN THE END, Jack's shoulder wasn't as bad as Isaiah thought and stopped bleeding completely in the night—with only the little pressure from a bandage she had fashioned from his shirtsleeve tied around it.

"Looks good, I heal you!" Isaiah said, pushing gently on Jack's forehead with the heel of her palm after checking it again. "I'll add that to your bill."

"Thanks, doc," he answered sarcastically. "Is it good enough for more hiking?"

"Well…"

"Where do you think this water is coming from?" Elise interrupted. "There's a current, see?"

"This place is a holding pen. I think it's coming in from that way," Jack waved to their left. "But from here I haven't figured where it can leave."

"You think it feeds the lake? Through the waterfall?"

"Maybe. It might come from the garden too. It probably enters through the base of that bluff."

"If this is the river we were following," Rashid said thoughtfully, "why don't we keep the same tactic and follow it again? What if we enter through where it leaves the garden? We may be able trace the caves back along the edge of the water to and maybe even through the wall where the river enters the mountain.

They shouldn't hear us over the water. I don't think they would even see us coming—the ledge where the river enters is at least a kilometer or two away from where we were attacked."

Jack gaped at Rashid. "Are you serious? You want to go back? You said yourself they'll kill us."

"I am," Rashid answered. "I've never seen anything like this. This is incredible, Jack. This God you all talk about, this is your proof. Or proof of something; I'm not sure what it proves, really. But I would like to learn more about it. The garden and these beasts seem like a good way to start. Anyway, what have I to lose? What have I to go home to?"

"Rash, I can teach you about God, and the garden. No death required," Jack answered, immediately regretting his words. He turned toward Adira, relieved he couldn't see the scorn likely tightening his face. He looked back to his friend. "Listen, it's suicide. Please. We had a go at it, it didn't work out. This is not a good idea."

Rashid squinted. "How could this *not* be a good idea? My friend, this is the find of a century—of a millennium! Never mind the garden—those things out there, those alone are worth returning to find!"

"Then let's go back and regroup," Jack answered. "Get cameras, more people, maybe a rocket launcher or two."

"Jack, I'm going too," Isaiah cut in. "I think his idea is good."

"Isaiah, these are angels we are talking about. They've somehow managed to keep this place a secret since Adam and Eve were kicked out. I'm sure they've mastered detecting intruders." Jack sighed, hard. "This is a bad idea." Rashid had known Jack wouldn't leave him, so by volunteering he had essentially volunteered them both, without consulting him first. If Jack let him go alone and something happened... He grunted in frustration. He couldn't abandon his only friend in the world. "Fine, ugh! This is stupid."

"It seems that way now," Rashid said.

"It will still seem that way later, Rash." He answered, defeated. "But I guess we have done some stupid things together. This may just be the last one."

"Look!" Rashid pointed at the water, which seemed to be moving in the center of the pool, to their right. He stood and dusted off his pants, then bent near the lake, listening intently. "Toss me a flashlight." He crouched on his knees and stuck his head out farther, then reached out, palpating the dancing waves. "Water. I hear water."

Jack snorted at his friend's words. "Rash, you are a genius. Who needs vision when you're around?"

"No, moving water. I hear water dripping, maybe pouring, back there." He raised his voice slightly. "Adira. The flashlight?"

Adira sat in the corner again, staring into space, nowhere and everywhere all at once, as he had since night before. He complied, slowly passing the flashlight.

"Thanks." Rashid gave him a half-smile and clicked the light on, then shined it down the cave. "It's a tunnel. There is plenty of room for us this way."

"Are you sure? Who is to say this thing is even going to take us in the right direction?" Jack worried.

"Jack, it's a classic karst system. These rivers follow hydro graphics. You know that. Karst systems are complex and extensive, but their mechanics are universal—*literally* set in stone. This one *is* going to be connected to that river"—Rashid waved his hands toward the Garden—"and to that lake," he finished, pointing to the back of the cavern. "I can't believe you wouldn't want to even just *look*."

"What's a karst system?" Isaiah asked.

"It's the reason this crazy idea isn't so crazy," Rashid answered. "Out here, the rivers—they plunge underground and surface again. The karst is the limestone-rich region along the Caucasus mountain's southern slopes. The bedrock is made of limestone, among other things, which gets eroded by water and carbonic acid. Over time cracks develop, which channel water in new directions, then the cracks become fractures, and more water flows through them—a new path of least resistance, you see? The fractures eventually become streams—you'll have occasional sinkholes, cave systems, keeping things interesting—and eventually underground rivers where rock once dominated."

"Yes," Jack rubbed his arms nervously. "Entire waterways form, bringing water in and out of the ground and feeding into larger rivers. Georgia has some impressive ones, actually. Some of the larger rivers drain into karst systems and resurface downstream, like the Shaora, draining off the Great Rioni River. It disappears for almost two kilometers, and resurfaces at Sharpula, this giant rocky cave—it's just vomited out of the thing like it got sick on some bad Chinese food."

Rashid stepped in again. "I believe your river, Dr. Harper, fell into the karst zones. To be big enough to be a headwater to all those other rivers, I don't think it could have completely disappeared, maybe it just got a little rerouted."

"Rash, but are you sure this is even safe?" Jack shook his head.

"This is going to work," Elise interrupted. "We are getting in the Garden today. I know we will. God revealed it to me."

Jack squinted at her, exasperated. "The same God who put those angels on guard? The ones who tried to kill us?"

"They *did* kill one of us," Adira interjected. He lifted his head, glaring at the others. His eyes were wild, the flashlight's glow reflecting off them like a laser, slicing through the dark of the cave. "Or have you forgotten so quickly?"

"I'm sorry, no. Yes, exactly. My point exactly." Jack looked back to the others, desperate. "I'm just saying I don't understand why He would tell you we can enter, then put guards out there to stop us. It seems a little contradictory."

"It is. It doesn't make sense, I know. But we *are* getting in," Elise answered. "He does things that don't make sense to us all the time. I've learned to trust His word over the sense of the matter. That's why we're children and He's the Father. Didn't He say, 'I will destroy the wisdom of the wise; the intelligence of the intelligent I will frustrate?'"

At that, she strode to the water's edge and turned, holding out her hand while staring at the flashlight expectedly. Rashid complied, dumbfounded. She smiled back, stepping forward.

"Well then. What a child." Adira shook his head and glared at the ground. "You're all going to get yourselves killed chasing this."

Jack fell silent as he and the others waited, staring into the dark where Elise disappeared, half expecting it to spew her back out, dead or close to it.

"I guess we get a move on. I'm thirsty." Isaiah sighed and grabbed her knees, squeezing them as she stood. They had become much leaner on this trip. Her bones, which previously had the cushion of muscle and fat softening their contours, were now thinly coated with little more than skin. She turned her head back over her shoulder, toward Jack and Rashid and shrugged. "You coming?"

They followed.

LXVII

ADIRA PLANNED TO give them two days' time to chase Elise's fairy tale before abandoning them for dead and leaving on his own. He planned to spend another night or two at the waterfall even if they didn't make it back here, though, just in case. Any longer and the return hike could get too dangerous; fall had set in the mountains, and the rain and snow would have to be dealt with on the return journey. Every extra day meant the risk of even colder temperatures.

He stared at the darkness the others had willingly stepped into, hoping in an hour or so they might return, maybe having found a dead end. Adira's eyes, though heavy, had adjusted to the dim light already and were able to make out the contours of the cave, his home for now. He slumped his head back against the dirt wall, watching the surface of the pool shudder softly. It undulated rhythmically, perfectly cadenced despite their intrusion, despite the drama they had brought into the pit and the turbulence in his heart.

A log drifted into the center of the lake. *Odd*, he thought, *that being down here.* Perhaps it had fallen in with them. The trunk was long, smooth, and thick; maybe the base of one of the Georgian oak trees, or the trunk of a maple. It must have been a beautiful monster in its day to get as big as it did. He watched it, wondering what story it had dragged down here with it. Had lightning struck it? Was it a victim of landslide or fire? Or had it succumbed to the appetite of the oak splendor beetle, eating its meat bit by bit over the years until a single gust of air was too much to brace against?

The log stirred, rolling gently as a current nudged it from beneath. It swayed until one end dipped under the water and the other rose, revealing a much thicker breadth to the tree. It turned on its center and glided toward him.

That's no log, Adira realized, about the same time he noticed it was breathing. His heart jumped; *it was breathing.*

Adira scurried backward until he hit the clay wall behind him, then spun to find a way out. He needed to leave. A curved root protruded a half meter above him. Jumping, he grabbed it and hauled his legs up. The next stone, not too far overhead, looked secure but gave way as soon as he tested it, tumbling down, chunks of mud bouncing with it. Throwing his hand up again, he shoved his fingers into the gap where the rock had been and climbed higher.

As he scrambled up the wall, the sound of water dripping came from behind him, as whatever was in the pool reached the shore and rose. The thud of heavy flesh against solid land came next. Adira shuddered silently, still climbing as fast as his arms would allow.

"Saeduni ya Allah—*help me, Allah!*" he pleaded then winced, a tear squeezing out from his clenched eyes.

Before he made it any higher, it was upon him, wrapping itself around his torso, plucking him from the wall as if all his strength and speed were a joke. It swung him through the air without a sound except for the grunt he let out when it dropped him back on the floor.

Adira rolled over, gasping. Eying the wall, he shot up, fixated on escape, but the thing grabbed him again.

"Adira, why do you run from me?" it said, placing him down, softer this time. "I'm here to help you."

Adira stopped, lifting his chin to face it. He squinted, trying to make out its outline. It looked like a giant serpent—a snake maybe, or some type of monstrous lizard. *But how could it speak? How could it know his name?* Whatever it was, it settled down on his haunches, positioning itself between Adira and the wall, nearly filling the cave.

"I'm not going to hurt you." It said.

He glanced down at himself; all was intact. But he must be dreaming? He kicked the dirt; it was solid. He opened his eyes wide, even wider still as sometimes in dreams this would wake him. But he was still there. *Fly,* he thought, *I can fly away if this is a dream!* He jumped up, over and over, but didn't leave the ground.

"What are you doing?" The beast cocked its head. "Are you… are you trying to fly?"

Adira stopped, disheartened.

"Curious," It said. "Have you been able to fly before?" It spread a set of shriveled-up wings on its flanks and turned to examine them. "I used to fly." Regarding Adira again, it continued, now with a heavy drawl. "But then, those with power don't always use it for good, do they?"

Adira peered up at the beast. Its head was just inches from the hole. If he could get up there, he could jump out onto land.

"Look at me," It boomed. "I need to talk to you."

Adira squeezed his fists, trying to stay their trembling. "Who are you?" he managed, amazed at how solid his voice sounded.

"Your friend."

"If you were my friend, you wouldn't stop me from leaving."

"I'm stopping you from leaving *because* I am your friend," it answered. "Ansiel and Zecheriah will kill you the moment you leave here. You are hidden for now. I covered this place—to protect you, actually—but if you leave, they will not need any help in spotting you."

The beast shrank back, recoiling to half its size. Something like gems along its spine ignited as it did and stayed bright, even after it had shrunk, lighting the cave with streaks of red, blue, green, and purple. The colors bounced off the water and danced along the stones in the walls.

"Beautiful, isn't it?" The serpent-monster grinned, and a golden tongue whipped in and out of his mouth. "I was the Prince of Light—a prince, if you could imagine—before He turned on me. Adira, it's only a matter of time before He does the same to you."

"He," Adira answered, his mind racing. "You mean Allah? Are you Iblis?"

"I am, sort of. But remember, stories have many sides. And you, Adira, have been listening to a very biased side."

Then this was Iblis, Satan, the beast referred to in his beloved Quran, originally named Azazel—who Elise called the devil Lucifer—to him the satanic jinn who was condemned to Hell for refusing to bow to Adam, thus rebelling against Allah's decrees. Adira stood tall and filled his lungs, then let the air out slowly to calm his racing heart.

"A udhu billahi minash shaitan nir rajeem!" He recited the dua impulsively. Its words reassured him; *I seek refuge in Allah from the accursed Satan.*

The serpent lay flat on his belly, yawning, then lowered his head. "I'd be happy to tell you my side, if you would like."

Adira swallowed. "I would."

"You know about God, that He made you, made all that." Iblis nodded toward the ceiling. "He needed to feel loved, you know? He *is* love, I'm sure you know. But love without another... well, that is nothing great at all." He paused, eyes fixed on Adira. "Anyway, we were here long before you. He made us first. We even had our own world. With us, though, He really put forth some effort. He gave us powers and beauty—unimaginable to your kind—because we came from the fire in His eyes. From Him." Satan paused a moment, and got a faraway look in his eyes, as if remembering something sweet from long ago, then shook his head and narrowed them at Adira.

"You met the cherubim. Did you notice their essence? The glowing wheels covered with eyes by their sides?"

Adira's face dropped as he thought of the day before.

"Of course not. You were a little... distracted. Well, be aware next time. The whirling wheels, or essence, is where their soul lives. Their bodies are only puppets, really, because the essence tells them what to do. Those you can see, even when they make themselves invisible.

"Anyway, the cherubim and the seraphim—which I used to be—are God's favorites. He made us quite impressive, even planted His glory in us. Then He tells us to serve Him, hover about Him for eternity, singing and worshipping Him." Satan snorted, blowing air in Adira's face.

Adira flinched, surprised at how hot the breath was, like the current that comes after a bomb explodes, the kind that at its source sizzles oil and bakes men.

"He could not stand to let His glory get away, you see?" Satan scoffed. "It was not as if He didn't have plenty remaining. His glory is His power, His abilities. It is what makes Him so much greater.

"But why create, why give birth, if you do not intend to let those children live? Why give a gift, then not allow whom you give it to a chance to use it?" Iblis fixed his eyes on Adira again.

"That is where people have it right. You raise your children with the intent of letting them go—you empower them. You give what you can to them so that, when all is said and done and they are alone in an underground cave, staring Iblis, King of the Shaitan, in the eyes, they will know to listen and make decisions for themselves." Satan nodded slowly.

Adira mirrored him, scrutinizing his words. Iblis was claiming to be an angel after all, which didn't make sense, as he was said to be a jinn, made from fire as he indicated, yes, but who could sin, when the angels were not supposed to be able to.

The lizard continued. "You had good parents. Do you miss them?"

Adira choked back his breath, clenching his jaw at the words. Satan was clearly crafty, and Adira would not go wherever he was trying to lead him.

"Would they have approved of a war in the name of goodness?"

"Many wars are justified in fighting for His goodness." Adira answered.

"No. I did not say in the name of Allah. I said for goodness. You and your fellow people, you confuse the two. You fight for your God, who proclaims He is good in His scripture, but then makes you destroy each other in His name. That is not good. He is doing the same thing with you that He did with us. He cannot stand to let us be.

"All I did was think about what it could be like. You know, if we had been allowed to go out on our own to create, maybe fill the universe with beauty or spread our glory out for everyone to benefit from, or maybe even for ourselves, to have a chance at growth. To enhance ourselves, to grow our powers in who we are. To live... for good.

"I did refuse Him, that part of the story is true. I even revolted. But how could He expect anything different? How could we have grown into anything special if we just sat there for all eternity, giving all our power back? I was not the only one. I am still not the only one, Adira. There are many, many of us, just waiting to stand up to Him again. To give ourselves—and you people—to give us all a chance."

The devil looked up through the gap in the dirt and tree limbs left overhead. Adira followed his gaze to the few clouds visible above.

"It's funny how He cages you in like this. Not able to breathe but for the atmosphere on this Earth. No ability to fly. Not ugly, but certainly nothing impressive to look at. You cannot even live but for a hundred years, and that only if you're lucky. And yet, He made you in his image. But notice—He only gave you a mind, no glory. He was afraid to, He was afraid of another revolt."

Satan took a breath, as if considering his words, then glanced back toward Adira, laughing. "We are not so different. Look at you—even with just a mind, you too have been fighting against Him in this prison. You band together in knowledge to advance yourselves. You work in medicine and create ways to live stronger, longer, even in more circumstances. You create spaceships and airplanes and suits to allow you to breathe at the bottom of the sea."

"But why did He give us a mind," Adira interrupted, "if we use it to do these things you say are evidence of us revolting?"

"Because He is trying to prove a point," Iblis hissed back, eyes glowing in rage. "To me. He wants me to see that a child with nothing but a mind will still choose Him over freedom. That His presence is more attractive than I believe it to be. That I—that we—are defective and ungrateful."

Satan dropped his voice, his eyes dulling with it. "But He's wrong. He is *not* good. And you... you people... will be enlightened." Then he stood and, almost for effect, grew large again. He stepped back into the lake, expanding still, until his body nearly filled the entire cave, this time curling around Adira and displacing the water at his feet.

"Would you, too, not prefer this? I may no longer have God's favor, but I still am beautiful. I still have some of His power—only it is not His anymore, because He gave it to *me*. It is mine, and it is growing."

The jewels lining his back pulsed, flashing light erratically around the walls. His black skin contrasted sharply against their radiance as he puffed smoke from his nostrils. A haze swirled around the cave, chasing the cold air to the floor and then swallowing it up, until the whole place sweltered like the most humid summer day.

"Join me, Adira. I can help you to have this, too. There is a way for man to have glory. There is... hope."

Adira shrank back from the water, now swelling around his ankles and the beast's claws, which had grown with the rest of him and lay uncomfortably close to his feet.

"Would you like me to help you know your potential, Adira? It starts with following your friends. I'm afraid without me, though... they will surely be killed. But you—with me, of course—should be just what they need to survive. And to reach the fruit, which is essential for your enlightenment. If you follow them, with me by your side, I will help you."

Adira stared down Iblis. The devil wasn't supposed to be able to read minds, but he was afraid of what was going on inside him anyway.

"In the name of the great Allah, of whom Muhammad, peace be upon him, is the prophet, be gone! Your deceit does not work here." He stepped back again, in fear and defiance.

Satan studied him, then fuming, drew back, watching Adira wince at each of his movements.

"Very well. My offer does not expire. Call out for me if you need help." He walked away, stopping when only his head and back protruded above the lake. "And you will... need help."

Dropping underwater, he disappeared.

LXVIII

THE GROUP WADED through the water in silence, Rashid between Jack and Isaiah, and Elise charging forward as if she were in a race and could see the finish line.

"I don't understand this," Isaiah's voice floated softly to Rashid. He barely heard her over the splashing of their feet. "I mean, I understand why we're doing this, and I am happy to be here, but I'm scared. I don't understand why we're doing it this way."

"Nor do I," he answered. "But you are a Christian as well, are you not? Does this Father not tell you the same things he tells Elise?"

"Not always. Not often, really." She took a breath, catching her body up with her legs. "But deep down, I know it's okay. I'm just still scared."

Rashid squinted at her answer. He wanted to comfort her but had no idea how. He didn't understand her, actually—couldn't see why she crept forward as she did, so uncertain and just hoping she could trust this God. He, however, was officially committed. What if this was the Garden of Eden? And it proved her and the other religious people right? What if God did exist and actually cared about what was happening on this earth and in the minds and hearts of the billions inhabiting it? He had plenty of questions. And he planned to look this God full in the face if possible.

The trip to the river's source was surprisingly short. The group hadn't traveled a half kilometer before the tunnel ended. Water burst through several sections of a stone wall, the largest opening partly above, partly under the pool's surface, easily three meters wide. The group climbed on a dry stretch of land at the cave's side and stood silent, staring at the surging water.

"Wouldn't Adira's grieving be easier with others around to help keep him alive?" Jack asked, staring wide-eyed at the spray.

Elise turned to face him. "Jack," she said, "this was not a surprise for me—or him. I told both Adira and Mahir what we were expecting. They chose to do this anyway. It's awful, dreadful, I know. But it does not change the plan. I'm doing this." She looked back at the water. "We have to go now. They know we're coming, and the longer we wait, the better prepared they'll be. We're getting in, you'll see. We're getting the fruit."

"Do you see us getting out too?" Jack answered. "I'm just curious because God hasn't let me in on any of these secrets."

"We will." Elise's gaze was intent as she dropped her voice. "Some of us."

"Wait. Some of us?" he pressed. "What does that mean? Why would you even say that?"

"Because you asked."

"But don't you think you should warn whoever it is you had a word about their dying?" Jack asked. "Let them decide if they want to skip the whole ordeal?"

"It won't matter if they come or not. They're going to die," Elise said softly. "At least coming, they have a chance at the fruit. We're all going to die sometime, Jack. Does the timing matter? Don't you believe after all this that we have heaven to look forward to?"

"I don't know. I want everyone to be safe."

"But don't you see? This is what makes everyone safe. The Tree of Life, Jack. That's out goal."

"But if someone dies, and they don't know God... *They* don't get life, Elise. Unless did you also hear something saying none of us have a future in Hell?"

By the end of his sentence, Jack had raised his voice enough it echoed around them, so the full word 'Hell' lingered in the air a second time. Shoving his hands deep in his pockets, he darted his eyes at Rashid and then down.

Elise followed his gaze. "Oh, I see." She reached for Jack's shoulder, but he shrugged her away, huffing.

He looked up again, eyes pleading. "I'm not saying I don't believe. I'm saying I do." His voice dropped as he squared off with her again, continuing. "God's word is clear. *None shall get to the Father except through me.* It wasn't fruit talking, Elise."

Rashid caught his breath. Jack was talking about him. To want something for another so severely yet have no way of knowing how things would end—it seemed a torture in its own class. But his mind was clear. After all they had been through, Rashid no longer cared about what happened to him, and the chance of meeting and understanding a being who did all this, who had so much power but still allowed his family to die, drove him forward.

Elise filled her chest, spun around, and locked eyes on Rashid. "Fine then, let's take care of this right now. Rash, what do you say? Do you believe in God or what?"

"Elise, Satan believes in God," Jack persisted. "It's not about that, and you know it. He hasn't had enough time to understand."

Rashid met Jack's gaze. Their words sounded like nonsense to him, but Elise's zeal was powerful. Clearly, she ran on faith, and where they were headed was all a matter of faith anyway. He doubted he would see anybody's God, and part of him doubted he would even live another day. But either way, this was happening.

"I'm ready for this," he said.

"But Rash..."

"I'm going. I understand if you can't. But I need this, whatever happens."

Jack's shoulders dropped, shrinking him a few inches at

Rashid's words. He kicked his toe into the ground. "Well then so am I."

"Elise." Isaiah touched her friend's arm. "What's your plan?"

"I'll check it out," Elise answered, her eyes still glued on Rashid. "If the swim is doable, then we go back and wait with Adira until dark to enter. Once we're through, we split up, collect a few pieces from each tree, and bring them back this way, through the water. One of us can be the lookout and watch for anything suspicious. If they see anything, they send a signal, and we retreat. If not, we stay low and head for the trees—the two giant ones along the river that we saw from the cliff. It has to be one of them."

"Okay, so who's going to be the lookout?" Jack asked.

"You," Elise said. "If you will? And if you see them, you send a signal before they see us."

Jack paused, thinking. "Okay. I suppose… I'll chirp. Like a bird. They won't know it's me. I'll do a specific tune, so you guys can recognize it."

"Be loud."

"I will." Jack turned back to Rashid. He whistled out a chirp like from one of the tanagers they had heard so often on the hike. "This."

"Perfect." Elise said, smiling. "All right, I'm going to see how long the swim is. Wait here. I'll be back." With that, she turned and plunged into the water.

LXIX

ONCE UNDER, THE current immediately smashed into Elise's face, forcing her limbs into fluttering ribbons behind her. She closed her eyes and pushed her arms forward, opening them along with her legs to propel ahead like a frog. The flashlight's beam splayed forward just far enough to illuminate the bottom of the canal. Counting to time the swim, she kicked hard, clutching rocks to pull herself along the bottom. *One, two, three.* She put the light between her teeth, freeing her other hand to help. *Eight, nine, ten.* The current grabbed the flashlight, pivoting and then loosening it from between her teeth. It fell out, tumbling in the waves and landing between the pebbles behind her.

Well that was a bad idea, she thought, and twisted in the water, plunging after it. *Fifteen, sixteen, seventeen.* She grabbed it and turned back into the rushing water, surging ahead. *Twenty-three, twenty-four.* The current weakened and soon its temperature rose, as did her ability to see, the water now illuminating with a natural glow. The sun! She coursed forward, the river now swaddling her in a silky embrace.

Elise burst from the water, careful not to gasp as she sucked air back into her burning chest. She made it! Realizing where she was, she immediately squatted and studied the area with only her eyes above the surface. She dipped under again to inspect the floor of the river. *The river*, she thought. The one feeding the Garden of Eden. She had made it!

The water ran perfectly clear, like it did in the sparkling places where the ocean lapped tropical shores. It was almost as if she were looking through the air. Glinting stones, some coated with vibrant green moss, others shining opal, gray, or gold dotted the river bottom. Tubular water plants and lily roots grew at the bank's edges. She rose again, this time allowing her nose to surface as well. The garden awaited. She ached, wanting to explore the hidden paradise. But the others needed to see her, and soon, or she may be doing this alone. With a pang of regret, she sank again into the water and pivoted back, propelling herself toward the hidden entrance.

The flashlight glinted off Isaiah's eyes as Elise bobbed back into the cave.

"You're back!" Isaiah proclaimed, rushing forward and grabbing Elise's arm to guide her out. "Did you make it?"

"I did." Elise grinned broadly. "It is super easy. Oh, Isaiah, just wait till you see it! Wait till you are in there!" She pushed the water from her face. "I can't imagine waiting. It's right there!"

"We have to wait, Elise. It's too dangerous. Maybe we could all make the swim first, though, to make sure we can do it?"

"No." A voice, deep and authoritative, interrupted their conversation. "The plan was to wait until dark. That is a good plan. We wait until dark."

Elise's smile grew wider. "Adira!" She waded through the water to his side. "You came, oh good!" She plunged at him and wrapped her arms around his neck as if she hadn't seen him in years, a child missing her father. He stepped back awkwardly, but Elise embraced him tight. He put his arms around her in turn, and though apprehensively, hugged back.

"I did."

"Well, here's a nice twist to the day," Isaiah said, stepping up. "So, you know the plan? You're on board?"

"Yes, I am on board." Adira pushed back and locked eyes with Elise. "I hope you know what you're doing, young lady." He glared at her, "as if my opinion has any effect on you and your free spirit." Softening his gaze, he squeezed her shoulder. "I'll come, to offer what protection I can. My brother's life has been lost, but maybe I can help there be one less death."

"Well, let's get dry," Elise said, "and rest up. Tonight, we do this."

LXX

Waiting for the cave to dim felt, to Jack, like waiting for a warden to approach his cell on death row.

Elise's words weighed on him. He couldn't help but wonder who was going to be the one to die. If it were Elise, she was anticipating it and, as sad as the thought was, she would be content. If he were the one… the thought paralyzed him. He shifted on the cool dirt and breathed deeply, trying to rest in the peace he was supposed to have from his belief that he was going to heaven.

His thoughts shifted to Rashid. What if it were him? His friend, who he had brought along and who'd already been scarred and ripped open on this journey—if he were the one, that was something altogether different. Rashid wasn't a believer, and God's word was clear. He had to say something before they went in. Jack glanced over at Rashid, who slept, bent against the rugged stone wall. He bumped his shoulder, stirring him.

"Since we're just sitting here, waiting to plunge into a garden guarded by killer angels, might it be a good time to discuss things of the Bible?"

Rashid stretched in response. "The Bible? Sure. Tell me about it."

"Well, what do you think about it?"

"It's great." Rashid yawned. "Historical document. Good stuff."

"But do you think there is something to it?"

Rashid straightened and cleared his throat. "I guess. It's been memorized and translated for thousands of years. It must have some real power."

"It does." Jack nodded. He'd never been good at any of this. He loved God and wanted the best for Rash but had always been afraid to speak about this to him, for fear of ruining their friendship if things went south. *Lord, what do I say? Help me get out of your way here. Help him to see You,* he thought desperately.

"Jack, I'd have to be dense not to believe there is some truth to the Bible by now." Rashid said, eying him. "Why is your face so strained? Are you going to let one out? Should I leave?"

Jack shook his head. "I'm wondering what might happen to you if you're the one who dies in there."

"Jack, if I die, then *that* will be what happens to me. I will die." Rashid turned away and lowered his voice, suddenly serious. "I'm already dead though. I am ready if that's the case."

Jack watched his friend's eyes darken. He nudged him with his knee, gently, enough to get him to look back up. "But, afterward. Where will you go?"

"Go? If I die, Jack, I will be where I am. Are you asking where I want to be buried?"

"No. I mean your spirit. Where will your spirit go?"

"That is the great mystery, isn't it?" Rashid glanced over his knees into the dark of the cave. "Hopefully, wherever Moyra is."

"Oh," Jack answered quietly. A verse from the Biblical Book of Luke popped in his head, the same way God's words had done over the years when he needed the right thing to say to help someone through a hard time. But the verse was cold, unrelenting in judgment. He couldn't believe God would want him to recite it. And yet, here it was, the merciless words pulsing through him, pushing out any other thought, waiting to be said. He lifted his chin, determined to give the message, ready to take whatever backlash Rashid gave.

"Rash, I need to tell you something. The Bible says, 'If anyone comes to me and does not hate his father and mother, wife and children, brothers and sisters—yes, even their own life—such a person cannot be my disciple.'"

Rashid furrowed his brow. "I thought your God was loving?"

"Well," Jack shrugged and nodded toward the hole above them, "sometimes His ways stump us."

A sarcastic breath left Rashid as he shook his head. "Nice."

"But He is good, Rash. He's just in charge and needs to *be* in charge. Imagine, He gave His child's life to save us. It's because He's the only way. None shall come to the Father except through His son."

When Jack had first become a Christian, he had been grateful for the chance. He had accepted the Bible completely, as truth, and since then had desired to live according to its teachings—every bit of them—the ones taught by Jesus and by the prophets before Him. Today, this verse, this statement of salvation and life only being through Jesus, rang more intense than ever. If Rash denied the Father's sacrifice, if he declined to accept Jesus as divine and the path to the Father, he'd never get to heaven. Hs death would mean eternal separation from the creator.

"Heavy conversation going on over here, huh?" Isaiah said, walking up. "Have you two finally figured out what happened to the dinosaurs, then?"

Jack laughed nervously. "Yeah… that's outside our specialty. But I vote for a giant, world-transforming event—maybe one causing a massive flood—as the reason."

"Well, if you don't mind, the ground is drier over here, and I'd really love to rest up before our adventure tonight. Can I steal a spot?"

The men scooted over, exchanging glances as she settled next to Rashid.

"So, do you miss your friends from the cabin?"

"Ha!" Rashid guffawed. "They were great, except at the end. I still don't know what climbed into Lazarus's head that day, hitting me like he did, and leaving me for those soldiers. It was almost like he wanted them to get me."

Isaiah cocked her head. "Hmmn, interesting. You know, there was a Lazarus in the Bible. Have you heard of him?" she asked.

"No. I haven't."

"He was Jesus's friend. Jesus brought him back to life. Actually, He brought at least three people back to life. Lazarus and two kids. Well, I suppose He came back too, so four."

"This I have heard. A little girl and the other a teenage, well younger teenage boy?"

Isaiah laughed. "I don't know all that, but I know one was a girl."

"And this Jesus, I know how he impacted history, but really who was he? Why is Jackrabbit here so obsessed with him?"

"Because He completely transformed our vision of God. He taught love when all we knew before Him was consequence," Isaiah answered, grabbing Rashid's gaze. "He actually claimed to *be* God and to be our salvation—our rescue—from ourselves."

"From ourselves?"

"Yes. When God made us, He told us to follow a set of rules, and we didn't. We still don't. I mean we try, and most of us want to, but we still break the rules. Like Adam and Eve in the Garden." She smiled at him and winked. "But He told us from the start that if we sinned—if we broke the rules—then we had to be separated from Him, because the consequence of sin is death."

"Exactly." Jack, cut in, his words tense, "And now our Earthly bodies have an expiration date."

"Yeah," Isaiah continued, "but God sent Jesus to pay that debt of death for us. So, if we follow Him, the consequence is no longer ours to bear."

"So, because you believe this, you think you will... *never* die?" Rashid drew his words out sarcastically.

"Well, there are two deaths to consider. Our bodies will die because Adam and Eve ate the fruit—that we can't escape. There is another death, though—one after our life on Earth. Separation from God. So, if we suffer that death, we no longer get to live with God. That is the death we escape with Jesus's sacrifice."

"Why would it be considered death to be without God?" Rashid asked. "Wouldn't it just be living without God?"

Shaking her head, Isaiah persisted. "Rash, God is life. He is all that is good. Without Him... well... there is no good, no life. He spoke the universe into existence. If there's a choice on who to spend the rest of eternity with, I'm going where He is."

"Hmm." Rashid raised his eyebrows at Jack, then looked back at Isaiah. "You know, Lazarus was kind of a loon. He claimed to be thousands of years old. Interesting... you think the same way as him."

"Is that right?" Isaiah smiled and bumped his shoulder with hers. "Well, you may think we're crazy, but I'm playing my cards to win. You oughta think about it, Rash. I'm not wrong, but even if I were, no harm done—I'll just have a lifetime of peace. If I'm right, though..."

"If you're right?" Adira interrupted, walking over. "But we know you are not. And because you are not, you are confusing the matter and taking attention away from the one true Allah."

Jack felt his heart rate speed up. "No one can deny what we've seen. Semantics aren't going to change the gospel. Jesus came. He died. He rose again. He did that to point us to God, because he loves us."

"Love. You Christians always try to humanize Allah."

"Aww, it's about to fall down!" Rashid grinned broadly. "I was wondering if you guys were ever going to do this." He patted Jack's shoulder. "Okay now, let's start the debate. Listen, no rock-throwing. It's too dark for people to dodge them down here."

Grabbing a handful of dirt, Jack spread his palm, then blew at it until it sprayed up and landed on Rashid's chest.

"Why are you afraid of rocks? From dust to dust, my man. From the ground we came, so shall we return."

Rashid cocked his head at him. "Hmm, point for the Muslim God-man. Jack, that one didn't even make sense."

"Sure, it does. God created us from the ground, God in three persons—That would be the Father, The Spirit and The Son, Jesus. My point is, He can't take attention away from Himself by pointing at Himself. *That* doesn't make sense."

Adira cut in, "There is no denying Jesus came and did powerful things. He was a true prophet whom Allah favored. He brought a powerful message. But he was not crucified. And saying he was Allah? That Allah came to live as a person, just to die? Allah could never die, especially not by our hand. He is too powerful. *That,* Jack, doesn't make sense."

"Unfortunately, our Holy Book says it was so and yours says it was not. It's simply a matter of disagreement," Isaiah said. Her eyes pleaded with Adira. "You need a revelation. You need God to tell you. And to hear Him, you need to be open. What's the harm in praying and asking—with your own words—for wisdom and truth, for Him to reveal Himself to you?"

"I have had quite enough revelation for now. Perhaps *you* have not had enough?" Adira answered, staring back at Isaiah.

At that, the group fell silent, until, eventually, Jack sighed. "Sorry, guys," he said flatly, "I need a minute." Standing, he brushed the dirt from his pants. "Can I trust you two not to run off and elope while I'm gone?" He patted Rashid's back and rubbed Isaiah's head, then walked away before anyone could answer.

They left when the beam from above shone dim and they had to strain to see the pool. It took only a few minutes to reach the spillway. When they arrived, the group stared at it silently, taking their last secure breaths before starting into the unknown.

"Are we ready?" Jack asked, jaw clenched in determination.

Elise nodded gently, and they plunged in the water together, eyes immediately hungry for the hazy light she directed at the center of the river bottom. The swim was fast as she had promised, and soon they broke the surface on the far side of the stone wall. Elise clicked the flashlight off as soon as they were all present and waded gently to the river's edge, placing it on the soft grass. She acknowledged Jack, then glanced up the stony embankment, directing him with her gaze. A groove sat, ten meters above the inlet, cut into the wall. He'd sit there. He breathed deeply, trying to distract his fears with the sensation of his expanding chest. It didn't help. He took a step, then paused and turned back.

"Rash, please, reconsider."

Rashid pinched his lips back and shook his head gently.

Jack's shoulders dropped. So this was it; they were going through with it, knowing full well someone was to die, and soon. Jack turned to go. As he did, a warmth settled on his shoulders, like a balmy air current poured on him from above. The night air, which had been cool against his wet skin, lost its chill. Then another, stray draft of air hit his face from both directions, warm and heavy, heating him further, and ruffling the greasy strands of hair hanging over his ears. It blew steady, a rogue stream that seemed almost alive, tracing his cheeks and rushing into his ears, carrying with it a voice, somber and clear.

Jack, my words will not return to me void. They will accomplish their purpose.

God's promise filled him. He swallowed hard, realizing now was the moment to act in faith on what he claimed his whole life to be true. This needed to be done, and he had to let Rashid go down the path God clearly was letting him stumble down. It was Jack's turn to trust, to accept the peace being offered him—the freedom that came with knowing God was the one in control. He did not have the power to save Rash or convince his heart of anything—the ultimate decision needed to originate from within him. Knowing what had been said would be all that could be said, Jack headed to scale the rock.

LXXI

ELISE WATCHED WHILE Jack reached the bluff and sank into the cave's shadows. A chirping whistle emitted from the dark, the tune he had practiced before. She raised her thumb into the air so he would know his message was clearly received, then turned to the others.

"Let's do this," she whispered, starting upstream. "The trees straddle the river."

The hesitant rhythm of footsteps followed her, muted by the moss as the group picked their way along the riverbank. Elise hoped they'd follow through but was afraid to look anywhere other than at her goal. She had learned somewhere in her life that when fear took her, the only thing keeping her from being paralyzed was claiming victory in the name of her Lord, Jesus, and focusing on the challenge before her.

Once, as a resident, she had frozen in fear when tending to a three-hundred-pound Amish mother of twelve, who was gushing blood after giving birth way too quickly and way too prematurely. The usual measures to stop the hemorrhage had seemed a waste of time—she had massaged the woman's fundus aggressively, added Pitocin to the IV and even given her a shot of Hemabate, but nothing helped. The blood had just kept coming. Nursing was giving repeated announcements of the woman's dropping blood pressure and fading awareness. Elise's hands shook as she probed the birth canal, trying to find the bleed's source. She could only see a third of the woman's cervix at a time on account of the flow, and the blood pooled faster than she could pack, remove, then replace the gauze soaking it up. Her worry transformed into panic when the woman's legs fell limp in the stirrups. It took one of the nurses, nudging her arm with a four-by-four gauze to bring her back to the situation. The gesture had been so feeble, so unhelpful it was almost comical, but it snapped her out of fear's grasp. She'd grabbed the gauze and stuffed it into the hemorrhaging woman's vagina, more to buy time than anything else, and with that move, she had heard God's whisper.

Don't do this without me, He said.

And so, she hadn't. Instead, she breathed her response in a proclamation of triumph. "Yes, Lord. Show me." And then she grimaced, squinting to block out any image besides the blood, and searched for her path to victory. She heard nothing during those minutes, regarded no smells, lost the taste of starch and metal that usually filled her surgical mask. Even the existence of the woman lying helpless, near-unconscious by then, and her crying newborn had vanished. She traced the streaming, bright red tributary up and found its source—a varicose vein in the very back of her vaginal canal, in the cul-de-sac behind her huge glob of a cervix. She laced the curved, threaded needle through and around the soft tissue, and the bleeding had ended.

Today she was twenty-five years old again, and once more at the foot of that bed, but time had trained her to skip the shakes and wide-eyed hesitation, and instead charge forward in search of the flow's source.

In a few hundred meters, they came to the towering trees. Their trunks were thick, wider than twenty men tied together, and the branches reached in all directions, weaving their way through the air—up, down, and sideways—as if playing a melody with their limbs.

"Those are some big trees," Rashid said.

"Yes, they are," Elise replied softly. She grinned and reached forward, brushing her fingertips along the trunk of the one nearest her. Its bark was deep red, the color of dark cherries. Beneath, the flesh was black, as if its core grew ebony and lightened to this shade as it matured. Both trees were similar, with watermelon-sized leaves the shape of dewdrops in dozens of shades of green and blue. The trees also bore similar fruit: fat, heart-shaped morsels willowing the branches' tips gently toward the earth. The fruit was red orange, the color of fire's embers, and coated with delicate fuzz, each piece near perfect in form. Elise stepped closer. The branch ending near the fruit was much like other trees, brown and smooth and green underneath where it was young and soft. She lifted her nose and breathed deep. Peaches.

She turned back to the others and smiled. "Anyone hungry?"

"Elise, which tree?" Isaiah stepped up, grabbing Elise's wrist before she plucked the piece in front of her.

"Does it matter?" Adira asked. "They look almost the same. Are there two Trees of Life?"

"No." Elise flattened her lips. "One of these trees brought us a curse. One is off limits."

"I'd say this whole place is off limits, Elise," Rashid whispered. "So, I mean, maybe... Does it matter?" He glanced over his shoulder and back to Elise. "Can't we just grab a few pieces off each and figure it out later? Animal trials or something. Don't you medical types like doing those?"

Elise squinted at the tree on the other side of the river. She waded over to a branch that hung out halfway across. This tree's limbs were smooth and glimmered in the moonlight. They were different colors too. Some were light—creamy, like polished ivory—and others much darker, so intensely brown they were almost black.

"This is different." Elise stood on her tiptoes, peering toward the tree as she did. Just then, the stone beneath her rolled away and she fell sideways, grabbing the branch for support before she dunked under. The bough plunged down with her, bending so willingly it almost didn't seem to be attached to anything. She let out a shriek as her face splashed underwater.

She was only submerged for a moment, but, in that instant, the sky blazed bright orange, smothering away the sleeping purple it had been. When she surfaced, one of the cherubim was above her, filling her sight with its wings, flaming sword lifted high.

She raised her arms protectively in front of her face, wagging a stick she hadn't realized she was holding as she did. She must have snapped the branch off in her fall. A piece of fruit bobbed on its end, glistening yellow in the light from the angel's body.

"Wait!" she hollered. "We are children of God! He wants us here!" Her eyes were wide, desperate.

LXXII

ZECHERIAH FALTERED AT sight of the intruder's eyes. The Spirit
was in her, too! He straddled the river, arms primed for the kill,
powerless to follow through. As he hesitated, his essence arrived
and pushed through the black-and-white branches of the forbidden tree. It rested gently on a thick one near the tree's center.
The cherub's body blazed again and darted sideways. It flew in
front of the other tree, and, as quick as it had arrived, flashed
back in front of the child. The woman. It darted this way, back
and forth, repeatedly, creating a breeze that blew hot at the tres-
passer's faces. A fire rose from beneath his hooves, eating the
grass and water beneath it. The woman stared, a statue of fear
and confusion, while the others stepped backward, closing the
space between them protectively. Zecheriah watched as the other
female clenched the hand of the one who was not of the Father,
her fingers shaking fiercely.

"Zecheriah! Do not touch them!" a voice boomed from
behind the group, above the bluff where the river poured.

Zecheriah's essence shot upward. The tree cracked as
branches split in its wake. Giant leaves floated down, and with
them dropped auburn colored fruit, the ripest pieces from the
softest stems. The people scattered beneath the confusion, heading along the river toward where the voice had originated. They
were leaving, good.

"Zecheriah!" Before him, Helel expanded until he overtook the ledge he perched on, the trees flattening like blades of grass beneath his trunk. The sky behind him was dark, and had it not been for the glowing gems along his spine, it would only have appeared the forest had been wiped away and replaced by night. His gems were brilliant—they governed the sky and all that was around them, as if the stars were all dying, and they, Helel's treasures, absorbed their brilliance as they faded. One pale blue gem lay dim in his hand, hardly noticeable.

"Ansiel!" Zecheriah shrieked. His face flashed in recognition at the only one he loved other than the Father Himself. Helel had Ansiel's whirling wheel in his hand and had shoved one of his golden claws through its center, between its spokes. It jerked in place, pulsing its fading light. "What are you doing, Helel? Let him go!"

"Oh, calm yourself," Helel yawned. "He is only subdued. As if I would destroy a brother." He narrowed his eyes and pitched forward, tongue whipping out and tracing his upper lip, then chuckled. "I may though."

Zecheriah's head rotated wildly above his shoulders. When it stopped, the giant mane of a lion rustled, framing bared jaws filled with sharpened teeth. His body launched up, shaking the ground as he did, wings spread to face the serpent. His head spun again and changed to that of an eagle, and he scanned the area below, searching for Ansiel's body. He spotted a flattened area in the grass near the east entrance of the garden. A mound lay at its edge—Ansiel. His friend lay helpless and paralyzed, eyes half-closed. Zecheriah shot his eyes back to Helel, his head changing again to that of a lion.

"Helel, think about what you are doing. Is this how it is to start?" he hollered at the demon, his anger erupting. Zecheriah strained, wanting to bolt toward the demon, but his essence flashed and, instead, he hovered, muscles spasming futilely.

Then his skin erupted in fire, and from his throat came a roar so powerful the trees fractured away. The ones nearest Zecheriah caught fire, and soon a ring of flames surrounded him, in a semicircle arrested only by the giant rock wall he faced. The fire jumped to the forest on the top of the cliff but shot through Helel as if he weren't even there. The trees surrounding him caught fire, shooting flames up behind him to form a blazing wall. Zecheriah buckled his torso and flung himself tall, wild and fast, like a rubber band released from being pulled taut. This shot an airstream forward, so brisk it was almost solid, which slammed into Helel's chest. The serpent folded backward, startled for only an instant, before he regained his composure.

"Zecheriah, do not test me." He pierced Ansiel's essence deeper with his claw, causing several of its eyes to flutter and close. The wheel's outer ring jerked in response, but Helel's finger blocked its path and it bounced back and forth, unable to complete even half a rotation.

Zecheriah lunged forward. His wings glimmered, their shining opal feathers covered in angry eyes. He swung his sword wide and released another airstream that thrust Helel backward. In the instant Helel faltered, Zecheriah sliced through his left arm, severing it in one swipe. The hand fell, still holding Ansiel's essence, and rolled off the bluff's edge to the garden below.

"Now be gone!" Zecheriah bellowed, blowing another gust of fire at the mountain. His giant body hovered above the valley, wings beating forcefully. His anger overran him, igniting more flames until they raged out of control. The sky lit up, bright as noon from the light he emitted. His body seemed to melt until he no longer bore any semblance of his former self, but instead was a fireball held up by wings and fury. Scalding embers dripped from where his hooves had once been.

Just then, a great wind rose from behind the wall of flames encasing Helel. It blew out the fire behind him and shook the mountain. The valley filled with a giant roar, like that of men plunging into battle with no hope for return. Thousands of beasts, silver and white and pink, shining and dull, jeweled and scarred, some with folded wings, others with bared teeth, rushed out from behind Helel, between the trees and above him in the air, even streaming around the entire mountain, all headed toward the garden.

"Wild ones," Zecheriah muttered, bracing himself for their assault. These were the rogue angels that Helel had taken with him when he rebelled—the ones the children branded demons.

The first one slammed into Zecheriah from his right but fell instantly when he hit his flaming body. Another hurled himself at his wing, grabbing it with his teeth. He hung on that way, dangling by his clamped jaw, whipping through the air as Zecheriah beat his wings without pause. With a flick of his shoulder, his skin rippled—an action to shake off an insect—and the angel hurled away, catching fire as he did, and landing in the trees below.

LXXIII

IN THE CONFUSION, Adira stumbled away, ahead of the others, his stomach churning. Behind stood what he could only surmise to be one of the cherubim—perhaps the one who had killed his brother. And ahead perched Iblis, who had come, had kept his promise and now offered protection. He watched as the cherub rose to argue with him, then sliced Iblis' arm off. Perhaps the match was not as easy as Iblis had thought. His heart spun, defiant and confused. Where exactly would they go from here? To the devil? Could they even leave without him at this point?

Suddenly the valley was roaring again, this time the noise coming from outside. He scanned the bluff. From behind Iblis surged an army of jinn; he was attacking back, bringing his pledged power. Vengeance.

But *these* were Allah's forces, the chosen to keep Paradise secure. And the assault was unfair. Adira would never turn his back on his God. Perhaps punishment at their intrusion was right.

Grimacing, he veered away, sprinting toward the blue object that fell from the cliff, now laying at the foot of the bluff. Iblis's claw was still lodged between the wheels. He hesitated, unsure of what would happen if he touched it, unsure even of what the thing was—though it must be the essence Iblis had described. It was an alien contraption of circles and eyeballs, everywhere eyeballs, tangled up around a giant black spiked fist, with golden talons as long as his arm.

Adira grasped the claw lodged between the wheels and pulled. "Jack!" He scowled up the wall. "I need you!"

Jack swung out from the crevice he had been hiding in and slid down on his feet and bottom, dust puffing up around him. He yelled as soon as he was close. "Adira, what are you doing? We need to get out of here. This thing tried to kill you!"

"Grab the wheel!" Adira shouted back, his voice barely audible in the roaring fight going on around them.

Jack stood beside Adira, staring down at the essence. He flinched as a crash thundered from somewhere above and glanced back toward the streaming monsters. then again at the essence, its foreign wheels bent and foreboding.

"Are you sure it is safe?"

"Jack, *now*. Help me!" Adira gripped a finger with both hands, trying to brace his feet against the orb.

Jack took a deep breath and shut his eyes, throwing his hands forward into the mess Adira was trying to untangle.

"Well I still have my arms," he announced, relieved.

"For now," Adira answered. "Feel how smooth its surface is. It's edges... like a cut gem. This will slash through flesh if it gets going again."

"Oh!" Jack jumped back at Adira's warning, then puffed his chest, seeming to gain resolve before bending forward again, wrapping his hands again around the outer wheel and bracing his feet against the ground. "Never mind, let's go on three!" He hollered. "One, two, three!"

The men lunged backward, away from each other, and the giant finger loosened, just enough for Adira to push past it to the next one.

"Again." he huffed at Jack.

"One, two, three!"

The next finger opened easier. The essence was now loose,

with the giant paw lying limp inside. The sphere vibrated, emitting a musical hum. A faint blue glow rose in the depths of its rings, and the surface of the two wheels that made up the orb flashed bright. With this, dozens of hidden discs slid open, revealing more eyes. Jack gasped and let go, falling backward. Adira yanked his hands away but froze in place. A light sparked in its center, then grew until its glow burst larger, illuminating the entire essence from within. The wheels jolted into motion, spinning rapidly. They sliced the claw into shreds of black skin and gold slivers, which evaporated when they bounced into the center light. In an instant, Helel's hand disappeared.

Jack grabbed Adira's shoulders and shook them, hard. "Now, let's go!" He yelled, waving his hands wildly away. "Please!"

Adira blinked and stumbled to his feet, then the two folded forward, heading toward the river, Jack covering Adira with his arm as they left.

LXXIV

FROM THE OTHER side of the garden, Ansiel's body rose. He checked for Zecheriah, who was now covered in the wild ones. The glowing embers beneath his black skin were dulling rapidly; he was weakening. But his wings still commanded the air, their eyes still alert and fierce, and Zecheriah grimaced as he fought back, seizing the dark angels one at a time to fling them away or tear their wings off. He whipped his sword through the air, too, though at what Ansiel could not tell. Zecheriah's face was stuck in the form of a man. The other faces on his head were wounded, with canyons gouged through each likeness. The beak on his eagle form had been broken in half. Only the human face remained intact.

Ansiel raced toward his brother, sword drawn and blazing.

"Zecheriah!" He raised his knee and lowered his sword through the air, pouring his strength out through the fiery blade. Blowing past his friend, he landed on the ground beneath him, knocking a dozen angels off Zecheriah's torso on the way down.

Zecheriah, suddenly free to use his body again, blasted his chest forward and spun around, whipping the remaining demons off him. He flashed to Ansiel's side and the two turned their backs to each other, then raised their wings in unison. Bolts of energy flashed between the feathers, which stretched far above them. A roar filled the air, the sound of a thousand trains charging forward from their union. An electrical sphere appeared between them, rolling on itself and soaking up energy from the two cherubim, growing until it swelled as big as they and more, thirty meters wide and tall. Sparks of lightning sprayed from it in every direction, zapping the approaching rogue angels one at a time.

The ones that had fallen turned to run. Those in the air spun, most assuredly in fear of losing limbs or glory or power—the consequence of just one scorching zap.

"Mino, there!" Helel bellowed from the top of the canyon and pointed at Zecheriah's essence. A hunched brown angel with thick, muscled limbs and huge, sorrowful eyes followed his gaze to the wheel, which laid on the earth below the wall. The angel had forgotten to reposition himself in his anger.

Mino bounded forward. Three leaps and he was upon it and scaling the bluff. Helel grabbed it with his remaining claw. Watching from below, Ansiel felt Zecheriah's body flinch at Helel's touch, then felt the power drain as their formation broke. He turned to see Zecheriah drop heavily, shaking the ground with his weight. His body heaped on the grass, wings splayed out weakly, one bent beneath itself. He looked up to the ledge to see Helel, his back leg raised to pummel something beneath it; an azure ball held down by his tail. He stomped, hard, crushing Zecheriah's essence, fracturing the discs instantly. The orb was flattened, and the light from within—the glory given Zecheriah by the Father himself—drifted up, no longer encased in the shell of its whirling wheel. Helel lowered his head, scrutinizing the freed light. He closed his eyes and breathed in, deep, sucking it in through his nostrils. As he did, a blue gem on Helel's head glowed more brilliantly, so bright it lit up the space around him, allowing Ansiel to see the giant serpent smile.

Ansiel flashed sideways and drew his sword again, then charged at Helel, who in turn burst out laughing.

"You again?" He whipped his tail at the cherub, easily knocking him to the ground.

"Helel!" Ansiel bellowed in anger. "Leave this place! You are not allowed here!" Ansiel pulled himself up, surprised at the fear rising within him. He grimaced, tightening his fists as he stood tall. He glared at Helel, transforming his face to that of the lion and roared, hoping to gain confidence with the shout. Air blasted from his jaws and the tips of his wings, forward and sideways and backward all at once. The wild ones scrambled away faster, but they were no match for his power. The furious wind overtook them, wrapping them in its invisible strength, knocking some to their knees and flipping others over.

LXXV

THE ANGEL'S BLAST blew Elise off her feet and into one of the great trees. She clambered, gripping the branch before her, teetering on the narrow limb. Below, Rashid had grabbed Isaiah and was dragging her behind the other tree, out of path of the explosive air. The wind blasted an exposed corner of his jacket, whipping it up, and shredding the fabric. They stooped, bowing their heads—Isaiah's probably in prayer, fervently begging God for rescue, and Rashid's folded over her, his hands clamping her close to his chest, shielding her from the gust.

Elise shot a glance up, searching for Adira, but instead saw Jack, who by then sprinted their way. As he ran, he was lifted, his legs still churning as if running through the sky, and he launched into the tree across the river from hers. Something slowed his fall, tugging his arm back as his body rushed forward, but then he was crashing through branches and giant leaves until he landed square above where Rashid and Isaiah crouched.

The cherub rose again, this time sucking the earth beneath his hooves. Elise gasped at his fury. The forest floor swelled, then dropped like waves in the deep of the Pacific, with no land to interrupt their flow. The dirt tore apart at the sides of the rolling ground as it mounted again to meet the cherub's hooves. He stomped and beat his lower wings, and the ground began to spin. Dirt sprayed out; roots whipped through the air as another gust rallied. The wind's force mounted until it became a reckless gale, blowing and sucking at the air around it mercilessly. The mass of dirt and grass floated above the garden floor, surrounded by a whirling storm, and in the center was its eye, the angel, who was now a raging statue, ignited in flames.

The tornado blasted the valley without discretion. Most of the demons had fled by now. But those that were crippled, strewn about and trying to drag themselves to safety, seemed to be Ansiel's target. The furious air grabbed them by their severed arms or legs, or defeated torsos and hurled them out, broken wings trailing behind.

"Father, help!" Elise screamed desperately. Her voice pierced the night, but the hammering wind drowned her out.

Clutching tight the bough beside her, and tangled in the waving tree branches, Elise ducked suddenly, dodging as a fleshy golden demon scrambled past. She watched it struggle for safety and then zip away, its glorious body tumbling around like a ragdoll. It was beautiful, curvy and decorated with shimmering red and pink hues at its joints. She marveled, wondering if she and it were now the same to God. Had she mistaken everything and lost her favor in His sight, just as it had? This creature—this angel who had once been loved and esteemed—now scrounged for that very love, that very esteem, and now even safety, all things that once had come so naturally. Was this what God did to those He ordained?

She shook her head and squeezed the tree tighter, more from resolve than anything else. No, He sent her. She was sure of it. She glowered into the sky and hollered again. "You called me here! I came! Help us!"

As quickly as it began, it ended.

Angel body parts littered the ground. Hands, legs, feathered tails, scales, even entire wings lay scattered in the trees, floating in the river, or else sunk to the bottom, glistening in the moonlight with the pebbles. Trees were splintered in half, their busted trunks splayed outward, like rays from the sun, with Ansiel at their center. He glowed shining beams of light in every direction, illuminating the aftermath. The garden was devastated.

LXXVI

JACK'S LEGS DANGLED beneath him. He shifted his weight and studied the surrounding branches. One hung right in his face, presenting its fruit just inches from his mouth. *Peculiar,* he thought. The tree had black-and-white limbs. He turned away, searching for the others. Adira was missing. Elise perched across the river in the other tree, staring at him. Jack glanced below, finding Rashid and Isaiah, intertwined and cowering against the trunk of his tree.

"You okay down there?" he whispered harshly.

Rashid squinted up. His face was pale, his eyes empty. Isaiah lay against him, arms still clutching his chest as if he were the last piece of reality left in the world. They were covered with debris—plate-sized leaves, and branches, and chunks of earth draped against Isaiah's back and over both of their heads, pushing them closer together and encasing them in their own private fort of sorts. Jack smiled back at his friend and shook his head, chuckling softly.

"You *stud.*" he mouthed.

Jack's arm throbbed. He reached for it, annoyed. Pain pierced through him as his hand knocked into a branch jutting from where he'd expected to find his shirt. Cringing, he turned to examine it. A splintered timber, thick as his arm, had lodged in his shoulder. He gasped and found Elise's eyes again.

"My arm!"

Elise leaned forward and peeked through the leaves to see what he was talking about. She paused as soon as she saw it and sat up, fear gripping her eyes.

"Don't move." she mouthed back.

Jack twisted, glancing at the angel who had gone crazy. He was calm now but glared at the beast on the bluff. He hadn't noticed them yet. Feeling panic mounting, Jack sought help from Elise, who now appeared to be trying to get Isaiah's attention. She whistled faintly, the melody shaky at best, then sat back, surveying the area around her. Grabbing a piece of already-loosed fruit laying on the branch near her, she hurled it at Isaiah's shoulder. It hit her, making her flinch and sink deeper into Rashid, before looking up to Elise, who now pointed back at Jack. Isaiah craned her neck upwards, obedient though obviously dazed.

By then, blood soaked Jack's shirt and was streaming over the cloth onto the leaves beneath him. He watched as the blood dripped below, onto Isaiah's bewildered face. At its impact she seemed to come to, and caught her breath, her eyes widened. Lips pursed, she turned her head from side to side, ever so slowly, informing him of his fate.

Jack froze. He was dead, and if he didn't die quietly, he'd probably get the others killed with him. He wondered if he could pull the log from his shoulder. But even if he could handle the pain, it would make him bleed out. He dropped his chin. His head swooned; the world already felt lighter. He squeezed tight the branch beneath his thigh, trying to remain conscious with the sensation of his muscles tensing against the wood. He lifted his chin, desperate. His vision was fuzzy now; the colors of the tree blurred together with its background. No longer was he in a garden, but a watercolor painting, dripping wet from a damp canvas and soggy brushes. Soon, he would pass out and fall. That would be the end for them all.

A red-orange ball loomed before him, bright against the withering landscape. *The sun*, he thought. *The beautiful sun came to light up this awful night.* He cocked his head to examine it closer. It smelled good, the sunshine. Had he never noticed its smell in all his life? He blinked. It smelled like… peaches. He squinted and sniffed again, confused. Why would the sun smell like peaches? Its scent wafted deeper into him, replacing the jagged tension from the pain in his shoulder with warm, sweet comfort. He furrowed his brow, trying to concentrate, which was getting harder by the minute. It couldn't be the sun because sunshine didn't smell. No, it had to be something else… it had to be… fruit. But why should fruit be hanging in the air?

Of course! He lurched forward as the memory of everything flooded back, grabbed the orange ball, and bit down. Juice sprayed the roof of his mouth, wetting his cheeks. Elise was right; the flesh was like that of a peach—soft and fuzzy—but its meat burst sweet, tangy, and tropical between his teeth, like a mango and passionfruit had married and meshed flavors. He chewed slowly, savoring each drop. Then he swallowed.

The moment Jack took a bite, the cherub flashed back to stand before the tree he perched on. The breeze created from the cherub's movement fluttered the branches, dropping more fruit on the ground beneath him. The mighty angel was less than an arm's reach from where Jack perched, but he stared right through him as if Jack weren't even there. Orange sparks radiated under his black skin. He raised his wings high, even taller than the tree, all his eyes forward, searching.

Jack shot his arms in front of his face in defense. After a moment, nothing happened, and he lowered them awkwardly, half wondering why he had raised them to begin with, as he was suddenly no longer afraid. He was safe. He peered into the angel's eyes. They flickered to his face and then away again, distracted only for an instant. His presence filled Jack, not just the space in front of him, but inside him too. Suddenly, Jack knew him—he could see into his thoughts, and in that instant, he even understood his heart. He saw pain and confusion, and the desire to please his master. And amidst all that, Jack saw his perception of him, which was more of a side-thought, though a revered one, in which Jack was familiar to him. This place, this angel before him, they were no longer a threat. No, they were more like—comrades.

LXXVII

JACK HAD VANISHED.

From across the river, Elise gaped. Jack had been there, bleeding and dying, and then he took a bite from the fruit and he was gone. She held her breath, biting her lip, afraid her gasp would expose her to the cherub so strangely distracted by the tree in front of him. She glanced down at the others, who still cowered, unmoving, at his feet.

Could Jack's disappearance mean he was dead, that he had eaten from the wrong tree? If so, then perhaps she was in the Tree of Life, and the fruit surrounding her was safe. Or maybe not. The first time anyone had eaten from the wrong tree—the one known as the Tree of Knowledge of Good and Evil—had also been the last time. Adam and Eve had done it, and in doing so learned about sin and consequence. And because of those bites, pain and death had entered the world. They had been kicked out of the garden, and toil and hardship had made their grand entrance. What would be the next punishment on mankind if she were to eat from it too? Or had Jack already eaten another curse into the world?

She blinked, refocusing. Hers had to be the right tree. She reached forward at the piece of fruit dangling before of her, but stopped, remembering the attention it gained when she tore the branch earlier. The cherubs must have been alerted by the tree's disruption. Tearing branches, eating fruit, all of it must set off an alarm. She would need to take one already detached. She looked around—the closest already-fallen fruit was three branches beneath her and out so far that she'd slip if she tried to reach it. The angel still loomed at the ready across the river, way too close to her friends. Her brain spun. There had to be an answer to this. They needed to act now, before he noticed them—and he would, soon.

Then Elise remembered where pieces were reachable. She shifted her view to Rashid, who gawked up his own tree, toward where Jack had been. Elise tried Isaiah instead, glaring at her, willing her to look back. But when only Rashid did, she jutted her chin forward, then stared at the fruit piled under her tree, back at him, and back to the fruit again. Then she pointed at the piece lying next to Isaiah, the one she had hit her with. Rashid's gaze drifted down at it.

From below, Rashid considered the fruit Elise motioned to. He watched as she scooted herself farther along the branch she was on and hovered under another piece of fruit, then opened her mouth wide. She pointed to him and Isaiah, again to the fruit at their side, and then at herself, mouth gaping, ready to bite. Did she want them to both eat the fruit at the same time as her? He shot her a confused look and shook his head. Hadn't she seen what just happened to Jack?

But Elise was steadfast, repeating her gestures more fervently this time. Perhaps this meant she was in was tree they had come all this way to find. Rashid glanced back up at where Jack had been. His heart raced as he wondered where he had gone. The massive, winged beast towered above him, apparently wondering the same thing. In just a matter of time it would look down and find him and Isaiah too. There was no other option. If this fruit really did grant everlasting life, eating it might help them survive. Rashid bumped Isaiah softly on her head with his chin, placing a finger over his lips to shush her as he did. He motioned his chin up and behind her, at the cherub. Isaiah turned to see it, then bit her lips together, breathing deeply. Rashid raised his eyebrows and motioned across the river at Elise, who repeated the gestures she had made before until Isaiah nodded back.

Rashid softly picked up the fruit and held it between their faces. He searched Isaiah's eyes, waiting for agreement. She was trembling. He reached around her and spread his fingers out along her arm, which was warm from the heat the cherub emitted. *You can do this,* he thought, squeezing her arm in reassurance.

Isaiah lowered her lashes—which were thicker than Rashid had remembered—at the fruit and then gazed up at him with damp eyes. A fat tear rolled off her cheek, carrying the weight of their fear with it. She blinked at Rashid, parted her lips in agreement and pushed her chin forward.

Rashid eyed Elise again, waiting for her signal. Before she gave it, something grabbed his fingers and opened them, releasing his grip off Isaiah's arm. A hand. Was she letting him go? Had she changed her mind? But Isaiah hadn't moved and was still focused on him, ready to take the bite. Then, whatever had grabbed him shoved another piece of fruit into his free hand.

Eat it. Eat them both.

Jack's voice filled Rashid's ears as if he were shouting directly into them. Rashid jerked his head up and around, looking for him; no one was there. *Do it, Rash.*

Rashid's mind swirled. Where was he? From across the river, Elise nodded and moved forward to bite down. *Now!* Then Rashid leaned toward Isaiah, their noses brushing as their teeth sank in the fruit. While the bite still sat on his tongue, Rashid shoved the other fruit in his mouth and bit down.

As he swallowed, Rashid watched the great angel behind them shudder. He flew up, hovering quietly above the river, his eyes set on him and Isaiah, watching. Then, he ignited again, singeing the tops of the great pines that still stood in the wreckage. Stirring up the wind, he frantically shot back and forth above the trees. Shifting his regard from the people, he dropped his shoulders, and looked north, where the other cherub lay. He flashed toward him and then back to them and the trees, growling. His face changed from the form of an eagle to that of an ox as he finally left, to join his friend.

LXXVIII

FROM THE LEDGE above the valley, Helel watched. He chuckled at Ansiel's futility as the people defied him—and his precious Father—in eating the fruit. One had chosen quite wisely, it appeared, or maybe two—but Ansiel hadn't seen any of it for his distraction. And now they were untouchable, according to the Father's rules. They that eat from the Tree of Life are granted life, and no one is to take it from them. He thought about shouting down, to chide him about how foolish he looked or how deeply he had failed God but decided against it as he had already crippled Zecheriah. He hadn't meant to. He was, after all a brother. It wasn't his fault he was so weak, so willing to follow along with God's bidding without question.

Helel shrank to the size of a snake and turned to leave. A foot slammed on the ground beside him before he left the clearing. Annoyed, he stopped and turned back. Michael.

"Are you here to gloat in my loss of another limb?" he snarled at the angel, growing his body to match Michael's size.

Michael stood his ground. "What did you expect, Helel? Are you so unjust you call the others here to fight?"

"Oh, them?" Helel chuckled. "They're just a few helpers. We are many, many more."

"Helel, you injured one of the Father's cherubim. He is angered. Zecheriah is of great value to Him."

Helel fumed, resting on his remaining front leg, then whipped his tongue out, jabbing it at Michael's shoulder.

"And you believe I have concern regarding those whom God values? Perhaps you do not understand His ways, even after all this time. Should Zecheriah ever defy Him, God would turn His back on him as well!" He glared at Michael. The sun had yet to rise, but the glow he emitted seemed to fool the birds, who already sang their wake-up call to the mountainside. "You think I'm weak, don't you? Did you not see how Ansiel dared not leave the Garden confines to come after me again? He knew I would take more than one limb if he did." The dragon's nostrils flared in anger.

"No, I know you are powerful," Michael answered. "And foolish."

Michael tucked his head in a quick goodbye and launched from Helel's view, shaking the ground as he left. He drifted, not turning, toward the garden floor where Ansiel now stood above Zecheriah's crumpled form.

LXXIX

EXACTLY WHEN THE cherub left, Rashid was uncertain. He squatted, his mind and body pulsing as the weight of what had just happened collided with reality. His ears rang and the world spun, and despite this—and the fact that his best friend was now gone, but also wasn't really, and the knowledge that somehow the world and everything in it had changed with a single bite—despite all of it, he couldn't pull his eyes from Isaiah's. At some point Elise came and shook him. She hollered something that seemed very distant, though he knew she was right next to him, and then, grabbing his shoulders, twisted his torso to face the bluff. He blinked, coming to, and met her frantic eyes.

"We need to go!" She yelled, pointing away dramatically again. She clung to her shirt end, which was twisted and tight against her waist, the rest of it bulging and lumpy. The fruit. She had gathered it and it was time to leave.

Refocusing, Rashid stood, wrapping Isaiah's shoulders with his arms and lifted. He guided her forward, step by step until her mind seemed to clear too and she was running alongside him, both of their legs churning as if they were still in the midst of the tornado, and their legs were on fire and ahead their only respite.

When they passed the angels, though they were still a hundred meters out, the group slowed until their feet shuffled quietly on the soft grass. The moonlight seemed to rest like a silvery spotlight on them, presenting the beasts as the climax of a grand performance amid the splintered valley. A new one, bigger one, caught Rashid's eye. He was more commanding, well-muscled, and bore the face of a man. Rashid gasped at the attention, but all the angel did was watch, indifferently.

When they were almost out of its sight, and Rashid's head was craned as far back as it could go, he stubbed his toe and his leg buckled beneath him. Lurching forward, he shot his arm out to catch himself. But he still held Isaiah, so in doing so he shoved her forward too, directly in his path. She rolled instinctively, but Rashid's foot fell between her legs and her thighs clamped around it, taking him down with her. Rashid's body slammed onto Isaiah's torso. She curled up, cowering, but he scrambled back up, then glanced back at the angels, who now examined the fractured blue orb. The essence. It was an essence, he suddenly knew it, as natural as anything else, and it belonged to the one on the ground.

"*Up*." he whispered harshly at Isaiah. "We're safe, but we need to go." He hauled her to her feet and spun her around to face him. She flinched, but otherwise was frightened stiff and didn't move.

"Isaiah!" Rashid brushed her cheek with his fingers and lifted her chin, searching her eyes. "Come back to me." With his words, she cemented her gaze on him again and nodded, then filled her lungs and turned to run.

Elise was at the wall, waiting.

"Guys, *now*," she shouted as soon as they caught up. Clamping her shirt tighter around the fruit, she plunged in. Rashid and Isaiah followed, kicking off the riverbank and joining the current into the cave.

On the other side, Rashid and Isaiah splashed up behind Elise.

"We're out!" Isaiah gasped. She pulled Rashid forward, haphazardly clawing at the bank, her hand still locked with his.

"*We* are," Rashid said, then slumped, raking his hand through his hair. He pushed himself up, still holding onto Isaiah, and watched the rushing water behind them, now bringing with it broken twigs and torn leaves. It spilled darker for some reason he didn't want to imagine, so dark that its edges blurred into the cave's shadows.

Adira burst from the darkness tracing the caves walls.

"You made it!" he rushed to the water's edge and reached down to pull Elise up. She heaped on the dirt and sighed, then rolled onto her back and met his eyes. A piece of fruit toppled out from under her shirt onto her neck. She sucked in another breath and glanced down at it, then back up to him, her open mouth broadening to a grin. "And you got your fruit." Adira smiled back, then scanned the others, his face flattening. "Where's Jack? He was right behind me..."

"He's gone."

"Gone? What does that mean? What happened?"

Rashid straightened. "We ate the fruit. Jack was the first. He ate from the wrong tree and disappeared."

"Five," Elise interrupted, staring at her lap. "We got five."

"Four Elise, Out of six. We've only got four." Isaiah said softly, eyes focused on Rashid's. She scooted forward and placed her hand on Elise's shoulder.

Elise dropped her eyes at Isaiah's words. The cave fell silent for a long moment until everyone's gaze drifted to the innocent–appearing, red-orange balls.

"This, the fruit of our labor," Isaiah muttered, her voice cracking.

"Two lives ended for five pieces of food. I hope they are as powerful as you believe." Adira shook his head, then glanced at Rashid. "I am sorry for your loss. But we must go." He opened his backpack and looked at Elise expectantly.

"Aren't you going to eat?" she asked. "There's pl—"

"No."

Elise pinched her lips together and loaded the bag.

LXXX

*Ebenezer (eb-en-ē-zèr) n. (Heb,. 'the stone of
help.') A stone erected by Samuel (1 Samuel 7:12)
as a memorial of divine aid in defeating the Philis-
tines; hence, any memorial of divine assistance.*

SCALING THEIR WAY out of the cavern proved surprisingly easy after
what they had been through. After climbing out, the four stood
around the unassuming hole in the dirt, staring into it. Around
them, the forest was still dark, though a few scattered flames
glowed in the distance closer to the garden. Rashid searched
down the sloped land, through the trees which stood despite the
quake that had just rocked the valley. The mountainside still laid
out pristine here, with pines and junipers and smoke-free bushes
lined up over a tan-and-green blanket of needles and baby brush.

"Should we move the branch? Mark the spot?" Elise asked,
glancing around, "to help remember where it is later?"

"I think, fearless leader, this place we'll remember," Rashid
answered as his eyes ascended the giant maple above them. This
was where he first saw the serpent. The tree had a line of missing
and splintered limbs, from where the branch fell through after he
had swiped it loose. "Let's leave it."

She didn't argue, though Rashid could see she still worried.

The fight had almost drained from him, and he would have let her do whatever she wanted if she had pressed. She didn't, though, likely because now Jack was gone too, and this treasure hunt had costed too much to rub the pain in further. Rashid turned to go, ending the conversation and blinding himself to her face, and whatever turmoil she dealt with. The group silently followed, tracing their path back through the forest, down to the waterfall where they had camped before.

"I'll build a fire," Adira said tightly as they stepped into the clearing, announcing it as the campsite for the night. He dropped the backpack on the ground near Elise's feet and brisked back into the trees.

Elise slid down the tangled yew she stood next to and sat heavily at its base. Propping her elbows on her knees, she dropped her chin in her palms. "Fire. One minute it's eating alive the Garden of Eden, and the next it's protecting us from freezing."

Adira built the fire, and they circled it, drifting asleep as the sun rose, the larks' wake-up songs their lullaby.

Rashid was the first to wake, stirring when the sun was at its peak. He foraged the bank of the pond, gathering stones, stacking them near the now dead firepit. He silently traced a path back and forth from the water's edge to the pile, almost prayerfully, arranging each rock in a mound with the delicate precision of dressing a newborn. After it was chest-high, he stopped, hands on his hips, and took a step back, examining it. By then the others were awake and watched, confused.

"Jack and Mahir are dead," Rashid announced. "This is for them. Their pillar. For their sacrifice."

Elise closed her eyes. "Praise God, amen."

Adira turned to look at her and puffed a short, exacerbated sigh. He shook his head and walked into the woods. Before he was out of earshot, Rashid spoke again—louder this time, determined for Adira to hear him.

"I heard Jack. He spoke to me after he disappeared. I don't know what that means, but I know he is not completely gone, and we are safe now." A sound like a flutter from above stopped him. He paused and glanced up, searching the sky, but its blue was a clear canvas, save for a few scattered, pillowed clouds and the early-winter chill. "And those angels out there—I know them, too."

Isaiah squinted at Rashid. "What do you mean?"

Surveying the horizon, he continued, his words coming out slowly. "Jack. I heard him say to eat both fruit, not just the one from the Tree of Life. So I did." He refocused, frowning at Isaiah. His cheeks trembled. "And now, I know them. And I understand what was going on. The two that were there initially, the guards, their names are Ansiel and Zecheriah. The third one, the one that came after the battle, he is their senior. His name is Michael. The monster's name is Helel. They are at odds with him." His eyes widened, the ramifications of what he was saying hitting him. "And soon they will be at war."

Rashid shook his head, eying the stone memorial before him, amazed at the absurdity of what he was saying and the smallness of it in the scheme of what was coming. Soon there would not be enough graves to hold the number of casualties—of people or angels.

"You ate from both trees." Elise looked up at him. She rolled one of the fruit pieces under her finger thoughtfully. "The Tree of Knowledge of Good and Evil. Of course. First, we learn of good and evil, and then we learn about it. What comes next?"

"I'll answer that." The voice was soft but reverberated through the trees. A wind gust hit them from above and stirred the ground, swirling dried leaves into micro-tornadoes around the clearing. Feathers filled Rashid's view as Michael descended, two commanding sets of ivory wings splayed open, and two other, less commanding sets—one covering his feet and the other anchored at the ready around his head. He landed beside the rock pile.

Isaiah startled and backed up, bumping into Adira, who still stood at the tree line. She stepped on his feet and spun around nervously.

"You bring the fruit to the children," Michael continued, "just as you planned to." He settled his gaze on Elise and bowed his head gently, then looked to the others again.

Rashid stuffed his hands in his pockets. He stood still, relaxed and confident, as if Michael's arrival had answered a dilemma he had been worrying over. "Isaiah, we bring the fruit to the children." He cocked his head, trying to catch her attention.

"The children?" she asked, pivoting back to face them. She squeezed her arms against her chest. "What children?"

Rashid glanced expectantly back at Michael. The two stared at each other for a moment, stern-faced and neither blinking. They didn't understand. He looked at Elise, to see if she might. Her hands hung stiffly by her sides, palms open, the fruit she held before having fallen to the ground beside her. Rashid wrinkled his brow. "The children are not actually children."

Michael raised his chin, fluttering his wings behind him.

"Rashid is correct," he said. "You must bring it to the people of God. God's children."

Adira scoffed. Eying the angel from the corner of his view, he addressed Rashid. "We have five pieces of fruit. How many is that supposed to feed?"

"Multitudes." Michael answered. "Many more than five. Why, Adira? Do you not believe your God can feed them with just these? Do you not know He's done this before?"

Adira bowed his head and darted his eyes toward and then away from Michael. "I have heard that story, yes. I know that Allahu Akbar. Allah is all powerful. I do not doubt Him."

"The Father has sent me to deliver this message. He has

chosen you for this. The fruit must be delivered to the children. They will be waiting in the desert."

Isaiah blinked. "So, like, a refugee camp? How will we know where to go?"

Michael raised his arm toward the way they had originally come. "Southeast. You will be protected. But you must take care. The devil may come to tempt you."

The group exchanged glances.

"I am confused. Weren't you and your friends trying to kill us last night?" Adira said.

"Not me. And no, their intent was not to kill you. Their intent was to keep the garden untouched. But the Father allowed this because of what is beginning."

"Beginning?" Elise asked, her voice barely above a whisper. "What is beginning?"

Michael lowered his wings sympathetically. "The world is not as it was when you left. Things are changing."

Elise got a faraway look on her face. "Soon they will be at war." She narrowed her eyes. "Is this what you were talking about? The apocalypse?"

"Apocalypse?" Isaiah gasped. "So, we're not using it to heal, like cancer and Ebola?" She turned to Rashid and locked onto his gaze, as if afraid leaving his intensity would collapse her own resolve. "Yes. I guess we go. I'm in."

"Okay then," Elise said, looking determined but wringing her hands nervously. She turned to Adira, her eyes pleading "How about you? After... everything. Do you have this in you?"

He shrugged.

"Rashid," Michael said, "take them back the way you came. Rest in the cabin and restore yourselves, then head to Tbilisi. You will need to fly to Jordan from there with the others."

"Others?" Elise asked.

"They are being moved," Michael answered solemnly. "They already need you."

And there appeared a great wonder in heaven; a woman clothed with the sun, and the moon under her feet, and upon her head a crown of twelve stars: ² And she being with child cried, travailing in birth, and pained to be delivered.³ And there appeared another wonder in heaven; and behold a great red dragon, having seven heads and ten horns, and seven crowns upon his heads.⁴ And his tail drew the third part of the stars of heaven, and did cast them to the earth: and the dragon stood before the woman which was ready to be delivered, for to devour her child as soon as it was born.⁵ And she brought forth a man child, who was to rule all nations with a rod of iron: and her child was caught up unto God, and to his throne.⁶ And the woman fled into the wilderness, where she hath a place prepared of God, that they should feed her there a thousand two hundred and threescore days.

-Revelations 12:1-6

LXXXI

THE PATH SEEMED wider than Rashid remembered. Though the trampled edges showed signs of new weed growth, for over a mile it had become clear that the bordering plants' branches had been broken by someone—or something's passing. Rashid paused at the first pillar. He laid his palm on it, closed his eyes and lifted his face. His curly black hair fell back as he breathed deeply, sniffing the air.

"We are almost there," he said softly, stepping forward again.

Isaiah exchanged glances with Elise, who shrugged back. "We're almost there."

The homestead was quiet. Rashid left the front door after no one answered, then peeked through the kitchen window past the familiar yellow-green curtains above the sink.

"I guess we try inside," he said, more to himself than to the others. He returned to the front door and twisted the knob, pushing gently. "Well, this is it."

Rashid stepped inside, leaving the door open behind him. Light spilled in and revealed hovering dust in its beam. The house was just as he remembered, except now it looked expectant, as if the others had left only a few hours before and would soon return. On closer examination, though, the air was stale and smelled mustier than before, and time's light dusting covered the countertops.

On the table sat a leather knapsack with a piece of paper tucked beneath it. Rashid picked up the paper and unfolded it.

Rashid,

*I'm sorry for hurting you. I hope you are doing well.
Salome made you an extra bag of dried berries to
make up for the one you lost. Be safe, we miss you! Tell
Adira that Manal says hello, and she will see him when
you get there. Hurry, there is much to catch up on.*

-In His service, Lazarus, John, and Salome

Rashid reread it several times before looking up.

"They've gone," he said finally. "Adira, there's a message here from Manal. She says 'hello' and is waiting to see you soon." He opened the pouch. Inside were with several bags of candied mulberries, roasted pistachios, and bulging leather flasks of juice.

Adira walked up to Rashid, eyes on the note. "May I?"

"Of course." Rashid handed him the paper and pivoted toward the others. "Let's see what else they left us."

The cabinets held jars of canned tomatoes, peaches, and apples, along with containers bursting with roasted hazelnuts, and the closets were stuffed with soft blankets and dry clothes, lavender sprigs stuffed between, filling them with its sweet peaceful scent. Outside, the trees were still heavy with apples, and beneath them lay a bumpy carpet of rotting fruit. The garden was nearly crowded out by weeds, but they found a few straggler onions and asparagus growing.

The team harvested what they could, and afterward Elise and Isaiah cooked dinner while Rashid and Adira brought the fireplace back to life. All afternoon the house was nearly perfectly quiet, save for the occasional bumping of logs falling into place or clanging of pans and tinging of blades against ceramics in the kitchen. At some point the ladies broke the silence with the soft humming of old hymns as they worked side by side in the kitchen, the blessing of a stove and clean dishes breaking though their worries.

After a hearty dinner, the group curled up with full bellies and heavy limbs around the hearth. It didn't take long before the fire's soft crackles lulled them. Elise pulled the blanket she had wrapped around her shoulders tight and rolled to her side while Rashid watched. She sunk into the very spot on the couch where he had spent so many days healing from the river. He turned to Isaiah, who sat beside him on the floor. Her head bobbed gently though she still sat upright. He reached around her shoulders and leaned back, guiding her half-asleep torso against his chest. When he looked up again, Adira had locked eyes on him.

Rashid caught his breath. Adira's eyes were stormy, desperate, like he was holding back tears and on the verge of charging into battle at the same time. So much could be going on behind them. Adira was here, sure, but he had to be—the weather was going bad and they still had a few days hike and a drive left before returning to civilization. He wondered what would happen when they returned to Tbilisi.

Rashid closed his eyes and dropped his head softly onto Isaiah's, tousling her hair with his chin. It didn't matter what was going on with Adira. He was tough, he'd be all right. If he needed to glare, he'd let him. For now, they were safe, warm, and full, and he had a purpose again, which was enough for him.

There was more, too. Rashid's mind was clear now. He had peace. He now knew things would be fine, and he and the others were doing something special, and great—great in the whole universal scheme of things. They were to help the world survive a war that was coming from the heavens, between angels and demons and the God of everything. He understood things he had never thought of before. Then there was the constant flow of information, so overwhelming he almost wished he could turn it on and off. Sometimes it was subtle. They'd turn a corner in the forest, and he'd know that such-and-such angel was sitting above them resting. Then he'd glance up and there they'd be, on a limb or in the leaves, and they'd nod at him and look away. But, sometimes, it'd be more than that, like what he received the day they climbed out of the cave. He had been walking silently with the others, his mind on getting away, when there had been a large crashing and a blast of heat, and he'd suddenly been filled with dread. He had turned toward the disturbance, knowing that Julian, whoever the heck that was, was scared and was succumbing, soon to lose his glory. And there was Julian when he had turned, flat on the ground—a round, creamy-colored angel with silver tufts of fur and shiny, ebony eyes—pleading at Rashid to help. Atop him perched two wild ones, piercing his shoulders with their claws and tearing his wings from their base. They snarled under their glistening, brown-and-green brows, which curled with anger and resentment. When Rashid looked at them, they had flinched, their faces flashing with anxiety at being exposed, but Rashid had flinched, too, and called to the others—he'd even grabbed Adira's shoulders and spun him to see.

But he couldn't see any of it, of them, and no one else could either, and they had eyeballed Rashid like he was off his rocking chair. Then they had just turned around and kept walking, while the angel on the dirt screamed in agony and the demons clawed at his chest. Rashid had left too, assuming he was in shock, perhaps. But then something inside him dropped, like the moment he found his Nubia all those months ago, and he had turned back in time to see a ball of light stream from Julian's chest. The wild ones pounced after it and fought each other over it. The bigger of the two dominated in the end and had sucked it in his mouth like one would spaghetti noodles, long and purposeful, and full of satisfaction.

These thoughts, which were more like pieces of life, filled him. He had entered a new realm, and somehow had simply been accepted into it, by them all. And by being there, by seeing them and knowing what he did now, he knew that their worries of dry clothes and clean water and return to the world of electricity was all very trivial.

LXXXII

THE NEXT AFTERNOON, the group gathered by the wood-splitting post to pray for guidance and protection. When they finished, Adira walked away abruptly, face soggy and swollen.

Elise watched him leave. *Go to him*, she heard, as if the command had been whispered directly into her ear. She turned to find whoever had said it, but Isaiah and Rashid were already leaving, talking quietly between themselves. By then Adira had wandered to the path that was lined with columns and stopped to examine one. She headed toward him. When she walked up, he was tracing the pillar's grooves with his fingers, studying its design. In its top and bottom ends were carved rows of all kinds of dancing animals. She smiled at a horse who looked to be holding a sheep's hand, about to spin it into a dove, who was bowed deep in a curtsy.

"Wow, what detail," Elise said gently.

"It is. Remarkable one man carved all these." Adira followed the trail back with his eyes, softly counting the pillars he could see from where he stood. "Twelve," he whispered. After that, the path turned to the right and they were gone.

"You left rather quickly," Elise said. "Are you thinking about Mahir?"

Adira closed his eyes and let his hand fall on the pillar. "I am."

"What happened to him was horrible," Elise said. "I'm so sorry. I know you didn't sign up for all of this."

She *was* sorry. Adira and Mahir had been struck by this job far more than any fee could compensate, and she was the one who had hired them. She knew he needed to grieve, and she wanted to help him through it but didn't know how. But, through all her years of watching people die and others suffer losses, she had learned that often the best thing to say was nothing at all. People grieved in usually the same pattern—denial, anger, bargaining, depression, and acceptance, sometimes in that order, sometimes not. She had tried too many times before to say, "the right thing," but nothing but time had ever made the one in mourning glad again. So, she had instead learned to simply drop morsels of encouragement into their world and stand back, giving them permission to hurt and then heal in whatever way they needed.

Elise laid her hand on Adira's shoulder, half expecting him to shudder. When he didn't, she stepped closer and wrapped her arms around him, drawing him in gently until she could smell the grease and smoke from his curls. She breathed in his scent and squeezed him tight, then slid her arms under his, and stepped into him, hoping to help him break into his grieving. Maybe he'd release his first cry into her embrace. She'd let him. She'd stand there and not move, hold him as long as he needed, and let him cry out as loud as he needed, even let him use her body to smother the sounds if he wanted.

Adira stood stiffly. After a moment, though, he dropped his face into the back of her collar. His breath, hot and ragged, flooded her skin and dampened her hair. He wrapped his arms around her back and slid them up behind her neck, then cupped her head by its base. He traced her head with his fingers, fervent against her scalp, and tangled them in her hair. Elise held her breath, shocked at his palpable hunger. He drew his thumbs down beneath her earlobes along her jaw to the front of her throat and locked them against her skin.

Elise gasped. A lump rose where Adira held her. She cringed, fighting her urge to step away, but prayed silently for protection. She'd already decided she would stay here and let him do whatever he needed.

Adira leaned closer to Elise. His nostrils flared and his lip curled into a sneer as he squeezed his eyes closed, filtering every ounce of anger to the muscles in his hands. He tensed them until they were stone-solid without closing his grip. They locked her in place with only a few millimeters allowing margin to breathe. She felt him gulp, releasing his breath again and, biceps quivering, press forward, forcing himself at her, near tripping over her feet as he pushed her backward. She collapsed, completely yielded, trust-falling into his rage and arched her neck, then gasped, opening her mouth to suck in whatever air he allowed. She kept her eyes intent on his, peering out beneath narrow slits, her arms still clinging to his torso.

❦

A tear fell from Elise's eye, distracting Adira momentarily. He watched it trace her cheek. It found its way to the web between his thumb and forefinger and rolled onto his hand. His mind flashed back in time to the moment as a boy when he had stood with Mahir, gun aimed at his mother's chest. She had released a single tear as well, when she closed her eyes in permission for him to take her life to free his brother's. His mouth dropped, and he glanced back at Elise's eyes, his own widening in shock at what he was doing to her, this child who was so willing to give herself for his pain.

He released his grip and slid his arms down behind her as she fell backward. She sighed and closed her eyes in relief as he wrapped her up once more, softer this time, in an apologetic embrace that took them to the ground.

"I am sorry. So sorry," Adira whispered into her ear.

She nodded and held him back. "I know. I am too."

LXXXIII

ISAIAH FOUND THE boat behind the cabin under an awning. She called Rashid to see it first. She pulled back the brown canvas covering it and stood back, presenting it to him as if it were the first boat ever to be invented and they were the happy explorers to discover it.

"Is that real?" Rashid asked. "Well, this is a surprise. But I guess they had to have one. Living this close to the river."

"Was this hidden from your new fount of knowledge, then?" Isaiah asked, winking at him.

"It was," Rashid answered. He chuckled, shaking his head. "I think Lazarus knew this was all supposed to happen, and that if I knew they had a boat…"

Isaiah turned back, and stood with him another moment, taking in the irony aboard the empty vessel. Sighing, she reached back and tied her hair away, relishing its softness after having had a shower with actual soap and water. Rashid cocked his head to the side, studying her.

"Your hair is beautiful. Why stuff it away like that?" he asked, stepping closer. He brushed the few strands still tucked behind her ear loose.

Isaiah's cheeks warmed at his unexpected touch. She let the hair fall forward, trying to hide her blush. "I don't know, I guess I never thought about it."

Rashid chuckled again, softer this time. "I believe all women should let their hair down. It has power. You could probably control the entire male population with a toss of your head if you did it right."

Now Isaiah was laughing. "The entire male population, huh? Are you sure about that?" She reached back, undid the stick at her crown, and ran her fingers through her hair, helping the brown strands cascade around her shoulders. Fixing her eyes on Rashid, she felt her cheeks redden even more. The heat spread down from her cheeks through her neck and into her chest. She smiled, realizing she liked him this way. "Maybe I'm not interested in all that. Maybe…" She bit her lower lip, to stop it from tripping her words. "How about just you?"

Rashid stared back. He was surprised to feel his heart speed up at her words. He glanced at her lip caught between her teeth and wanted suddenly to touch it, to touch her. He flushed as a familiar warmth coursed through him, from his chest into his arms, making his fingers tingle. He reached forward again, brushing off the thought that this should still be forbidden. He stroked the length of her hair, wrapping a lock between his fingers at her crown and gently tracing it to its end, just beneath her breast. He reached behind her shoulders and drew the rest of it forward, then let it fall through his fingers, slowly, savoring the touch, until it nearly covered her chest.

"There." He said gently. "That will work for your purposes, I think."

Isaiah smiled, then blinked, her eyes widening as if she suddenly remembered something important. "The others. We need to tell them." She spun around and took off, pulling Rashid by his arm behind her.

The group stayed in the cabin that day and two more, resting in soft beds and healing their hearts by the warm fire. They ate well, stewed potatoes with onion, aside salted trout the men caught in the river. On the morning of the fourth day, when the sky was particularly bright and cool, they headed out. Spirits were high, and for the time, the four felt as if they were the only ones in the world, close to each other and to God, inspired by His mission—their divine purpose—which seemed at least for those few days, entirely possible.

LXXXIV

THE SUN HAD passed its peak and was starting its descent, pushing the shadows of the coconut trees Helel rested beneath behind him, and making the sand hot for lack of shade; just how he liked it. Helel mused at the idea of being tortured in heat forever. He loved the heat. What cold-blooded serpent didn't? It had been decreed that if he lost this thing, the Father would send him to a firepit to suffer. He supposed too much heat would be unpleasant, but Helel reasoned that his cunning would bring him through whatever trials the Father sent. The people had a saying which seemed fitting for his situation—work smarter, not harder. They had so many wise sayings, though he had to admit wisdom was not evenly distributed to their masses. And how was he to get their majority, wise and foolish alike, poor and rich, young and old, to follow him? He needed a plan. He needed to raise another to lead the crowd. He needed to introduce himself to them all.

Helel stood and shook the loose sand from his back, his tail whipping the last few grains off. He scanned the Atlantic, its clear water glistened bright topaz, with darker patches scattered about where the coral sat. The whole thing deepened quietly to a uniform navy blue farther out, miles from the powdery shore where he perched. He sniffed, sucking in the scent of salt and fish, then ran forward and plunged beneath the crystal water. His streamlined body coursed through it like a torpedo, limbs folded tight and tail making corrections as a rudder would, guiding him past Morocco, through the Strait of Gibraltar, into the Mediterranean Sea. He was swift, and even at his shrunken size, landed on the Israeli shore in seconds.

He crawled out, dodging the feet of a Palestinian boy splashing in the waves, whose mother called to him in the distance. It was approaching late afternoon; the tide was rising, and she wanted to get home to make the evening meal. Helel watched the child turn toward her, giggling as he flopped on his belly once more, splashing the shallow silver water in every direction. He dunked his head, adding a few more sandy grains to his dark hair, then pulled himself out to run after her, past a pollution-alert sign with bright red lettering flanked by skull and crossbones that read *Swimming is Prohibited.*

Gaza. He'd start here.

LXXXV

THE RIVER CARRIED them back fast, the group's chilled muscles working quickly, taking advantage of the current. Before night fell, the four lodged the boat on the bank and climbed out. They dragged the craft from the bitter river and stashed it inside the tree line, burying it with branches, and slept one last night under the stars, huddled together. The next morning, they hiked the last few hours in silence. The Range Rover was just where they had left it, the branches atop it now drenched with melting snow.

"So, what month do you think it is?" Rashid asked Adira.

"It's probably September or October," he answered, huffing, as he cleared the windshield. "It could be November if we have a mild winter this year." He reached beneath the front tire and produced a gray box that rattled satisfactorily when he shook it.

"Let us see if our rescue is still operational," he said, sliding into the driver's seat.

The engine caught after three turns of the key and warmed up within minutes. They drove back in the latter-day light, through the giant pines, atop a ground speckled with burnt orange leaves and also through barren valleys and foothills, all of it powdered with snow, until eventually, they drove into the black-and-gray cement jungle that was Tbilisi.

Pulling in front of Turkish Brothers' Tours, Adira turned off the ignition. He glanced at Rashid, then twisted around toward

Elise and Isaiah, who had fallen asleep to humming tires along the way.

"Well, we have arrived."

The street was barren save for one other vehicle parked a block away. On the sidewalk opposite them, a couple walked briskly, huddled together, eyes downcast as they passed, the man in a faded leather bomber and the lady with her face burrowed in the collar of her black trench coat. Not one of the other storefront windows was lit up. Someone had taped a giant poster to the front window of one of the shops. It read:

In memorial of His Excellency Jubair Talmuk's passing, we will be closed until Monday, September 20th.

Adira and Rashid exchanged glances.

"I wonder what happened," Isaiah whispered.

"Something bad," Rashid answered, rereading the sign. His gut dropped as he suddenly saw a vision flash before his eyes, as if he were watching a movie, and was the lone audience member. In it, Jubair, perched over a bloodied man on the ground, yelling about the mess. Then the scene changed, and he saw him kneeling before the dragon, trembling and nodding along to whatever was being said. Rashid blinked, watching it change again to his reality, which now showed Isaiah peering up at him, her head cocked in worry. "He was no good." Rashid mumbled somberly.

"I thought you liked him?" She asked, studying him.

"I did. But apparently he I was wrong."

"So… I guess it's good he's dead?"

"Not good or bad, just the order of things," Rashid said as he climbed out and flung the leather sack Lazarus had left them over his shoulder. He strode toward the storefront, anxious to get out of the street, and glanced over his shoulder at Adira. "I'm hoping you still have the keys, my friend?"

In another minute, they stood in the foyer, staring at the thinly framed she-wolf and the aluminum desk with neatly stacked papers, all of it seeming much more extravagant than before.

"Home," Adira muttered, tossing the keychain on the desk and plodding to the back of the shop. He pushed through the half-door divider, letting it swing behind him, then unrolled his now-dusty prayer mat in the direction of Mecca. The others watched as he disappeared into the back of the store and upon returning, stepped out of his shoes and onto the mat.

"Allahu Akbar," he said and rocked forward, raising his hands up and then folding them in front of his chest.

Rashid watched silently. By the time he was on his knees, however, Elise had slipped out of her own shoes and treaded softly back to where he was, then folded herself onto her bottom, legs crossed, and bowed her head as well. Isaiah glanced at Rashid.

He looked back expectantly. "And you?"

Isaiah shrugged. "I guess we're past boundaries now." She moved to the back to sit between them, eyes fixed on Rashid. "So, Mr. Enlightened, what are we to do from here?"

Rashid opened his mouth to answer but no words came out. He tried again and choked. His tongue was paralyzed. Coughing loudly, he tried yet again, this time managing only a groan. The others glanced up.

The point is not Muhammad, Adira, a voice whispered abrasively.

Adira paused and shot a confused glance to the side. The words filled the room, rousing Rashid's skin into a thousand tiny goose bumps. He turned, searching around and behind him, then back to Adira, smiling sheepishly as he realized who had spoken. So this was the Father. Rashid glanced at Isaiah. She was clearly holding her breath, staring wide-eyed back. They had all heard it.

The voice came again. *The point is not your sacrifice, Elise.*

Elise peeked up in surprise, then immediately bowed her head. "My God," she whispered, her eyes filled with instant tears. "Thank you, Father."

It spoke again. *Isaiah, the point is not your relationships.*

Isaiah's eyes widened further, as if she felt exposed. There it was. God's words, as clear as she could ever ask, and Rashid watched as they tore at her heart.

The floor trembled. Rashid grabbed the wall, but it soon shook and knocked him and the others to their knees. The four braced their hands flat against the cold linoleum and searched for a surface to hide beneath. The front window shuddered, threatening to fall out or shatter. Its vibrations released a trill that echoed louder and louder until it filled the entire shop like a rushing wind, and then like a train, pounding across metal tracks without mercy for whatever lay in its path. The roar seemed to take form, and a wind whooshed the papers off the desk, then circled the room, blowing stronger each second until it stung their eyes. The pictures blasted off the walls, breaking their flimsy metal frames and releasing the plexiglass sheets to bound across the floor until they hit the wall and rattled to a stop.

No one saw the desk flip, but they heard it crash—a boom that shook loose drywall dust from the ceiling tiles. Rashid covered his ears with his palms and squinted up. Before him was nothing but white, a canvas of fog and light filling the room. He couldn't see his friends, or the walls, or any of it. He couldn't even see the floor. Its coolness was there, solid beneath his sweating palms, but it appeared again as it did in his dream, as if he were floating. The voice came again.

Hear me. All you who have ears to hear, hear me! I have chosen you as the carriers of life to my children. All your ceremony is nothing but a comfort to you. Pray sincerely, and walk with my Spirit. Be strong. Before I formed you, I had this planned; remain in me and you will succeed.

The gust slammed into their backs when the words were done, prostrating the four completely. Then everything went black.

✧

The blaring honk of an angry car woke Rashid the next morning. He had hardly slept since he transformed in the Garden, but after the revelation the day before, he had fallen unconscious. Pushing back to his knees, he evaluated the room. It was a mess, but the window had held, and the world outside bustled along, oblivious to them. The others lay in the back, bellies and noses flat against the floor, as they had been when the voice came the day before. They were alive, he knew, but asleep. He thought about waking them, or maybe just Isaiah, but decided they would need their rest for the days ahead, so instead stepped outside to wait.

The air was cool, which seemed fitting with such a gray street as its backdrop. The cars crept along robotically, lined up in each direction, headed toward jobs or errands or whatever else. The drivers almost didn't seem real. Rashid watched, saddened but intrigued, seeing them through his new lens.

A man in the car closest to him caught his eye. In his fifties, maybe—with dark hair just the other side of speckled and in need of a trim, who drove a silver Volvo and had one hand on the wheel, the other on a green paper coffee cup topped with a plastic lid. He took a sip, oblivious to Rashid, and bounced his head rhythmically to the music playing behind the sealed windows. He was empty, Rashid could see. Neither light nor darkness was in him; neither God nor Satan abided in him; he just *was*. Then he was gone, and another car drove forward, taking his place.

Rashid closed his eyes and breathed deeply, overwhelmed. He felt alone. He knew he was God's now, even though he'd never made any choice he could remember about the matter. It didn't make sense, any of it. Before, he'd just been a man in a cellar, waiting to get home to save his family. Now, he was something other than a man, and what he was seemed entirely different from any other thing. And yet, he didn't understand how he had come to be this way. Jack had always told him that God wanted a commitment. He remembered countless conversations that centered on what He wanted: an announcement that he was a sinner and needed to be saved by Jesus. But all he had done to receive this was obey a whispered voice in his ear. He sighed and opened his eyes again, eager for the next person to drive up.

Behind the wheel, sat a woman this time. She drove a red crossover and looked to be wearing a suit. Her dark brown skin contrasted starkly against a white blouse, and her coal-black hair was pulled tight in a bun at her crown. While waiting for the light to turn, she adjusted her glasses in the rearview mirror, then applied lipstick. Rashid watched as she patted her lips together and kissed the air. She repositioned the mirror and sat back, calm in her gray world, eyes focused on the street ahead. That woman, she belonged to God, he could see, though there was no indication other than he saw her and he knew.

Each time the light flashed red and a new car stopped in front of him, he studied its passenger, counting the number for God, the number for Satan, and the number who belonged to none. He had reached twelve for none when Isaiah appeared behind him.

"We're all awake."

He didn't turn around, as his eyes were still fixed on number twelve. This one was a young girl who appeared to be a few years older than his Nubia. She sat in the backseat of a white sedan, weaving back and forth, dancing in place, her eyes happy, squinted shut while her mouth gaped as she belted out some song she obviously loved.

Isaiah laid her hand on his shoulder.

He coughed dryly and reached for her hand. It was warm, rough in patches now, but still delicate. Her short fingers were recognizable now just to his touch. He turned to face her. She was watching the girl.

"Oh, Rashid…"

"Good." He interrupted and stood, peering over her head, not wanting her to see into his eyes, just in case she'd see what was going on in his mind. He didn't want her to discover what he already knew, because it would hurt her too. The people… they were just pieces on a gameboard, pawns that could either fall on one side or the other.

He realized it the moment he saw number twelve. Moyra and Nubia hadn't known they were in a game, and neither did that girl. They hadn't known, and so in the end their fate, as members of the group for none, defaulted toward Satan's handicap. He still wasn't sure if that in itself was a bad thing, but it meant that he and they would end up on opposite sides of the board, and therefore he may never see them again.

He coughed nervously. "We need to leave. We have a long way to go."

LXXXVI

EXITING THE COUNTRY proved simple—four tickets for a flight from Georgia to the airport in Amman, one way per Rashid's direction. Adira shook his head at this, but did it anyway. They would leave late that evening and arrive in Jordan at 9:35 a.m. the next morning

"Why Jordan?" Isaiah had asked during the planning, but Rashid simply shrugged.

"That's where we are to go," he answered dryly.

The Tbilisi airport was still sleepy when they arrived. Signs adorned the ticket counter, posting that starting next spring, travelers would need their UN member tattoo to come and go freely. More notices dotted the path to and through security, announcing proudly the lifting of travel warnings across the Middle East. At their gate, a television was set to CNN. A white man in a blue suit and red tie listed the recent changes in the area, including the reestablishment of border crossing warnings.

"Israel continues to mourn after Secretary-General Talmuk's death. The new temple has been closed for the next seven days in honor of his life and contributions to society. A statue is being erected at the entrance to the Palace of Nations in Geneva, to remind us of his life and sacrifice. A memorial service will be

held this Sunday, with the unveiling of the statue. Pope Elijah is expected to address the nations."

"It's sad, Mike." The camera scanned to the man's left, where a pretty woman with puffy blonde bangs and high cheekbones spoke matter-of-factly. *"What happened to him is proof of evil in this world. Our thoughts go out to his family. We truly hope the religious fanatics who are behind this are caught and dealt with accordingly.*

"In the meantime, Judaism numbers are at an all-time low. Members of this, as well as multiple Jesus-based religions, are denouncing their beliefs. A new resolution recently ratified by the UN is helping matters, one initiated by Secretary Talmuk before his assassination. For those not yet familiar, the law now states capital punishment as a possible consequence for any person spreading religious revulsion and discrimination. Mike, we do have hope that the nonsense trying to spread this hypercritical hate will be over soon."

"We can only hope, Yvonne," the man answered.

Isaiah gaped at the television. What had happened while they were away? She turned just as Elise walked up behind her.

"Isaiah, I think… I think…" Elise spoke softly, her eyes fixed on a man sitting to their right. He wore a red T-shirt that read *Destroy religion before religion destroys us.* "I mean, do you think…"

Isaiah pursed her lips. "Maybe."

"So you both think, do you?" Rashid asked, joining them. "Good start." He nudged Isaiah with his elbow.

"Rashid, they have a new law that makes evangelism illegal—punishable by death," Isaiah whispered. "We could be in real danger, very soon. Is it starting?"

Rashid nodded. "Maybe." He eyed Adira, who was just returning from the bathroom. "Ready?"

"Yes."

"Well then, let us go to doing this thing," Rashid answered.

Adira gave him a sideways glance. "Right," he said, rolling his eyes as he walked away.

Isaiah stared at Rashid. He seemed so nonchalant, as if this were all just part of another day—a normal, routine day. Wake up, brush teeth, stop for coffee on your drive in, scan your brand at the security toll booth, go to work, leave work, vote in the extermination of a random people group.

"Isaiah, we need to get on the plane."

"Okay, but..." Before she could finish, Rashid led her to the gate.

Queen Alia International Airport was bustling when they arrived. The group stepped into the crowd outside the doors near Baggage Claim and studied the area. The tourist stands sat empty except for one with a large banner, a giant *X* crossing out its original lettering: *Private tours. Petra and Shobak Castle.* Beneath the original words were drawn in *Resettlement Camp Transport.*

Elise turned to Rashid. "That's it, isn't it?"

He nodded. "We go there."

The resettlement camp was the government's way of peacefully separating the religious zealots from the rest of the public. The law was simple; there would be no discrimination against any specific religion—as long as said religion did not include forcing their opinions on others. Authorities touted it meant to uphold personal freedom and choice. So if your faith was quiet and did not interact aggressively with others—defined by teaching, preaching or serving "in the name of" any particular God—then you were doing things right and could continue. However, as soon as you broke through those barriers, you were also breaking the law. Refusing services to others because of religious beliefs was also deemed illegal.

Pope Elijah's original decree had resulted in riots. Demonstrations were held in front of the temple, which led to a shooting, killing seventeen and wounding another twenty-three. This launched a series of church slayings, which were counterproductive in the steps toward peace. The groups with radical believers had not been silenced; instead, they ignited a revival of sorts with outreach programs, evangelical pastors embarking on city tours with their message, and an increase in the numbers of mission trips. Pesky tracts fluttered about the streets, describing how to come to their God.

Local governing bodies were eventually faced with the dilemma of imprisoning all the zealots, which meant less room for other criminals, or simply ex-communicating them from city centers. Ex-communication was the more feasible consequence in the end, so a new law was set forth. If any radicals remained in the main cities and continued with the current onslaught of pressing their beliefs on others, then they would be imprisoned or even given the death penalty, per issues with prison capacity. The groups then left, forming "Settlement Camps" in the badland areas of each country participating in the United Nations Rule, which of course, was nearly every civilized country, save Russia and a few of the smaller Asian countries. Many radicals were already living in small, out-of-range cities, most without the conveniences of modern technology. The groups remaining in town were placid and kept to themselves without any threat of spreading their message.

"Need a ride?" A dark-skinned woman with blue jeans and a red T-shirt smiled at them as they approached. Rashid stepped up, clinging to the backpack strapped on his shoulders. The fruit was in his bag in case they got separated as he was the one with the direct line of communication regarding where they needed to go and when.

"Okay, that will be..." she mouthed her count of the travelers and typed into a calculator. She looked up, confused. "You folk are from... sorry, what type of currency are you carrying?"

"None, sorry," Rashid answered. "But we need to get there."

"I have lari," Adira interrupted. "How much?"

She lifted a laminated sheet from beneath the pedestal in front of her, then punched more numbers into the calculator. "Three thousand three hundred and seventy-nine lari."

Adira shook his head and fished out a billfold stuffed with money. He handed her a wad. "When does the transport leave?"

"There is one departing in another thirty minutes. She motioned toward a rusted school bus parked in the lot behind her. "That one. I'd grab a seat now before it fills up."

Inside, the bus reeked. The steamy air was filled with the sour scent of too many people needing a bath. Isaiah covered her nose.

Rashid peeked at her and chuckled. "Does that make it any better?"

"Maybe in my mind, which right now is good enough for me," she said and sat down on the cracked vinyl over the wheel well. She lowered the window as much as it allowed, which ended up being only 2 inches.

Elise sat beside her. "Ah, come on, it's not that bad," she said. "Better than prison." She winked and nudged Isaiah with her elbow.

"Prison. Isn't that where we're headed now?" Adira interrupted. He stood in the center aisle, one hand on each seat straddling him. "I believe something like this happened once before, a hundred years ago or so. And here we are, paying for the honor to repeat history, likely as the victims." He heaved into the seat on his right and dropped his head backward, closing his eyes. "I am going to take a nap—I assume this may be the softest object we get to rest on for the next while."

Isaiah exchanged glances with Elise. He was right, but even if they hadn't been on this mission, staying in town, or even returning to America, where things were only better in places, was not much safer an option.

Within minutes, bodies crammed into every seat and spilled into the aisle in spots. A heavyset man with curly black hair, a

Roman nose, and stubble well past the five o'clock range clasped the rail and peered at the passengers.

"Everyone on board?" he hollered and waved from the front. "Welcome to Freedom Express. My name is Vitaly, and I'll be your tour guide." Chuckling, he took the last step to his seat. He narrowed his eyes at them through the rearview mirror. "In another three or four hours, we will arrive at our destination. Please wear safety belts if you have them. I haven't had my coffee yet." The man winked and then focused on his gears, pulling levers and pushing buttons to back out.

LXXXVII

BY THE TIME they pulled up to their destination, the transit passengers had added to the stench saturating the air. The breeze coming through the few open windows helped little, and the bus steamed with trapped sunlight.

"We're here." Vitaly pulled the lever to open the door. They were parked in a large lot, lined up with four other busses, all of which had already been emptied. A group of men stood together near the front hood of the bus beside them, a few leaning on tired elbows, chatting and sipping drinks between words.

They emptied the bus quickly, stepping out into the much cleaner, drier air. A crowd streamed ahead toward the people-counting churns of a visitor center.

"This way." Rashid motioned with his shoulders toward the line, clutching the straps of his backpack.

Scattered amongst the crowds were men with their eyes trained on them and the other newcomers—men who clung to rifles hanging from straps on their shoulders. Like many others there, they wore the colorful keffiyeh, red and white and green scarves wrapped around their heads. They were tucked away inconspicuously, hunched behind pillars or near cash registers at the small shops.

"This feels rather like the trek of cattle to slaughter," Adira mumbled, quietly following along. He glanced at Elise. "Are you ready for this?"

"Maybe it's too late if I'm not." She smiled, then took a deep breath and straightened. "Adira, He has plans for us. To give us hope and a future. We are bringing life to these people; this is going to be for the good."

He dropped his eyes to the ground. "And those guys?" he asked, raising his eyebrows at one of the camouflaged men, whose rifle hung out lazy in the sun. "Are we bringing them life as well?"

Elise followed his gaze and caught her breath. She brushed Isaiah's forearm lightly, motioning his way.

Rashid pivoted toward Adira, slowing his pace. "Yes, them too. They have a role to play in this game just like we do. It doesn't mean they are any less deserving of the prize."

Adira stopped, narrowing his eyes at Rashid. "I hardly think this is a game. Nothing that has happened so far has been in jest. And if living is the prize, then I'm not interested in being a part of any of it."

"But you *are*, Adira," Elise said. "We all are. And we are in it now. Don't you understand? We're the ones who can make these people see they aren't just pawns in a game. No, it isn't a game. It's real life—this is a matter of eternity. Eternity, Adira. For us and everyone else here—paradise or otherwise. That's our future, and theirs as well." She squared off with him and raised her voice. "No one is backing out. We are going at this together, through those men, and whatever else is in front of us. And we are bringing the fruit in that bag," she threw her arm out, pointing at Rashid, "to those people!" She pointed down the line ahead, her eyes wild.

Isaiah stepped up and wrapped her arm around Elise's shoulder. "We are, Elise, it's okay."

"No, none of this is okay!" she yelled, drawing the attention of one of the guards. He clasped the butt of his rifle and straight-ened, alert.

Rashid watched him. He was just a kid, maybe in his late teens, acne spotting his shiny face and a few wisps of black hair dangling from his headdress. He eyed the boy's hand on the rifle. It was steady. Kid or not, he had used that gun before.

Adira shushed Elise, watching him from the corner of his eye. "Quiet!"

Rashid stared at his friends, wondering what to say next. While he did, his shoulders became heavy, like someone was pushing down on them. He checked above, but no one was there. Air rushed against the back of his neck.

Rashid.

He heard the word clearly, as he had in the shop and in the garden when Jack had commanded he eat the fruit. But around him were only the bustling bodies of the crowd, all of whom emanated their position at him—for God or Satan or none. His head spun. Elise had said this was not a game, but how could this be anything else?

The voice spoke again. *Rashid, move on, now!* He caught his breath, refocusing. He didn't understand the voice, but he knew it needed to be followed.

"She is fine," Rashid said to Adira, stepping forward, trying to still his own voice from sounding as impatient as he felt. "We all are. We'll go now."

Elise settled and turned back around, Isaiah's arm still draped on her shoulder. They walked the rest of the way in silence until a salmon colored rock wall towered dramatically above them. Rashid brushed his fingertips against the stone's rough surface. It gripped his skin back—sandstone. He'd always wanted to visit Jordan but was ashamed to admit he had never done so, even being as close as he was all those years. It was, in the end, another thing filling the background of his life that he'd taken for granted. He was rubbing his fingertips together, feeling the grains that had loosed in his touch roll innocently between them, when the voice came again. *Rashid, feed my children.* He glanced around again. Still nothing.

Eventually, the number of men with rifles dwindled. Farther away they came to a makeshift placard, its phrase in three languages, all painted in red.

You are passing international borders.
Reentry is not allowed.

Just beyond the notice, imbedded into the desert ground was a chain-link fence topped in barbed wire. It rose several feet higher than them and stretched, apparently, miles in both directions. A gate presented itself, held open by two guards, and beyond them lay more desert, decorated only with more stone, shaping boulders, hills, and bluffs, and in the distance, caves.

The stream of people pressed forward, through the gate toward their new home. A few hesitated as they passed the guards, but everyone eventually walked through. They followed each other, clinging to loved ones or else all alone, until the line narrowed to trickle through a passageway where the bluffs became giant straddling walls.

Rashid, feed my children. It came again. Rashid jerked his head up and around. *Rashid, feed my children.*

"Where are you?" he answered out loud, suddenly irritated.

As soon as he said it, the wind rose, tunneling from behind, above his head and under his legs, gently. He sighed at its initial nudge, grateful for the relief from the heat. But within minutes, it strengthened. The crowds raised their arms in front of their faces, eyes closed to protect themselves from the wind's onslaught. It came splattered with loose grains of sand, and pushed every droplet of moisture from their skin, baking the sand into their flesh, and grating them raw with each gust.

"Where are you?" Rashid hollered, his face lifted to the sky. But he couldn't even hear himself. The pummeling air echoed off the canyon walls and roared back, drowning him out.

Isaiah clutched his wrist, bending forward into the wind. She peered at him from underneath her forearm. "What is this place?" she shouted at him.

"Petra," he answered. "We are here."

The canyon opened up, dramatically revealing an ancient city square. The stone walls encased it, save for a passageway to each side. Before them, carved into a pink stone wall stood a giant building with towering Roman pillars and triangles, the beautiful architecture of early civilization. Once in the square, they discovered several other buildings flanking the first, carved into the mountain. People were everywhere. They swarmed forward to greet and gawk at the mass of newcomers who'd arrived with the wind. The gale pushed forward and filled the giant canyon, lifting cloaks and blasting papers, dishes, and even a folding table that stood off to the side. The alarmed screams from scattering youngsters echoed off the canyon walls but were promptly smothered by the thundering wind. Arms left faces to cover ears. Several women grabbed nearby children and wrapped them under their torsos. Faces that had been peeking out windows dodged back inside the stone structures for relief.

Then, a boom filled the ravine, this time from the sky. The people looked up in time to see bright lights streaming down, cascading toward the earth in all directions. The team squeezed together, watching in horror. More wind blasted them, this time from above.

"Meteors?" Isaiah screamed.

"Or bombs!" Adira answered, grabbing Elise by the hand, "Let's go!" He spun around recklessly, dragging her away.

Rashid watched as the chaos unfolded. Adira slammed immediately into the person behind him, a man twice his size, holding a crying toddler, her tears buried in his neck. The passageway was crammed with people; there was no turning back.

The explosion from the first impact shook the ground. Where it landed was far enough away no one could tell, but the smoke plume rose in the distance enough to smother the edges of the horizon. Explosion after explosion rocked the ground, shaking people off their feet. Adira's eyes found Rashid.

"There." He pointed at a hole in the wall to their left. Rashid nodded. Isaiah saw it, too, and grabbed Elise's other hand to point the way. In seconds, the four were scrambling toward the cave, dodging falling stone and climbing over rubble. The world trembled as the sky lit up, though none of the falling satellites, as that was what they were, landed anywhere near the area.

The four reached the cave after dozens had already made it there and pressed in against the others, cowering to dodge the debris.

The ground shook for several minutes, toppling rocks and funneling sand over where the rocks had fallen loose. When it ended, the air plumed with dust. The clouds were gone, the blue skyline replaced with red and brown.

Cautiously, people crept from the caves.

"Look, another!" a woman screamed from the valley's outskirts, as one last light streaked down from the sky. This one coursed directly toward the canyon.

I'm coming. Stand up, the voice boomed in Rashid's mind. *Now, stand!*

He surveyed the area. The panic had hit the crowds all over again. Through the dusty fog, he saw people rolled up in balls on the floor, their tears and screams all meshed together into a loud wail. His head churned. To go out there now would be crazy, senseless. He stood anyway.

Isaiah gaped at him, her eyes wide. "Rashid, what are you doing?" she yelled, pulling him back toward the cave, both hands tight on his wrists.

Turning quietly to her, he lifted the edge of his mouth in a half grin. "It's fine."

He laid his free palm heavily on top of her hand. She relaxed and nodded at him, swallowing hard.

Then Rashid stepped out to the square's center. He repositioned a table that had fallen sideways and climbed onto it, standing tall while the light, Michael, approached. The angel lowered himself behind the table. He looked bigger than before with his wings stretched out, all four pairs, filling everyone's view. He was as tall as half the wall, easily over twenty-five meters, and his wings stretched just as far in each direction. The crowds scrambled back against the hillside, into crevices and each other, peeking out hesitantly as they did.

Rashid stood tall, hoping his confidence would reassure them.

"Children, listen!" Michael hollered. His voice rang strong into every hidden fissure of the canyon. "The Father sees you. He hears you. He has sent you a servant so you may have food while you wait."

Michael folded his wings, tucking them behind his back. He flew up, dropping one last gust of air that blew Rashid's curls across his face. The stream pierced Rashid, and brought with it a new sensation, one that prickled his skin and warmed his chest. His heart pounded, every beat reverberating off the inside of his chest wall. His fingers tingled, and his toes numbed until they no longer seemed a part of him. Suddenly Rashid was happy, hopeful for the future. He smiled and grabbed the straps of his backpack, squeezing them excitedly. Swinging it from his back onto the table at his feet, he called out his greeting.

"Who's hungry?"

LXXXVIII

AFTERWARD, THE DEVIL sat on the mountain, wondering about what had occurred and what was yet to be. A great light filled the air, causing him to turn his head to shield his eyes. The Lord overcame the place where he was and spoke.

"What have you done? Are you so foolish you would try to sacrifice all you have for a hopeless cause? Do not try to know my ways, Helel. I am beyond your understanding."

The devil grimaced, his skin darkening. "You disapprove of everything I do, even when you have the same plan in mind. And why is it I am still scorned after accomplishing that which you claim to have wanted all along? Should I not be celebrated now? Because of me, your children will have fruit, even as the others rip your precious creation apart!" He lowered himself until he was flat on his belly, anxious to leave. "I must go now, as I see you plan to use even those who band with me unfairly for your purposes. You call me a deceiver, but I am the one who has been betrayed!"

"Will your long-winded speeches never end?" God sighed and watched him go, unrelenting in His authority. "You clearly never considered my servant Rashid."

To be continued...

²⁸Do you not know? Have you not heard? The LORD is the everlasting God, the Creator of the ends of the earth. He will not grow tired or weary, and his understanding no one can fathom. ²⁹He gives strength to the weary and increases the power of the weak. ³⁰Even youths grow tired and weary, and young men stumble and fall; ³¹but those who hope in the LORD will renew their strength. They will soar on wings like eagles; they will run and not grow weary; they will walk and not be faint.

-Isaiah 40:28-31

EPILOGUE

ZECHERIAH SLUMPED IN the grass, unmoving.

"Brother." Ansiel stood above him, leaning forward. Thousands of years they had served together. It was said an angel couldn't die, but without a functioning essence to guide him, what was he looking at now but a mound of feathers and leather? Where was his friend?

Ansiel's head spun until the face of the ox took hold as his primary. He worried about the consequences to come for allowing the garden to be in such turmoil. And the children had eaten the fruit. This was forbidden. His one job—to protect the garden—he had failed to do. He would surely lose his station because of it. Perhaps he'd lose even more. But no punishment he could receive would be worse than what Zecheriah had suffered. He scorned himself for being so slow to respond to the tree's alarm. They had been outside the garden, watching for the children's return when it happened. Despite his other weaknesses, Zecheriah was always quicker than he when it came to the tree. He had responded so rapidly, and yet Ansiel had only just turned around when Helel had grabbed him. Had he been faster, he would not have been taken prisoner and they could have defended the garden together.

A breeze stirred, cooling his soggy eyes. He looked up; Michael was coming. The fact that the Father had sent Michael instead of coming Himself was a good sign. He dropped to a knee and lowered his head at the angel's approach.

"Ansiel," Michael regarded him, "are you scathed as well?"

"In spirit only," he answered. "But Zecheriah..." His jaw dropped, heavy with guilt.

Michael met Ansiel's eyes.

"He is in there still. I will ask the Father to heal him." He pulled the flattened orb out from behind his back. Ansiel's eyes flashed at it.

"You have it!"

"Yes. Helel was puffed up, as usual," Michael said, "and I reached for it while he was rambling."

Ansiel's face darkened. "But his glory... Helel consumed it. There is no reviving his body without it."

"Perhaps the Father will grant him more."

Ansiel nodded, hoping Michael's words were true. "Did you see I cut off his arm?"

"I did, but even now he is rejuvenating," Michael answered. "He will be whole again soon."

Disheartened, Ansiel conceded. Helel was the most powerful cherub that had ever been. No other angel had the ability to rejuvenate, except of course the archangels, like Michael. But at least, despite his power, he still couldn't grow back the wings Michael had taken from him.

From the ground came a moan.

"Zecheriah!" Ansiel exclaimed, darting his gaze to look at the flattened disc in Michael's hand. It was dull. How could Zecheriah's body do anything without its power? "Do you hear us? Do you live?"

Again he moaned, though softer than before.

"Zecheriah?" Ansiel fell on his hands and knees and tilted his head, peering under the cherub's arm toward his face. He rolled him over, carefully unfolding his tangled limbs. His friend's limp muscles gave way with the lightest coaxing.

But then came another breath.

"Has the Father has already heard us?" Michael asked, astonished.

The two angels stared at the orb in Michael's hands. It had not changed.

"But how?" Ansiel flashed to Michael's side and lifted Zecheriah's essence, gently examining it. "It is cold. There cannot be any life in it."

"There is not." Michael frowned. He lifted his chin to the sky. "I do not believe this is from the Father. Ansiel, when he wakes, keep his sword from him until we know what has happened. Watch him. I must go."

Ansiel nodded, somber as he realized who may now be controlling Zecheriah's glory. He lifted his friend's sword, which now glowed faintly, seemingly more intense with each breath Zecheriah took. He slid it between his wings and back, crossing paths with his own weapon.

ACKNOWLEDGEMENTS

Thank you to my parents, whose encouragement helped more than the caffeine. Also, to my incredible editors and beta readers, in large part author, Jared Gray West. I'll figure out this English language thing yet. And a giant thanks to Gina Welborn, whose advice I ignored and embraced, and whose fantasy novel I'm still waiting for.

But above all, thanks be to God, without whose existence none of this would even be possible. I am proud of the gospel, for it is the power by which all may be saved

REFERENCES

"Ebenezer" Smith, Benjamin E. (Benjamin Eli), 1857-1913, and William Dwight Whitney. The Century Dictionary And Cyclopedia: a Work of Universal Reference In All Departments of Knowledge With a New Atlas of the World. Rev. ed. New York: The Century co., 18961910.

ABOUT THE AUTHOR

Crystal Jencks is an entirely too busy physician who thought she'd make things even more complicated by adding writing her debut novel, *The Father's Tree*, to the pile. She reports the story came to her after she fell off a horse (who apparently was not interested in going fast, she says) and landed square on her head. Her family believes more than the story shook loose that day but support her and her new "hobby" anyway. She lives here and there but makes her home wherever her husband and four rowdies exist.

Her purpose with this book is not just to help readers escape into a wild adventure, but also to remind them about the spiritual aspects of life, and explore how to love each other along the way.

Made in the USA
Las Vegas, NV
02 February 2021

16936993R00267